Carl Weber's Kingpins:

Greensboro

Carl Weber's Kingpins:

Greensboro

Trinity DeKane

www.urbanbooks.net

Urban Books, LLC
300 Farmingdale Road, N.Y.-Route 109
Farmingdale, NY 11735

Carl Weber's Kingpins: Greensboro
Copyright © 2025 Trinity DeKane

ISBN 13: 978-1-64556-684-7
EBOOK ISBN: 978-1-64556-696-0

First Trade Paperback Printing April 2025
Printed in the United States of America

10 9 8 7 6 5 4 3 2 1

This is a work of fiction. Any references or similarities to actual events, real people, living or dead, or to real locales are intended to give the novel a sense of reality. Any similarity in other names, characters, places, and incidents is entirely coincidental.

Distributed by Kensington Publishing Corp.
Submit Orders to:
Customer Service
400 Hahn Road
Westminster, MD 21157-4627
Phone: 1-800-733-3000
Fax: 1-800-659-2436

Carl Weber's Kingpins:

Greensboro

Trinity DeKane

The Beginning

Greensboro, North Carolina

September
Early Saturday Evening, 5:30

"Aye, shawty. I miss yo' li'l ass already," Tyrone told Bridget.

Tyrone had just returned from a very relaxing and life-changing summer with his sister. He met who he considered his wifey.

"I miss you too, boo," she sighed into the phone.

"Look, let me call you right back. I need to call Kendra and let her know that I just touched down."

"All right. Call me back too," she commanded.

He laughed at the tone in her voice, almost demanding.

"I got you, girl!" He laughed.

He hung up and dialed Kendra's number.

"Hey, sis. I just made it back to town. I was calling to let you know. I guess you're busy. I love you, and thank you for letting me chill for a while."

As Tyrone sat at the stoplight, he replayed his message. Once satisfied, he sent it. When the light turned green, he turned down Church Street, heading home.

He called Bridget back, and they talked as he drove.

***

Carlos and his boys were out making their rounds when Tyrone's car caught Rick's attention.

"Man, do you see who I see?"

"Hell yeah! Shit, your connect was dead on when he told us where to look for this li'l bitch. Pull up on young'un!" Carlos ordered.

The man driving Carlos around busted a quick U-turn in the middle of Church Street. Carlos picked up his cell phone and called his crew following close behind them. He ordered them to position themselves in front of the white Impala that was a few cars ahead of them. As the guys moved around as instructed, Rick moved quickly to the left lane, then swung quickly back into the right lane and pulled up quickly to the bumper of the white Impala.

Tyrone, who was inside the white Impala, looked in his rearview mirror, rolled his window down, and waved his arm, gesturing for the car to go on around him. However, he soon realized that they had no intention of moving around him. As they boxed him in, he was forced to turn off Church Street and down the short dead-end street that led to Barksdale Alley.

He sat in his car and surveyed the situation, and he sighed, "Man, I'm not gon' let them kill me sitting in this car! I picked the wrong night to come back home."

Once Carlos pulled up, he immediately stepped out of his car, along with the driver and the four guys who were in a Yukon.

Carlos laughed as he realized that Tyrone was contemplating his possible options. "Aye, young blood, come talk to me."

Tyrone shook his head and got out of the car. "What's up? What is this all about?"

"Aye, I just wanna talk to you. I need to get a message to your brother and his crew," Carlos told him as he advanced on him. "You see, they been going against the grain, and they know that's not the way to do business. Sean had an agreement with my partna that they would move what they were going to move, and we'd move our product. But lately, they've been moving everything, and that's not the way to do business."

"Yeah, but that ain't got shit to do with me," Tyrone replied.

"True, true. But you see, somebody got to take the heat, and since your brother is hiding, then"—Carlos shrugged—"it's got to be you!"

Bam!

Carlos punched Tyrone in the face, causing him to fall backward on his car. As he swung a second time, Tyrone blocked him and punched him in the face. Carlos rubbed his jaw and laughed. As his boys moved forward, Carlos raised his hands.

"Don't do shit! I got this!" He laughed. "You got some balls, nigga! Let's get it!" Carlos sneered.

As the two men began fighting, Tyrone lost his footing and fell. Carlos stood over him and began beating him relentlessly.

"Get the fuck up!" Carlos growled as he stood at a full stance, wiping blood from his knuckles.

Tyrone struggled to sit up, grimacing as pain shot through his body. He knew that they weren't going to let him live, and he wasn't going to bitch up near the end. "You can kill me, but you know my brothers are gon' make sure they find you, then kill you and your whole damn family!"

"Man, let me kill this little nigga!" one of the guys with Carlos cried as he pulled his gun out.

Carlos stopped him. "Didn't I tell y'all that I had this? Let him have his final words."

"This ain't the final word and you know that! Hell, I ain't afraid to die, so let's get it over with!" Tyrone laughed in pain, but the laughter ended in coughing, causing him to spit a glob of blood from his mouth. He looked up at Carlos. "You know my brother was right. Niggas like you are bitch made. It shouldn't take you so long to pull that trigga!"

Carlos laughed, "Yeah, well, at least I will live to see another day, li'l man. And the brother you speak of so highly, he's next!"

Pow!

Carlos shot Tyrone twice in the face.

"Let's go!" he yelled as he pulled his phone out to call his partner to inform them that Tyrone was dead. They weren't supposed to kill him, but his trigger finger was itching to shoot the boy.

"Slight change in plans. He's dead."

"What?" the person cried. "You were supposed to rough him up, not kill him."

"Deal with it, man! Fuck," Carlos growled before hanging up.

Sean Toby Love
Sunday Afternoon, 1:00

Sean had just returned to Greensboro after riding out to Charlotte to drop a package off to his brother. He couldn't stand the man his brother had become. He was a pussy and a traitor in his eyes for leaving and relocating to Charlotte. He was more like their mother in so many ways. In Sean's opinion, Brent thought he was better than them and never wanted to get his hands dirty with the business that got him where the fuck he was presently. He had a nice home as well as a successful business all built from drug money! And now, due to a bad business deal, he had to return to his roots.

Once Sean hit Florida Street and drove a quarter of a mile down, he pulled up to Jackie's apartment and blew the horn to his souped-up Cutlass Supreme. When she walked out, he rolled down his window and yelled, "Bitch, come the fuck on! I'm tired and ready to go home and get some sleep!"

"Damn, bae, you can come in and lie down. I'm sure your kids would like to see you!"

"Listen, I'm not trying to do all that. I gots to get home and handle some business. Just come on and suck my dick so I can go!"

"Fine, but can you give me a few dollars first? I need to go to the grocery store, and I need gas in my car," she replied, getting in the car and putting on her seat belt.

"Damn, it's always something! Fuck!" He fumed as he pulled out his wallet and gave her $200.

"You act like this little bit of money gon' hurt you! Nigga, you best be glad I haven't had your ass up for child support," she sneered and rolled her eyes.

"If you ever do that, I'll break your rusty-ass neck, bitch! You know fuckin well I'on play that police shit! Don't say shit else to me until we get to where we going," Sean growled.

He turned his music up, with Diamond D's "Was It Really Worth It" blaring from the speakers. He leaned to the left with his head bopping, and he pulled off.

He drove to their spot down in Guilford County, two dirt roads over from his house. Once they were parked next to the pond off Kerr Chapel Road, he pulled his pants down.

Jackie was always spooked by his eleven-inch dick. They had been fucking for over nineteen years, and she still wasn't used to it. She gagged something awful every time she sucked it. He knew she couldn't swallow it all, but he always seemed to grab the back of her head, pushing it down until she felt like she was going to vomit. She remembered the one time she did vomit. She thought he was gonna kill her the way he slapped her around. But hell, it wasn't her fault. His dick was just too big to be sucking.

She looked at Sean and grabbed his meat and began sucking it. Her head bobbled, saliva seeped from her mouth, and her jaws were hurting, but she sucked him fiercely. After they were done, she jumped out the car to spit his cum out. She hated when he insisted that she swallow that shit.

Before she could get back in the car, Sean's phone rang. "Let me call you back. I'm handling some business. All right, bae."

She shook her head, realizing he was talking to his bitch.

"I guess that's your bitch, huh? I wonder what she would say if she knew I existed and your kids," she said.

"Get your dumb ass in this car before I leave your ass out here! You say the dumbest shit!"

"I can't stand you!" she cried.

"And yet you suck my dick and fuck me whenever I ask. Okay, you can't stand me. You know what position you play in my life, so stop trippin'!"

Jackie got back in the car and stared out the window without uttering another word. She was going to make Sean respect her if it was the last thing she did. He didn't waste any time pulling back into traffic after he dropped her off. She hated that her flesh was so weak for a nigga who refused to wife her or spend real time with her kids. He damn sure wasn't going to continue using her home, her kids, nor her body if he didn't give her what she wanted—a commitment!

She walked into the house, and her oldest son, Troy, was bagging up some dope.

"Give me a bag, and then get Li'l Rob to ride with you to drop it off to Knowledge," she told him.

"But, Mom!" Troy started.

"But, Mom, my ass, just do what the hell I said!" Jackie yelled as she snatched a dime bag of crack from Troy's hand and walked to her room. Once inside, she sat down on the edge of the bed, pulled her pipe out, and sucked on a glass dick that always made her feel good.

She pulled on it again, and once she was high, she put the pipe down and stretched out across the bed. She closed her eyes and thought back to the day she met Sean.

Jackie was forced to grow up quickly at 15 years of age, living with her cousin Kia Love. Her mother had been arrested and convicted of murdering her best friend and Jackie's father when Jackie was only 10, and then she was sentenced to two life sentences in prison. Kia, who was 19 at the time, agreed to take her in because she was family. Instead of being a responsible caretaker, Kia allowed Jackie to do as she pleased. After only six months of staying with her, Jackie had gained a reputation as the neighborhood jump off.

She met Sean at a party that Kia was having at her place. After a few dances, along with a few drinks, he asked her out and she agreed. A few nights before their big date, Kia walked into her room smiling. "You know Sean really wants you. Are you going to fuck him or no?"

"Girl, I'ma do whatever he wants as long as he looks out for me. He is a real baller, and I'ma bag that nigga!"

"Bitch, you betta!" Kia laughed as she walked out of Jackie's room.

The night of their date, Sean picked her up and took her to The Sushi House. Jackie didn't know how to tell Sean that she didn't eat that, and when she did, he blew

out an exasperated breath and drove away. When he
pulled up at Burger King, Jackie frowned, looking at
him like he had lost his mind.

"Really?" she asked, frowning up at him with one
eyebrow raised and the other one down.

"We fucking or no?" Sean asked her.

"Are you taking me to a better spot?" she replied.

He pulled off and pulled into China Inn. "This is as
good as it gets!"

She sighed, "Cool!"

"We're gonna get it to go. My dick is already hard," he
said as he stroked it, staring at her long legs.

Jackie stood right at five feet seven inches. She was
brown skinned with a thick frame. She always wore
braids that made her look like an Indian in Sean's
opinion.

They walked in and ordered their food to go, and
thirty minutes later, they were enjoying their food at the
Ramada Inn in Greensboro.

"You think you can handle this dick?" he asked.

"I'ma try my best!" she replied, smiling.

Jackie didn't pay too much attention to Sean as he
undressed because she was too busy trying to get her
own clothes off. She had been watching him all day, and
she couldn't wait to see what he was working with! She
giggled lightly as she thought about what she had told
her homegirl earlier: "Call me a ho, call me whatever you
want, but I'm going to get that dick tonight. I'ma put it on
this nigga!"

As she lay back on the bed and opened her legs, inviting him to slide up in her, he smiled and shook his
head. He turned her on her stomach, lifted her hips up
in the air, and slid inside of her hard. "Oh, fuck!" she
whimpered. She was open from that point on.

She picked up her cell phone and called her old flame. She had plans for Sean!

Sean
Sunday Evening

Sean headed down the road to drop off some money to his main chick, Melanie, who was gonna take it to his distributors. Melanie was a woman he was introduced to by one of his major connects, and he figured he'd keep her around because she was good for business. She knew the drug game inside and out and played no games! He knew Jackie didn't like it, but he didn't care. All Jackie ever was to him was a fuck and his baby momma. When he first met her, she was for the streets, and he didn't have to try that hard to get her. They had fucked on their first date. He continued to fuck her and was hypnotized by her wetness. He started raw doggin' her after a while, quickly learning that good pussy led to great responsibility. Children!

Sean parked his car in Melanie's driveway, grabbed his bookbag, and got out. While he was walking up to the door his cell phone rang. "Yeah?"

"Sean, it's Ms. Howell. You need to come home now!" she cried.

Charlotte, North Carolina
Brent Tino Love, 38 years old

Brent sat in his five-bedroom brick one-story home and looked at his schedule for the next week. Brent and Sean were brothers and were as close as any siblings could be until Brent decided to trap off on his own. He always talked about distancing himself from the family business, but he always seemed to get snatched back into shit, which pulled him deeper into the game. He knew Sean was angry with him for leaving home, but because of his brother's deceptive ways and his mismanagement of business funds, he didn't stray too far from the family business. He wanted so badly to leave that lifestyle alone, but if he did, he knew that he would be cast out of the family, which would only lead to his demise.

Brent looked at the package that his brother had brought him, checked its contents, and then stuffed it in the safe behind the picture of his parents.

"Aye, Truck, come here right quick," he yelled out.

A few seconds later, Truck, who stood at six nine and 225 pounds, walked in. "Yeah, what's up, Tino?" he asked, using his middle name.

"Listen, call Tony and ask him to meet me at the trap later on," Brent told Truck once he walked in.

"Okay. Ariana is waiting for you downstairs."

"All right, tell her that I will talk to her later on. You remember what I asked you to do?" Brent asked.

"Yes, sir."

"Put it in motion for today," Brent ordered.

"I'm on it!" Truck replied as he walked out to do as he was asked.

Three Hours Later

"Get that bastard in the shed and strip him down to his drawers! Get Ariana up here too, 'cause if that bitch thinks she is going to play me like a clown, she got another think coming! Nigga," Brent growled as he walked into the shed over to Tony, who was being held up by the arms by Tim and Bishop, "you were supposed to be my boy, yet you fuck my girl and steal from me! I can guarantee you this—you won't fuck over nobody else after tonight!"

As Tim and Bishop, Brent's top thugs, struggled to get Tony's big ass out of the room, Brent's phone began to ring.

"Yeah, speak your business!"

"It's me. You need to come home now!" Sean explained.

"Shit, I'm in the middle of something, bruh!" Brent replied, recognizing his brother's voice.

"Yeah, well, your brother was killed early this morning. They found his body this morning," Sean told him.

"What? What you mean? Man, hell naw!" Brent exclaimed as he fell back against the door of the shed.

"They claim they don't have any leads. Man, Pops and Moms isn't doing too good, so we got to handle shit for them. Man, I'm calling Kendra and everyone else once I hang up with you."

"Man, not Tyrone! Fuck! Somebody gon' die! I will be en route to you in the next few hours," Brent boomed.

"All right, bruh!" Sean said as he concluded the call.

Brent felt like his insides were churning. He raced to the main house and headed to the liquor bar. He stood at the corner of the bar and poured a drink. He downed it in one gulp. After three more, he heard the front door open, and he turned to see Truck pushing Ariana through the door.

"Take her to the shed. I'm coming in a few."

Truck nodded and pulled Ariana behind him, kicking and screaming for Brent to explain what was going on.

"Shut up, you nasty-ass bitch! You will soon find out. Aye, Truck?"

He turned and looked at Brent. "What's up?"

"Strip her li'l dirty ass down, too," Brent ordered.

"Got it, boss."

Brent sat down and pulled his cell phone back out and called his best friend, Lisa. "Baby girl, you wanna take a trip with me?"

"Damn right I do. What's the play?" she asked.

"To be honest, I don't know yet. Just be ready to leave about four in the morning. If you can, make us a little breakfast to eat before we leave. Call me back in about an hour. I got some business to tend to."

"All right, I got you. Aye, have you seen my sister?" Lisa asked.

Brent peeped around the corner and stared out the window at Ariana being slung into the shed. "Nope!"

"Okay, well, I will call you as soon as I have the seats booked," Lisa sighed.

"Cool."

After Brent hung up, he walked out of the house to the shed. When he walked in, he stared at Ariana and Tony.

"My once most favorite people! What do you got to tell me? Huh?"

"Man, I don't know what you are talking about, bruh!" Tony cried.

"Are you sure you don't know?" Brent asked.

"Man, if I knew, I wouldn't be asking. Come on, man, you know I'd never betray you."

The other guys in the room looked at each other, waiting for Brent to explode. To their surprise, he laughed.

"Oh, yeah? So, Ariana, are you gonna stand before me and lie too?"

Ariana didn't say a word as she hung her head.

"I didn't think so. Tell me something, how long have you been going out?" Brent asked as he took his Glock out.

Ariana began to talk quickly. "It was nothing! I swear we only had sex once! Please, baby, you got to believe me!"

Brent frowned with a shocked look at first and began laughing. "If you think this is only because you fucked ol' boy here, trust me, it's not just that. I can get pussy anytime I want it. Your sister has been wanting to give me the ass for years, sweetheart, and I should've taken her up on it 'cause she is more real than you have ever been. But I think I can fix that just as soon as I have your ass out the picture. Where is my fucking package?"

"Huh?" Ariana asked.

"My shit! Where is my shit?" Brent shouted as he walked over to her and pointed the gun at her shoulder.

"I don't know what you're talking about!" Ariana cried.

Pow!

A scream erupted from Ariana that could heal the deaf.

"I'ma ask again, where is my shit?" Brent asked, pointing the gun to her upper thigh.

"I . . . I . . ." she stuttered.

Pow!

"Wrong answer!" Brent growled.

Ariana screamed once again as the bullet ripped through her thigh.

"Tony, my man, my man, where is my shit?" Brent asked as he walked over to where he was standing.

"Li'l nigga, I ain't scared of shit you can do to me. You a young-ass bitch nigga who just got off by shooting a female! Nigga, fuck you and all that you stand fo'!" Tony stormed.

"Listen really close to me. I don't want you to fear shit! See, I just learned that my li'l brother was just killed, and I'm pissed, so trust me, I'm about to have Tim untie you 'cause I need to vent. I'ma let you get a few touches in, and then I'm gonna kill you with my bare hands. Once I'm done with you, I'ma focus on that bitch." He paused as he looked up at Ariana, who was leaking blood from both legs and breathing heavy from the pain. "If she doesn't tell me what I want to hear, I'ma kill her ass too!"

Brent stepped back and took off his T-shirt. He placed his gun on the side table and pointed to Tony. "Untie that bastard!"

As soon as Tony was untied, Brent advanced on him with a black look in his eyes.

He laced Tony's face with two hard, quick jabs, which sent him staggering backward, doubled over. He rushed forward and helped him to a standing position and hit him with an uppercut that sent him flying backward. Every hit that Brent laid on Tony was precise and hard, with a force that brought forth blood and spit. He didn't focus on body blows. They were straight facial connects. He felt tears stinging his eyes with each blow as thoughts of his little brother filled his mind. He was disconnected from the fight even though he was whopping Tony.

Tony's face began to swell, and his eyes began to sag, but this had no effect on Brent as he continued to beat him relentlessly. Tony fell backward, and Brent kneeled over him with devastating punches.

When he felt that Tony was close to death, he stood up and looked over at Tim. "Hang this nigga back up and bring me my axe."

"Yes, sir!" Tim replied as he rushed to do as he was asked.

"Man, I'm so sorry about bruh! He was a good kid!" Bishop said as he walked over to Brent.

Texas
Kendra Tiara Love
Saturday, 10:36 p.m.

Kendra walked in from the club and sat down in her recliner. Her feet were killing her, and she was starving but didn't feel like eating. She glanced down and saw that she had a message from Tyrone. After she listened to it, she noticed that she had a missed call from Bridget but decided that she'd call her the following morning. She was tired and needed to sleep. She walked into her bedroom and collapsed on the bed fully clothed. As she closed her eyes and eased into a nice sleep, the shrill of her cell phone interrupted her peace.

"Fuck!" she yelled. She pulled her cell phone from her coat pocket and shook her head as she noticed the number calling.

"What's up, big brother?"

"Kendra, it's Sean. You need to come home now."

Kendra knew that if Sean was calling her of all people, it had to be very much serious. He didn't like her and hated it when she was around.

"What's wrong?" she asked.

"They killed Tyrone!" he replied.

"Who?" she screamed.

"We don't know. We got the news this morning after eight. I've called almost everyone else," he explained.

"I'm on the first flight out tomorrow."

"Good," Sean replied before hanging up.

Kendra stood up and walked to the kitchen. She reached into her cabinet and pulled out her vodka and a shot glass. She poured a huge shot of vodka and cringed as the liquid set fire to her throat. She sat back in her chair and shook her head. "Damn it!"

After she took two more shots, she picked up her cell phone and dialed the only person she kept in contact with from her home state.

"Hey, Taye, it's me. Can you pick me up at the airport tomorrow night? I will text you early in the morning to let you know what time."

"You know I got you. Shall I tell anyone that you're coming?" Shantae asked.

"No, don't say shit to anybody," Kendra answered.

"Oh, fuck, a real bitch is coming home! Yes, it's about time, too, 'cause Greensboro needs a little order!"

Kendra didn't say another word. She hung up and walked to her bedroom to pack her bags.

Sean

Sean hung up after talking with Kendra and walked to the den where his mother and stepfather were sitting. His mother was sitting with her head laid on Omar's shoulder, sobbing, and he was sitting like a brick wall. No emotion, no movement. It was as if he were a statue.

"I called the family, and everyone should be in tomorrow," he told them.

"Is he coming too?" Omar whispered as he smoothed Le'Tera's hair back.

"I don't know. I left him a message. We will see if he shows. I'm going to get Rosa to fix the rooms up and set up the parlor to accept guests," Sean told them.

"Thank you, son. You are very much appreciated," Omar told him.

Sean nodded and walked away. He had to put on a strong front for his parents, but inside he was dying. Tyrone was most likely killed behind some bullshit that he had done, and it was eating him up inside. He low-key prayed that the cops didn't find his murderer because he needed to find them himself. Everyone knew who they were, and the streets better be ready for the bloodshed that was coming. He wasn't going to rest until he killed the bastards responsible for his brother's death.

After speaking with Rosa, Sean walked out of the house and through the cornfields. He remembered the one and only time Tyrone had asked him if he would teach him the family business. He would've obliged, but he knew that his mother would have a whole hissy fit, and as bad as he was, his mother was worse.

He closed his eyes as his brother's voice rang in his ears.

"Aye, bro, go back dere and get John. I need him to finish planting the rest of this corn so I can go handle some business," Sean told his brother as he turned the corn planter off and jumped down.

He took his gloves off and stomped his feet to remove the excess mud from his boots. His dirt-stained jeans fit him perfectly, showing every sexy groove of his lower body. His gray T-shirt was drenched with sweat and coated with dirt also.

He took his hat off and wiped his forehead as he walked past Tyrone.

"Can I ride with you?" Tyrone asked as he followed Sean.

"No, I got to do this solo. Yo, go get John like I asked," Sean retorted as he headed into the house.

"Hey, Ma, those collard greens smell good," he commented.

As he raced up the stairs, he heard his mother mumble something, but he couldn't make it out. He only had two hours to make it to his appointment, which was over an hour away. That was one of the problems about living so far out in the country.

He shook his head as he remembered how disappointed Tyrone was that he couldn't go. He stayed so busy making runs that he never had time to spend with his younger brother.

"All he wanted was some time! Fuckkkk!" Sean cried. He shook his head. "I can't let this break me. Fuck, man. My li'l nigga gone!" Sean stood in the middle of the field, his eyes bloodshot, and his skin tingled as he clenched his fist. "Li'l bruh, we gon' get retribution. Believe that!"

He knew that if he was having a rough time, Kendra was definitely suffering inside. Omar and Sean had first contemplated telling Kendra after she arrived home, but they knew that she wasn't going to uproot herself from her business to come home for just any reason. Of all of them, Kendra's bond with Tyrone was tighter. He always spoke of moving in with Kendra when he turned 18, and she was ready for him.

Sean didn't too much like Kendra as a person, but he loved her as his sister and was going to be there for her and everybody else through the family's sorrow.

Sean walked back toward the house, and once inside, he saw his mother asleep on the couch with her head resting in Omar's lap. They had given her a sedative to calm her down. It was rough on them all.

After he watched his parents for a moment, he walked to his bedroom and grabbed his other cell phone. He had five missed calls from his fiancée, Melanie, but he wasn't ready to talk to anyone else at that moment. He flopped down on his bed and lay back with his arm thrown over his eyes. He couldn't fathom anyone wanting to hurt Tyrone.

Tyrone was so different from the rest of them. All he ever wanted to do was to graduate from school, then college, and start his own business. He knew that his brother didn't respect him or what he did, but the fact was he was still his brother. When he found out who was behind his death, he was going to see that someone paid for his brother no longer being present on earth. He also knew that he wouldn't be alone in the task!

Chapter 1

Going Home

Kendra

The Next Day, Sunday Morning, 5:30

"Good morning, ma'am. Would you like something to drink or maybe something to read?" the tall Mexican stewardess asked Kendra as she settled down in her seat.

"Yes, a bottle of water will be fine for right now, thanks."

"Here you go, ma'am. If you need anything else, don't hesitate to ask. I hope you enjoy your flight with us today."

"I'm sure I will," Kendra replied as she placed her headphones on.

"Good morning, this is your captain speaking, and I would like to welcome you all aboard Flight 796, destination Greensboro, North Carolina. Please buckle up and turn any electronic devices off as we prepare for takeoff."

After the captain gave out his instructions for the flight, Kendra sat back, closed her eyes, and relaxed as the plane took off. She hated having to return to her home. She had worked so hard to distance herself from them. She hoped that she could go in, handle her business, and slip away again. She knew her brothers were going to make it hard for her.

Her mind was filled with so many perturbed feelings about going home. She had created a wonderful life in Texas, and she wasn't going to lose everything that she had built on her own. But she also wasn't going to leave North Carolina without finding out who had killed her brother and why!

She closed her eyes, and as the plane took off, her mind wandered.

It was a Friday morning, and Kendra was awakened by the shrill of her phone. She looked at the time on it, shook her head, and groaned. "What in the hell? Yes?" she answered.

"Sis, please call Mom and ask her if I can come stay with you. I can't take this shit any longer. I don't have a good feeling about shit!" her little brother, Tyrone, whispered quickly into the receiver.

Kendra sat up, wiped her eyes, and snatched her bonnet off. "What's going on? Do I need to make a trip there? Because I will!"

"Sis, I just need to get away. Pops is trying my last damn nerves. He wants me to become something I'm not, and Sean is sucking up so fucking bad trying to take Brent's spot that he ain't thinking straight! I just can't take it! Please, sis!"

"I got you! I will call her as soon as I think she is up. Listen, try to get some sleep. I will call you right after I talk to her."

"All right," he replied before hanging up.

Kendra looked at her clock once again. "Four thirty. Let me get some more sleep before I have to call this woman!" She lay back down and tossed and turned.

Later that morning, after Kendra woke up again, she called and spoke with her mother about Tyrone coming to stay with her for a while. Her mother agreed after Kendra pleaded with her for a few minutes. Her mother told her that she would let him visit with her, but only after school let out for the summer in June. She made Kendra promise to take care of Tyrone while he was with her, and Kendra assured her that she would.

After she had gotten off the phone with her mother, she called Tyrone to let him know their mother's decision. He thanked her repeatedly, commenting that he hoped the time would pass quickly.

When she hung up with him, she got up out of her bed, walked to the kitchen, and put on a pot of coffee. While the coffee was brewing, she took a quick shower, brushed her teeth, and put on her favorite sundress. She put her bedroom slippers back on and walked into the kitchen area. She grabbed a bagel and put it in the toaster. She wasn't hungry, but she had to put something on her stomach. Otherwise, she'd get sick. She poured a huge cup of coffee, putting hazelnut creamer and light sugar in it for a sweeter taste. After she ate her bagel, she took her cup of coffee out on the patio and sighed as she took in the beauty of the city. She loved living in Texas, but she hated being so far away from her brother, especially when he needed her.

She grew up a problem child and was sent away after she committed a crime that her father deemed unnecessary. She laughed at the irony of it all because her father was the leader of one of the most ruthless gangs in Canada.

She learned about the family business by mistake when she was only 8 years old. That mistake proved to be her awakening.

As she drifted further in thought, she remembered that day like it was yesterday.

"Arrggg!" sounded from the back of the Love family estate.

It was only eight o'clock in the morning, and Kendra, always being a curious child, jumped up out of her princess bed and sprinted to the window to see what was going on.

She squinted as she tried to see what her brothers were doing. Her father walked out of the storage building he always kept locked, and then he went back in carrying something shiny, long, and black or silver. Kendra ran to put her shoes and robe on, then snuck past her nanny, Ms. Kane, who was cleaning her father's office. Once she got downstairs, she opened the door quietly and ran down to the shed. She peeped into the small opening around the window, catching a glimpse of a man tied to a chair, and he was bleeding. Her brother, who was 17 at the time, was smashing the man in the face with a shovel. His head snapped back, and instead of Kendra looking away, she was in awe of what they were going to do to the man next. Just as she was getting into the scene, someone grabbed her arm.

"What are you doing out here? Come on here before your father finds out you are out here!"

Kendra jerked away from Ms. Kane, glaring at her with a sinister look, and took off running back to the house.

Ms. Kane followed her in and finished cleaning while Kendra stood at the back door waiting for her father to come back inside. Suddenly, she heard a loud bang. She jumped, but she refused to move from her spot. When her father finally walked in, Kendra approached him, looking more behind him than at him. "Daddy, I heard someone crying. Can I see what's going on?"

"Kendra, go back to your room now and forget what you think you heard!"

"But, Daddy!" she protested.

"Now!" he growled.

Kendra looked at him with defiance, but eventually, she turned and stomped up the stairs.

Ms. Kane stood at the top of the stairs with a smirk on her face, which infuriated Kendra even more.

Kendra sat on her bed, but again curiosity got the best of her. She walked to her father's room and stood in the doorway. "Daddy, how come Sean and Brent get to see and I don't? It's not fair!"

"Girl, if you don't get out of here . . . I said what I said, and I mean it. Forget what you saw and heard."

"You're mean!" Kendra cried, folding her arms across her chest.

"Young lady, if you don't . . ." he thundered, grabbing for his belt.

Kendra took off running to her room, slamming the door behind her.

She refused to come out when told to come down to eat breakfast. Later that day, her brothers and father disappeared, once again leaving Kendra alone with Ms. Kane.

When she walked out of her room, she went over and stood at the window, looking for her father's truck. When she realized it was gone, she walked through to the kitchen to fix a sandwich.

In passing, she saw Ms. Kane standing at the top of the stairs on a two-step ladder, cleaning the chandeliers. Kendra hummed as she skipped to the kitchen. She fixed a bologna sandwich and raced back up the stairs, bumping into the stepladder, which tilted, causing Ms. Kane to fall over the banister. Kendra stared at her body sprawled on the floor and smiled as she bit into her sandwich.

"I'm sorry," she whispered, still smiling.

As she sat down at the top of the stairs, she finished her sandwich and waited for her father to walk back in.

After what seemed like hours, she heard her father's truck pulling back up, crackling the gravel on the dirt road that led to their home.

When he walked in, followed by Brent and Sean, he gasped at the scene. When he looked up at the steps, he whispered through clenched teeth, "What did you do?"

"Nothing! She fell! Daddy, I'm thirsty," Kendra replied as she skipped down the stairs.

Sean laughed, only to get a harsh look from their father.

"Call 911!" he ordered. "Brent, take Kendra to my room and keep her there until I ask you to bring her down. Dammit, I don't need the police here checking for shit. Sean, don't call nobody. We will handle this shit how we handle everything else."

Kendra sat down at the bottom of the steps looking innocent, but her father knew better.

Hours later, after disposing of Ms. Kane's body, Kendra's father and her two brothers huddled in the office. Kendra stood at the door and listened to her father and brothers discussing what to do with her. Brent was the only one who was opposed to her going to boarding school, but in the end, she was shipped off.

Kendra snapped back to the present and shook off the thoughts from her past. She began to prepare herself for what was to come. She wasn't sure if Wake County was ready for the storm that was brewing. Blood was going to be shed!

"Damn, my brother is gone!" She began to sob.

A few hours later, the airplane landed on the strip of the Piedmont Triad International Airport. Kendra shook her head again, as she was very distraught and miserable. The only good thing about being back in North Carolina at that point was seeing Taye. Taye was her best friend, and she hadn't seen her in years.

After she got off the plane and gathered her bags from baggage claim, she walked outside.

"Hell fucking yeah!" she heard her friend scream. "Here, let me help you with your bags."

"Hey, Taye! You look just as weird as you did the day I left!" Kendra laughed.

Taye's hair was in a curly Afro, and she was dressed in a long red skirt with purple leggings, a red and purple shirt, and a pair of black boots. Her colors were always grunge in Kendra's opinion.

"Hey, you know me. I follow and create my own style," Taye admitted.

"Yes, we have to catch up before I go back home," Kendra suggested.

"I'm so sorry about Dre, Kendra. I heard about it once we got off the phone last night," Taye told her.

"It's a lot to process, and I thank you. Let's get to the house," Kendra murmured, not wanting to talk about her brother's death. She hadn't absorbed the fact that he was gone. They left the airport without delay.

En route, Kendra's phone beeped, and she had three more messages from Bridget. She called her back after listening to the inaudible messages.

"What's up, Bridget?"

Bridget was sobbing. "Something happened to Tyrone last night."

"How do you know?" Kendra asked, frowning.

"We were on the phone. Please tell me that you've heard from him."

Kendra began to cry, which gave Bridget her answer. "Nooooooo!"

The scream that erupted from Bridget's mouth sent shivers down Kendra's back. She hadn't even considered Bridget's feelings. She and Tyrone had become close.

"Bridget, pack a few clothes and catch a flight. I will send you everything you need to get here, and I will have someone pick you up when you land."

"Okay," she replied, then hung up.

Kendra could hear the pain in her voice as she disconnected the call.

Brent
Sunday Morning, 10:00

Brent pulled up to the intersection of Kerr Chapel Road and Old Stoney Creek Mountain Road and sat at the crossroads contemplating what he was going to do about his family dilemma. He hadn't been home in years and was wondering why his brother had been killed. He was sure it had something to do with Sean's bullshit. He pulled off from the intersection, and five minutes later, he was pulling into the gated home that his family owned. The grounds were still well kept. As he traveled down the gravel driveway, he took in the view.

"Looks like they got more cows," he whispered to himself.

"What did you say, babe?" his companion asked.

"Oh, nothing. We're here," he announced.

She sat up and took in the scenery. "You grew up here?"

"Yes, me and my two brothers and sister," he replied.

"Why don't you ever talk about your family?"

"There ain't much to talk about," he answered, shrugging his shoulders.

"Are those the only siblings you have?" she said, continuing to pry.

"I have another brother and one other sister. They stayed with our father when he and my mother called it quits. Listen, I don't want to relive my family drama right now."

Lisa turned her head and decided not to press the issue. She felt like she was traveling down a road in a movie scene. Everything was beautifully laid out. She saw chickens, horses, cows, goats, and even a llama. As they approached the house, Lisa's eyes grew wide with excitement. The house was three stories high, and it was wide.

"How many square feet would you say this house is?" Lisa asked.

"About seventy-five hundred. Trust me, it wasn't all that to grow up in," Brent replied as he pulled up to the house and parked.

He got out and walked around to open Lisa's door. He grabbed her hand and helped her out. He walked into the house and called out for Rosa, the maid. When she appeared, he instructed her to get a few hands and get their bags out of the car. He then asked where his stepfather was.

"He is in the study, where he has spent most of his time since Tyrone's murder," she answered.

"And where is Sean?" he asked.

"He took one of the horses out early this morning," she replied.

"Okay, I'm going to see if he is at the stables. I will be back in a few minutes," he told her and walked out of the house after ensuring that Lisa was settling in okay.

Sean

Sean galloped up the gravel driveway and laughed as he saw Brent walking out on the porch with Lisa. He already knew that their father was going to flip out. Why would he bring that bitch to their house when they were going through what they were going through? He nudged the horse's side as he rode past the house to the stables.

Once he slowed his horse to a halt, he jumped off, brushed his jeans off, then led the horse into the stall and gave him some water. He wasn't in a rush to see Brent, but evidently, Brent was ready to see him. Sean surmised this as his brother walked briskly to the stables. As soon as Brent walked in, Sean greeted him with a half hug.

"When did you get here?" Sean asked.

"I got in earlier this morning. Listen, I'm just gon' come out and ask. Was our brother killed behind some bullshit you got going on?"

"I don't even know! We don't know who killed him or why, but I will find out once the funeral is over," Sean explained as he took his gloves off and walked toward the house.

Both men stopped short and stood silent for a moment as they took in the reality that a funeral was being planned for their little brother.

"I see you brought your chick with you. You can't just leave right after the funeral. You do know that, right?" Sean asked.

"I know, Sean. She is here for moral support. I will be taking her back to Charlotte and coming right back the following morning," Brent assured him.

"I was just checking, bruh," Sean mumbled. He knew that Brent wouldn't be the only person suggesting that it was his business dealings that got Tyrone killed, and until they found out who killed their brother, the streets wouldn't be safe. They would fill them up with the blood of all involved in the murder.

"Is anyone else here yet?" Brent asked as they continued to the house.

"No, you're the only one so far. I'm guessing everyone else will be here shortly," Sean replied.

As they reached their parents' house, Sean could see their stepfather and mother, Omar and Le'Tera, sitting on the porch. Le'Tera was crying uncontrollably, which was too much for Omar to handle at that point.

"They took my baby from me! Why? He never bothered anyone!" Le'Tera was screaming.

"She started hyperventilating, so I brought her out here for some fresh air," he explained once they were within earshot.

The pair raced forward to help comfort and calm their grieving mother.

Kendra

Kendra and Taye didn't talk much on their way to Kendra's family home. Kendra appreciated Taye for not pushing her to talk about Tyrone and giving her space to think.

Tyrone had just left her home after spending the summer with her and couldn't have been home but a few hours before he was killed. He was supposed to have stayed another week, but he received an urgent phone call to return home. He didn't say what the issue was, but she knew it had to have been important for him to have left like he did.

"Taye, I appreciate you driving me home. It's been a long time since I've been here," Kendra whispered, attempting a little small talk.

"Sis, you know I got you and anything you need from me during this time. I'm here for you. Dre was like a brother to me," she commented.

"Yes, I know, and I will keep you updated with the arrangements for his funeral," she said as her voice trailed off. "I just can't!"

Taye reached over, grabbed Kendra's hand, and gave it a light squeeze, then grabbed the steering wheel again with both hands, wondering if Kendra would be okay after everything was said and done. She admired Kendra so much for leaving home and finding her own path in the world. Kendra didn't get involved in the family business unless it was necessary. She made her money the legal way and always encouraged her to get out from under her family's thumb as well. Taye wasn't going to announce it to Kendra just yet, but she was about to take her advice.

Chapter 2

Brent, Sean, and their parents were sitting on the porch when Taye's car pulled up.

"Looks like Kendra is here," Sean sighed.

"Finally! Maybe she can talk to Mom and calm her down," Brent whispered to his brother.

Sean gave him a hopeful yet bleak glare and walked down the steps to greet Kendra. Kendra got out of the car as soon as they were parked, and she grabbed her bags.

"Hey, everyone," she said as she walked over and gave Sean a half hug along with Brent.

Lisa walked out the door and smiled. "This must be one of your sisters."

"Yes, it is," Brent informed her.

Kendra walked up the steps, ignoring Lisa, and headed straight to her mother. She wrapped her arms around her mother's neck, and the two wept together.

Brent cleared his throat. "Hmmm, we will get your bags out and put them in your room."

Kendra nodded and followed her brother into the house. She walked through the front door and stopped in her tracks. Everything looked exactly the same as when she was last there. She sighed, took a deep breath, then exhaled before she headed down the short hallway leading to a stairwell. As she ascended the steps, she could feel Tyrone's presence approving of her return home. As she reached the top of the stairs, she felt a lump rising in her throat as she glanced over at Tyrone's bedroom door.

It was open slightly, and without having to guess why the door was cracked or who was inside, Kendra forced her legs to move. When she pushed the door open, her mother was seated on her brother's bed, her body looking frail and slumped. She was looking down at Tyrone's graduation picture, ignoring Kendra for a few seconds.

Kendra talked to her mother almost daily via Duo, but it had been close to eight years since she'd been physically with her. She stared at her without saying a word, and as she watched on, she saw her mother's shoulders begin to tremble. Her mother then held her head up and let out one of the most horrific screams she had ever heard. The scream was filled with anger and pain. Kendra felt every sting of her scream.

She walked forward and bent down in front of her mother, sat back on her knees, and laid her head in her mother's lap as she hugged her around her waist.

Le'Tera grabbed Kendra's hair and began to massage her head as they both wept. After ten minutes, Kendra finally lifted her head. "What are we gon' do without him, Mommy?"

Le'Tera shrugged. "Baby girl, I honestly don't know."

Kendra stood and wiped her eyes with her hands as she stood and sat down on the bed next to her mother. "Whatever we do, we will get through this together."

Le'Tera looked at Kendra and nodded. "Yes, we will."

"Mom, we have to get things situated. We got to hold it down for li'l bro. He had his own flair, and I think we need to send him off how he would've wanted."

"I just can't think about that right now. Listen, you and your brothers get it started. Please! I can't do it."

Le'Tera started crying again, so Kendra wrapped her arms around her mother's shoulders and held her close and tight.

Finally, after thirty minutes of grieving, Le'Tera was ready to greet the family who had started arriving at their home.

She and Kendra headed down the steps. Brent and Sean walked forward, stood, and waited for the ladies at the bottom of the stairs. Once Le'Tera hit the floor, Brent hugged her tightly, followed by Sean. Le'Tera felt comforted knowing that almost all of her children were home.

"Has anyone heard from Nigil?" Le'Tera asked.

"We called them, but we haven't heard back from them yet," Sean replied as they walked into the front parlor.

The news of Tyrone's death spread quickly through Wake and Alamance Counties. By midday, a lot of the family's relatives and friends had arrived to show their respects. They brought in food, drinks, and their Bibles, laying prayer upon them.

Le'Tera sat in the corner of the front room, staring out into space. Her eyes were red, and her hair was tousled. Kendra stared at her nervously. She knew that losing Tyrone was hard on all of them, but she was concerned that her mother would never recover.

"Mom, do you want me to fix you something to eat?"

Her mother sat still for a minute, then shook her head no.

"Mom, you have to eat," Kendra sighed.

"I'm not hungry. Y'all go ahead and eat. I'm okay," she whispered.

Kendra walked down the hall toward the kitchen. She was going to fix her mother a small plate of food and would cram it down her throat if necessary. As she hit the threshold, she bumped into a solid body. She looked up angrily. "Watch where the fuck you're going!"

"Whoa, li'l lady, you bumped into me," the man retorted.

"What the hell are you doing back here anyway? We are receiving guests in the front parlor," she questioned as she finally focused in on the older gentleman in front of her. He was tall, heavyset, and sexy as hell. The gray in his beard and hair accented his olive complexion. His shoulder-length, wavy hair was up in a ponytail, and he reeked of sawdust and sweat. His jeans were dirty and clung snugly against his muscled thighs. When she finally stared into his light brown eyes, she gasped silently. They held a hint of gold around the iris, and they were slanted. When he spoke, his deep voice sent chills all over her body. As a reflex to the effects of being close to him, Kendra rubbed vigorously at her arms.

Suddenly remembering why she was there, she sneered, "Move!" She pushed past him and continued on her way.

He looked at her and smirked at her bossy demeanor. "Ma'am, I'm sorry for your loss. Please accept my condolences," he told her.

Kendra didn't say a word as she continued to fix her mother some food.

Chapter 3

Monday Morning

As the family sat down at the table to eat breakfast, the doorbell sounded off loudly. A few moments later, the maid was leading three men dressed in suits into the room.

"Ma'am, these detectives are here to see you!"

Le'Tera stared at Rosa as if she had grown two heads. "Have them wait in the parlor, Rosa! We are about to have breakfast!"

"Mom, breakfast can wait. Let's go see what these gentlemen have to say," Kendra suggested.

"Y'all go! I don't want to talk to them unless they are here to tell me that they caught my son's killer!" She turned and faced the detectives. "Are you here to tell me that?"

"Uh, no, ma'am. We were just hoping—" one of the detectives started.

Le'Tera held up her hand. "I don't care! If you all are going to talk, go in the parlor!"

Le'Tera picked up the huge spoon and began placing food on her plate. Kendra looked at her brothers, confused at her mother's behavior. However, when she looked to them for support in convincing their mother to talk, they too refused to talk.

"We have nothing to say!" Sean replied before he accepted the spoon from their mother to fix his plate.

"Oh, for God's sake! I'll go talk to them myself!" Kendra replied. She followed Rosa into the parlor with the detectives close behind.

"We'd like to offer our condolences to the family, and we have a few questions for you," the taller detective started.

Kendra couldn't help but notice how nervous the officers were. "Do you have any suspects yet?" Kendra asked with her arms folded.

"Um, no, ma'am, we haven't. But trust us when we say that we won't stop until we have them in custody," the shorter officer replied.

"So, what's the purpose of you being here? Look, this has been a rough time for us and I'm doing my best to give y'all the benefit of the doubt that you will find out who did this, but I'm not sure that you will. You are here to ask us questions that we for sure don't have the answers to. No, my brother didn't have any enemies. No, my brother wasn't into any shady shit or in the streets, and no, I don't have any further information for you. My brother is dead! Shot and beaten!" Tears swelled in her eyes, and as they dripped down, Kendra stomped off and raced upstairs.

She felt vomit rising to her throat. As she ran into the bathroom, she heard Brent at the door. "Kendra, you all right?"

Kendra slid down to the floor, grasping the towel and pulling it down with her. She wiped her mouth and began thinking about Tyrone. The day before he had left, they had a real heart-to-heart.

"I love you, sis! I don't want to leave!" he told her.

"Well, you only have a few more months before you turn eighteen. You just hold on a li'l longer, li'l bro."

"You know Brent is trying his best to get me to join the family business, but I just don't see that being a part of my life. I wanna break free just like you."

Kendra hugged him and promised that he had a place with her in Texas.

"Nooooo!" she let out a scream as she grappled with her present reality. She stood after a few minutes, and when she walked to the door and opened it, Brent was standing there waiting for her.

He didn't say a word. He hugged her and kissed her on the top of her head. "We gon' be okay. Once we find out who did this."

Kendra pulled away and stared up at him. She wiped her eyes, and she knew exactly what he was thinking without him saying a word.

She nodded, letting him know that she was ready for whatever they had to do. She walked away and found herself standing again in Tyrone's room.

Kendra sat down and rubbed her hand across the burgundy comforter on his bed. She lay down, grabbed his pillow, and began crying. Tyrone was the only normality in her life. Everything she had accomplished in life she did for the both of them because she knew that he didn't want to follow in his brothers' footsteps. Before he left her, they had spoken about him joining her company and becoming COO once he graduated from college.

They had plans!

She thought back to the day that she caught him and her assistant, Bridget, together for the first time, and his reaction was priceless. She laughed out loud between her silent sobs. He had been there about a week, and he was familiarizing himself with the company. Kendra had suggested that Bridget show him the ropes while she finalized a contract deal with a new artist she had just taken on as a client.

"Kendra, come now! We have to go to the funeral home to make the arrangements and to view the body. Mom isn't going," Brent called out.

Kendra sat up and wiped her face with her bare hands. "Coming!"

She stood up and walked out of the room, closing the door quietly behind her.

As Kendra trotted down the stairs, the man who she had encountered the previous night was standing next to Brent. He didn't seem as interested in her as he was the night before. He ignored her once she joined them. She walked purposely into him, then stood next to Brent as she rolled her eyes at the man. He huffed a short laugh.

Sean could feel the tension and decided to see if he could clear the air. "Kendra, this is our farmhand, John Enoch. He and Tyrone were close, and I've asked him to accompany us to the funeral home."

"Farmhand, huh? Well, it's nice to meet you. I guess." She frowned.

John tilted his black Stetson hat and smiled just briefly. "Nice to finally meet you formally."

"Where is Brent? I thought you said y'all were ready," she said, ignoring John.

"He should be down soon," Sean assured her.

When she glanced over at John, he was eyeing her as if he was studying her. His eyes spoke no hidden messages, and she couldn't get a fix on him. She looked at his hands. She could tell they were working hands, and they were huge. He could easily cover her oval face with one hand. She couldn't help but wonder if he could've had something to do with Tyrone's death. Just how much did they know about him?

As if reading her mind, John loomed over her, and he spoke, "Never in a thousand years did I imagine that Tyrone would gain his wings before I did. He was a great kid, and I won't rest 'til whoever is responsible for his death is laid out in the cornfield."

She didn't know why, but she believed him. Finally, Brent was ready, and they headed out.

The Funeral Home

As Sean pulled into the parking lot of the funeral home, Kendra's pulse quickened, and her breathing increased. She could feel the sweat building in the palms of her hands. She balled her fists, and then relaxed them. She could feel the tears gathering in her eyes. As she dropped her head and took in a deep breath, she felt Brent grasp her hands.

"I know, baby sis. I feel it too."

She glanced over at him and wiped at the tears that fell, nodding.

Once they were parked, they exited the car and walked toward the door. As they got closer, Kendra paused. "I can't do this." She began to cry uncontrollably.

Sean and John stopped and walked to her, each positioned on opposite sides of her. "We are right here," said Sean.

Kendra took a deep breath and swallowed hard. "Okay, I'm ready."

They walked inside and saw that Brent had already located the funeral home director and was talking to him. As they approached the two men, they heard Brent ask to see Tyrone.

"We don't usually allow the viewing until the body is prepared. We just picked the body up this morning," the director explained.

Kendra shook her head. "Listen, my brother didn't ask what you usually do. He asked you to show us his body, now."

The director looked at the group and smiled. "I must warn you that seeing the body right now won't be easy."

"First of all, the body has a name—Tyrone Love. Secondly, like seeing him dead and dressed up will be any easier. Just take us back there," Kendra replied darkly.

The director reluctantly agreed and asked them to sit in the office while he prepared Tyrone for viewing. After thirty minutes, a lady walked in and asked them to follow her to the back. As they did, they slowly looked into the various areas of the funeral home. Nervousness set into a few of them, and the smell of antiseptic filled the air.

As they approached a closed door, the lady turned. "I am truly sorry for your loss."

She opened the door, and they walked into a cold room that was dimly lit except for where Tyrone lay stretched out with a sheet covering his body. Kendra began to sob as John helped her to the table. As she finally stood over him, she bent down and kissed his forehead. It was cold and hard.

"He looks like he is just sleeping," she whispered, wiping the drips of snot from her nose. She laid her head on his chest and closed her eyes. Her body was shaking as she let out a horrible scream.

"Not my brother! I love you. You didn't deserve this," she said to him, and suddenly her body went stiff. She stood up, wiped her eyes, and turned to look at Brent.

She didn't say a word, but he knew that his sister had left the building. Mentally. He, himself, couldn't get over how swollen and bruised his brother's face was. He could see where the bullet had entered his head, right above his left eyebrow.

He didn't say a word as the funeral director walked in. "I am sorry, but we really have to get started on the planning. I have another appointment after yours."

They followed the man to his office, and after finalizing the details, they all headed out.

"Man, they fucked over our li'l brother, and we gon' have to find out who was behind this shit. I don't want to bring Dad in this because he is stressed the fuck out. I ain't never seen him like this, bruh."

As much as he hated agreeing with Sean, Brent knew they had to avenge their brother's death, but hell, where were they gon' start?

"I'm wit' it, bruh. Let's get the funeral over wit' first," he replied.

John stood between Sean and Kendra. "Should I clear out some room for another cornfield?"

Sean nodded. "Immediately!"

Chapter 4

Carlos

Carlos was sitting in his office, looking over the contracts for his next big show. He had been so busy doing other people's bidding that he hadn't had time to really focus on his own business.

"Carlos, someone is here to see you," Sabrina, his club manager, informed him.

"Who is it?" he asked.

"Nautica. He said it's important," she replied.

"Okay, show him back, but we need to have a meeting later this afternoon. We have got to do something about bringing in more clientele, or this club is going to get shut down soon."

She nodded with her hand on the doorknob. "Just holla when you're ready."

A few minutes after Sabrina left his office, there was a knock at the door. The door swung open before Carlos could say, "Come in." He sat back in his blue leather office chair and gawked at his guest. "I mean, what's good, bruh?"

As Nautica and Havoc, another one of Carlos's top goons, walked in looking grisly and furious, Carlos noticed that they left two of their goons standing right outside his door. He couldn't help but wonder if they were there to keep someone out or keep him locked inside. Either way, he knew things were about to escalate.

"Shit, I'm just coming to have a li'l chitchat with you. Why don't you have that bitch out there bring me a shot of something strong?" Nautica replied as he sat down. His muscles were very visible through his button-down shirt. He loosened his tie and sat back.

Carlos cleared his throat as he eyed Havoc. "You want something too?"

"Naw," Havoc replied, never removing his eyes from Carlos.

Carlos called for Sabrina to bring in two shots of 1800.

After Sabrina brought the drinks and left again, Nautica downed his drink in one swallow. His face twisted a bit from the sting of the liquid, but he shook it off and cleared his throat.

"We got wind of what happened the other morning, and I got a question," Nautica started.

"What questions do you have?" Carlos asked, frowning.

"What the fuck were you thinking? Have you lost your goddamn mind? Huh? You know that certain shit and folks are off-limits! You just opened a whole can of worms you aren't ready for, and to top it off, you got my muthafuckin' brother involved!"

Carlos stuttered trying to reply. He could tell that Nautica wasn't trying to hear any excuse.

"Answer me, dammit!" Nautica growled. At the same time, Havoc walked over and punched Carlos in the gut.

Carlos doubled over, but Havoc reached down and forced him to sit back up.

Gasping for breath and drooling, Carlos grumbled, "It was a business deal, man. I got this under control."

Bam!

Havoc punched him once again, and just like before, Carlos doubled over coughing and moaning. "Come on, man. I promise I'll fix it."

When Carlos finally sat back up, Nautica was holding a Glock and pointing it at his head.

"Man, that's not necessary. Come on now. I got this," Carlos begged with his hands up.

Nautica stood and placed the muzzle of the gun under Carlos's chin. "Nigga, you got what? Huh? You probably just got my little brother killed over a 'business deal.' Driving you around like he yo' chauffeur and shit! If my brother gets killed behind this shit I'ma have to go to war with them fools! I promise you, you gon' regret this 'cause what I'ma do to you is gon' be ten times worse than what them Love boys gon' do to you. Fix this shit quickly. Oh, and you on yo' own with this. My men aren't available to you."

Carlos nodded. "I understand."

Nautica looked at Havoc and shook his head. "Can you believe that this fool just started a war with the worst bastards he could think of this side of the mountains? Stupid ass! Fucking with people he don't know shit about."

Somewhere deep down, Carlos felt the need to respond, "I know exactly who the Love boys are. I got this under control."

Slap! Havoc open-handedly slapped Carlos across the face.

"You really don't get it, huh? You fucked with the wrong dude. Bruh, not my hands nor any of my shooters will have any part of this, and if I ever catch you around my brother again, I'ma chop yo' head off. Understand that. Let's go, man."

After placing his gun in its holster, Nautica straightened his shirt. Havoc smiled at Carlos and walked toward the door. Once they exited, Carlos limped to his private restroom and rinsed his mouth, as it was bleeding from the hard slap that Havoc had delivered.

He grabbed a wad of tissue and placed it at his lip. Once the bleeding was under control, he grabbed a second wad of tissue and walked to his desk. After he sat down, he grabbed his cell phone and called his connect. While he waited for them to pick up, he placed the tissue back at his lip.

"Yeah, what's up?" his connect answered.

"Are you sure you gon' be able to control yo' family?" Carlos asked harshly.

"I told you I got them. They're too busy planning the funeral to worry about anything else. Let me handle them, and you do what you need to do," his connect replied.

"Man, I hope so. I'd hate to have to kill you too," Carlos growled and hung up.

He leaned back in his chair and closed his eyes. His heart was thumping wildly. Had he fucked up? He shook his head as the realization that he may have done just that sank in. Not only did he have to worry about the Loves, but he had earned a new foe in Nautica Banks, a man who learned everything he knew from the man responsible for teaching the Loves the secret of battling a war: Nautica's father.

The Loves

Before leaving Greensboro, Kendra received a text from Bridget, Tyrone's love interest, whom he'd met while he was visiting Kendra over the summer. She had arrived and was at the airport. Kendra asked her brothers if they'd mind taking her to the airport in Greensboro to pick her up. She knew that they wouldn't mind, but she also knew that they had a lot to figure out with Tyrone. It was almost mid-afternoon, and they still had to go and speak with their parents about the arrangements they had made.

"Do this," Sean started. "Get her an Uber and have them meet us in Mebane. That way we can all meet up in forty-five minutes or so, versus us having to drive over an hour there and back."

Kendra agreed, and after scheduling the Uber trip and alerting Bridget of the plans, they headed to Mebane.

Once they arrived, Kendra got out, and when Bridget walked over to hug Kendra, Sean began to cough. "She's . . . she's . . ."

"Don't even say it!" Kendra warned as she glared daggers at his head.

He laughed hard for the first time since they'd been back home. He leaned in and whispered, "She's a cracker!"

Kendra hit him and shook her head. "She is just white on the outside."

"Oh, my God, Kendra, I just can't believe that this has happened," Bridget cried as she hugged Kendra tighter and tighter. Kendra could feel her body shaking.

"Come on, let's go to the house," Kendra murmured as they got in the car after Brent helped her put her bags in the trunk. When they arrived, John took Bridget's bags in as she and Kendra sat on the front porch for a while. The wind was blowing, and the sky was filled with clouds. They could smell the water from the pond. The crickets and owls were filling the air with their sounds.

"It's so peaceful sitting out here. I can see why Dre spoke so highly of it. I never realized that your family owned so much land and crops out here," Bridget started. "Are you sure there won't be an issue with me being here?"

Before Kendra could answer, a large commotion was occurring inside the house. Kendra stood up and raced into the house.

"This ain't the time nor the place for your bullshit, Jackie," Sean was yelling.

"These are your kids, and they deserve to be here! I'm sicka yo' ass treatin' them like fuckin mules! They are your children, nigga!" Jackie yelled back.

When Kendra ran in, she searched the room, and her mother was nowhere to be found.

"I know who kids they are. And you're right, they do deserve to be here, but you don't! You're just a mistake I made that led to these other mistakes I made! I own the fact that they're mine, but it don't mean I don't regret it. Fuck you talkin' about, ho! Get yo' dirty ass on outta here and," he continued, looking at his boys, "if y'all don't like what I just said to y'all mammy, well, you can leave with her. Just know that I got a great memory when it comes time to give y'all some money."

As Sean continued his tirade, more cars began to pull into the driveway. Sean looked out the door and realized that his crew had arrived. He looked back at his boys. "Matta fact, Troy, come with me, and, Li'l Rob, see your mother out, then come back in here and help get some of this stuff cleaned up."

Troy glanced at his mother, unsure of what to do.

"Now!" Sean growled.

Troy jumped and hurriedly followed his dad outside.

"See, that's why I never wanted to be bothered with this family. They can't even act civilized at a time like this. It's no wonder one of 'em got killed. It was bound to happen," Kendra overheard her Aunt Louise mumble.

"What did you just say, you ol' hag?" Kendra asked as she turned to face her elderly aunt.

"I . . . I didn't me—" she started.

"Naw, yo' ol' bitch, don't get tongue-tied now! Say what the fuck you just said. My brother was a perfect kid. He didn't get involved with bullshit, and for you to say . . ." Kendra paused. "Say it again. I dare you."

Without saying another word, Kendra lunged at the woman. As she grabbed at her, her aunt's wig slipped off and onto the floor. Kendra slapped her across the face, and Louise fell to the floor. Everyone watched, but no one dared to move in the older lady's defense.

John rushed over and picked Kendra up as she was about to stomp the woman.

"Put me down dammit! She deserves to get her ass whooped! Did you hear what she said? I'll scratch those old, beady eyeballs out dat bitch's head! Put me down!"

John didn't say another word as he wrestled Kendra out of the house, fists flying and legs kicking. Once he was at his trailer, he set her down on her feet.

"Calm down, li'l baby. Look, I know that you're angry, but what the family don't need right now is you in jail. Use that head of yours."

Kendra balled her fists as she stood glaring at John. "I don't give a fuck about none of that shit."

As she attempted to walk around him to head back to the house, John pushed her backward roughly. "Chill the fuck out now! Yo' momma needs all of y'all surrounding her right now. Besides, who gon' watch out for your homegirl? I know you didn't fly her all the way out here just to leave her alone in a place she knows nothing about."

Kendra began to cry. She covered her face and fell into John's chiseled chest. He wrapped his arms around her and held her tightly.

John could feel Kendra nuzzling his neck. He tried to pull away, but she gripped him tighter.

"Please," she whispered.

"This isn't the time," he began.

"It's the right time for me. Please don't say no," she whispered as she kissed him softly on the lips.

"I don't want to take advantage of you," he replied.

"Well, let me take advantage of you," she replied. She needed to feel something because since she had learned of her brother's death, she barely felt anything other than darkness.

She pressed her body against John's and gripped his dick. "You seem ready to me," she whispered as she kissed him again.

"I don't want you to hate me in the morning," he again protested.

"We will worry about 'in the morning' then. Right now, I'm trying to feel you inside of me. I won't take long at all."

He laughed, "Shit, ma'am. Well, let me g'on ahead and oblige you then." He lifted her up and carried her up the stairs into his mobile home.

She started laughing. "This ain't no *Gone with the Wind* kinda party, John. Put me down."

She and John laughed for a minute. They sat down on the sofa, and she looked over at him. "We ain't got to do nothing. I don't know what came over me. I think it's just I feel so lost. You know? Like I'm in a nightmare that won't end. My brother was a great person. He didn't deserve to die. All that replays over and over in my mind is what his last moments were like. Was he scared?" She looked over at John. With a mask of anger, hurt, and confusion, she sighed, "He deserves retribution."

John nodded and wiped the tears that were falling. He leaned over, grabbed her by the face, and kissed her deeply.

She closed her eyes and gave in to her desires. He stood and undressed, and she was taken aback by how sexy John was. He was muscular all over. His bowlegs made him even more attractive. She also took in the sexiest part of him—his bullet wounds. He had three as far as she could see, which meant to her that he was a warrior. She stood after he finished undressing and allowed him to remove her clothes. Once they were both naked, he stretched her out on his couch and opened her legs. She closed them and shook her head.

"We ain't got time for all dat, cowboy."

"You talk too damn much. Shut up and move yo' hands," he replied as he swatted her hands away.

She frowned, wondering who the hell he thought he was talking to as she did as he told her.

He turned her body so that she was sitting up, facing frontward on the couch. He got down on his knees and slid her toward him until her bottom was on the edge. He lifted her legs and placed each one opposite one another on his shoulders. She gasped as he dipped down and began tracing her clit and pussy opening simultaneously. He sucked on her clit, then stuck his finger deep inside her as he continued pleasuring her. He could feel her walls contracting as he slowly slid his finger in and out. He slurped and nuzzled her pussy just as she had his neck earlier.

"Oh, fuck! Eat this pussy, John!" she moaned.

She began to buck her hips faster, keeping in sync with his finger. As he pushed into her deep, she could hear him let out a moan.

He pulled her down on the carpeted floor, positioned himself between her legs, and pushed deep inside her slowly. They both let out a sigh of pleasure. Kendra lifted her legs and wrapped them around his waist. A few minutes later, they were both climaxing and clinging to one another.

Kendra pulled away from John's embrace and sat up. She avoided looking at him as she began feeling around for her clothes.

"I appreciate that. I gotta get back to the house and help Bridget settle in," she told him.

He sat up on his elbow and stared at her. "No problem, love. I'll walk you back up."

He stood, showing his magnificent body, and as bad as Kendra wanted to drag him back down to the floor, she knew she had to get back to check on everyone. She finally turned her gaze from his naked body and continued dressing. Once they were both fully dressed, they walked back to the main house.

Upon entering, they saw that Le'Tera was in the process of cleaning up and putting out everyone who wasn't family.

"I'm tired, this has been a long day, and y'all gots to go. I appreciate the visit, but I'm done wit' it," she was fussing.

Kendra looked around and noticed that chairs were overturned, the curtain in the parlor was hanging from the rod, and the television was smashed.

"What happened?" Kendra asked Brent, who was sweeping the floor.

He looked at her and nodded in Le'Tera's direction. "Momma whooped Aunt Louise's ass after you left. Where have you been anyway?"

"Yo' farmhand decided to rescue Louise from my wrath. He took me to the pond. I wish I'd stayed now. I could've helped Mom."

Brent laughed, "That short lady didn't need any help. She needed that outlet. John did the right thing taking you outta here. Mom can restrain herself and knows when enough is enough. You don't."

Kendra hit him on the arm and laughed, "I'm not that bad. I've made a whole change in my life."

"Whateva. You need to go rescue your friend from Lisa. She's been talking her head off since she's been here."

Kendra looked around and saw Bridget sitting on the sofa and Lisa sitting next to her, her mouth speed chatting. Before she could walk over to Bridget, her mom stopped her.

"Who is this white girl you done invited to my house?"

Kendra turned. "Ma, can you keep your voice down?"

Le'Tera got louder. "I will not lower my voice! Who is that white girl ova dere?"

Hearing Le'Tera's question, Bridget nervously stood and walked over.

Kendra sighed, praying that her mother wouldn't make her out to be a liar. She had told Bridget that no one would trip about her being there, but at that moment, she wasn't so sure. "This is Bridget. She works for me and was also Tyrone's girlfriend."

Bridget nervously stuck her hand out. "I wish we were meeting on different terms, ma'am. Tyrone was special to me. The night he . . . well, the night that this happened, we were on the phone, and I heard . . ." Bridget began to cry, and Le'Tera embraced her before Kendra could.

Kendra frowned because whatever Bridget was going to say seemed worthy of hearing. She wasn't going to press her about it, at least not yet.

After a few moments, Le'Tera released Bridget. "Go and clean yourself up. We will get through this somehow."

Bridget walked to the restroom, and when she walked back out, she walked out the door and sat down on the top step. She looked around and closed her eyes. She hadn't known Tyrone but for three months. They hadn't had enough time to explore a relationship.

She began to sob silently. Kendra walked out and stopped in her tracks as she watched Bridget's shoulders shaking. She moved forward and sat down next to Bridget.

"I'm sorry for all this crying. I feel so empty. It's not fair, Kendra! We didn't get to do anything we talked about. Dear God, how can this hurt me so much? We didn't know each other long, but, Kendra"—she paused for a moment—"I felt like I'd known him my whole life."

"I know, baby girl. I'm hurting too." Kendra sighed.

Bridget looked up. "I'm so sorry. I have no—" she started.

"Don't you dare say what I think you're going to say. You were Tyrone's first love. I didn't see it at first, but y'all were meant to cross paths, no matter how brief." Kendra smiled as she wiped her face.

"I heard it, you know."

"Heard what?" Kendra asked, already knowing what she was talking about. She just needed to hear it.

"I heard them kill him. He called me and didn't disconnect the call when they pulled up on him. I heard the man say that he was going to kill him because of something Sean did that interfered with their business. Tyrone knew they were going to kill him. I couldn't hang up, even though my heart shattered. I didn't want him to be alone. It's crazy, I know, because I wasn't there physically, but I—"

Kendra gulped and shook her head. "Don't say no more, Bridget. We got a long week ahead of us. I need a stiff drink."

As they walked in, John was still there, talking to Sean and Brent. Kendra was mentally drained and didn't care what they were talking about. She just wanted to take a shot and go to bed. As they walked in, John and Kendra stared at one another, sharing a knowing look. The intimacy that they shared earlier would be continued at a later date.

Kendra was the first to break eye contact. She walked to the kitchen with Bridget behind her. After she grabbed a bottle of tequila from the refrigerator and handed two shot glasses to Bridget, they walked upstairs.

Chapter 5

The Funeral

Thursday

The day before the funeral, Taye and Kendra took Bridget to a few of Tyrone's favorite places. They wanted to give her a piece of Tyrone that she could take back to Texas with her. Kendra was glad that they decided to go out because she needed to avoid seeing John as much as she could. She was starting to feel like their one night of fun was a mistake. He wasn't doing anything to pressure her, but her body was. Every time they were around one another, her coochie started doing the waltz. She needed to stay focused, and that man was definitely a distraction.

Taye brought a bag and decided to stay a few nights with Kendra. She wanted to give her friend the emotional support that she knew she needed. She also quickly bonded with Bridget and hated that she and Tyrone didn't get to see their future blossom.

They awoke and said a quick prayer. No one wanted breakfast, and outside of a sigh here and there, the house was quiet. Everyone was lost in their own thoughts. By the time everyone showered and got dressed, the funeral car had arrived.

As they packed into two family cars that would be in use for the service, Bridget felt a cold chill go over her body. She couldn't help but smile. As she started crying, Taye wrapped her arms around her and assured her that she and Kendra would be next to her. She nodded and got in the car.

As they rode, Sean's phone kept beeping, but he refused to look at it. He had his boys riding with Le'Tera and Omar.

The family chose to not have a viewing of Tyrone's body. They wanted to have a quiet family funeral at the church and bury him in the family's mausoleum.

Twenty minutes later, the family cars arrived and parked. The family exited the cars and walked down to where Tyrone was to be laid to rest.

Sean, Melanie, Kendra, Taye, and Bridget got out of the first car, and Omar, Le'Tera, Brent, and Lisa got out of the second. Le'Tera instructed everyone to walk ahead of her. She had to gather herself. It was the first time that she'd been away from the house since Tyrone's death, and the reality that she was leaving her son behind a cement slab grabbed at her heart.

Melanie linked her arm with Sean's, and they headed down to the graveside service. A few people were already there waiting for them. As they approached, the attendees stood out of respect for the family.

Sean glanced over to his left and saw Jackie standing in the back row with Troy and Li'l Rob. They stepped forward as he got closer, waiting for Sean to approach so they could join him and the family. However, Sean turned his head, leaving the boys hurt and Jackie fuming.

One by one the family members were guided to their seats, but before Le'Tera walked to her seat, she stopped and grabbed Li'l Rob's hand and pulled him and then Troy out toward her.

"Come on," she replied, throwing a disgusted look at Sean. She hated how he treated her grandsons and was at her wits' end with it.

She asked a few people to move a row back so that the boys had a place to sit. Once they were seated, Le'Tera walked and stood next to where Sean was sitting with his arm resting on Melanie's lap, and she sneered, "Move down! I wanna talk to you about how you treat them boys. Soon!" she whispered as she sat down.

Melanie overheard what she said and rolled her eyes.

Le'Tera caught her and laughed, "If I weren't burying my son today, I'd snatch those thangs out'cho head."

"Ma!" Sean cried softly.

Le'Tera looked at him. "Don't talk to me, Sean. Just don't!"

Sean sat back and stared ahead, waiting for the service to start.

Suddenly, the sound of tires traveling up the gravel road sounded. Everyone's attention was drawn to the cascade of cars pulling up. The first two were dark gray Range Rovers, followed by two black Cadillac Escalade ESVs and then another gray Range Rover.

Brent looked at his mother. "I guess they decided to attend."

Sean shook his head and gave Omar a side glance. "I got a feeling that a storm is about to brew."

As the huge entourage of men exited the vehicles, Clinton Love stood in the middle, fixing his suit and tie before descending the hillside to greet his children. Two of the men stood firm at the second Escalade with their arms clamped in front of them. Omar moved in front of Le'Tera as if guarding her from Clinton.

"Listen, we aren't here to start any trouble. I just want a word with my family," Clinton Love assured Omar once they were standing eye to eye.

"I really don't think that you should be here right now. I mean, where were you when he needed you?" Omar asked. "I'm his father and have been since he was a baby! You don't belong here."

"Omar, please," Le'Tera whispered.

Omar stared at his wife, then shook his head and threw his hands up. "Fine, but only because of you!"

Clinton and his brother, Craig, walked forward and stopped in front of Le'Tera, and tears gathered in Clinton's eyes. "My son is gone, huh? Trust me when I say that there will be hell to pay!"

Le'Tera nodded her head, giving him her silent approval. Clinton walked over to his other kids, who were seated in the front row of the mausoleum. He shook their hands, then pulled Brent and Sean to the side. Kendra watched through tear-filled eyes as her only sister, Christine, finally exited the car and headed their way.

Le'Tera grabbed at Kendra's arm and whispered, "She looks just like you."

Christine was Kendra's half sister. Before their parents split, Kendra had learned that her father had started a new family, which was why he and Le'Tera split up, but not before Tyrone was conceived. Omar stepped in later and assumed responsibility for the boys.

Because her father decided to send her to a private school at 11 years old, she had never really gotten a chance to interact with Christine, which caused her to feel slighted and sour toward all of them, including Tyrone for a good portion of his childhood. It wasn't until he reached his early teens before they bonded. Kendra had a hard time forgiving her mother and father for sending her away. They kept every one of their kids, who all had a murderous past, yet she was the only one who was put away. She learned, though, that they did it for her own good, and she had grown to appreciate it.

Once she hit 18, she was ready to fly on her own. She used the money that she had saved over the years to move to Texas and start a talent management company. It was a small firm in the beginning, but she and her small team—Bridget being the first person hired—worked tirelessly for success, and after signing two top-name clients, they were fast-forwarded into success. Her company had gained notoriety, which landed them on a list of the top twenty most successful management firms. She and Christine finally connected, and they visited each other in the beginning, through the summer, but suddenly it stopped. Life took them in different directions, but they maintained contact here and there.

"Hey, baby girl," Christine said as she approached Kendra. She gave Le'Tera an empathetic smile. She had never met Le'Tera, but she had heard so many good things about her from Tyrone and Kendra.

Kendra hugged her tightly. She was glad that they decided to show up. "Hey, sissy. Are you okay?" Kendra asked once they let each other go.

"I'm good. I know you're having a rough time. How are you, Ms. Le'Tera? I wish I were meeting you under other, more pleasant circumstances."

Le'Tera smiled. "Thanks, sweetie."

Christine hugged her sister once more before heading over to the front row where Clinton was seated alongside Brent, John, and Sean. They were the pallbearers, and Clinton wanted to assist them. He had played a minimum role in raising Tyrone, but it didn't hurt any less knowing that he was about to place Tyrone's body in an above-ground grave.

Throughout the funeral, Sean noticed that Melanie was texting off and on. Twice he saw her phone ring, and she flipped it upside down. She saw him eyeing her, so she smiled, placed the phone in her purse, and placed her arm around Sean's shoulder.

Sean, Brent, John, and a few others helped push the coffin in its position in the mausoleum with Kendra going in behind, placing three white and purple tulips on his plot. She kissed her hand and placed it on his casket. "Love you, little brother."

After everyone was out, the door was sealed once again.

Le'Tera was half carried to the car, but she made sure that her grandsons were with her in the family car. They pulled off and headed back to the farm.

Sean, Brent, John, and Clinton

Sean, John, Melanie, and Brent climbed into the Escalade with Clinton and headed to the farm.

"I need to drop her off at the crib right fast." Sean looked over at Melanie. "Let me see your phone."

"Why?" she asked, frowning.

"Melanie, if you don't do what the hell I said . . ." he growled.

Clinton and Brent pretended to not hear the exchange between the couple.

Melanie looked at him and shook her head. "Here!"

She handed him her phone, and he opened it up. He scrolled through the messages, and after reading what he found, he placed her phone in his pocket.

"What the fuck, man?" she asked.

"We just buried my brother and you sitting there conducting business?" he asked.

"Listen, somebody gotta do it. I understand you and your family are going through something, but we still gotta eat, Sean. You couldn't focus on it, so I did it for you. I got yo' back," she told him.

He looked at her and started to hand her the phone back, but he changed his mind.

"Try that bullshit wit' somebody else. That was disrespectful as fuck, B."

She rolled her eyes and sat back in a huff. He cut his eyes over at her, and after three minutes, he snapped, "Here, man!"

He gave her the phone, then looked at Brent. "I got a text during the service, and my guys found one of the guys responsible for Tyrone's death. The boy been bragging about the murder. They got him tied up in the barn. John, when we get there, I need you to get some thick rope. I feel like baptizing the bitch in the pond before we kill him."

Clinton nodded his head with approval. "I'm with it."

They dropped Melanie off and then drove down the dirt roads leading to their barn. They had several acres of land, and they knew that no one would be able to hear or see what they were about to do.

As they pulled up, four men stood outside the barn with machine guns, and the others were inside, beating the young man they had scooped up. They could hear the screams echoing from inside the barn as well as the wild noises from the dogs barking and horses neighing inside.

After they got out of the Escalade, they greeted the men standing outside. When they entered the barn, Sean quickly realized who the kid was. He sat down and dropped his head, then stared at John. "Ain't this some real fuck shit?"

"Not really, 'cause we ready for war!"

"Are we?" Sean asked.

"My guys came here ready to shoot up some shit, so yes, we are ready for war!" Clinton assured him, putting an emphasis on "we."

"Who killed my brother, nigga?" Brent was growling as he punched the boy in the face.

The boy's head wobbled, and blood flew, but he refused to talk. After a few more punches and still no answers, Brent pulled his gun. The boy could barely hold his head up.

"Wait! Wait! Don't kill him. I got this, bruh," Sean said, putting a halt to Brent's assault on the boy. Sean grabbed his phone and dialed Melanie's number.

"Baby, can you send me Nautica's number?"

"Sure thing, babe," she replied before hanging up. A few minutes later, he was dialing his number.

Nautica

Nautica and Havoc were sitting at the local high school, watching Havoc's nephew's football game, when Nautica's phone began to ring.

"Yeah?" he answered.

"Hey, bro, this is LT. We got a real tough situation that needs to be addressed. You see, my guys just picked up your little brother 'cause word is he was involved in my brother's murder. I mean, what do you think I should do about this?"

Nautica's face turned black and contorted into an awful scowl as he listened to Sean. Havoc knew without even asking who was on the phone and why.

"I know who did it, bro. I can give you his info. Just don't hurt my brother. Let me handle him." If he replied with anything crazy, his brother would definitely have his head on the chopping block.

He had to use his common sense to reason with Sean. He knew that Sean didn't want to kill his brother, because if he did, he wouldn't have called him.

"Who the fuck was it, bro? 'Cause your brother definitely ain't talkin'. As a matter of fact, let's just do this: you and your squad is going to handle this shit for us, and your brother will walk away alive. I can't say he will be unscathed, but he will be very much alive."

After Nautica ended the call, he looked at Havoc. "Call our top shooters and send them out. Tonight!"

Back at the House
Kendra, Taye, Christine, and Bridget

After they arrived home from the funeral, Le'Tera and Omar went to their bedroom while Kendra, Taye, Christine, and Bridget went to the den. Christine was lying across the daybed with her arm thrown over her face. Kendra was in the bathroom, trying unsuccessfully to hide the fact that she was crying. Christine didn't usually show a lot of pained emotions. She looked at that type of display of emotions as a weakness.

Kendra finally walked out of the bathroom. Bridget was balled up on the couch, crying uncontrollably, while Taye was sitting at the foot of the couch, patting her legs to console her.

Having seen and heard enough crying, Christine sat up on the daybed. "Shit, y'all gon' stop all this damn crying. Dre wouldn't want y'all acting like this. Taye and Kendra, y'all already know that. C'mon now. Let's get dressed and go take a few shots for our brother."

Kendra nodded as she smiled and whispered, "I am so glad you are here. Do you know of anyplace we can go?"

"I know the perfect place," Taye answered.

"Well, all right, let's go get dressed and head out. I'll be the designated driver," Christine told them.

Two Hours Later

As seven o'clock approached, the ladies were dressed and ready to head out. Before they left, Kendra noticed that her brothers hadn't returned and neither had John. She already had a feeling that they and their father were out seeking retribution, something that she wanted to be privy to.

She walked to her mother's room door and knocked lightly. Omar opened the door seconds later.

"Is Mom good?"

He nodded. "She's finally sleeping."

"Good. We are about to head out for a while. I will keep my cell on me, so if you need me, call."

"Okay, baby girl," he replied before shutting the door.

Kendra walked back down the stairs, and they left. Forty-five minutes later, the girls walked into C Lounge, a popular nightclub on the west side of Greensboro. It was one of the only elite jazz clubs in the Triad area. There was always a live artist spotlighting there, and it was full of the most prominent people around.

As they chose a table in the back, Taye motioned for the waitress to come over. She ordered a round of drinks for everyone. Kendra was putting on a great front, but the pain from losing her brother was taking a toll on her, and Christine could see it in everything she did. She grabbed Kendra's hand and gave it a squeeze.

After a few drinks, Kendra had convinced Christine to get up on the stage and sing. It was karaoke night, and Christine decided to oblige her. She felt that it would loosen Kendra up a bit. Christine stood on the stage and thought about her brother, Tyrone. She smiled and began singing "Missing You" by Missy Elliott.

As she sang the song with perfection, she had unbeknownst caught the eye of the club owner. She gripped the microphone, and she moved her head as the melody flowed from her lips.

Chapter 6

Carlos

"Who is that young lady on stage?" Carlos asked his head waitress.

"I'm not sure, but I can find out for you," Tracy replied.

"Okay, yes, do that. I like her sound," he told her.

Tracy looked at him and laughed, "I bet that's not all you like."

"Go back to work, Tracy," he ordered without looking at her again.

Christine finished singing, and when she got back to the table, they had a few shots poured. She downed the first two that were set out for her, and then she sat down.

"Girl, you chose the right damn song, but later I'ma need you to put down some Mary J." Kendra laughed, hugging her.

"Thank you." Christine smiled.

They sat at the table, taking shots and sharing happy memories about Tyrone. Christine was just happy that they were out enjoying themselves.

Carlos walked out of his office just in time to see the young lady he was fixated on earlier in the evening exit the stage. She didn't once glance in his direction even though he silently willed her to do so. He shook his head as he laughed inwardly at the thought, cursing himself. "Damn, nigga, who are you supposed to be, Magic Mike?"

He leaned against the door ledge of his office and pulled on his cigar as his gaze followed the woman.

Just then, JD, his club manager, walked up. "I need you to sign these forms, Carlos."

Carlos took the forms and signed them. When he handed them back to JD, he nodded toward Christine. "Send her to my office. With her voice, we could definitely use her here."

"Right away, sir," JD replied and walked away.

Before JD could make it to the other side of the club, gunshots rang out.

Pow! Pow!

Everybody scattered, leaving an open view of the floor, and lying on the floor was the very lady he had hoped to talk to. He instantly grew angry and began shouting orders to his men. "Call 911. Now! Listen, I want y'all to find out who the hell is behind this shit!"

He ran over to the woman, kneeled, and smiled as she looked up at him. He leaned over and whispered, "Be very still. You have been shot, but the ambulance is on the way. You will be just fine. Just hold on."

Christine's eyes fluttered open, and she smiled, rubbing her upper arm and feeling the nick and the small amount of blood that was present. "No, no. I'm okay. It's just a flesh wound."

Carlos smiled. "What's your name?" he asked.

"Christine."

"Christine what?"

"Kent," she replied, giving him her mother's last name. She had never changed it to Love after she learned that Clinton was her father.

Before he could reply, some guy asked to speak to him, and a look of concern gripped his face. He turned his attention back to Christine. "I have to go, but if I give you my phone number, will you call me?"

She nodded. "Yes."

He helped her up, and they exited the club through the back door. He and Christine hopped in the back seat of his car, and he had his driver pull around to the side and drop Christine off at the corner of the club.

"Would you like for me to take you home?" Carlos asked.

"No, no, I came here with my sister, and I can't leave without her. Listen, I'll be okay."

"I understand, but I have to go handle some things right now. Can I get your number?"

"Of course."

After he got her number, Carlos headed off to his house. Only a select few knew where it was located.

"That hit came from Nautica. It was his man's truck that opened fire on the nightclub," his head of security told him.

Carlos sighed, "It's war then."

Kendra

Kendra was drunk, but not so drunk that she didn't realize Christine wasn't with them. Kendra frantically searched the crowd for Christine. She was pushing forcibly through the large group of people. Everything was in chaos.

Ten minutes passed when finally Bridget, who was also looking for Christine, tapped Kendra on the shoulder. "There she goes right there!"

Kendra followed Bridget with Taye behind her.

"Oh, my God! Are you okay?" she cried once she got close enough to realize that Christine had been hurt.

"Yeah, it's just a graze. Let's go before these folks start shooting again! I ain't got my gun with me," Christine replied. They hurriedly walked to the car. Once everyone was in the car, she started it up and sped off.

Kendra was mentally done. She needed something to soothe her soul, and she knew exactly what it would take. When they turned down the long dirt road leading to the farm, Kendra looked over at Christine. "Let me out right here. I need to clear my head a bit."

Christine shook her head. "Hell no, Kendra. What's wrong with you?"

"I just need time to myself," Kendra whispered.

"Well, when we get to the house, you sit on the porch and clear your mind there, but I'm not letting you out here. We still got five minutes to go before we get to the house."

Kendra sighed. She knew it was no good to argue with Christine. Once they pulled up to the front porch, Kendra got out and sat on the bottom step leading to the house while all the other ladies went inside. Bridget stopped briefly.

"I'll be in in a little while," Kendra said as she pulled out a blunt to steady her nerves.

She knew it wasn't right to use him for sex, but with the feeling that John gave her, she would gladly suffer whatever karma threw her way. She stood up and walked down the path leading to John's trailer. She knocked on the door, but there was no answer. She turned the doorknob to see if it was open, and to her surprise, it was.

Kendra fell across John's couch and clumsily began taking her clothes off, then began searching Netflix for a movie to try to relax. She had lost her brother, her heart, and damn near lost her sister earlier at the club. She didn't wanna know what was in store for her family next, and she didn't wanna think about it. She pulled a blunt from her pocket. Five minutes into the movie, she fell asleep with the blunt unlit, still in her hand.

Nautica and Sean

Nautica and Havoc were sitting in Havoc's 1969 Oldsmobile, smoking and drinking. Nautica's phone rang, and he answered it solemnly, "Yeah, tell me you got him."

"Man, we missed. The club was crowded," the caller explained.

"I didn't tell y'all to shoot up no damn club. I said to kill Carlos. That means you walk up to him and blow his fucking brains out! Fuck!" Nautica ended the call and shook his head. "Goddammit, I oughta let them kill Rick's damn ass. He should've never dealt with that boy!"

Havoc sat back and sucked his teeth. "We can just kill those Love boys and be done wit' da whole thang."

Nautica laughed, "They hands reach long, bruh. When you in the game, you move smart, not crazy."

"Yeah, but you don't move scary either, bruh. You letting them boys bitch you up for real," Havoc replied.

Nautica looked over at Havoc and smiled, showing his gold fronts. "Now see, it ain't scary. It's surviving. If you ready to die, then you go after them."

"If I have to die for something, it's gon' be dat," Havoc boasted.

"That sound about stupid. You won't be able to appreciate the feeling of being respected 'cause you gon' be dead. Make it make sense."

Havoc laughed, "Bruh, give me that darn blunt. No mo' weed fo' yo' ass!"

Nautica looked down at his phone and nodded his head. He dialed the number that Sean had called him from.

"You got some good news fa me?" Sean asked as he answered the phone.

"There was a little snag," Nautica answered.

"Meet me at the football field ova by Bartlett Yancey School in forty-five minutes." Sean hung up without letting Nautica respond.

Sean called a few of his shooters and told them to suit up and meet him at the ball field as well. He left John and Brent at the barn, but his father, Clinton, went with him.

When Nautica pulled up to the football field, he saw three cars near the GO BUCCANEERS sign. He parked close to where Sean had asked him to meet him. He noticed that Sean, along with a few of his other goons, were sitting on the bleachers. Although there was little light out there, he noticed that the one person he didn't see was Rick.

"Man, I'ma take out as many as I can before I stand there and just let that nigga kill me. You heard?" Havoc said as he placed his gun in his pants.

Nautica laughed, "Just chill, man. I got this."

After he tucked away his gun also, Nautica and Havoc got out of the car and walked over to where Sean was. Havoc was ready for war, and despite what Nautica had said earlier, he wasn't going to cower.

"Aye, just know that I ain't lying down without a fight. It's because of Nautica that I don't kill you myself."

Sean laughed, and two of his guys stepped forward. "Chill, y'all. I got this." Sean stood face-to-face with Havoc. "Nigga, I think you need some straightening, and I don't mind giving it to ya. Now, when I whoop yo' ass, I'ma need you to understand"—he paused and looked at Nautica—"yo' boy gon' owe me one. Feel me?"

Nautica looked at Havoc and shook his head. "Aye, man, what we get if he wins?"

"Yo' brother," Sean replied as he stepped back.

Havoc smiled. "This what the fuck I'm talking about!"

"Learn to respect, nigga. You gon' have to show me what you built of. You wanna kill me, let's get it," Sean sneered.

The two men squared up while Nautica took a seat opposite Sean's crew. Havoc swung first, connecting each blow that he delivered, facial hits and body shots, and the last two sent Sean diving to the ground face-first.

He rolled over quickly and shook it off. He immediately jumped to his feet. "Goddamn, that big boy got some strength behind his punches. But now it's time to teach him a li'l something."

Sean began throwing blows: face, body, body, face. He danced around, avoiding any blows that Havoc threw. Havoc fell and lay on the ground, chest hurting, face swelling, and he was sure his nose was broken.

"Naw, nigga, get up. Lesson ain't ova yet. Got a few mo' things to teach you!"

Havoc looked at Sean and regretted escalating the situation in the first place. Sean didn't stop! Nautica sat back and dropped his head. There was nothing he could do at that point.

Nautica's attention was drawn to a man walking up with his head bent downward. He didn't know what was going on, but he kept his eye on the man. Something about him seemed familiar, but it was too dark to tell. Minutes later, the fight was over.

Sean walked over, breathing heavily and sweating profusely. He sat down and closed his eyes to catch his breath. When he reopened his eyes, he noticed that Clinton had finally gotten out of the truck and was sitting on the bleachers. Nautica and one of Sean's guys were helping Havoc to the bleachers, and once he was seated, Nautica walked over and stood next to Sean.

"Say, bruh, what's gon' happen with my brother?"

"Have a seat," Clinton said without looking at Nautica.

"I'm good, bruh," Nautica replied without looking at Clinton. "Listen, just tell me what the deal is so we can be on our way. Is he dead?"

"First off, muthafucka, you were asked to sit down, or do you not know who you're talking to?" Clinton asked as he lifted his head.

Nautica frowned. Was it really him? "Are you fucking kidding me? Pops?" Nautica whispered.

"Sit down," Clinton again ordered.

Five years earlier, Clinton had invited Sean to his home in Florida, and upon arrival, he was introduced to his half brother. Nautica, whose name was Nathaniel Love, was the offspring of the woman with whom Clinton had cheated on Le'Tera, causing the first stage of their marriage breakdown. Clinton offered Sean and Nautica wealth if they didn't tell anyone that Nautica existed. They both agreed and decided that they'd respect one another and stay within their own corners of the hood.

"Listen, y'all need to fix this to where both my sons stand after this. Your beef ain't wit' each other. Outside of me, you're all he has, Sean. Remember that," Clinton said.

"I don't owe his brother shit, though! No, I'm not handing Rick over to you. Get your goons in order and bring me Carlos's head. Simple. You see, they took something that meant the world to my momma, and somebody gon' pay. So, I'ma hold on to Rick 'til you do what you need to do. I promise I won't kill the li'l bastard, but each day that you make me wait for Carlos, I'ma spill some of that nigga's blood. I promise I won't kill him, though," Sean informed Nautica. He then stood up and walked to the truck, leaving his father and Nautica to talk.

"I'll try to convince him to send Rick home, but you gotta make this right. I lost my son, and yes, Rick is your brother, but Tyrone was blood too. Fix it, son." Clinton walked away, following Sean's path.

Havoc glared at Nautica as he was gripping his bruised ribs. "Brothers, huh? Now that makes more sense."

"Shut the hell up. You ready to go? Can you make it to the car with yo' bad ass?"

"Yeah," Havoc whispered shamefully.

"You can't earn yo' respect getting beat the fuck up." Nautica laughed as he helped Havoc to the car. "Told you not to try him. It runs in the blood."

Chapter 7

Sean and Melanie

The next evening, Sean was at Melanie's house talking business with Clinton and Nautica. They were making arrangements to pick up a shipment of drugs that they were supposed to have retrieved before Tyrone's death. Since the funeral was over, they decided to make the run, get back to package it, and distribute it.

Melanie was across from them, sitting Indian-style in a pair of jogging shorts and a tank top. Her curly Afro was glistening. She was texting out orders to their crew. She was popping her mint bubble gum, causing Sean to snap.

"Goddamn, Melanie, give that gum some rest. Just snap! Snap muthafuckin' snap! That's all the fuck I'm hearing. Take dat shit outta yo' mouf or swallow it! Either way, chill on that poppin' shit, B!"

Melanie glanced over at him and rolled her eyes. She wasn't about to let Sean get under her skin. She continued to chew her gum and text. A few minutes later, pop! She popped her gum loudly. When she finished laughing, she looked up, and Sean was standing in front of her with a look of rage on his face.

He grabbed her around her throat and started to squeeze. "Bitch, I know damn well you ain't trying me."

Melanie's eyes began to water, and she began to shake, but not from fear. "Nigga, if this ain't leading," she choked out, "to us fucking, then get yo' dick beatas off me!"

She began hitting him and kicking. He jumped back. "Well, stop fucking playing wit' me. You already know how I am, B."

"And you know how I am too. Fuck you sayin', bitch!" she retorted. "Listen, y'all handle y'all shit somewhere else 'cause my house is closed!" She stood and walked off in a huff with her gray and white slippers flopping.

Sean glanced over at Clinton and Nautica, who were gazing at them, enjoying the show.

"Damn, she put all of us out!" Clinton laughed. "You betta go handle that, son."

Sean gave Clinton an "I wish I would" glare while following Melanie.

Melanie rushed into the bedroom, slamming the door behind her. Sean was on her ass, and after he busted through the door, he slammed it also.

"Now you hear me, and you hear me good, Sean. If you eva handle me like that again in yo' natural-born black-ass life"—she took a quick breath—"I'll snatch yo' nut sacks off and plant them where you plant yo' bodies!"

Sean took the last three steps that were separating him from her. "I let you get away with that bullshit in front of Pops because I ain't wanna embarrass yo' ass and it was kinda cute." He reached out and grabbed her curly Afro near the nape of her neck, causing her to momentarily stand on her tiptoes and bite her lip. "But if you ever threaten me again," he said, moving his hand from her hair, grabbing her under her chin, and gripping it, forcing her head back, "I'll blow that mouth slap off yo' face."

Melanie swore she saw the blackness that encased his soul right then, and she swallowed. As scared as she was, she was just as turned on. She decided to play Russian roulette. "Nigga, you ain't gon' do shit to me!" He couldn't do anything but fuck her up physically or fuck her period. Either way, she had shot her shot.

Sean could hear the defiance in her voice and knew that it wasn't coming from a hostile place but a sexual stance. He again let his hand slide to her throat and applied pressure, but this time, the look that frightened her before was a look that made her pussy throb.

She bit her juicy bottom lip, and the look of desire wasn't mistaken. "You know I know how to finesse my savage!"

"Shut da fuck up and get on yo' knees!"

"Yes, baby," she replied as she took her clothes off. Once she was naked, she turned and assumed her position on the edge of the bed.

Sean pushed his pants and boxers down to his ankles and began to massage his dick. As it got harder and harder, he began to rock his hips back and forth. He moved closer to Melanie's ass and took his finger and rubbed it between Melanie's ass cheeks. He groaned as he felt her warm and extremely wet pussy. He removed his fingers and slid his dick in her slowly, feeling her ass tense with each thrust. He began to move quicker, purposely drawing moans and groans from Melanie. She was speaking inaudible words as her face was buried into the pillow. He reached down and kissed her back, ran his fingers in her curls, and snatched her head up.

"What you say, B? Huh? When"—he slammed into her once hard—"I"—he pushed into her again hard—"tell"—he growled once more—"you to chill da fuck out, that's what I mean."

Sean pulled out and shot his cum on her butt.

"I know you playing, Sean!" She stood and turned, facing him.

Sean pushed her back on the bed and laughed while pulling his pants up. "Man, chill, B. You needed some act right. You didn't deserve the dick I just gave you! Man, go take a shower so we can go on and get some food."

Melanie sat down on the bed, glowering at Sean as if she could strip the skin from his body. "Dat's fucked up."

"Gotta stop playing and listen sometime. Do the right thang, B." Sean laughed as he walked out of the bedroom, leaving Melanie horny and furious.

He walked into the room where Clinton and Nautica were sitting.

"Had to handle that shit. Yo' feel me," he said as he tapped Clinton on the shoulder.

"Boy! I know goddamn well you ain't just put yo' pussy-smelling hands on me!" Clinton fussed as he jerked away.

"Yeah, good pussy though, Pops!" Sean laughed.

"Boy, I don't give a damn if that bitch was a pure gold mine! Go bathe yo' ass!"

Nautica sat back, laughing at the exchange between his dad and brother, slightly envying their relationship.

"Well, I'ma go and join my boopie in the shower." Sean laughed as he walked back to their bedroom.

Once Sean was out of earshot, Clinton looked at Nautica. "I think we need to be heading on out. Seems like those two gon' be busy."

"Bruh ain't right, Pops." Nautica half laughed.

"We're stuck with him," Clinton replied as they headed out the door. He put his black brimmed hat on and buttoned his coat.

"You sure about dat?" Nautica asked lowly.

"Positive," Clinton replied, glaring at Nautica sternly.

"Just checking, Pops."

"That betta be the reason. I'd hate . . . never mind. Let's go grab some food."

Nautica paused, staring at Clinton. *Did he just threaten me?*

He slowly followed him, knowing at that moment he'd never measure up to his precious son. He would have to keep one eye on Clinton and Sean.

They got in his truck and drove off.

Back in the house, Sean had undressed, walked into the bathroom, and opened the shower door. He got in and stood behind Melanie and pulled her against him. "Round two?"

He reached her, rubbing her clit while kissing her neck. She closed her eyes and tilted her head back, enjoying the way the water massaged her face and chest while his fingers massaged her clit. She opened her legs, giving him full access to her.

"Tell you what," he whispered, "you can finesse my savage ways as long as I can finesse yours." He moved his mouth from her neck to her ear and nibbled the tip of it, causing her to shiver. "Deal?" his deep voice drawled.

All she could do was nod.

He bent her over, and with one swift motion, he was inside her once again. This time, he took his time hitting and caressing the walls of her pussy with his dick.

He turned her around to face him and lifted her up. She instantly wrapped her legs around his waist, and he pressed her back against the wall of the shower and fucked her so good that she came three times in fifteen minutes. After they were finished and their shower was complete, he grabbed a towel and wrapped it around his waist. "Next time I won't be so nice, dammit!"

She laughed, ran, and jumped on his back as he was walking by the bed. They tumbled over on the bed. She climbed on top of him and stared at him. "I do love you. I love you. I love you," she whispered, singing it to the song by GQ.

"You betta know it, B."

She kissed him and proceeded to get dressed. Sean started getting dressed, and as he was buckling his belt, his cell phone began to ring. He quickly pulled the small end of the belt through the loop and answered, "Yeah?"

"Bruh, the cops got yo' baby momma's house lit up right now," the caller informed him.

"What the fuck?" Sean groaned.

"Yeah, it looks like they taking Li'l Rob to jail. I figured you'd wanna know," the caller replied.

"All right, hit me back when they leave." He hung up. "Fuck! What the fuck else can go wrong?"

"What's wrong, babe?" Melanie asked.

"Li'l Rob just went to jail," he replied.

"Leave his ass in there a day or two. He'll be inclined to be more careful," she said as she sat on his lap.

Sean said as he laid his head on her back, "Shit, I would, but you know I can't do that."

"How else is he gon' learn? You know that boy could use some straightening. He has been careless one time too many, Sean," she said as she stood up and walked to the door. "At least tonight. Let's go get some food. We can worry 'bout him tomorrow."

"You right. Let's go." Sean put his phone in his pocket, and they walked out.

John

When John left the barn, he drove straight home. He was exhausted and needed a breather. When he pulled into his driveway, he noticed that his television was on. He knew that he hadn't left it on, so he eased out of his truck and closed the door quietly, although he knew that if someone was inside, they knew that he was outside. He quickly pulled his gun and eased up his steps. When he unlocked the door, he found Kendra asleep on his couch. He stared at Kendra lying on the couch. All he could smell was her perfume and alcohol. He didn't know where she had been, but he was happy that she was there.

He walked to his kitchen and poured a glass of juice. He sipped his drink and smiled once more. He was very much smitten by her, and he loved that she was sleeping peacefully, with no panties on, on his couch. She had deprived him of her time, but he understood why. She wasn't there for a country romance. She was there to bury her brother. He knew that she was probably using him as an escape from the tragedy, but he didn't care. He set his glass down on the side table and took his clothes off. He was about to take her to another level. He stared at her as he massaged his shaft. As it sprang to life, he walked over and stood over Kendra. He turned his head sideways and smiled. He could tell that she was a sound sleeper, but tonight, she was about to awaken to the wonderful world of dick.

He eased down and lay behind her, lifting her left leg so he could slide in her warmth. As he slid his dick in slowly, he felt her pussy begin to throb. He pushed in more and she moaned loudly. He pulled out quickly and eased it back in. He moved up a bit more, sliding her hips toward him, and began to move at a steady pace, pausing to nibble on her back. Kendra arched her back, pushing her ass back against him. She was angry as shit with him, but damn, he felt so good.

John slid his dick out slowly until just the tip of the head was in, refusing to move as he felt Kendra's ass twitching. She began rotating her ass, and he pulled out a bit more. The head of his dick sat right at the edge of the opening of her vagina.

"Tell me why you deserve this dick," he whispered.

Kendra closed her eyes and swallowed hard. She turned and looked into his brooding eyes and shivered. He had never looked at her in such a way.

"Did you hear me?" he growled as he slapped her across her ass.

She cried out as he pushed into her hard.

He slowly ground into her as he gripped her hips. She closed her eyes as she felt her walls begin to tremble. He continued to fuck her, rubbing her nipples, knowing that they were one of her hot spots. As he again slapped her across the ass, he flipped her over on to her stomach and raised her ass. He had never hit her in anger, but he was going to punish her. He slid in deep and hard as he slapped her ass and dipped down. Kendra cried out and tried to move forward. Again, he gripped her hips and dipped down deep and hard inside of her. She was shocked at this side of John, and it was both pleasurable and frightening.

"Why do you deserve this dick, Kendra? Huh?"

He slapped her across each ass cheek, then opened her cheeks up, took his thumb, and began massaging her asshole. He didn't put his thumb in, but she prayed he would.

Kendra wasn't thinking about answering any questions and prayed that he'd feel offended by her stubbornness. She wanted him to beat her pussy and asshole like she had violated him.

And he didn't disappoint her. He fucked her hard while talking shit to her. She needed to feel the pain and pleasure he was giving her. It made her feel something other than the nothing that she had been feeling since learning of Tyrone's death. Afterward, John and Kendra lay next to each other, out of breath, but completely satisfied. After ten minutes passed, Kendra sat up, but John pulled her back down.

"Aht, don't get up yet. Let's just enjoy this moment."

Kendra looked at him and noticed the way he was looking at her. He was catching feelings, and she wasn't ready for those kinda problems, and she told him just that.

"John, you do know that I'm leaving in two days. I have a business to run in Texas, and I'm sure my employees and clients are ready to resume business as usual."

"You just lost your brother. I'm sure they'd understand you taking some time off," John whispered. "Shit, if they don't, fuck it. You got money, Kendra. Yo' family got money."

Kendra sat up once again only to have John grab her and pull her back down as he had before, but he wrapped his legs around hers so she couldn't move away. She struggled a bit, but it was an unsuccessful attempt.

"I'll let you go when I'm ready. Chill, shawty. If you're leaving in two days, then I'ma need a li'l bit mo' of yo' time and sweetness," he said as he placed his hand between her legs. They were in the spooning position. John used his thighs to open her legs and began massaging her clit once his hand reached her wetness. She closed her eyes and swallowed hard as she felt a new wave of sensations engulfing her body.

John took his time and reacquainted himself with her body.

Kendra could feel his dick throbbing against her ass, and a small amount of warm precum began wetting her ass. She pushed her butt against it, ready for round two, but John refused to give her the satisfaction of his dick. He wanted to taste her. As he released her legs and rolled her over on to her back, he stood up. "Don't move, I'll be right back."

When he returned, he had a warm, soapy washcloth and cleaned her woman cave. Afterwards, he feasted on her, leaving her body shaking and wanton. She needed to feel his penetration. Once he finally entered her, she felt like her body and soul were doing somersaults in a ray of warm sunlight.

She wrapped her legs around his waist and arms around his neck, grasping at his head. He leaned up and stared at her as he continued to fuck her. She looked at him and started to close her eyes.

John grabbed her around her throat and kissed her. "Look at me."

She turned her head sideways, but he turned it roughly back to face him. He dipped his head to kiss her, but she turned it before he could, causing him to straddle her. He got on his knees, never pulling out of her, moved her body downward just a bit, placed the heel of her feet on his shoulder opposite one another, and began power driving her pussy.

Kendra could feel every bit of his dick, and even though he was trying to roughhouse her ass, she was enjoying it. After they were finished, he whispered, "You can leave early in the morning. I'll tell them that I found you drunk asleep by the pond and let you stay with me."

"Or we can just acknowledge that I'm grown and ain't gotta explain shit to nobody," Kendra replied as she stood up. John lay on his side, propped up on his elbow.

"I have to go, John. You know, we went to this club and my sister was shot."

"What? Does Sean know about this?" John asked as he stood up and started putting his clothes on.

"I'm not sure, but it was just a flesh wound. Someone just literally started shooting up the place."

John put his boots on and shook his head.

"What are you doing?" Kendra asked as she noticed John grabbing his gun.

"I'm walking you back up to the main house. I can't let you go up that path by yourself. You know, snakes and all."

Kendra laughed, "I found my way down here on my own, sir. I'm sure I can get back to the house just fine."

"You did indeed. You had a li'l taste for Big J, huh?" he joked.

Kendra blushed a bit. "I did."

John smiled. "We are here anytime you need us, Miss Lady."

Kendra watched him move closer to the door. "Well, since you insist on walking me back up, let's go."

They walked up the path in silence, both wondering if they'd have more intimate moments or if this was their last time together. When they reached the back of the house, John stopped Kendra.

"Just let me feel them juicy lips." He kissed her and walked away afterward.

Kendra shook her head. "He's trying to make it hard for me to leave."

Kendra walked into the house and heard Brent arguing on the phone. She assumed it had something to do with Tyrone, but she was too tired to inquire about it. Whatever it was, she'd find out the following morning.

She walked into her room and sat down on the bed. Bridget started stirring around a bit, and Kendra whispered, "I didn't mean to wake you. Are you okay?"

Bridget sat up, her blond hair falling across her face. She pushed it back, and her swollen eyes and puffy red cheeks told Kendra that she was not. Kendra sat down and hugged her friend.

"It's okay, love. I get it, and I know its gon' take some time for both of us, but I'm here with you. Okay?"

Bridget sniffled. "I heard the man's voice."

Kendra frowned. "What man?"

"The man who killed Dre," she whispered.

"I know, sweetie. I know that's haunting you like crazy. It may sound weird, but I'm glad Tyrone wasn't completely alone when he died."

Bridget shook her head. "I meant tonight. At the club. The man who killed Dre was at the club. I couldn't see who it was because of all the commotion, but he was there, Kendra."

Kendra's face told several different tales as she soaked in the words that Bridget had just spoken. "Huh? Why? I mean, why didn't you say anything afterward?"

"There was a lot going on. The shooting, Christine getting shot, and then on the way home, you were in a mood. I didn't want to do that to you, but when I fell asleep, it's all I dreamed about. The voice. Tyrone refused to go down like a bitch though. He stood up 'til the end." Bridget began to cry as well as Kendra.

Taye walked in and shook her head. "Sis, it's gon' be okay. I've decided that I'm gon' go back to Texas with y'all. You need someone with you right now."

"That sounds great." Kendra laughed as she wiped her face. "Let's try to get some rest, okay? Shit been crazy."

"I agree," Taye replied as she lay down next to Kendra. The ladies soon fell asleep.

Carlos

Carlos decided that he wasn't going to his home in the city. He needed to hide out while he figured shit out. Outside of the six guys who worked for him in the streets, he didn't have anyone to turn to. But then it dawned on him that he had one person who could help him out of his current mess—the person who put him into it.

As he traveled outside the city limits, heading in the opposite direction of Wake County, he called the man responsible for his current situation.

"Aye, I'm going to the mountains. You know where. Get at me when you straighten shit out with yo' peoples!"

Carlos didn't give them time to respond. He hung up and began staring out the window. He was tired and hadn't had any sleep. He tried multiple times to catch a nap, but every time the driver had to press down on the brakes too hard or people began honking their horns, he would awaken. He wasn't really concerned about them Love boys. He was more afraid of what Nautica was out to do to him.

His home in the Fontana Mountains was secluded and a safe haven for him. He gazed at the steep hills as they got closer to the mountains. He figured he'd eat, take a shower, then retire for the night. However, not before he called the lady he had the pleasure of running into at his club. He wasn't going to miss out on getting to know her.

Chapter 8

Sean

Sean woke up, and after dropping everyone off at the airport, he headed over to the apartments where Jackie lived. He sat across the street and watched his sons walk out with a huge black man, talking and walking to a Durango truck. The man had all the signs of a narc. Sean prayed that he was wrong and that Li'l Rob wasn't trying to sell him and his family out.

After the Durango pulled out, Sean followed it for a while. The guy finally pulled into the driveway of a gray house with burgundy shutters, and a garden of flowers decorated the huge porch. Sean drove past slowly, giving the man a nod as he continued down the road.

Sean wasn't dumb by far, but he'd blow that whole house up with everyone inside if they were indeed cops and had turned his son against him.

Four hours later, Sean had his answer. As Sean was eating his hotdogs, his cell phone rang. "What's good, TK?"

"Listen, Li'l Rob is in the front room, asking to re-up. What do you want me to do? Something doesn't feel right about this, man. He ain't never came here without you."

TK had just confirmed what Sean had been thinking: his son had gotten out of jail to destroy him.

"Call bruh and 'em right quick. Tell them to clean up and prepare for an inspection. Nothing, and I mean nothing, is to be moved out or in. I need at least two guys at each location, and tell the guys on the street to take a couple of days off until I say otherwise. No money will be made for a few days. I'll handle Li'l Rob."

Kendra, Taye, and Bridget
One Week after Returning to Texas

Kendra walked into her building and greeted everyone as politely as she could. Being back wasn't as easy as she thought it would be. Her last few days at the office, Tyrone had been there. She was happy to see Bridget at work, sitting at her desk. Taye eyed her and waved. Afterward, she and Kendra walked into Kendra's office.

Her employees all gave her a solemn, "Good morning," as they could see that she wasn't in the best of moods, which was understandable.

As soon as Kendra sat down behind her desk, she turned her focus to her computer. She clicked the mouse to open the file of a potential client she hoped to sign to her management company. She suddenly turned her chair around and glanced at the plaques on her desk. She earned them, but they meant nothing to her at that moment. She shook her head and looked downward.

Taye shook her head. "Kendra, are you sure you're ready to work? No one will blame you for leaving."

"No, I got a whole team depending on me. If I don't make money, they don't," she retorted quietly.

"Well, in that case, get yo' feelings in check while you're here. You got a whole other hat to wear today. You're a boss, and you gotta suck up that pain and do what you came here to do. Make money," Taye told her.

Kendra knew Taye was right, and she nodded. "I just need a few minutes to get my head straight."

"I understand, babes. You got this, and I'm here for you. You're like a sister to me. We're family, so I got yo' back. Tyrone wouldn't want you to fold right now."

"I know. I'ma go wash my face right quick. Be right back. Aye listen, while I'm in the restroom, can you listen to a few tracks and let me know what you think? I'm trying to establish if my potential client has what it takes to be a star."

"Sure I can," she replied.

Kendra handed Taye an iPad and scrolled down, clicked on a folder, and pushed play. She handed Tyra the iPad and walked out to the restroom.

When Kendra returned, Bridget was sitting in the chair opposite Taye.

"How are you today, Bridget?"

"I'm okay," she lied. Truth was, she felt like her whole world was over. She had fallen for Tyrone, and he swore to never hurt her, but the pain that she was feeling had her thinking he had lied unknowingly.

"Okay, I can tell you're not, but we gotta work, babes. Listen, when my ten o'clock gets here, have them wait in conference room C and make sure there are drinks present please," Kendra told her assistant.

"Yes, ma'am. I already have copies of our marketing package along with the contracts ready. Would you like me to place them on the table now or wait?" Bridget asked.

"Wait until I call for them, and, Bridget, I thought we talked about your appearance. You represent my company and me. Therefore, you need to add some flair and sexiness to your style. We have to entice our prospective clients to allow our firm to rep them."

"But—" Bridget started but was quickly cut off.

"I've been doing this for years, and my determination to succeed is why I have one of the top management firms in Texas! Just do as I asked. Please," Kendra replied.

She walked over and closed her office door, then sat down at her desk, pulling out her Gossip lotion and applying it on her arms and neck. She stood up and checked her appearance in the full-length mirror that was in her personal bathroom. She practiced different smiles, trying to decipher which one didn't look so forced. Although she was in mourning, her dark skin seemed to glisten like silk.

She was a beautiful woman and wore her clothes well. Her apple-bottom ass was firm and jiggly in her blue and white pinstriped pantsuit. She had a bit of a stomach, but she didn't mind it at all. Her breasts sat up perky thanks to the support bra she wore. When she smiled, the small gap in her teeth made her more attractive, in her opinion, and the burgundy highlights in her hair set her appearance off.

She walked back to her desk, sat back down, and began reading over the file of her prospective client while Taye continued listening to the music samples that Kendra had given her.

Devon Gray was a young, talented rapper. At least, he would be after she finished with him. She just hoped Bridget didn't stick out too much. Bridget had been with her firm for years and was good at her job. However, being that she was the only white girl in the firm, she stuck out and often dressed like a plain Jane. It was unbelievable to Kendra that Tyrone could've fallen for someone like her. She had never wanted to mingle with her staff outside of business activities, but Bridget had become special to her since Tyrone's visit.

As she stood to go and inspect the conference room, she pulled her suit jacket down and adjusted her shoulders, then walked out. As she walked down the hall, she was greeted by a few more of her employees. She had three marketing agents and two in-house attorneys who contributed to her company's success. Unique Management Firm managed models of every nationality and size. They also managed musicians and actors. She had made millions from making others successful. She had worked long hours and at times went days without sleeping at the beginning of her career, and it all paid off.

"Hey, Kendra. How are you today?" Charles asked as she passed by him.

"Hey, Charles. Listen, I need you to sit in on my morning meeting. It's going to be in conference room C."

"Aye, you're the boss. I will be there." He smiled.

"Thank you." Kendra smiled as she continued on her way.

When she entered the conference room she sighed. She remembered showing Tyrone all the pictures of all the clients she had helped or still worked with that she proudly displayed on her wall. She remembered how his face beamed as he acknowledged her accomplishments and couldn't wait to join her in her endeavors, but a horrible fate intervened.

"Get your head into this!" she scolded herself, remembering Taye's words just moments earlier. She cleared her throat and walked to the table.

The cherry-oak table that sat in the middle of the room was shiny and clean. The room was prepped for the meeting just as she had asked.

"Um, Kendra, I'd like to have a word with you if it's possible," Charles said from the doorway.

"Can it wait? I really don't want to lose focus on what's about to happen. Let's have lunch, okay?" she replied.

"That would be great."

Charles was one of her longtime friends as well as her top attorney. He had helped her close over ten high-profile deals that were also highly profitable.

The two walked out of the conference room, and she asked everyone who was going to be present in the meeting to join her in her office so that they could go over all the last-minute details. She also wanted to lead her team in prayer before the meeting. It was a ritual. She was far from a Christian woman, but she figured no harm no foul.

After Kendra said a quick prayer, which concluded their brief meeting, Bridget announced that their prospective clients had arrived and were sitting in the conference room, awaiting their arrival.

"Let's get 'em!" She laughed.

As they exited her office, they walked down the hall, steps in sync. As they walked into conference room C, everyone entered and took their seats, with Kendra walking in last. She loved the dramatics of their entry.

"Welcome to Unique Management Firm!" Kendra opened the conference by introducing her firm to the group of guys before her. She paced the floor, expressing the importance of having a management firm like hers to represent each one of them. She stood, pointing to the board showing the geographic area that she would target as well as a promise to come up with the right plan to promote Devon.

As she turned to look at the guys, she noticed that Devon was staring at her ass. When he looked up and realized that he had been caught, Kendra thought that he'd look away shamefully. Instead, he smiled, letting her know in no uncertain terms that he wasn't shy or embarrassed at what she noticed. She looked away anxiously and continued to deliver her proposal.

Once they were finished, they all stood talking and agreeing that the firm was what they were looking for. She shook each guy's hand only to have Devon hold on a little longer than the others. She pulled her hand away, smiled, and walked over to shake the two other members' hands. When she turned to walk to retrieve her files from the table, she bumped into Devon. He stood staring at her, biting his lip.

She stuttered, "Excuse me."

"You good, baby girl," he told her, making no attempt to move. So, she stepped around him, grabbed her folders, and walked out of the room. Once she was in her office, she closed her door and leaned against it.

"Lord chile, these young ones getting a bit too much for me."

Taye looked up. "Oh, yeah? Why you say that?"

"One of my younger clients just tried to push up on me. I swear, I'm not ready for that, but if I ever decide to, I'll have that li'l boy singing love songs instead of rapping."

She walked over to her desk and sat down. She closed her eyes and thought about John, their last night together, and how she left without saying a word. He probably wasn't thinking about her.

"Taye, if I tell you something, you gotta promise to not tell another soul, not to mention browbeat me about it."

Taye looked up. "What's up?"

"Girl, when I was at the farm, I slept with John."

"The farmhand? Bitch, when?"

"Shit, a couple of times. That man, I tell you. He is just oh, my Godddttt!"

Taye frowned then laughed as she watched her best friend's eyes twinkle. "Damn, he got you like that? Not Kendra Love."

"Exactly! That's so not me. I don't do that love shit." She shook the thought from her mind, and before Taye could comment on the love statement, there was a light knock on her door. "Yeah, come in."

Bridget walked in. "Hey, boss lady. Just reminding you about the event at Trinity's Lounge tonight. The new artist you've been trying to get signed with UMF will be there."

"Oh, yeah, are you going to be able to attend?" Kendra asked while looking past Bridget to Devon and his team walking out. As he walked by, his eyes met hers, and he started smiling as Kendra shifted in her chair. As she cleared her throat, she looked back at Bridget. "So are you?"

Bridget frowned. "Well, I wasn't, but I can if you need me to be there."

Kendra smiled. "I can tell by your facial expression that you'd rather not. But that's something you're going to have to get over if your goal is to move up in my company. You have great potential, honey, and don't take this personally, but you got to get some of that whiteness out of you. You don't have to go tonight, but I'ma need you to step it up!"

"I . . . I'm ready to do whatever I have to do to excel in this company. Being the only white woman here, I have a lot to prove. I can do this. I can also bring a lot to the company with a different appeal for a whole new outreach to people, which means more revenue for Unique Management Firm." Bridget sounded like she was pitching a sale, which Kendra caught.

"You know, I like the sound of what you are saying. I tell you what, set some time aside Monday for lunch, and we will talk. But right now, we gotta get back to work. We will shut down around four so that we can get ready for this show tonight."

"Yes, ma'am!" Bridget replied excitedly.

Kendra ended her workday being updated by her team of all the progress the company had made in her absence. They kept her updated by email while she was gone, but they all needed to discuss everything as a whole team in person. Kendra was proud of how well they kept things together. She had to also give thanks to Bridget for delegating the workloads to the appropriate people. She had an eye for who was best at pulling in clients based on the category of management that they required.

After the meeting, Taye joined Kendra in the hall in front of her office and they left. Kendra called Christine to check on her as they left the building.

"Hey, sis, how are you feeling?"

"I'm good, sis. Have you talked to Clint?"

"No." Then Kendra paused. She didn't miss the reference of Clinton by his first name and not by "Dad." "Is everything okay between you and him? I noticed how you avoided him during Tyrone's funeral."

"Um, yeah, it's all good, sis. He just been so tied up with Sean that I haven't spoken to him much. It's cool. What you got going on?"

"Work as usual. You know how that goes."

"Yeah, I do. Listen, let me call you back later," Christine said.

"Okay, talk to you later." Kendra hung up and sighed. She didn't know what was up with Christine and Clinton, but she prayed they worked it out. She herself had never been that close with their father, but it wasn't a relationship that troubled her as she was sure it was troubling Christine. She got in her car and drove home.

Chapter 9

While Kendra was getting dressed for the event, her phone beeped. She glanced at it and smiled.

John: You left without a bye, Miss Lady. How you doing?

Kendra: I do apologize, sir. I'm good. Call me.

Kendra pressed send slowly. She wanted to talk to him, but she didn't want to seem too anxious. Once the text confirmed delivery, she sat down on the bed and waited. She didn't have to wait long.

"You missed me, huh, shawty?" he asked.

She laughed, "Maybe just a li'l bit."

"I'ma make you fall in love for the first time, li'l lady."

"How you know I ain't never been in love before?" she asked flirtatiously.

"You really want me to answer that?" he retorted. "The way you stared in my eyes as your pussy gripped my dick, and the way your arms grabbed my head when I tasted you. Shit, if I'm wrong, please tell me now. I'on wanna be just an average lover. I'll step my game up."

She dropped her head and smiled as she twirled the end of her lace on the hat that she was going to wear. "Well, you may be right, but still. What makes you think I'ma fall in love?"

"First, are you saying you gon' give me a shot? Don't think we should be having this talk if it's just talk," he inquired.

Kendra had never let herself out there much, and she wasn't sure if it was time. She sighed. "Let's take it slow and just let things play out."

"So I'ma put a pin in this conversation until later then," he replied.

They sat silently on the phone, and Kendra could hear Sean in the background yelling for John to meet him in the barn.

"Sean just pulled in. I'll call you back."

"All right," Kendra replied.

After she hung up, she walked into the front room where Taye was waiting. "What you think?"

"Girl, it screams sexy professional," Taye replied.

"I'll take that. You ready?" she asked.

Taye nodded. "As ever!"

They walked out and headed to the club. When Kendra and Taye walked into the club, they searched the room. She spotted Devon and his team and headed in their direction. As she walked through, she was shocked to find Bridget sitting across from where her clients were seated, waiting for her. She looked beautiful in Kendra's opinion, wearing a lovely pantsuit that fit her perfectly. Her blond curls were in a messy but sexy ponytail with a Chinese pin adorning her hair, which brought out the gold specks in her brown eyes. She wore a pair of blue heels that tied around her ankles. Her brother had the opportunity to love a real one, in Kendra's opinion. She was angry when she first learned about Tyrone and Bridget, being that, one, she was years older, and two, she also worked for her.

She had to shake the thought of Tyrone from her head. She had to be able to focus on her clients. Taye grabbed her hand and gave it a squeeze. She could sense her friend's pain.

Kendra smiled. "I love you, girl!"

"And the feeling is mutual, boo. Let's get a drink."

As they stood at the bar ordering their drinks, Kendra hugged Bridget. "Thank you for meeting me here. I know that it's not easy trying to get back to business, but we both got to. You won't have to go through this alone.

Bridget was kinda scared to go to the event at the club. After all the racial conflicts going on around the country, she didn't want to end up on the wrong side of the war.

"You look lovely tonight."

All three ladies turned and saw Devon standing behind them, cheesing hard.

"Thank you!" they all replied.

Devon laughed, "You're all welcome. I hope I can get a dance later on before you leave."

"Who?" Kendra asked.

"Shit, you. That's who."

Bridget spat out the liquid that she had just drunk, coughing continuously.

"Oh, um, yeah, sure," Kendra replied.

"Good. I'll be back for you in a few." Devon smiled and walked away.

"Boss lady, him wants some of yo' goodies!" Bridget stated.

Kendra burst out laughing at Bridget's juvenile statement.

Kendra sipped her drink slowly, and before she could finish it, Devon was yet again approaching her.

"Let's dance." He pulled her up and whisked her out to the dance floor. They danced for about two minutes when they were interrupted by a female who looked to be about 17.

"Who is this fat-ass bitch you all wrapped up with? See, if I had known you were going to act like this, I would've stayed at home."

Devon laughed as Kendra turned quickly and checked the young lady who had just approached them. "Little girl, if you don't go sit your ass down somewhere and behave . . . I'll send him back to you just as soon as my fat ass is finished with him! And trust me, if I weren't here in a professional capacity, I'd beat the brakes off your bony ass! Now run along before I take him home with me tonight!"

Kendra felt that Devon could've easily checked the whole situation and told his friend that she was his new manager, but he was intrigued by the exchange between the two women. The young lady stared at Devon, waiting on him to check Kendra. But when he didn't, she spun on her heels and stomped back to her seat, tripping over her own feet.

"Listen, I don't know what you think this is, but you got it all wrong if you think anything more than business can happen. I don't roll like that, and if I did, that little display right there would've been the end anyway. I don't do young'uns nor childish drama."

"I'm old enough to have you calling me daddy though! Don't let the age fool you. Besides, it can't be more than, what, a three- or four-year difference? I can handle it all!" he countered.

Kendra groaned, pulled out of his grasp, and walked away. Devon laughed but took in the view as she walked away.

Kendra walked back to the bar where Taye and Bridget were standing, talking, and shook her head. "Y'all, I feel sick to my stomach. That boy just really tried me."

"Girl, nooo!" Taye laughed.

"I told you!" Bridget sang.

"She been drinking?"

Taye laughed, "A lot!"

"Huh, I wasn't gone that long," Kendra replied, looking at Bridget.

She was sitting on the swivel stool at the bar, bopping to the music. Her ponytail was loosely hanging, and she was sipping her drink through a straw.

"Chile, she took two quick shots with that lady right there," Taye explained.

Kendra turned to see who she was speaking of. The lady saw Kendra looking and waved at her with a drunk grin. Kendra waved back and started laughing. "Damn, well, she needed this."

"Yeah, we all did," Taye replied.

"Let's go dance," Bridget suggested. She hopped off the stool and started dancing her way to the dance floor.

"Damn, they gon' laugh at us. Look at her," Taye whined as she and Kendra slowly walked to the floor. "She all uncoordinated and shit!"

"Fuck it!" Kendra laughed.

Finally, the time arrived for the showcase, and when they announced Devon's name, Kendra searched the room for him. When she saw him, he was sitting with his arm draped across the shoulder of the girl who had approached them earlier. The girl turned her head and kissed Devon before he stood. Kendra laughed. The last thing the girl had to worry about was her. Kendra half wished that she was the type just for spite.

Kendra checked out the crowd's response to Devon's performance. She peeped how they performed, but they weren't really interacting with the audience. She studied their weak spots and their strengths. After the performance, Kendra spoke with Devon and his team, thanking them for inviting her to see their show.

"Okay, we will sit down tomorrow with our team and decide the best route for you guys. Bridget will call you to set up your next appointment once we have a solid plan in place," Kendra explained.

"Damn, why you can't call me?" Devon replied with a mischievous grin on his face.

"Again," Kendra started, ignoring Devon's question, "Bridget will call you tomorrow. I really enjoyed the show."

"Hell, you were the show for me," Devon replied, licking his lips and flashing his golds.

"Man, listen—" Kendra started.

"Okay, okay. I got it." He laughed. He tapped his homeboy and pointed backward. "Let's go, man."

After they walked away, Taye looked at Kendra. "This might be a problem, boo. For real. Not all money is good money."

Kendra laughed, "Girl, listen, I'll give it to someone else before I lose this account."

"I don't feel so well," Bridget whispered. Her face had turned red, and her eyes were shaky.

"Let's get her home!" Taye laughed.

"Shit, I think we should get her to the bathroom first. I'on think she can hold whateva she tryin'a hold in."

"You take her, and I'll call a cab," Taye replied.

"Come on, Bridget," Kendra said as she helped her to the restroom.

About twenty minutes later, they were heading to Kendra's place. She decided it was best if Bridget stayed with her for the night and she could go home the following day.

As soon as everyone lay down, she texted John.

Kendra: Are you up?
John: Yep, sure am. How was your night?
Kendra: Crazy.
John: How so?
Kendra: Call me.

Seconds later, she and John were talking. She talked to him until four twenty that morning. When she hung up, she smiled. He made her night so much better.

Chapter 10

Sean and Melanie

Sean and Melanie were returning from a lunch date that he had planned for her. He was enjoying his food until he received word that one of his houses had been run up in by the police.

Troy: Aye, bruh, we got smashed in on. You know?

Sean: Is everything good? Y'all all healthy?

Troy: It's all good. We had everything ready for inspection.

Sean: Good. I'll holla at y'all in a few.

Troy: That's what's up.

After they finished texting, Sean got undressed and hopped into bed, and Melanie joined him. As they lay there, she kept staring at him.

"Babe? What's going on?"

He began playing in her hair and gave her a half laugh. "My son is trying to set me up, and I'm torn on what to do."

Melanie sat up and looked down at him. "He what? How you know?"

"They ran up in Jackie's shit and busted his dumb ass. Lucky for them, nothing was found in the apartment. He had sold to a few undercovers, and they finally snatched his li'l ass up."

"Okay. That don't mean he snitched though, babe."

"B, listen, he got out the next day. I didn't post his bond. His broke-ass momma didn't post his bond. Then he shows up at one of my houses looking to re-up. He knows that's not allowed. And then," Sean said as he sat up and started putting his clothes on, "that same house gets run-up in. I know it was him."

Melanie licked her lips, contemplating if she should say what was on her mind or just remain quiet, but she couldn't hold it in. "Sean, what would you do if it were anybody else?"

"You know what I'd do, but that's my son, Melanie."

Melanie shrugged her shoulders. "All I'm saying is that if you don't, ain't nobody gon' respect you and you gon' lose everything you worked hard to get. Hell, someone might feel that they can kill you, but you got to go do what feels right to you."

Before Sean could pull his pants all the way up, she smiled.

"Want me to suck yo' dick before you leave?"

Sean bent down and kissed her. "I'll be back later. I gotta figure this shit out."

"Okay, babe. Aye, whateva you do, I'm wit' you," she whispered.

"I know it, B." Sean walked out with a heavy load on his shoulders.

He got into his truck and placed the key in the ignition. He gripped the steering wheel tightly, then released it. As he sat in the driveway, he realized what he had to do. He started the vehicle and backed out. As he drove off, he called Jackie.

"Hey, we need to talk. Who there?"

"I have a friend ova," she replied.

"Male or female?" he asked as he turned onto the interstate.

"Sean, why? What's up with all these questions?"

"Male or female, and please don't try me, especially when I'm on my way ova there," he warned.

She was quiet for a second.

"All right, I'm about to pull up. Bet not nobody be there when I get there, Jackie."

"I hear you, man," she replied and hung up.

Sean shook his head and laughed. He pulled up to Sheetz to get gas and condoms.

"I ain't fucking that ho raw," he whispered to himself. He didn't want to fuck her period, but he had to make her believe that he was coming back to her.

Sean pulled up where Jackie lived and parked. He didn't want to be over there, but he had to see Li'l Rob. He got out of the truck and turned, pushing the lock button on his keychain. As he approached, he heard several voices inside. He hit his side and kept his hand there just in case he had to blow a bitch's brains out. He was licensed to carry and never left home without his registered gun.

He opened the door without knocking and walked in.

"Hey, Dad!" Troy greeted him.

"What's up? What y'all up to?" he asked as he sat down next to Troy.

He looked over at Jackie. "You look mad. You mad?"

Jackie rolled her eyes. "If you're here to see your kids, then visit with them. I'll be in the kitchen." She got up and walked out. Sean laughed.

"We playing *Madden*. You wanna play?" Troy asked once Jackie was in the kitchen.

"Why not?" Sean took his light jacket off and grabbed a controller. "Start it back over."

Troy did as he was told as he, his friends, and Sean started their game. After an hour, Li'l Rob finally walked in.

"Damn, boy, where you been?" Sean asked.

"Hey, um, Dad. What are you doing here?"

"Damn, I can't come see y'all?" Sean asked.

"I guess. Where Ma at?" he asked.

"She went in the kitchen," Troy told him.

"Okay," Li'l Rob replied.

He walked into the kitchen, avoiding eye contact with Sean. Sean sat there and stared at the kitchen doorway, wondering what was going on.

"Your turn, Dad," Troy announced.

"Oh, okay. Listen, this gon' be Daddy's last game. I need to talk to yo' momma."

After they finished, Sean walked into the kitchen where Jackie and Li'l Rob were. They seemed to be huddled together whispering and stopped when he walked in.

"Jackie, let me holla at you right quick," he said.

Jackie looked at Li'l Rob and smiled. She stood and followed Sean to the bedroom.

"Sean, what are you doing here? You already told me how you felt at your mother's house. I don't have time for this bullshit anymore."

"I want to try to make this work. I need to be with my kids and you. Let's go to the lake for the weekend and see if we can create some family moments."

Jackie folded her arms. "Whateva, Sean. You don't have to say all that."

Sean stood and walked toward Jackie. When he reached her, he stood directly in front of her and smiled. "You gon' give me some pussy?"

"Sean, hell naw! I knew it was something. What, Melanie won't give you none?"

"I broke up with her. I told her that I wanted to work things out with you," he lied.

Jackie was quiet for a while until Sean began to caress her hips and thighs.

"You gon' tell the boys to pack? We leave in the morning," he whispered as he slid his hand in her jeans.

She closed her eyes as he began to play with her clit.

She pushed him away and frowned. "Sean, if it's me you want, then why not wait 'til we get to the lake house to make love? Can you just hold me?" she asked.

He sighed, "If that's what you want."

He didn't care one way or the other as long as she agreed to the trip. He got his confirmation as he undressed to go to bed.

"Li'l Rob, Troy, pack y'all an overnight bag. We're going out of town tomorrow."

Sean could hear Li'l Rob groan, "Mom, are you serious? Why do I have to go?"

"Because I said so. Now go get packed up and order something from Uber Eats."

Sean shook his head. "That boy hates me."

Jackie turned. "He's just having a rough time right now, and he just feels like you turned yo' back on them."

Sean nodded. "I get that. Come on, let's get some sleep."

Later that night, Jackie looked over at Sean, who was snoring like crazy. She reached over and grabbed his phone off the nightstand. She typed in a code that she had memorized, and to her surprise, it was still the same: his mother's birth date.

She took a few selfies of her and Sean and sent them to Melanie from his phone. If he was lying about their breakup, she was going to definitely pull the trigger on it and dead it for good.

When they woke, she fucked him like she was trying to prove something to him, and she almost tricked him. Afterward, he got up still determined to figure shit out with Li'l Rob.

"Aye, I need to go get my bag. I'll be back in about two hours. You gon' be ready, man?" he asked.

"Yes, we will. Can you pick up some snacks for the trip?"

"I gotcha," Sean answered as he walked out of the apartment.

Sean walked into Melanie's house and saw her sitting on the couch with a gun. Her eyes were swollen and red. Her curly hair was wild and looked dry.

She looked up at him and wiped her nose. "So that's what you doing?" she asked.

"What are you talking 'bout, B? I came to get a few things 'cause I gotta make a run for a day or two," he replied. He didn't dare move from his spot.

"Naw, nigga, this what we doing?" she repeated, taking aim at his feet.

"Don't do nothing stupid, Melanie. I told you what I was doing."

"Well, tell me where you been," she said with an expressionless face.

Sean hadn't ever seen her like that and wasn't sure if he was going to make it out alive. "I'on know what you think you know," he started.

"Let me tell you then," she started as she stood up and grabbed her phone. "I do know that you were laid up with yo' nasty, pussy-hustling baby momma last night. How do I know? 'Cause I got this picture last night from yo' phone," she replied as she tossed it at him.

Sean looked at it and then back up at her. "Girl, this an old picture. Stop trippin'."

"Yeah, nigga, I rode past the trick's house, and guess whose muthafuckin' car was there? You wanna take a guess, bitch?" she sneered through clenched teeth.

"Okay, let me explain," Sean pleaded.

Melanie started crying, and when she wiped her eyes, Sean quickly reached up and grabbed her arm. As they wrestled, the gun fell from her hand, and Sean backed her up against the wall.

"I hate you! I hate you!" she cried over and over.

"Man, chill out, Melanie, and listen!" he yelled as he slammed her back hard.

"Get away from me! Let me go, you bastard!" she screamed.

Sean didn't know how else to get her to calm down, so he slapped her. Melanie glared at him and screamed loudly as she dived at him, scratching his face. Sean picked her up over his shoulder and carried her kicking and cursing into the bedroom. He dropped her down on the bed and held her down.

"Chill the fuck out, B! Listen to me. I'm trying to figure this shit out with Li'l Rob. I'm just trying to make them think I want to be a family."

"So that means you gotta fuck that nasty bitch?" she asked.

"I used a condom," he replied.

"Get off me, get yo' shit, and leave. I'm done. You know she fa everybody, nigga, and condom or not, you dirty."

Sean released her and laughed, "Melanie, I pay every bill in this bitch. I buy you every muthafucking thing you want. Ain't nothing you hurting for. Any other bitch who pulls a gun out on me, scratches my face, or even talks to me how you do would be dead by now. I love you, but I got to do this."

Melanie sat on the bed, staring down at her hands. "Sean, I may not hurt for anything, but I'm damn sure hurting." She laughed. "But you don't understand that. And at this point, I'm ova it. Go do what you got to do. I'll see you when you get back."

Sean turned and pulled some clothes out of the dresser. "I promise I'll make it up to you. B, you know it's us, right?"

"I guess. I'm gonna go to the store right quick. Can I have some money?" she asked.

"Yes. You know where it is," he replied.

She walked over to him and hugged him. "I understand why you're doing this, and I'm here for you. Do what you got to do, but come back for me, nigga. Not right back. And protect yo' dick."

Sean smiled. "I love you, B."

"Right back atcha."

She went to the safe and took out $500 and locked it back. As she walked out, Sean followed right behind. He locked the front door and walked her to her car. He opened her door and leaned in for a kiss. She quickly moved her head.

"Now you know I ain't gon' let that happen. Sean, although I said I understood, I'ma need a li'l time. Okay?"

Sean hated it, but he would give her that. At least she wasn't trying to kill him again. "Okay, I can respect that."

Chapter 11

Charlotte

Brent

Brent was sitting in his office with Shock and Fizz, his top goons and business associates. They were both smart, and they helped Brent out of many snags while creating his company. He was greeted with good news on the business front, but they still didn't have a clue as to where his product and money was. He knew that Ariana and Tony had spent some of it, but it wasn't possible for them to spend that much money and get rid of that much dope in such a short time.

"Man, I'm gon' have to just eat that loss. I'm too tired to even stress about it. I appreciate you guys for all the work you did while I was away. I'm gonna be back and forth for a while until we find out what happened to Tyrone, so I'ma need y'all to keep bringing in these clients. I mean, damn, y'all snagged Bobby Vane, one of the world's wealthiest engineers in the nation! We should focus on that, and whatever happens with Sean when I tell him that the money is gone will just have to happen."

Shock, also known as Jeffery Alston, nodded his agreement. "I'm with it. We can definitely find some top-end developers to start building the houses on the north end of Charlotte. We can also find some funding to help us."

"Let's get started on that," Brent replied.

"On it, boss," Jeffery replied.

As the men walked out, Lisa walked in. "Hey, you haven't heard from Ariana, have you?" she asked.

Brent shook his head. "I doubt she's gonna call me. She and Tony stole from me, and I called them on it. I can only surmise that they are living it up off me."

Lisa shook her head. "I hate she did that, but I don't put nothing past her. What you got planned today?" she asked.

"Probably whatever you got planned. Can we spend the rest of the day together?" he asked.

She smiled. "Yes, we can."

Brent stood and followed her out the door. He had no intention of ever telling her where Ariana was.

They walked out of the office and spent the day together doing nothing at all. She took him back to her place, and they cuddled up on the couch and watched movies, and Brent was just fine with that. He knew that Lisa was meant to be his, and he was going to make it happen.

Sean

When Sean pulled back up to Jackie's house, he got out of the truck and walked into the apartment. "Y'all go put y'all stuff in the truck. I need to holla at y'all momma real fast."

Sean pushed Jackie, who was standing in the front room, into the bedroom.

"What the fuck were you thinking going in my phone? Why would you send a picture to Melanie? That was some fucked-up shit. Stay the hell out my phone!" he sneered as he mushed her in the face. Jackie flew back on the bed and hit her leg on the side bottom railing. She cried out, and Li'l Rob ran in.

"Leave my momma alone!"

"Boy, who the hell are you taking to? Ain't nobody fucking wit yo' mammy. Go get in the goddamn truck and chill out before I beat yo' ass!"

Li'l Rob swallowed hard as he heard the tone in Sean's voice. He did as he was told but only after making sure his mother was okay.

"Man, let's go!" Sean growled and walked out of the room.

Seven minutes later, they were on their way to the lake.

Three hours later, Sean had pulled into the driveway of the lonely cabin. It was surrounded by woods, and the lake was just a few steps away. It was beautiful but deserted.

They got out of the truck and followed Sean inside. As he pushed the door open, Troy and Li'l Rob were directed to a room on the left while Sean and Jackie stood in the living room.

Bam! Bam!

A loud noise flowed from the bedroom. Jackie attempted to go check on the boys, but Sean grabbed her by the back of her shirt.

"Sit down!" Sean ordered with his gun drawn.

"Sean, what is this?" she asked as she slowly walked to the couch.

"Bring my son out here now!" Sean ordered.

A few of Sean's goons walked out with their guns on Li'l Rob.

"Son, why? Just answer me that?" Sean asked once Rob was standing in front of him.

"Why what? Why did I try to take up for mom? Because I'm tired of you being mean to her. We've been just fine without you!" Li'l Rob answered.

Troy was taken out of the house and escorted to the truck, where one of Sean's guys stood watch over him.

"No, why? Wait, let me rephrase that. When did you become a snitch? Huh? Yo' was gon' turn on yo' daddy, boy?"

"Pops, please listen. I didn't do it!" Li'l Rob cried as he stood staring into his father's eyes.

Sean's eyes filled with tears as he listened to his son lie. He had all the proof he needed that his son was a snitch.

"All this time I thought you were a loyal soldier. Nigga, I fed your ass, I clothed your ass. I spent thousands of dollars making sure you didn't want for shit, li'l nigga, and this is what you do?" Sean asked as his voice cracked.

Everyone stood watching and wondered what was going to take place. Sean had always preached that any type of disloyalty from anyone wouldn't be tolerated.

"Sean, just listen to him! Don't treat him like he is a paid hand. He's your son!" Jackie cried.

"No child of mine would betray me!" Sean sneered as he grabbed Li'l Rob by the throat and started squeezing. "I hate liars, and you betraying me is the worst thing that anyone could do to me! You once told me that you hated me. Well, you will die hating me! It's because of me yo' bitch ass is in this world, and I'ma take you out."

As Sean continued choking Li'l Rob, his youngest child, an eerie silence fell upon the room.

The onlookers were shocked at what was taking place. Jackie broke the silence that hung over the room as she ran forward, fist flailing.

"Noooo! You bitch-ass nigga! Let my baby go! Damn you!"

Before she could make it all the way over to where Sean was killing their son, Scott's big ass grabbed her and held her tightly. She fought him as hard as she could but to no avail.

When Sean stood up, he didn't say a word. He didn't look up for a long period of time. His body was shaking, and his heart was breaking!

"I'll never forgive you, never! I'll see you dead soon, you bastard! By your hands, our son died, and by mine, you will! I promise you that!" Jackie cried.

Sean shook his head. "Baby girl, that I truly believe. I know you will come for me." He reached around to the back of his pants and pulled out his .45. Pow! He shot Jackie in the chest, striking her heart and killing her instantly.

"Aye, man, clean this shit," Sean ordered, emotionless.

When he turned, he saw Troy standing in the doorway, staring wide-eyed. He didn't budge a muscle. Sean walked over and escorted him back to the truck. He turned to Scott, asking, "What did he see?"

"I don't think he saw you shoot them. Just the aftermath."

"You not sure? I oughtta kill yo' ass right here!" Sean growled, staring at Troy in the back seat. "Listen, help them clean this while I take Troy to my mom."

"All right."

Sean got in the truck and turned to face Troy. "You want something to eat?"

Troy shook his head. Sean stared down at Troy's legs and saw that he was trembling.

"Listen, son, whatever you think you saw, it wasn't what you thought. And don't say a word to anybody, 'cause the same could happen to you. And we don't want that, do we?"

Troy shook his head.

"Good. Now put yo' seat belt on so we can go."

Kendra

For a week, Kendra and her team worked diligently finding the right marketing tactic to introduce Devon to the masses. They reached out to every major broadcaster, online and abroad. Kendra appreciated the fact that it kept her a bit too busy to think about the troubles and losses in her life. She hadn't forgotten that her brother was killed or that the murderer was still breathing, but she had a life.

The only thing she didn't like was the fact that Devon kept making advances on her. She kept him at bay mostly by ensuring that anytime they met, someone else would be around. He was so persistent that it made her sick when everyone else thought it was adorable.

She would never mix business with pleasure. She'd never lower her standards to deal with such a loose-lipped kid. He was everything that John wasn't, and that made it much easier to ignore his advances.

"Kendra, don't forget you have an appointment at one o'clock. We already received all the photos that we requested from the photographer this morning," Bridget informed her.

"Yeah, I'm looking over them now. She is very beautiful. I just checked my email, and there are about twenty companies looking for a fresh, new look to represent their companies. After the meeting and she signs the contract," Kendra said as she stood up and adjusted her suit jacket, "call a few of them, and let's create a buzz using these three pictures. Let's see what kind of money these companies come at us with."

"Okay, I'm on it. I wanted to tell you that I started seeing a therapist to help me through this depression, and I don't want to step on yo' toes, but I think she might be able to help you as well."

Kendra picked up two manila folders and looked down at them. "Go through the emails that I forwarded to you and make the calls. I can handle my own depression." Kendra walked out of her office, leaving Bridget feeling like she should've kept quiet.

Kendra walked out into the hallway and saw Taye sitting at the table in her event-planning conference room, working with a team she had put together to coordinate the trail ride event for one of her clients. Taye had been a great friend through everything and a great assistant. She had almost the same educational background as Kendra in business, and her presence definitely complemented Kendra's business.

Before she walked into the room, her phone rang. She looked at it and saw that it was John. She smiled and texted him back quickly.

Kendra: Hey, handsome, I'm going into a business meeting, and I'll call you back once it's over.

She put her phone back in her pocket and walked into her meeting.

Thirty minutes later, everyone walked out of the conference room laughing and shaking Kendra's hand. When Gloria, the model who was there as a potential client, hugged Kendra, Bridget knew that Kendra had sealed yet another deal. After everyone left, Kendra gave Bridget a thumbs-up and smiled as she walked back into her office.

As Kendra sat down behind her desk, she called John back. "Hey! How is your day going so far?"

"It's going," he replied. "I miss you though."

"Awwww, so we're doing all this mushy stuff, sir?" she asked, smiling hard. Anytime she talked to him, he made everything seem better.

She leaned back and pictured John out at the stables with no shirt on, showing his abs with the love handles on the side that she had gripped anxiously and was ready to again.

As she started getting lost in her conversation, there was a knock at the door.

"Hold on a sec," she told him. "Yes?" she called out.

The door opened and it was Devon. "Hey, gorgeous. Look, I know you wasn't expecting me."

"And you're right, I wasn't. Devon, what are you doing here?"

"Well, if you hadn't been so quick to speak, I could've finished. I wanted to take you to dinner tonight."

"First of all, no! Second of all, who are you speaking to like that? I don't know what y'all young men are doing to attract a woman, but that's not the way to go. And thirdly, I'm very much involved. But even if I weren't, I wouldn't go out with you. You're very rude, womanizing, and you just—"

"You're just not me!" John spoke out.

"Dammit!"

Instead of Kendra pushing the mute button, she had pushed the speaker button, and John had heard everything.

"Aye, no skin off my back. I feel you, playa. I'd let a nigga know that she's taken also. Respect," Devon replied. Before he walked out, he left a piece of paper on her desk. "In case you change yo' mind," he mouthed.

Kendra grabbed the paper and tore it up and tossed it in the trash.

Kendra finished up her call with John and walked out to ask her marketing team to stay late so they could go over a plan to take their new client worldwide. It was time to expand their network and outreach sources. She held two more meetings, and by four o'clock, she was finished. She walked out and announced to her team that they'd be meeting in the main conference room. Everyone headed back and took their seats while waiting for Kendra to enter. Kendra walked back into her office and grabbed her laptop, tablet, and notepads off her desk. Her back was turned to the door, so she didn't see Devon approach.

"I like that view," he commented, startling Kendra.

"Devon, why the hell are you here?" she asked as she turned to face him. Her head was hurting, she was tired, and she was ready to relax. She didn't have time for Devon's bullshit.

"Listen, I want you, and you seem to be fighting me all across the board. If I don't get what I want—"

"Nigga, if you're threatening to cancel the contract, don't bother. I can do that now. Not all money is good money, and I promise I won't fuck you for your business. Who the fuck do you think you are?" Kendra was growing more and more disgusted by the minute.

Devon snatched her arm roughly. Kendra snatched away and chopped him across the throat. He grasped at his throat and fell backward, bumping into Kendra's desk, knocking a lot of her things to the floor as he went down.

Back in the conference room, everyone heard the commotion, and Taye was the first to rush inside with Bridget close behind. She opened Kendra's office door and found her straddling Devon, choking him.

"Kendra, sweetie, let him go. You gon' kill him," Taye urged her.

Kendra wasn't listening. She kept applying pressure as Devon's eyes bulged. His face was puffy and turning colors. He was grasping desperately at her hands, trying to pry them from his throat.

"I told him to leave me alone! He had no right to touch me. If I kill him, I'll be justified!" she growled.

"Kendra, please! Don't do this. What would Tyrone tell you to do?" Taye asked.

"He'd tell me to kill him," she answered but loosened her grip. She allowed Taye to pull her up.

"He ain't worth it, babes. You don't want to lose all you've worked hard to have for a lowlife like him," Taye said as she pulled Kendra off Devon finally.

Devon scrambled to his feet, rubbing his throat. Kendra scooted back into the corner and began sobbing. Taye squatted down in front of her and hugged her.

"It's too much, Taye. How am I supposed to do this without Dre? He was supposed to be here! He was taken from us, and for what? Then that fool come up in here snatching on me and shit! I'm tired, Taye. I'm tired!" Kendra continued to fuss, and Taye kept consoling her.

Bridget was leaning against the wall, grasping at her chest. She didn't know the pain Kendra was feeling from losing her brother, but she felt her pain from losing Tyrone. When Bridget turned, she saw a few of their team members looking in. She walked out and shut the door behind her.

"Go on in the office, and I'm gonna conduct the meeting. I have her notes. Go please. She is okay."

After she assured them that Kendra would be okay and they were heading back into the conference room, she quietly walked back into Kendra's office and started straightening up the mess that was left in Devon's wake. Taye and Kendra barely noticed she was there as they were still talking. Bridget walked out once Kendra's office was straight and headed to meet with everyone. As bad as she was hurting, she had to toughen up for Kendra's sake, and she did just that.

Christine
Early Thursday Afternoon

Christine and Carlos had been getting closer and closer. After four weeks of talking and spending one hell of a weekend in the mountains, Christine was falling for him hard. She decided to surprise him with a visit. When Christine pulled into Carlos's driveway, she decided to pull into the back because she didn't feel like walking all the way around. He had shown her where the spare key was if she ever needed to get in and he wasn't home. He offered her a key, but she refused it.

Christine walked into the house and down the hallway. As she approached, she heard Carlos arguing with someone. She tiptoed up to his office door, and she saw that it was cracked open enough to where she could hear what was going on. She stood back a bit, then leaned forward to see if she could get a glimpse of Carlos's visitor, only to realize that he had the guy on speakerphone.

She moved backward a bit after checking to make sure that no one had walked in behind her, and she listened to what was being said.

"Man, I need a few dollars so I can get out of town! You owe me that!"

"Nigga, I don't owe you shit! Who the fuck are you trying to handle?" the caller growled.

"It's not like that, but . . ." Carlos sighed. "Come on, bruh. Help me out. I am falling short in a few places, and I need some money to even out."

"I'ma help you out and suggest you never call me again. You were paid graciously for helping us with the hit on Tyrone, but I have no need for you any longer, and like my man told you last night, you need to get lost now. I am not giving you another dime!"

Christine covered her mouth to stifle the gasp that she felt coming. Had she heard that nigga right? Was he the one who killed her brother? She fought back the urge to bust up in the room and kill Carlos with her bare hands.

"All right, bruh, but I must warn you—"

The man hung up before Carlos could finish.

Christine moved back quickly, turned, and quietly walked out the side door. She couldn't believe what she had just heard. She had been sleeping with the enemy the whole time. That bastard was the reason that Tyrone was dead.

She got into her car and put the gear in reverse and allowed the car to coast down the driveway. Once she was far enough away, she started the car and drove off as quickly as she pulled up. She immediately called Brent and told him that she needed to talk to him.

She drove to the nearest rest area and parked. She had to get her mind right. What was she going to do? The voice of the man she had heard on the phone with Carlos was very familiar indeed. She didn't want to tell anyone about the traitor, but she was definitely gonna tell everyone that she had found Tyrone's killer, and God forbid the person who set it up tried to get away before she had time to check them.

When Brent answered, Christine told him what she had learned.

"Christine, we're gonna need you to see Carlos one more time. Call the nigga up and tell him that you had to handle some business, but you will see him this weekend."

She groaned, "Why the fuck are we waiting? We can kill him now! I can do it myself!"

"Christine, I need to talk to Sean and see what he wants us to do."

"You do what you need to do, bro. And I'll do what I need to do," Christine sneered. "You know, Sean doesn't need to be aware of everything. He ain't focused on shit but what concerns him, as usual. I got the nigga in my grasp, and I'ma deal with it, Brent. We can tell Sean after it's done."

Brent sighed, "You right, but I need a souvenir back."

"Man, I ain't fucking with you," Christine replied and hung up.

Saturday Night

Christine walked into Carlos's house and began to call out his name. "Carlos, where are you?" she yelled.

A few seconds later, Carlos peeped out the door and smiled as he motioned for her to come into his office. She shifted her purse to her other shoulder and walked into his office.

"Hey, baby," she greeted him as she kissed him on the lips. "What you got going on tonight, babe?"

"Oh, I'm just working on a few business contracts and managing my money," he replied as he sat back down behind his desk.

"I just needed to talk to you about a few things, but right now I just want to relax."

"Hmm, we can talk now. This can wait," he replied.

"Do you know that I love you?" she asked as she slid her pocketbook to the side.

He looked at her long and hard. He didn't know what to say. He knew that she loved him, but she never said it. He felt the same way, but he never trusted his heart to any woman before, not even his first wife. "Come here!"

Christine smiled. "Finish your work. I'ma roll up right quick. We got all night."

He smiled and looked back at his laptop.

"Can I get the ashtray?" she asked as she pulled out her blunt wraps and her bag of weed.

He turned and reached behind him and grabbed it from his bookcase. As he handed it to her, their fingers touched, and he looked up at her. The look that they shared was nothing less than pure love. She sat back down on the couch in his office and busted the blunt open. As she rolled the blunt, he continued to look at the computer screen and the paperwork that was on his desk.

"What exactly are you working on?" she asked without looking up at him, licking the edges of the blunt.

He sighed, "I'm going over my books. Something isn't adding up. With all the expenses paid out for stocking the bar, payroll, and entertainment, I still should be bringing in twice as much as I'm making. I think someone is ripping me off, and if I find that I'm right, all hell is going to break loose!"

"Yeah, I can understand that, bae."

"I pray I'm wrong. I've only trusted two niggas with my books, and one is my best friend."

Christine dipped into her pocketbook and pulled out a second bag of weed and rolled another blunt. As she licked it, she looked at him. "Maybe you need a woman's eye," she suggested.

He laughed, "Maybe so."

She looked up at him and smiled as she met his gaze. "Why are you looking at me like that?"

"Do you really like me?"

"My feelings for you are like none that I've ever had. You are the only man who has ever stirred up my feelings like this. Every time I'm around you, my heart beats twice as fast. When I'm not with you physically, I'm thinking of you. I can't shake it, and that's why I'm here tonight. I just need to share my innermost feelings with you," Christine answered, staring him in his face. "Do you like me?"

"Yes, I do. Come here," he said as he slid his chair back, giving her room to sit on his lap.

She stood up and walked over to him with the blunts in her hand. She sat down on his lap and kissed him on his neck before she looked at the computer. "So explain to me what I'm looking at."

Carlos showed her the inventory cost sheet, the spreadsheet for what was bought, as well as the payroll. He also showed her the receipts from paying the entertainers who lined his stage. After matching the paperwork with what was on the computer, they found that he was correct. Someone was stealing from his nightclub.

She lit their blunts, and they smoked as they went over everything once more. As they finished up, Carlos put his roach in the ashtray, and Christine did as well. She turned to face him with her legs spread on either side of him. Again, she kissed his neck. "Let's talk, babe."

"I'm ready," he replied as he cupped her buttocks.

She frowned at him as his eyes crossed up. "Babe, are you okay?"

"Yeah, I am," he replied as his words kind of slurred.

She laughed, "Buzzed up that quick, huh?"

He moved his hands and slowly raised them to his forehead and rubbed it. "I'm a little lightheaded, but I'm straight, so let's talk."

She stood up and looked down at him. "You know, for four years I've been alone. No family, nothing. I searched all over for the one person who could change that for me, and I found you."

Carlos's head dipped. He tried to look up, but his head bobbled.

Christine continued to talk. "I have been so lost, Carlos, since the night I learned of my brother's murder. Carlos! Are you listening to me? Hold your head up, bitch!"

Christine raced over and pushed his head back so that he could see her.

"My brother was killed a few weeks back. His name was Tyrone Love. I know it was you who killed my brother."

Carlos tried to speak, but he couldn't.

"That codeine that I laced in that blunt is working. It won't last long, so let me get started."

As Carlos drifted off to sleep, Christine walked over to her purse and grabbed two sets of handcuffs and some wire. She cuffed Carlos's feet together and tied his arms around his back and handcuffed his wrists together. She then got on her cell phone and called Kendra. "It's done. Come in through the side door."

When she hung up, she sat down on the couch in his office, then jumped up again and grabbed his laptop. "What is on this bitch?"

About an hour later, Carlos woke up to a room of unfamiliar faces. "Christine, what is this?" he whispered.

"Oh, shit, I didn't properly introduce myself to you before. My name is Christine Love, and this, sir, is your karma! You should've known that shit would come back around for you." She laughed.

"Who the fuck are these niggas you got in my home?"

Priest, Christine's right hand she had flown in the night before, walked over and slammed his fist into Carlos's face.

"Aye, no one touch him! This is all me! He has a safe behind that picture, and I am moving the money that is in his bank account to another account. Oh, and, Priest, once we're done, light this bitch up!" Christine ordered.

As Christine sat on the couch looking over Carlos's books, he glared at her. "I trusted you, Christine! I fell in love with you!"

Christine looked at him and laughed, "Yeah, well, I loved my brother also, and you ripped him from my life. The night that you killed my brother, nigga, I ached for your life to cease even though at that time I didn't know your identity. It was by pure luck that I walked in just as you were talking to someone about how you killed my brother."

He dropped his head and knew it was over for them, but before he took his last breath, he was gonna drop one last huge bombshell on the Loves. He was going to tell them the truth about the hit that was put on Tyrone!

Sean
Thursday Morning

Sean sat in the hotel with Clinton, discussing ways to bring in more guns for the team and to sell. They had a major connect who was looking to buy some heavy artillery and was willing to pay a hefty fee for them. Clinton had a friend who was in the army who could get him everything he needed.

"I want you and Nautica to capitalize off this play. So, you two will need to work together in this," Clinton explained.

"Yeah, but, Dad, why are you constantly trying to throw us together?"

Clinton stared at Sean. "All these years, haven't I made sure that you didn't want for anything? I've never steered you wrong, have I?"

"No, sir," Sean replied.

"Everything I've done has been for this. You two together, you'd be untouchable. You two will run these streets!"

Sean was about to reply, but his phone interrupted him. "Hey, Ma. Troy good?"

"Yes, he's fine. I have something to talk to you all about, and it's important. I've called everyone except you and Kendra. Can you call her? We will be having dinner Sunday around four. I really need y'all to be here."

"Oh, okay, Mom. You know I'll be there. Mom, are you okay? What's wrong?" Sean asked.

"I will tell you everything when everyone is here tomorrow. I love you, son," Le'Tera said before hanging up.

Clinton looked at Sean. "Is Le'Tera okay?" Clinton was genuinely concerned. Le'Tera was a woman whose heart he could never possess but whom he obsessed about even after they split. Sean kept him informed about everything that Le'Tera and Omar had going on.

Sean shook his head. "I don't think so. She wants me to come to dinner tomorrow for a family discussion. Whatever is going on, it's serious. I can't handle another funeral. I hope she isn't announcing that she's dying."

"We're not claiming that!" Clinton replied. "Whatever she needs, we will make sure she gets it."

Sean sat back chewing on the toothpick that he had in his mouth. "Damn!" Sean could hear the pain in his mother's voice. All the sleeping and crying she had been doing . . . Was she carrying something heavier on her shoulders than Tyrone's death?

Sean always had Clinton's back when all his other kids barely acknowledged him. Christine was raised by him, and yet he couldn't understand why he could never really bond with her. He put up with her. He shared his thoughts with Sean.

After a few minutes, he heard the door to the room close hard. He walked out of the front bedroom of the suite and saw Christine sitting on the sofa.

"Hey, Dad, I need to stay here for the night if that's okay," she told him.

"That's fine. Your brother is here and going through something. We'll be out in a few minutes."

"Okay," she replied.

Sean had so many questions. He stood. "All right, Pops, I'm about to head out. I'll check on you tomorrow before I go home."

"All right, son. I might just go myself. Offer her a li'l more support."

"She might like that. Okay, talk witcha lata," Sean said as he walked out the room and into the front room. "What's up, Christine?" he said as he walked by.

"Hey," she replied.

"Well, damn, I didn't roll over on you this morning. No need to be so angry," he replied.

Christine gave him a warning glare, and he laughed.

"Well, fuck you too, sis. See y'all later," Sean said once more as he walked out.

After he was gone, Clinton looked at Christine. "What's wrong wit' you?"

"Nothing, man. Is it okay if I stay here for a day or two? I got some business to handle," she asked.

"Now you know you can. Why ask such a stupid question?" Clinton asked as he walked back to his room.

"I'll be back in an hour or so," she yelled out.

"Yeah, that's fine," he replied as he walked to the bathroom.

Christine walked out, leaving Clinton lost in his thoughts.

As she headed to the elevators, she called Nautica. Christine and Nautica had been talking for a couple of days discussing the similar issues that they were having with Clinton. On Saturday, after she dropped Kendra off at the farm, she called Nautica and asked if they could hang out.

It was still early, and she needed to smoke. He agreed and asked where she wanted to meet.

"Where you at? I'll pick you up."

He texted her the address, and she put it in her GPS and headed his way. As soon as he and Havoc got in the car, she pulled off. They drove around until she found a low-key area with very few people around. She parked

*and twisted up three blunts, then passed one to Havoc
and Nautica. Christine lit hers up first and took a long
drag from it.*

"You seen yo' father?" Nautica asked her.

*"Not yet. I'm going there later to spend the night. I
don't want to, but I just don't want to go stay with those
Loves tonight. Don't get me wrong, I have no issues with
them, but I discovered something, and I just can't see
myself staying there."*

*"You know Clinton upholds everything that Sean does.
I'm done with that man," Nautica told her.*

*"I need you to help me on something, but you gotta
keep yo' end of the bargain or it won't work," Christine
said.*

He pulled on it. "Sis, whateva you on, I'm on."

*Havoc was in the back seat, laid back, high as all
get-out. "Y'all know I'm wit' whateva, and if you want, I
can handle Sean's ass, too. I owe him."*

*Nautica laughed and passed the blunt to the back so
he could hit it. "He done already showed you that you
ain't a match for him."*

"Man, I was geeked up!" he roared.

*"Aye now, Havoc, if you say so." Nautica looked over
at Christine and shook his head. "He not though."*

Christine laughed and Havoc sat up. "Man, fuck you!"

*They all started laughing, and Christine looked over
at Nautica. "I need yo' help with something."*

"I'm all ears."

Christine had filled Nautica and Havoc in on her plans,
and once they were all in agreement with the plan, she
had dropped them back off at Havoc's and driven back to
the hotel.

Chapter 12

Texas

Kendra

"Kendra, Mom wanted me to reach out to you and ask if you could come to dinner next weekend. She said something about taking care of loose ends with us," Sean informed Kendra once she answered.

"Is she all right?" Kendra asked.

"I can't answer that. Look, I have to go. I just . . . hold on," Sean said.

Kendra glanced over her paperwork while waiting for Sean to get back on the phone.

"Okay, I'm back. Aye, John, can you go plow the fields back over by the clearing? I want to plant some creasy greens. Okay, sis, I'm sorry, but again, I don't know what's going on with her, but I'm sure whatever it is, y'all can manage it. I got too much going on right now. I can't handle much more. I will be at the dinner, but if she is sick, you gon' have to step it up with her."

"You're such a dick, Sean. You literally don't care about anybody but yourself!" Kendra fumed.

"You can feel how you want, but at the end of the day, I've been here through everything with Mom."

"Because you chose to. I didn't! I was sent away when I was young!" Kendra argued.

"Yeah, and guess what? Just like Brent, you strayed from the family. You left that girls' school and kept moving. So, fuck what you or anybody think at this point. I will be at the dinner, but whatever the issue, y'all can handle it."

Kendra opened her mouth to respond, but Sean hung up.

"What?" she growled aloud as she stared at the phone in her hand. "No, the hell he didn't just hang up in my face! Oooo!"

Kendra tried to call Sean back, but he sent her to voicemail.

"Fuck it!" she yelled.

She then sat back in her swivel desk chair, frowned, and sat back upright. "Clearing for some creasy greens?"

She instantly texted John: Who died?

John: Nobody. Why you ask that?

Kendra: Why you working the fields?

John: How you know that?

Kendra: I was on the phone with Sean just now.

A few minutes went by before he replied.

John: Nobody, Miss Lady.

Kendra: Okay.

Kendra knew that if they hadn't died, someone was about to. Had they found Tyrone's killer and just decided not to tell her? As she dived deeper into thought, there was a knock on the door. "Yes?" she called out frustratedly.

"Hey, your two o'clock appointment is here," Bridget informed her.

"Okay, I'll be out in a moment. Take them to conference room B," Kendra told her.

"Gotcha, boss lady," Bridget replied before leaving.

Sean

Sean hung up with Kendra and sighed. He had arrived home twenty minutes earlier and called Kendra as he headed straight for the barn. He took his hat off and wiped his forehead. He hated having to sound so harsh about their mother's condition, but he couldn't watch his mother die if that was indeed the reason that she wanted everyone there.

He was nervous about seeing his mother and needed to delay it as much as possible. He was having a rough time facing her after what he had done, which was why he had been spending so much time with Clinton.

Le'Tera had a way of seeing things in him that no one else could. She knew when he lied and when he was in pain or troubled. He hadn't slept very much after what he did to Li'l Rob and Jackie. He had to keep Troy away from mostly everyone so that he wouldn't be tempted to tell them. And the looks that Troy gave him spoke louder than any hateful thing he could've said. He couldn't blame him though. He had completely lost it. He had made a rushed judgment to kill his child, and now he was feeling the pain. He played things off well around others and wore a mask that said everything was okay, but deep down, he regretted taking his son's life.

He was about to take a shower and go spend time with Melanie. She kept him sane when all else failed. He had given her the space that she had asked for, but it was time to see her. He hadn't spoken to her for a while, and he had planned to call her, but he decided that he was going to just show up. That way she couldn't tell him no.

It took Sean less than an hour to get showered and dressed. He ran down the stairs and hopped in his truck. He didn't see Omar or his mother, but he knew they were there.

As he started his truck and pulled out, he turned his music on and headed toward Melanie's house. When he finally arrived, he pulled into the driveway and stopped. "What in the hell?" Sean got out of the truck and looked around. "No, no, no! This ain't right!"

Melanie's house was completely empty. He dialed her number, and as soon as she answered, he began yelling, "What the fuck, B? I know you playing right now!"

Melanie laughed, "Umph, what kind of fool do you take me for? Did you really thing that I was gon' ride fa ya ass after you went and fucked that skank? You made yo' decision. Now deal with it. And don't worry looking for me or your li'l stash in the house 'cause I took it. I earned all that." She hung up the phone, and he began stomping.

"Shit, shit, shit!"

He raced up the stairs and used his key to get in. As he walked in, he heard a fantastic echo of his entrance into the empty house. He walked into the room and saw the safe open and empty.

He leaned back against the door and began to bang his fist against it repeatedly. He had never felt so betrayed. He pulled his cell phone back out and called Melanie again.

"The number you just dialed is—" the recording started.

Sean growled loudly and smashed his foot through the bathroom door. As he exited, he knew that he wasn't going to see Melanie again.

Chapter 13

Saturday Evening

Kendra had arrived at her family's home around six thirty. She had texted Christine to let her know that she had arrived safely and hoped to see her before she left on Monday. She didn't stop at the main house first. She headed straight for John's trailer. When she saw him, her face lit up. She was finally standing face-to-face with John. "So, what we gon' do tonight?"

"I'ma just hold you tonight," he joked. "But I did miss you."

He grabbed her from behind and wrapped his arms around her waist. They walked to his truck and got in. She looked over at him and laughed.

"What's funny?" he asked.

"You," she simply replied.

"What about me?" he asked as he pulled off and headed to his trailer.

She looked over at him. "Nothing."

It didn't take but a few moments to get to John's place. Once he parked and they were inside, he pulled Kendra to the bathroom.

"Take yo' clothes off, Miss Lady," he said as he put the lid on the toilet down and sat down on it, eyes glued to Kendra.

Kendra smiled and kicked off her shoes. She then began to take her pants down. "Remember when I tried to strip for you a few weeks ago?"

"Don't talk!" he ordered.

Kendra laughed and finished undressing.

"Come here," he told her.

Kendra did as she was told, and once she was standing in front of John, she smiled. "What can I do for you, sir?"

He laughed and slapped her on her butt. "The question is, what can I do for you?"

"Let me show you." She laughed.

They had sex for less than an hour and fell asleep. Kendra was definitely satisfied and was just happy to be lying next to him. They fell asleep entwined in each other's arms.

Sean

Sean had arrived home in a terrible mood. When he walked up the stairs, Omar was walking out of the bathroom and going into the bedroom.

"You okay, Sean?" he asked.

"I'm fine!" Sean snapped.

"Okay then," Omar replied, trying to hold his tongue from saying what he really wanted to say. He was getting tired of everyone snapping on him.

As Sean brushed past him to go to his room, Omar spoke, "You know I done damn near had it up to here with all this disrespect!"

"Well, move out! This is my momma's shit, man!" Sean growled. "You know what? Fuck it! I'ma go stay with Pops 'til morning."

Omar shook his head, waved his hands up in the air, and walked into the bedroom.

Sean used the bathroom, then walked back out of the house. He called Clinton and asked if he could stay the night.

"Christine is here, and she has the room, but you can get the couch," he replied.

"Okay, thanks. I'm on the way."

Sean hung up, and twenty minutes later, he was walking into Clinton's suite. He told him about the fallout with Omar along with Melanie leaving and taking all his money that he had in the safe over at her house.

"How much was it?" Clinton asked.

Sean looked up and dropped his head back down. "Over three hundred grand."

"Yeah, you a new kinda stupid, son. Ain't no way you supposed to leave that much money around any bitch. That girl really just robbed you. What you gon' do about it?"

"Ain't shit I can do, Pops. She's gone. I don't know where she is, and to be honest, I don't have the desire to know," he replied.

Clinton stood up and headed to his room. "Just plain stupid, I tell you," he fussed as he walked.

Sean lay down on the couch after spreading a sheet over it. He closed his eyes, and sleep hit him instantly.

When he awoke the following morning, he took a shower and put on the same clothes that he had worn earlier except his drawers. He put them in a small bag. He didn't mind free balling for a while.

Sunday Afternoon

Le'Tera had the dining table set beautifully as she waited for her kids to show up. "Troy, go wash up and get ready for dinner."

"Yes, ma'am," he replied.

Omar walked into the dining room and kissed Le'Tera on the cheek. He noticed how she only smiled as she walked into the kitchen.

He frowned and followed her. "Le'Tera, you been acting funny for two days now. What's going on?"

She smiled. "I'm just going through a little depression right now, Omar. I mean, my son did just die, or has that surpassed everybody's brain? Just because the funeral is ova don't mean the pain ain't still there!"

"Now goddammit, Le'Tera, don't do dat! He was like my own son!" Omar raged.

"Yeah, well, you don't act like it. Not once have I seen you really break down. Why is that? You know what? This is a talk for after dinner! My cornbread is done. Move outta my way!" Le'Tera pushed passed Omar.

Omar stormed out of the house. He sat down on the porch and shook his head as he stared out into the wooded area across the street. He didn't know what had gotten into Le'Tera, but they would definitely have to talk.

As he continued to ponder, John walked up. "Everythang good, Omar?"

Omar laughed, "Wife problems."

John laughed as he held up his hands. "Say no mo'."

Sean pulled up in the driveway with Clinton behind. Clinton parked close to the huge apple tree that sat next to the house. He got out and walked over to Sean.

"I can already smell that cabbage. Yo' momma has always been a helluva cook."

"That she has," Sean laughed as he grabbed at his muscular abs.

They walked in and sat down in the sitting room. Omar walked into the sitting room ten minutes later, and once he saw Clinton, he stormed back out.

"Le'Tera, what the hell is he doing here?" he yelled out, not caring who heard him.

"Fool, who are you talking about?" Le'Tera asked as she walked down the stairs.

"Clinton, that's who I'm talking about. Now, Tera, I can handle almost anything, but that man gots to get out of my home," Omar fussed.

Le'Tera followed Omar into the sitting room and froze at the sight of Clinton and Sean looking at their old family albums. "What is he doing here, Sean? This is a family dinner, an important family dinner, and he shouldn't be here," Le'Tera asked angrily.

"Well, Mom—" Sean started, but Clinton spoke up.

"I'm so sick of y'all acting like I'm not family. These are my kids, and technically you're still my wife, and this bum you've been shacked up with all these years is my cousin. So, if I'm not family, then what the hell am I?"

Le'Tera glared at him with her hands on her hips and squinched her eyes up. "You are so right, Clinton, but you've never been a father to any of my kids, and you damn sure wasn't a good husband!" she cried.

At that point, Brent and Kendra walked in. "What's going on in here?" Kendra asked.

"Yo' father here wants to discuss y'all childhood. Let's do that then," Le'Tera replied as she waved her hand in Clinton's direction.

Clinton laughed, "You act like you're so perfect, Le'Tera. Do you kids know who you really are? Huh? Do they know that you started all this? That you introduced the drug game to me?"

Kendra looked at Le'Tera. "Mom?"

Le'Tera nodded. "I did. That's true, but you introduced it to our kids and sadly allowed it. I will pay soon enough for my sins, but at least I know what mine are. You led our boys down a destructive path. You not only showed them the drug game, but you taught them that it was okay to take a life to get what they wanted. I had to send Kendra away because I didn't want her following the same path after she pushed our maid down the goddamn stairs!" Le'Tera shouted.

Kendra dropped her head and sat down on the arm of the couch. She still had nightmares about that day. She wasn't hurt by her mother's words because they were facts.

"You seem to forget who taught them how to dispose of the bodies after they killed them though. You fail to want to acknowledge who showed them how to invest illegal money into a farm. You helped them bring in millions off them dead bodies. You and yo' man there!" Clinton growled, pointing to Omar.

"I'll bury yo' ass in the cornfield, boy. Keep trying me," Omar replied as he stepped forward.

Le'Tera placed her arm out to stop him. "Let him talk. It's time my kids hear all this. I never taught them how to kill anybody, but yes, I taught them when it was necessary to kill a muthafucka and how to dispose of the bodies in a manner that would make it almost impossible to find. It was already instilled in them, but I made it profitable for them. Look at this farm and the grounds. We sell food and milk. We breed animals. We have all of this because of me, and like I said, I know I'ma pay for my sins. I know my karma is coming, but at least I know. I live in my truth, you sack of shit. We are both responsible for our kids' bad choices. Tyrone died, and for what? He didn't want to be a part of this, and I didn't want him to either. The one thing I can say is that you and Omar both wanted this lifestyle for him."

"Now that's where you're wrong, Le'Tera. I didn't want this lifestyle for Tyrone. Hell, I didn't even think the boy was mine. You raised some weak kids, except for Sean.

He's more like me than any of my kids. Brent was lazy. He wanted a life sitting behind a goddamn desk, pushing paper and shit. He fell down on his luck and looked to Sean for help. I don't respect that. If you stray away from the game, then you stay the fuck away from the game. When Sean told me what he had done, I intercepted the shipment. Ain't no free handouts around here!" Clinton roared.

Brent looked at Clinton. "So it was you? You took my shit?"

"You aren't made for that life. Yes, I did it. Sean told me who to contact, and I paid yo' nigga to take it. It wasn't hard. You don't even know when a muthafucka is loyal to you."

Brent stood and stormed out of the room.

"Sean, I tried my best to take you with me, but your mother made it clear that she'd fight me tooth and nail. I did what I could though. I kept y'all supplied with the best connections and product. That was my way of taking care of y'all."

"Clinton, get out of my house! But first, let me correct you on a few things," Le'Tera started. "Tyrone was all you, and you know it. I didn't sleep with Omar until after you were long gone. And Brent, he wasn't and isn't a weak man. He wanted better for himself, and I have no doubt that he will make a success out of the company that he built. He never needed you and never will."

Clinton stood. "Fuck y'all! And those two kids too. I don't need any of y'all." He looked at Sean. "I'll be at the hotel when you finish yo' dinner, son."

Before Clinton could walk past Omar, Omar punched him in the mouth. "Don't ever disrespect my kids like that!"

Clinton staggered backward but straightened back up quickly. He grabbed his chin and massaged it. He wanted to hit Omar back, but he was certain Le'Tera would act a fool, and he didn't have his gun on him. Instead, he smiled, nodded, and walked out.

After Clinton stormed out, Le'Tera held her head down for a second, and when she looked up, she glanced at Kendra and Sean. "Please, go get cleaned up for dinner." Her voice was low, hoarse, and filled with pain.

Kendra didn't know why, but she felt like everything she knew about her family was about to get worse. She stood and walked out.

Le'Tera walked to the back door and walked out. She saw Brent leaning against the tractor, smoking. She sighed and walked down to where he was.

"Don't you dare let that man cause you to look so defeated. Ain't nothing weak about you. You did something that most wouldn't do. You branched out and started your own life. You were ready to sacrifice damn near everythang for a new start, and it takes a strong man to do that. You hold yo' head up, boy. You hear me?"

Brent nodded but kept his head bent. "Ma, you know I always knew he felt that way about me, but hearing him say it, bruh, that makes it official. At least by me thinking it, there was a small chance that it was all in my head. Ya feel me?"

Le'Tera laughed and popped him upside the head. "I ain't ya bruh, bruh! Sean never lived on his own or sacrificed anything. He is something different is all I'm saying. Come on, let's go eat. Everything is gonna be okay."

Brent grabbed his mother's hand and kissed it. "I love you, bruh." He laughed as she swatted him playfully on the arm.

"Ditto, bruh." They walked hand in hand to the house.

When they reached the door, Le'Tera's cell phone rang. "Hello?" she answered as she walked through the door. "Go get cleaned up. Dinner will be ready soon," she whispered with the phone flat down on her shoulder.

Brent walked away, leaving Le'Tera to her call. "Sorry about that. Who is this?"

Le'Tera walked back out on the porch as she continued her call.

Chapter 14

Clinton

Clinton was furious. He couldn't believe that Le'Tera allowed Omar to hit him. He knew that if he had tried Omar, he probably would've gotten whooped. Omar was a strong man and gained a reputation for his fighting skills. He didn't have his gun, and he knew his kids probably wouldn't have helped him.

He pulled up to the hotel where he was staying and got out. He noticed a police car patrolling the area. He walked in naturally. He had a couple of ounces of cocaine in his pocket that he used for recreational purposes. Once he was inside, he walked quickly to the elevators and pushed the button. He turned slightly and watched the police car pull out of the parking lot and drive away. Once he was on the elevator, he got on and headed to his suite.

Christine was sitting on the couch, flipping through the channels when Clinton walked in.

"How was the dinner?" she asked.

"I don't want to talk about it," he whispered as he walked into the bathroom.

"Yeah, well, that seems to be all the time. Did I do something?" she asked loudly.

When Clinton walked back out of the bathroom, his eyes were glued to Christine's. The dark, sinister look on his face terrified her. She looked at her phone, slid it open, and tapped on it. She then stood up and stared back at Clinton.

"That damn Omar hit me, and then Le'Tera put me out!" he exclaimed, laughing as he sat down on the couch.

"You know, I overheard what you told Sean the other day. Did you mean all that?" she asked.

"Not you too!" he groaned. "What did you hear?" he asked.

"That I was a mistake, and that since I wasn't born male, I was a waste of shared cum. That's what I heard. Why even deal with me if I made you feel like that?"

Clinton laughed, "What is this, revelation Sunday? Yes, okay, yeah, I said it. Your mother was a whore, and I tried to save you from that lifestyle. Although I should've let the streets have your worthless tail. Y'all kids can't be bred from me. Y'all too softhearted."

Christine took a few steps toward the door and opened it as if she was about to leave.

"Or you could've killed me like you had Tyrone killed. You had one of your li'l eyes watching him and paid them to kill him. How could you kill yo' own son? That's lowdown even for you."

Clinton's eyes grew even darker. "I don't care what anybody say. That wasn't my boy! They tried to pass him off as mine, but it was time for my real son to join his brother and run these streets. They can do it!"

Clinton had blanked out and was seeing black. He was ranting so bad that he hadn't realized that Christine and three police officers were standing in the room, listening to his confession of killing Tyrone.

Christine had called Le'Tera and told her everything that she had discovered from Carlos, then had set a trap for Clinton. She had contacted the police the day before and sent them all the evidence they needed, but they also needed a confession to seal the case.

Clinton finally focused in and clamped his mouth closed.

"Mr. Clinton Love, you have the right to remain silent," the taller officer said as he handcuffed Clinton.

Clinton looked as if he could use his eyes to throw bullets at Christine.

"You ain't even begun to feel my wrath. I'ma make you mean the fuck outta that bullshit you just spoke."

Christine grabbed her coat, and after sharing the recording that she had just made, she walked out.

The Family Dinner

Le'Tera stood in the doorway of her kitchen, feeling like a knot was embedded in her stomach that kept tightening and tightening. She felt like each breath she took could be her last. Finally, she forced herself to sit down at the table. She stared down at her plate and didn't utter a word. When she lifted her head up, she glanced at each one of her kids, her eyes finally landing on Sean, who sat right next to her. He looked so handsome to her.

She looked at Troy and smiled. "Are you full, baby?" She figured he should've been. She saw two chicken leg bones and three rib bones on his plate with signs of the pintos, cabbage, and potato salad left on his plate.

"Did you fix dessert, Grandma?" he asked.

She smiled. "I didn't. How about I let John take you to get some ice cream? Whateva you want."

"Okay! But, Grandma, I got my own money." He laughed, pulling out a wad of cash.

She flashed Sean a look, wondering if he was okay with what he was doing to his son by introducing him to the streets like he had.

"Take him to get whateva he wants then, and it's still on me. You keep yo' money, baby." Le'Tera smiled.

"Yes, ma'am," he replied and walked out.

When the front door closed, Le'Tera cleared her throat. "Today has been one of those days, and I just hope that when we all leave this table, we have a clear understanding." She looked at Kendra, Brent, Omar, and then Sean.

She reached out and grabbed Sean's hands. "I failed you, son. I turned a blind eye to everything you did, even helped you to build by your mistakes instead of making you learn from them. You had two great boys, Sean."

Sean grimaced at "had." He then knew that Troy had told his mother what he did to Li'l Rob and Jackie.

"Momma?" he whispered, looking her in the eyes.

"Shhhh. It's okay, Sean. I can't blame you at all. It's our fault, that." Le'Tera dropped her graying head, her dreads beautifully wrapped up on her head.

She looked at Kendra and smiled. She let Sean's hand fall off the table.

"Can you pass me the chicken? And slide that plate of ribs on down," Le'Tera said. "I'm dying, everyone," she announced.

Omar dropped his fork. "Le'Tera? What?"

"I've known for a few weeks now, and I'm okay with it. What I'm not okay with is leaving my family so broken. I have to right my wrongs, kinda like cleaning my plate, you could say."

She placed the chicken on her plate and lifted her knife. Instead of cutting into the meat, though, she stabbed Sean in his hand.

"Uggggg!" he cried as he tried to move his hand. The knife stuck through his hand into the table.

"Ma! What the hell?" Kendra cried as she jumped up.

"Sit down right now, Kendra," Le'Tera ordered.

"Momma, please." Sean began to cry.

"Never in my life did I think that you'd turn out this way. Where is Li'l Rob? Where is Jackie? Huh? Tell me that?" Le'Tera was in tears, and her voice was cracking badly.

"Momma," Sean pleaded.

No one at the table dared to move, but it was all starting to make sense to Kendra and Brent.

"I won't let you destroy that boy like I destroyed you. I have to make it right, Sean. I know what kind of monster I am, but you a different breed, son. You will kill yo' own seed before you would a bitch who finessed you outta almost everything, son."

"But, Momma," he moaned. "I—"

"Sean, I brought you in this world, and I am going to take you out. Sound familiar? I didn't want to believe it when Troy told me what you did, but deep down, I knew he was telling the truth. Why, son, why?"

"Momma?" was all he whispered.

Le'Tera nodded her head. "Get out!" she ordered everyone else.

Brent paused. "Don't kill him, Momma. Please."

Le'Tera looked him in his eyes, tears glistening within them. "Leave."

Brent glanced down at Sean and shook his head. "Bruh, did you really kill Li'l Rob?"

Sean dropped his eyes.

Brent looked at his mother and walked out. He got in his car, and without saying goodbye to anyone, he left. He swore he'd never return.

Kendra sat on the porch and waited. Her heart was pounding, and she prayed that Sean's death was swift so that he wouldn't suffer. She could feel how pained her mother was, but she was the matriarch of the family, and Sean had violated the family extremely. Yet, she wondered how her mother would cope with knowing that she was no better than Sean.

She heard a loud pop sound and knew it was over. She huffed and shook her head. "Family!"

She heard the back door open and close and knew that Omar's guys were cleaning up the mess and about to bury her brother.

"Kendra, I did what I had to do. I pray you understand, but if you don't, then that's something you will have to deal with. I see Brent left, huh?"

"Yes, ma'am. Momma, are you really dying?" Kendra asked.

They could hear the ruckus coming from inside the house. Over in the cornfields, there was an area John had been clearing off earlier, and it hit Kendra. "John knew you were going to kill Sean?"

"That's something you have to ask that man. Yes or no, it's up to him to answer that. You know, I had changed my mind about killing Sean. I was thinking, 'Tera, you can't really be considering killing Sean.' However, Christine called me before I sat down at the dinner table, and you know what she told me?"

"What was it, Mommy?"

Le'Tera bit her lip and tears fell. "She told me that yo' father, Clinton Love, was responsible for Tyrone's death. She asked me if he had left, because she had something special planned for him. He killed my boy." Le'Tera shook her head, and her legs began to shake.

"Oh, Momma," Kendra cried.

"That's why I couldn't let Sean live. He was exactly like his father. I couldn't die knowing that I let him live. Troy deserves better, and I think you and John would be perfect parents to him. He has no one else, Kendra. A life away from this foul place would do him wonders. He deserves a chance to live."

"Me and John?" Kendra asked.

Boom!

"Man, roll him to the left. You gon' tear up all Miss Love's stuff," they heard coming from inside.

Le'Tera rolled her eyes and frowned. "Handle my baby with care, dammit!" she yelled out.

"You worried about handling him with care after you just shot him, Mom? Really?"

"Kendra, if I had any other option, I would've taken it. Sean was evil, and I couldn't let him get away with that. Troy wouldn't have stood a chance. But even so, they will be careful with him. My heart is broken, and nothing in this world will repair it. But at least give me some peace of mind in knowing that you will care for Troy. Don't lie to me and tell me that there's nothing going on between y'all. I pay attention."

They could hear the back door close, and after a few moments, they saw the guys carrying Sean's body to the cornfield.

Le'Tera stood up and looked out into the fields. "I love you, baby girl, and I'm so very proud of the woman you are. Don't let anything break you down to this level."

Kendra smiled. "You're perfect to me. I can't say I understand any of this, but I'll never lose respect for you, Ma."

"At least someone hasn't," she replied. And without saying another word, she walked back into the house.

Omar stood in the hallway, staring down at the floor, standing like a statue. When Le'Tera walked in, he glanced over at her.

She shook her head. "Not now."

"For fuck's sake, Tera, this is too goddamn much now. You . . . you just can't kill yo' own son and not . . . Man, Tera, whyyyy?" he asked.

"I couldn't let him live. Damn, do you not see that?" she cried.

"You didn't even say shit to me though!" he replied, throwing his hands up in the air.

"What would you have said if I told you?"

The look on his face answered her question.

"Exactly. I loved him enough to kill him," Le'Tera replied and walked upstairs.

Omar was on her ass. "And why didn't you tell me you were dying? Huh?"

"I just found out, Omar. I've made my peace," she started and looked at him. "With everything."

"Fine!" Omar slammed out of the room, causing the windows to shake. He decided that he was going to stay in the guest room until Le'Tera was ready to talk to him.

Chapter 15

Kendra

Kendra sat on the porch, refusing to go back into her family's home. As soon as John pulled in, Kendra walked up to him. "Can we, um . . . can we stay with you tonight?" He looked at Troy and smiled. "Indeed, Miss Lady."

Kendra, John, and Troy walked down the path behind the house without speaking. Troy was amped up and pointed to the cornfield where Sean's body was being buried. "Aunt Kendra, will it ever get better?"

Kendra glanced over to the area that was lit up and turned her head back quickly. "I hope so, Troy."

As they entered the trailer, John walked to the back room and prepared it for Troy. He then went into the bathroom and started running some water. Kendra sat down, feeling exhausted, and she hadn't even done anything.

When John reappeared, he walked over and grabbed Kendra by the hand. "Come on."

"What?" she asked as he pulled her to the bathroom. "John, we can't do that while Troy is here. Besides I can't."

John smiled. "You must not know me, huh? I ran you a bath. While you relax, me and Troy can watch a movie or something."

Before he could leave, she looked up at him. "You knew, didn't you?"

John didn't answer. "Take a bath. We'll talk once Troy is asleep."

Kendra took her clothes off and eased into the warm bath that John had run for her. She closed her eyes, thinking that she could ease her mind, but images of Sean and Tyrone kept springing up in her head. She swallowed hard and counted to ten. Her heart began to beat wildly. She clenched her teeth and fists. How had she been dealt such a fucked-up family? They turned so easily on one another, and it angered her. She wanted to shout, but she couldn't. She knew if she did, Troy would hear her, and he had been through so much in the last few weeks. She couldn't traumatize him by screaming.

Her head started banging, so she decided to get out of the tub and lie across John's bed. When she walked out, Troy and John were watching television.

"I'ma lie down for a while," she told him.

"Okay," John replied.

"Good night, Auntie," Troy replied.

"Good night. See you in the morning."

"Okay," he replied.

Kendra walked into the room and took John's robe off. She pulled the covers back and sat down. She didn't want to use his lotion, but she didn't have a choice. She put on the Suave lotion and rubbed her finger across the top of his Degree deodorant and put it under her armpits.

She lay down stark naked and closed her eyes. She lay there in the dark alone for fifteen minutes before John came in. She could smell the soap scent on him as he lay down behind her.

She turned to face him. "You knew, didn't you?"

"Yes, she told me everything a couple of days ago," he admitted.

"John, you . . ." she yelled, but then lowered her voice to a whisper. "You didn't say shit to me! Why?"

"That's family business, and y'all had to deal with that. She wanted to do it her way. When she told me what Sean did to Li'l Rob, I lost all respect for him. He had it coming, Kendra. You know it couldn't have happened any other way."

"And her dying? You couldn't tell me why?"

John frowned and sat up. "What? She's what?"

Kendra began to cry, and John lay back down.

"What am I gon' do with Troy? Huh? Can you imagine how fucked up he's got to be right now? I'm a grown goddamn woman, John, and I'm fucked up. How can I help him understand and deal with all this if I can't understand and deal?"

"We gon' figure it all out day by day together. Shit, I'on know how, but I'm ready and willing to work through the good and the bad with y'all."

Kendra turned and curled up into John's arm. She scooted her butt against him, and when she felt his bulge, she whispered, "Turn the television on."

"Kendra, I won't take advantage of you like that. Just rest, okay? You got a lot on yo' mind."

Kendra sat up with her double D's bouncing and climbed on top of him and kissed him on the lips. "Well, can you do me a favor?" she asked.

"Anything, Miss Lady."

"Don't stop me from taking advantage of you."

Kendra placed his manhood inside of her and slowly slid down on it. She began to move up and down, using her hand to cover his mouth as he moaned softy. He sounded like a hungry bear to her, and it made her grind faster but light enough to keep the springs from making too much noise.

She needed to feel John deep inside her, touching every part of her pussy. He reached up and grabbed her by her hair and pulled her head down to kiss him.

His hands then gripped her hips as he lifted her ass and slammed her down. She groaned seductively against his mouth. He let himself go, and he and Kendra rode every wave they created that night.

Clinton

Clinton sat in an interrogation room and waited angrily for the detectives to walk in. He couldn't believe that his child had turned on him. As he waited, he laughed, "The li'l bitch just fucked me over. She was more like her momma than I thought. Trifling!"

The detectives entered the room and began asking him questions about Tyrone. "Why did you kill your son, sir? Who was involved?"

Clinton could've told them everything they needed to know, but he decided that he'd let it ride. If he told them anything, they'd go after Sean, and he couldn't allow that. Sean was his first born, the alpha, and he did things for him that no one would ever know about or understand.

"I'm not saying shit," he replied.

"You lawyering up, huh? No matter, we got enough evidence to put you away for life," one of the detectives said.

"Use it then." Clinton shrugged.

"This is Sunday, so you won't be able to see the magistrate until morning for a bail hearing. I will tell you, though, you're going to be with us a long time."

"Man. I ain't do nothing! Let me out this bitch!" they could hear an irate inmate yelling outside the door.

"Take him on back as well. Mr. Love, welcome to our house." The detective laughed.

Clinton was processed in and was given a plastic bin with one blanket, one pillow, one sheet, and a few toiletries. He walked into the cell where there were over twenty inmates. He set his bin down, and right next to him a fight broke out. It seemed like half the dorm was involved. Some fell over on top of Clinton, and for five minutes, they were all going in. When the guards finally arrived and separated everyone, they found Clinton lying in a puddle of blood. They rushed him to the infirmary, where he was pronounced dead.

Nautica
Monday Morning

Nautica was fixing himself some scrambled eggs when his phone rang. "Aye, bruh, you a'ight?"

"Yeah, everything is good. I just left my bail hearing," Havoc told him.

"What's the numbas?" Nautica asked.

"Fifteen thousand," he replied.

"All right, I'ma send someone fa you in a few. Hit me back in a li'l while," Nautica told him.

"A'ight."

Nautica grabbed his burner phone and called Christine. "Can you go grab him?" Nautica asked when she answered.

"Yes. I got the call early this morning that Pops was dead," she told him.

"Umph," he replied.

"I gotta go collect his things. I already have a bondsman who's gon' get him. I'm going to pay him off in full after he gets him out. That way it won't look weird, you feel me?"

"Yeah, I do," Nautica replied. "Sis—" he started.

"I don't want to know any details," she answered before he could ask.

"Gotcha. Talk to you later."

Nautica, Havoc, and Christine had made the play of a lifetime. They had gotten rid of Clinton and were about to inherit his wealth.

Havoc intentionally got himself locked up on a felony drug charge, and when Clinton was brought into the jail cell, he instigated an argument between a few guys. Once they started fighting, he used that as an opportunity to stab Clinton. He had gotten the knife from one of the guards who owed Nautica some money. They reached out to him, and after he confirmed that he was going to be on the shift, they set their plan in motion.

Nautica really enjoyed the hustle and unexpected surprises that came with the drug game, but he was ready to build his own legacy somewhere else. Away from Greensboro. He hadn't told Havoc, but he and his wife were about to move to Florida and start over, far away from North Carolina.

He didn't care how Havoc responded. He could go with them or stay, but Nautica was getting out.

Le'Tera and Omar
A Week Later, Sunday

Omar didn't speak to Le'Tera for almost a week until Sunday morning when she asked him to take her to the cemetery. He agreed because he needed to go as well. He missed Tyrone a lot, and no one even cared about his feelings in the matter. He always kept a tight lip about things, which he felt was for the best. Nevertheless, he knew Tyrone knew he loved him, and that was what counted.

When they first arrived, Omar stayed back while Le'Tera approached the grave. She stood looking down at it and then bent down and wiped her hands across the tomb of the mausoleum. She slowly knelt and removed the dead flowers from the cement vase that was attached to the stone building and then replaced them with fresh flowers. She then grabbed her bag and pulled out *The Velveteen Rabbit,* a book she used to read to Tyrone when he was younger. It was his favorite book, and he had asked her if she would keep it for him because he wanted to read it to his kids when he had some. She enjoyed reading to all her kids, but Tyrone seemed to enjoy it more. She sat down on the small bench beside the structure.

As she began reading the book, she started to rock back and forth. Tears began to drop, and mucus began to drip from her nose. She jumped and turned as she felt Omar's hand touching her shoulder. She turned fully around and wrapped her arms around his neck, sobbing uncontrollably.

"My baby! My baby!" she repeated over and over.

Omar walked her back to their car with her head snugly resting in the crook of his neck. They arrived back home, and he sat with her on the swing and comforted her as best he could. They had been out there for less than forty-five minutes when Le'Tera finally looked up at Omar, who looked down at her. "I love you, Le'Tera."

"I love you more, Omar. Thank you for being the man you are. You have proven your love for me and my kids, and for that, I will always love you."

"Those are our kids!" he corrected her.

She smiled sadly. "Our kids." She stood up and smiled. "I'ma get some tea. Would you like some?"

"Yes, I would. You want me to go get it?" he asked.

"No, I got it. I need to do something to clear my mind. Today was a rough day," she told him.

"Okay, baby," he replied.

Le'Tera walked to the bathroom and grabbed some pills from the medicine cabinet and proceeded to the kitchen. She grabbed her pill crusher from the drawer in the kitchen and began to crush a massive dose of Fentanyl that she had obtained days earlier and placed an equal deadly dose of it in each cup of tea. She hadn't lied to the family about her dying. She just hadn't told them how. She had planned to kill herself and Omar the day she decided to kill Sean. There was no way she could live with herself after that.

After everything that she allowed Clinton to put her kids through as young children, she would never forgive herself. Tyrone, Sean, and her grandson Rob were all dead because she didn't have a backbone, and the worst of it all was that they couldn't properly bury and mourn Sean and Rob. Her grandson was dead because of what she allowed her son to be taught by his wayward father. Her two kids who remained would face a lifetime of regret and trouble because of what they had been through.

As she walked back on the porch with both cups, she smiled at Omar. "Here you go, honey."

Omar took the cup and slid over so she could sit back down next to him. She smiled as she watched him drink his tea. He took one big gulp and a second one before he glanced over at her with his eyes bugged out.

"What did you do?" he asked.

"I'm protecting my kids!" She began sipping her tea as well. With every sip, her throat began to burn. She could feel herself getting sleepy by the time she finished the cup.

Omar's eyes began to close also, and his breathing became shallow. He couldn't move, and neither could Le'Tera. As her body began to shut down, her head drooped over, and the cup fell from her hand. The couple died side by side sitting on the swing that he had built for her as an anniversary gift.

Two Years Later

After the discovery of Le'Tera's and Omar's bodies, Kendra and Brent both agreed to board up the house and farm and close down the business. With everything that they had to deal with personally, it took two years to make it happen. They sold off all the livestock, except for the horses, and burned down the cornfields.

"I'm gonna miss this place," John said as he wrapped his arms around her waist, resting his chin on her shoulder.

"I'm not. I don't ever want to see this place again." She sighed. "Too many awful memories. This land is tainted with so many souls, John. Even my own family. That soil could tell a lot of stories of the dead. I don't want to ever go back to this lifestyle. Ever!"

"I agree with that."

"You promise?" she asked.

John grabbed her ring finger and kissed the diamond wedding band that he had officially placed there the year before. "I do," he replied.

"Lord, that boy can't ever stay off that phone. Look at 'im," she laughed.

Troy was walking around the barn with his phone up in the air, trying to find a signal.

"Aye, John, can you come and help me pull the rest of this plywood down?" Brent called out.

"I sure can," he replied.

Kendra smiled as she watched her husband walk away.

She glanced down to where Troy was. "Get away from the edge of that pond. I don't want you to fall in."

Brent walked over to her and stared down at Troy. "Didn't you hear what Kendra said? Don't make me put yo' ass to work now."

John chimed in, "That'll work. Put that phone up and come help us knock this barn down so we can add it to the fire."

"Man!" Troy fussed as he stomped over to where John was.

Brent laughed, "He got to have that phone. Lisa is up at the house. You might want to go help her with some food. You know she can't cook."

Kendra laughed, "We'll go get something. I need to ride out anyway."

Brent looked down at his feet and back up at her. "Can you wait to go to the cemetery? I want to go with you."

"Really?" Kendra asked, shocked.

"Kendra, I'm never coming back to this place. We placed Mom and Omar there to be with Tyrone. She wouldn't have wanted it any other way, but this was never my home."

"Shit, bruh, mine either."

Brent laughed.

"What is it?" Kendra asked.

"The last real talk I had with Mom. We had a talk about using the word 'bruh.'" Brent stopped in mid-thought. "I can't come back here."

Kendra understood Brent completely. He was also suffering from her absence. It had totally slipped her mind that Brent, too, lost his family, and she felt so selfish by not checking on his well-being. They talked a lot, and he helped with Troy way more than she thought he would. Brent had stepped it up to make sure that they were all straight, but no one had checked on him to make sure he was good.

She looked at him and grasped his hand and gave it a squeeze. "Are you okay, bruh?" she whispered.

He looked down at her and kissed the top of her head. "Not even a li'l bit," he replied.

She looked at him for the first time in a long time and smiled. "Me either, but we're gonna get through this together."

"Facts, baby sis." He moved away from her and started to walk away.

Kendra's cell phone began to ring, and she answered it, smiling. "Hello?"

"Hey, sis! How's it going?" Christine asked.

"It's going is all I can say. Is everything almost planned?" she asked.

"Yes. We are on track," Christine replied.

"Good," Kendra replied.

"Hey, Kendra darling!" she heard Taye yelling in the background.

"Hey, boo. Y'all must be drinking," Kendra joked.

"Bridget is working this shit out. She's making sure we're doing what we're supposed to do," Taye replied loudly.

"Is Brent coming?" Christine asked.

"Hold on. Let me take him the phone." Kendra ran the phone to Brent, and when he looked down and saw that it was Christine, he laughed.

"What, bruh?" he said.

"Bruh my ass. You coming to the King's Ball next weekend?"

"Not sure yet," he replied.

"Fuck dat shit, dude. You either be here or we gon' visit you every weekend for the next three years," Christine fussed.

"Lord, I can't deal wit' dat. I'll be there, scout's honor."

"Whateva! Love ya, and tell Kendra that I'll call her back. Our drill sergeant is commanding our attention." Christine hung up, and Brent passed Kendra the phone.

"Did you hang up on her?" Kendra asked, laughing.

"She said she'd call you back."

"Well, I'ma go see if Lisa wanna ride with me to get some food. Mexican sound good?"

"Yeah, I'm good with that," Brent replied.

"John," Kendra yelled out.

"Yes, Miss Lady?" he replied, standing up and swiping the sweat from his face.

"Mexican food good for y'all?" she asked.

"Yes indeed," he replied.

She nodded and headed to the house.

For the first time in a long time, Kendra's heart felt full. With all the losses that her family had been faced with over the last few years, she still had family left. They had grown closer together and mindful of just how wonderful it was to share even the worst of times with real love. It was going to be a long road to travel, but they were all going to make it.

When she entered the house, Lisa was sitting on the couch in tears.

"What's wrong?" Kendra asked.

"After two years, they just called my parents and told them that they found my sister's body in a lake along with her friend Tony. Who could've wanted her dead? She was a very genuine person and never bothered anyone to the point where they'd want to kill her."

John and Brent walked in, and as soon as her eyes clashed with Brent's, he knew that she knew he had killed her sister.

"You? Was it you?" she asked as she stood up.

"I don't know what you're talking about, Lisa. Was what me?" he asked.

Lisa charged at Brent, but as she got closer to him, he punched her in the face, knocking her out.

Kendra stood and placed her hands on her hips. "What did you do?"

Brent quickly tied her up and gagged her. Kendra sat on the couch looking at Brent.

John stood next to Kendra and whispered, "I'm gonna go get Troy and keep him from coming inside until y'all figure this out."

"Y'all? It's him!" she fussed as she stomped her feet. "Goddammit, I told y'all this fucking land is cursed. We can't escape this shit!"

Brent looked at Kendra and for once agreed it had to be cursed because ain't no way this shit should've happened. He didn't know what he was going to do, but he had to figure it out.

Chapter 16

Brent paced the floor, wondering what he would say to Lisa when she came to. He loved her and didn't want to hurt her. How was he going to make her understand? Kendra sat on the edge of the couch, shaking her leg, angry at their current situation. "How the fuck does this happen? We were literally about to board up this house and be safe from its tainted soil. Brent, what you gon' do? Man," she laughed sarcastically, "this can't be life."

"Damn, Kendra, I didn't expect this bullshit to happen. You acting like you mad at me. Hell, you should be mad at her!" he stammered.

"Mad at her for what?" Kendra asked, confused.

"I told her to leave her phone and shit at home. Had she listened, we wouldn't be where we are now. How else would her folks have been able to tell her about Ariana?"

"Dude, still! What the fuck you gon' do with her?" Kendra asked as she stared at Lisa handcuffed and tied to the kitchen chair.

Brent rubbed his hair. "Man, sis, I'on know. It's all Clinton's fault!"

"Blame everybody else except yo'self. That's what it is, huh?"

Brent sat down next to Kendra and sighed, "I'm gon' deal wit' this in my own way. You go on down to the trailer with John and Troy while I make a few calls. Take Troy and go back to Texas tomorrow. I'll call you, and maybe my intelligent sister can help me figure this out."

"I got the answer for you now! Kill her ass! That will eliminate all the bullshit and be done wit' it." Kendra shrugged. "Anything else you do gon' lead to nothing but disaster."

"That's cold, Kendra." He sighed.

"But killing her sister wasn't?" Kendra stood and looked at Lisa, then back at Brent. "Whatever you decide to do, do it, but you asked me for my opinion, and that's it. Kill her, Brent. It may sound cold, but if you don't, you're going to prison for a long time."

Kendra kissed him on the cheek. "Don't leave me out here alone. Figure this out and stay safe. I love you." She then walked out.

Brent turned and stared at Lisa. How could he kill someone who held his heart so firmly in her hands? He never imagined that after two years they'd find Ariana's body. He hadn't heard anything on the news about them finding a body. He grabbed his cell phone and began sifting through the news section on his phone.

"Nothing!"

He frowned. If it wasn't on the news, then who exactly had found Ariana's body?

Kendra and John

Kendra walked into the trailer and sat down on the couch beside John. She looked over at him, and he gazed at her.

"I'm not sure what's going on or what will happen, but I can't leave Brent up there at that house alone like that. I need to talk with him, but I have to hear you tell me that you understand," Kendra mumbled as she reached out for John.

John allowed her to grasp his hands in hers. "Kendra, do what you feel you need to do."

John pulled his hand back and stood and walked to the back. Kendra sighed and shook her head. She had to go and convince Brent that he needed to get rid of Lisa immediately.

She followed John to the back bedroom and stood at the door, watching him as he packed his clothes.

"I promise, I'm just gonna talk to him and come back down here. We can leave in the morning. I will honor your wishes."

John looked at her and smiled. "I love you, and I'm glad you're thinking logically on this."

Kendra smiled, walked over, and hugged him from behind. She rested her head on his back and sighed. Truth be told, she hated, although understood, his position. Troy had lost so much, and he deserved a peaceful young adult lifestyle, but she wasn't ready to just let her brother go to prison for the murder of Ariana. If Lisa was set free, all their family secrets would send her and Brent to prison for the rest of their lives, and she wasn't about to allow that to happen. Brent had to fix it.

She lifted her head. "I'll be back in a little while. I'ma try to see where Brent's head is right now. Make sure you get all my stuff."

Brent

Brent walked out of the house after securing Lisa to the bed and headed down to the barn. He needed to clear his mind and figure shit out. He loved Lisa and wanted to be with her forever, but she'd never forgive him for what he had done to Ariana.

"Goddamn you, Clint!" he cried aloud. "Even dead, you're destroying my life!"

Brent kicked a tin pail across the floor of the barn. He paced back and forth nervously and then stopped and closed his eyes as a thought struck him. Lisa was the beginning of his problems. Her brothers, who were known in the Rocky Mount area as the most ruthless brothers in the state, were about to rain some real shit on Wake County if Lisa told them what she knew. They feared no one and didn't have a care about going to prison.

"What the fuck!" he growled frustratedly.

Kendra

Kendra walked into the house using her key. "Brent, where are you?" she called out.

She searched the downstairs area and headed upstairs after not finding him. As she opened up the door to her mother's room, she froze. She hadn't been in there since Tyrone's funeral. She closed the door and walked over to the bed. The room was dusty, and the windows were tinted with dust and old water spots. She turned and closed her eyes as visions of her mother's face danced in her mind. She wiped at her eyes and sat down on the edge of her mother's unmade bed, which had been untouched since her death.

She understood why her mother killed herself, but she didn't respect her decision. After all the lessons that she had taught her, giving up was never one of them—until the day she took her and Omar's lives.

"You were a coward! You took the easy way out, and I'll never forgive you for that! Do you hear me, Le'Tera?" she growled out in the empty room.

Kendra walked angrily out of the room with a fury developing inside her. Her life had been screwed up from birth, and the two main people who were responsible for it were dead. She walked down the hall, swinging the doors open.

"Please help me!"

Kendra turned, hair swinging in her face as she did. Her eyes were red, and her heart was beating fast. She walked to her old bedroom, and when she opened the door, she found Lisa lying on the bed, hands and feet tied together and handcuffed to the brass headboard.

"Kendra, please let me go. You know Brent is dead wrong. I promise I won't go to the cops," Lisa pleaded.

Kendra looked blankly at Lisa and walked over slowly. She hadn't heard a word that Lisa had uttered. Once she reached the bed, she sat down next to Lisa.

"You know, this was my room for eleven years. I always knew what my family was into. They tried to hide it from me, but when they discovered that I knew, they punished me by sending me away. At least, that's what I thought back then. But I learned that they did what they thought was best for me. I swore," she ground out darkly, "that I'd never come back to this bitch when I grew up, and I didn't until they killed my brother."

Kendra laughed as she studied her hands. "Lisa, I was taught that family love, protect, support, and even punish one another when needed. I can't let you go. And I . . ." Kendra turned to look down at Lisa. "I can't trust that Brent won't kill you. I have to protect him."

Lisa's eyes bulged out with fear. "Kendra, please don't do this."

Kendra nodded as she accepted her fate.

Brent

Brent walked back over to the house as he left the barn. It was always a place where he felt at ease. He thought that it would ease his mind to where he could figure out what to do about Lisa, but to no avail. As he stomped up the steps, he noticed that Lisa had stopped screaming. He prayed that she would be calm enough to listen to him.

As he opened up the door, he felt an uneasiness shaking his soul. He looked up the steps and ran up them two at a time. He slowly walked to the door that he had left closed when he left that was now open.

"Kendra, noooo!" he yelled and raced to the bed.

He pulled at Kendra, who was straddling Lisa with her hands wrapped around her throat, squeezing the last bit of life from her body, causing her to fall to the floor. Lisa lay motionless on the bed with her arm dangling off the bed.

"What did you do? Kendra, wha . . ." His words drifted off as he laid his head on Lisa's chest. He turned his head, trying to find a single heartbeat.

Kendra stood up and stared at Brent. When he looked over at her, she had the same innocent, wild-eyed look that she had when she was 11 after she had killed their maid.

"You don't know what you just did, Kendra," he whispered.

"I saved you! That's what I just did, Brent."

Brent stood up and waved his hand toward Lisa's body. "You just signed my death certificate, Kendra! You shouldn't have done this, dammit!"

Brent's hands were shaking, and Kendra took a step back. He looked like he was about to attack her, and if he did, she'd have to kill him herself, and she didn't want his blood on her hands. But she wasn't about to back down.

"Who the fuck are you afraid of? We ain't never been afraid of shit. If Sean were here, he'd have killed her ass and anybody else who came with her! The fuck you mean, your death certificate? Brent, you aren't just any nigga!

I done seen you murk several niggas when we were young. Y'all think I didn't see what y'all was doing. All those people y'all took back in that barn who didn't walk back out. All the bodies I watched y'all through the barn windows grind up and use to fertilize that goddamn corn. Y'all seeded this farm with blood, and now you stand in front of me scared? Get yo'self together, bruh, because if you don't, you might be fucking right. You're dead!"

Kendra walked off quickly because the way he stood staring at her, he was either about to cry or try her. Either way, she wasn't trying to deal with it.

Brent stood and watched Kendra walk away, and he slowly turned and stared at Lisa's lifeless body. He didn't want her to die, but maybe Kendra was right.

He covered her body up and walked out of the room, closing the door behind him.

He walked down the stairs and out of the house. As he sat down, he pulled his phone out and began to scroll through his contacts. He got comfortable on the top step, and when he located his right hand's name, he pushed the call button. After he attempted his call twice, Big T finally answered.

"What's good, bruh? You on your way back?" he asked, seemingly out of breath.

"Naw, but listen, let me ask you a question. Have you heard anything about Ariana?"

There was a brief silence before Big T spoke, "Let me go into another room right quick. Hold on."

"Wait a damn minute. You need to finish me off before you take that damn call!" Brent heard a female fussing.

"Shut that shit up. Hell, yo' pussy worn out anyway. I wasn't feeling shit—no grip, no suction. You can go the fuck on 'cause I can't nut off yo' pussy anyway, bitch. Who the fuck you think I am? Get yo' shit on and get the fuck on."

Brent could hear some rustling noises, and then he heard a thud. He shook his head, realizing that Big T had just knocked the female out.

"Bruh, let me call you right back. I gotta slide this bitch to the doe!"

Brent shook his head and looked at his phone as Big T hung up in his face.

A few minutes later, Big T was calling him back. "All right, bruh. I'm back. What's going on, B?" Big T asked.

"Listen, I'll tell you all that, but I need you and Truck to drive down here to the country now!"

"Text me the info, and I'll get with Truck, and we gon' be on our way," Big T told him.

"All right, I'm about to send it now. And aye, don't y'all ride dirty. Anything we need, I got already."

Brent knew that Big T was confused, but he wasn't going to say too much over the phone. After Brent hung up and texted Big T the address, he decided to call one more person to help him prepare for a war he knew was coming.

Brent walked back into the house and changed into his rugged jeans and T-shirt. He put on his gold Timberlands and grabbed his brimmed hat. When he exited, he walked down to where they kept their machinery and got on the mini backhoe to dig a hole in the middle of the field. It was surrounded by tall sunflowers. He surmised that if Lisa wanted to be buried anywhere on the property, it would be the sunflower field. She spent a lot of time there during their current stay on the farm.

As he drove the machinery up to the field and began working, Kendra stood staring at him from the trailer.

Kendra

Kendra sighed as she walked away from the window. She glanced over at Troy, who was sitting on the couch staring at her. She could tell by the look on his face that he had heard Brent start up the backhoe and knew why he had. He just didn't know who was about to be buried.

Kendra began to worry that nothing that she could do would keep Troy from the same fate as his brother or experiencing a savage lifestyle. But the look that she saw in his eyes was that of wonderment, curiosity, the look of wanting, wanting to kill. The look that she had on several occasions. She loved him so much, and she thought back to her and John's earlier conversation. She promised her mother that she'd take care of Troy, and she was going to do that if it killed her.

"Pack yo' stuff. We leaving in the morning. First thing."

She didn't wait for a response as she walked back to the bedroom. John lay across the bed on his back, looking at his phone. She sat down on the bed and began taking her clothes off.

"I'm about to take a bath. Can you make sure that Troy packs his things? I'll make the flight reservations when I get out of the tub."

John put his phone down on his chest and reached out and began stroking her back. "You know I love you, right?"

She nodded. "I do, and I love you."

"I know," he replied as he sat up and sat next to her. "We are doing the right thing."

"Right." She stood and kissed him on the lips. She grabbed her robe and put it on and walked out of the room.

John knew that Kendra wasn't thrilled about leaving Brent with a mess, but they had to concentrate on Troy. He walked out and headed into the front room. "All right, let's get those bags packed."

Troy stood up without saying a word and did as he was told.

Chapter 17

Brent

As the evening approached and the sun began to set, Brent was sitting on the porch smoking a cigar. He had his head bent, staring down at an army of ants that were creating dirt hills. He grabbed his Natural Light beer and poured it slowly over the anthills. Some scattered, and others sank instantly. He closed his eyes as his temples began to pulsate. He hadn't eaten, nor had he disposed of Lisa's body. She was still lying cold across Kendra's bed. He was waiting on Big T and Aaron to arrive. Aaron had texted him less than an hour earlier and informed him that they were about an hour away, so he was expecting them to pull up any moment, and once they arrived, he would have them help him bury Lisa and come up with a plan to deal with Lisa's family.

Brent looked up at the sky with tears in his eyes. "Damn, man, if this is life, I'm ready for it to be over! I see why you took your own life, Momma. Death is probably better than this shit. You were the only one who loved me really until Lisa, and now she is gone. I miss you every day, Mom. You would know what to do."

Suddenly, a name popped up in his head, and he knew exactly who could help him figure shit out. He pulled out his phone and put his cigar out. As he scrolled down and clicked call once he found the number, he said a silent prayer that they'd answer.

Big T and Aaron

"Man, I see why Brent's family chose to live so deep down here in the country. Everything is sectioned off and secluded. I haven't seen two houses yet that are close together," Aaron said.

Big T looked over to his left for a brief moment and saw a semi-wooded field FOR SALE. Some of the land had been cleared out, but the For Sale sign looked old and rusted. The words were faded due to the weather. He glanced back at the road. "I wonder how much they want for that."

"Shit, by the looks of it, you might be able to get it for cheap," Aaron replied. "You thinking about buying it?"

"Hell naw! I was just wondering." Big T laughed.

"I think our turn is coming up, bruh," Aaron announced as the GPS said, "In a quarter of a mile, turn left."

Big T slowed down as they approached their turn. "You have arrived at your destination." Big T turned down the dirt road, which was lined with trees on either side that hid the main property. Aaron turned down the music as they headed down the long driveway.

As they drove farther down, they saw a clearing and then the house and Brent's truck. The stalks of corn that were barely recognizable were wilted and brown. Big T noticed what he assumed was a freshly dug hole in the middle of an area where sunflower beds were growing. The area where the huge garden was had tall weeds growing up from the ground, and whatever vegetables had been planted there were long gone. When they reached the house, Big T whispered, "I betcha this used to be a bad-ass house!'

"Probably! I'd have loved staying down here," Aaron agreed.

The dirty white paneled house was huge. The shutters were barely hanging on, and the few ripped screens that adorned the windows were dirty as well. They parked behind Brent's royal blue F-150 and got out. Big T stretched his legs and arms, then cracked his back. Big T was five foot ten, 225 pounds, solid with a low-cut fade. He had brown skin with thin lips and a goatee that was trimmed neatly. He had a small amount of hair coming out from his outer earlobe. It was a family trait that all the men in his family wore proudly.

Aaron walked around and stood next to Big T. Aaron was shorter than Big T and Brent, standing at five foot six, stubby with short dreads. He had two gold teeth in the bottom row of his teeth. His facial hair was thinned and wildly spread across his face. Everyone in his family called him Pumpkin Head or Charlie Brown because of the size and shape of his head. Aaron wasn't the cutest man, but because of his bad-boy reputation, the women flocked to him. Since being a part of Brent's entourage, they had learned how to earn and keep the respect of a lot of individuals.

Before they could ascend the stairs, Brent walked out. "I'm glad y'all here. I gotta show y'all something, and then we gotta talk."

Brent walked back into the house, up the stairs, and into Kendra's room with Big T and Aaron following. "What the fuck!" Aaron grimaced.

They stood halfway in the room, gawking at Lisa's body.

"Man, don't act like you ain't never seen a dead body before," Brent told him.

"Man, that's Lisa. What happened?" Aaron asked.

Brent started to tell them everything, but with the way Aaron was acting, he decided to hold on to what actually happened. "She told me that she and her family had found Ariana's body, which brings me to this. Somebody done told them folks something 'cause Ariana's body been disposed of, right?" he asked, looking at Aaron, who fumbled with his words for a second.

"Um, yeah, yeah, you know it. I got rid of it."

"Whateva, man, all I know is when I find out who the snitch is, I'ma chop their fucking head off."

Before Brent moved Lisa's body out of the house, he asked Big T and Aaron to help him put up a chain and a NO TRESPASSING sign at the main entrance of the home. He didn't want any uninvited guests. He was going to inform Kendra of that when they left the following morning to take the back trail out.

After they successfully put up the chain and sign, they headed back to the house. They rolled Lisa's body in a quilt and toted her out to the area where Brent had previously dug the grave. As they laid her body in the dark, cold pit, Aaron shook his head.

"This shit gon' get real ugly, bruh. You know that after they don't hear from Lisa, all hell is going to break loose. It's gon' be hell in those streets."

"Yeah, man, her brothers ain't gon' just let a second sister disappear with no real explanation. Hell, I'm shocked they fell for the story we gave them about Ariana," Big T agreed.

Brent sighed as he stood back, wiping the sweat from his forehead. "Shit, it's not the brothers I'm concerned about."

Big T looked at Brent and nodded. "She would be the one to fear."

Brent laughed, "If my brother Sean were here, he'd tell me that I was a pussy for what I'm about to do, but this is about survival at this point, and anybody who gets in the way is on their own. As a matter of fact, I need y'all to toss those cell phones in the pond. Somebody is talking, and I won't let no man bring trouble to my do'step."

"Man, you should know it's not us," Big T commented.

"Even so, toss them." Brent repeated.

Brent stared down at Lisa before they started filling the grave. He remembered when he met Lisa. He had met her twelve years earlier and fell in love with her very quickly. Lisa introduced him to her brothers, who invested money in his business venture in an attempt to separate his life from his family.

Brent started his accounting business with the Harris family as his client. They used his legit business just like his family used their farmhouse as a means to launder money and make legal bank transactions to cover up their underground gun business. As the money began rolling in, Brent began to get greedy, skimming small amounts of money from the Harris accounts and others until he frittered it all away, causing his business to crash. It resulted in him having to do a few jobs for Sean, which undoubtedly pulled him back into the Love family's drama.

When Ariana learned what he had done, she took it upon herself at his father's request to further sink his ship by stealing from him. He couldn't allow her to get away with it. After killing her, he started seeing Lisa.

Brent couldn't help but think that if he hadn't been forced to kill Ariana, he wouldn't be in his current dilemma. If he had to blame anyone, he figured, Clinton was the best place to lay blame. Everything around him seemed to be falling at a point in his life when he felt like it was all coming together. Thanks to Kendra's meddling hands, he was burying yet another daughter, the last Harris girl. He knew hell was about to rain down on him. He had to lie low and let shit simmer. He had pulled Christine into his web of shit, using Kendra as the scapegoat. He prayed that she could make things right for him, but if all else failed, he'd pack up and leave the state. That was, if Ariana and Lisa's mother didn't find him first.

Kendra

Kendra awoke the next morning and had John and Troy put their belongings in the car while she walked up to the main house to check on Brent. She needed to apologize for killing Lisa and let him know that she'd help him in any way outside of getting involved with the situation with Lisa and the law.

As she approached the house, she noticed a car that she'd never seen before. She frowned as she walked around to get a closer look at the vehicle. She walked around the car and peeped inside to see if she could get a hint of who was inside with her brother. Frustrated, she walked up to the door and walked in.

"Aye, aye, who the fuck are you?" Aaron asked with his gun halfway pulled out of his pants.

"Who the fuck are you? You're in my shit, bruh," Kendra replied as she walked forward. She wasn't afraid of being shot because if he was going to shoot, he would've done so when she walked through the door, and if he had plans to kill her, then she was already as good as dead just being in there, so she wasn't about to give them the satisfaction of seeing her frightened.

"Man, that's my sister, bruh. Back the fuck up!" Brent told him.

By that time, John had walked in. "What the fuck?"

"It's okay, man. These my folks from Charlotte. They gon' help me finish boarding this house up."

Kendra walked into the kitchen and looked at Brent. "I need to speak to you privately, please."

John was looming over Aaron, looking like he wanted to steal off on him for even trying his wife like he just did.

Kendra smiled at how nervous Aaron looked standing so close to John. His eyes were averted, and as Big T walked in, he took that as his cue to move away.

Big T looked at John and walked over with his hand extended. "What's good? I'm Big T."

"I'm John," John replied, refusing to take his eyes off Aaron.

"Nice to meet you."

"Who you?" John asked Aaron.

"Um, my name is Aaron," he stuttered.

"You owe my wife an apology, young buck, or you gon' see me before we leave out," John told him.

Big T looked at Aaron and shook his head. He had never seen him look so frightened. Lately, he had been acting scared, and he didn't like it. Aaron looked at Big T, who threw his hands up. "Don't look at me. That's all on you, bruh."

Aaron nodded and walked around John and Big T and walked into the kitchen to eat his breakfast.

"Aye, do you want me to go ahead and put the food in the car?" Troy asked as he walked into the house.

"Yeah, you can. Kendra is outside talking to your uncle right now," John replied.

"Okay. Hopefully, she will be done soon 'cause I want to talk to Uncle Brent before we leave," Troy told him.

"These are Brent's associates, Aaron and Big T," John said as he introduced the two men to Troy.

"Hey," he simply said before turning to walk back out of the house.

"Was it a long drive?" John asked, trying to make some small talk as he waited for Kendra and Brent to walk back up from the basement.

Kendra and Brent walked down into the basement, and Kendra sighed, "I almost forgot this section of the house existed."

Brent laughed, "Me too. Up until yesterday."

"I'm so sorry about all this. I know that I made shit worse by killing Lisa, but, bruh, she was going to call the cops," Kendra replied.

"The cops would be easier to deal with. Kendra, everything that you thought that our family used to be, her family is ten times worse. Once they figure out that she is dead, I won't be too far behind." He sighed as he rubbed his head.

Kendra dropped her head and sat down on the bottom step. "What are you going to do now?"

Brent laughed inwardly because he noticed how Kendra used the word "you" when she was more to blame than he was. "I think we got it covered. I will figure this out. Don't fret," he said in a sarcastic manner that didn't go unnoticed by Kendra.

"Are you angry with me? I mean, if I hadn't killed her, what were you going to do, Brent?" she asked.

He shook his head and laughed, "You know what?" He paused. "I probably would've had to kill her too."

"Exactly. That's why I did it, because it would've been hard for you to do."

"Yeah, but, Kendra, it was for me to do. Not you."

Kendra nodded. "I get that. I'm sorry, bruh. Seriously I am. We are about to leave and head back to Texas. If you need me, call me."

"I got it figured out. No worries."

Kendra stood up, and Brent walked over and gave her a hug.

"Take care, sis," he whispered.

She didn't know why, but it sounded like a final goodbye to her. She stepped back and looked at him, tears gathering in her eyes. "Please be careful," she whispered.

Brent wiped the tears from her eyes and kissed her on the forehead. "I got this, baby."

She smiled, and they hugged once more before heading back up with everyone else.

Troy also hugged it out with Brent and said his goodbyes, and Kendra, John, and Troy left Brent to finish boarding the house up and dealing with what he needed to deal with.

Chapter 18

Charlotte

Scottie Harris

Friday night, the Charlotte Metro Police had the South Park neighborhood blocked off at the top and bottom. No one was allowed in or out. They had just apprehended Scottie Harris, a member of the notorious Harris brothers. They were known around Charlotte as one of the most ruthless families. They always covered all bases and left no trails of any crime that they committed—that was, until now.

As the police fought to escort Scottie, struggling against them, from his home, the onlookers were standing around with their phones out recording the scene.

"I knew he was a criminal. His kind shouldn't be allowed in this neighborhood," one of the white spectators growled.

One of the other black residents, who overheard the comment, looked at the man and glared angrily at him. "What the fuck you mean by that?" he questioned as he shoved the man.

The two men began to tussle a bit, causing two officers to rush over to separate the two men.

Detective Thomas Gage smiled as he shook the hands of a few officers on site. He was thrilled that he had one of the Harris siblings in cuffs. To him, it was just the beginning of a massive round-up that he was determined to see through.

"One down, three more to go!" He laughed as he walked over to assist the officers in getting Scottie in the car. Another officer was walking out of Scottie's house with a gun and a black bag filled with money.

"You know he ain't gon' talk, right?" Detective Patrick O'Dell pointed out.

"We don't need him to say shit about what he been doing. We got him on gun charges, and once we match that money," he said, nodding to the black bag being placed in the trunk of the police car, "then we got him on several charges that's gon' get him life. He will talk if he wants to ever see the streets again."

"Yeah, but don't count your chickens before they've hatched," O'Dell advised him.

Gage ignored him and walked toward his car. "You coming? I wanna watch them walk that bastard into the precinct."

O'Dell nodded and walked toward the black Crown Vic and got in. He looked at his partner and smiled. He prayed that he didn't get his hopes up about Scottie Harris squealing on his family.

Sunday Morning

Donna Harris stood at the podium, staring out at the attendees of her church. As her eyes landed on her two sons sitting in the front row, she smiled approvingly. "As I lay eyes upon my sons who have been faithful to their God by being obedient to their mother, I want to leave you all with this last word. Colossians 3:20 states, 'Children, obey your parents in everything, for this pleases the Lord.' May God bless each and every one of you."

She nodded at her sons, looked at her stewardesses, and nodded at them. She walked down the three steps leading to the open area of the church. She greeted her visitors, shaking their hands as they left. One of the stewardesses walked over and whispered something in her ear. She nodded and spoke with the next person leaving the church.

Once Thomas and Jason approached their mother, she smiled. "I need to talk to you two before you leave. If y'all can meet me in my office, I'll be in there as soon as we lock up."

"Yes, ma'am," Jason answered.

"Momma, can this wait 'til later? I have something to do right quick," Thomas said.

Donna didn't say a word, but she stared at him darkly.

"Yes, ma'am," he uttered.

"Good. I'll see you in a few minutes," she replied, turning to speak with one of the visitors to the church.

"Man, yo' momma be doing the freaking most," Thomas complained as he and Jason walked back down to the front of the church, heading for Donna's office.

As they walked in, Jason turned the lights on, and they sat down in the two chairs sitting in front of her desk.

"I wonder what this is about," Jason whispered.

"Like you don't know," Thomas retorted.

Ten minutes later, two of their mother's stewardesses entered and took a stance on either side of the door.

Thomas turned around, looked at them, turned back around, and huffed, "Do you see what I mean? They doing too much. Look at them standing there like they in the freaking army. Bruh, like we ain't all about to go to

Donna's," he fussed, calling his mother by her first name, "house and eat dinner. This whole conversation could've taken place then. She's just being extra for no reason."

"Is that right, son?" Donna asked from the doorway.

Thomas spun around and watched as his mother walked around her desk and sat down, looking at him, smiling.

"I mean, dang, Momma, we could have talked at dinner. Where's the lie in that? Then you got Evelyn and Sharon standing against the doe like they security guards or some mess," Thomas blurted out.

Jason stared at Thomas with his mouth dropped and eyes wide.

"Well, I haven't seen y'all in a few days. What's going on?" she asked, seemingly ignoring Thomas's outburst.

"You know, we do work, Momma," Thomas answered.

"You know, you getting real comfortable with your loose mouth and disrespectful tone, son," she said, shooting daggers at him. "Seems to me," she continued, "y'all been too busy to notice that Scottie ain't here. Where is he? Oh, and when was the last time y'all heard from Ariana and Lisa? Huh? Family business takes priority over everything else. Do I need to help y'all understand that?"

Thomas looked at his mother with a fire in his eyes. "Momma, Scottie is in jail."

"I know where the fuck he at!" Donna sneered, not caring that she was in the house of God or that she was a messenger for Him. "Tell me why he isn't sitting here with us."

"Scottie got himself locked up," Thomas replied, challenging Donna.

Donna laughed, "Thomas, I see you need a li'l act right. Let me help you out."

Before Thomas could respond, Evelyn stepped forward and hit him with a volt from a Taser.

"Uugggg!" Thomas cried out as his body jerked.

Jason jumped up and moved out of the way. He didn't know what was about to happen.

"Sit down, Jason," she whispered as she sat back in her chair and watched Thomas adjust from the shock. "Let's try this again. Why is Scottie not here?"

Thomas cleared his throat a few times and choked out, "I'll get him out in the morning, Momma."

"Tonight. Now, once Scottie is out, I need y'all to go find my goddamn child!" she ground out, screaming in the end. Donna's angelic face was in a scowl as she stared at Jason and Thomas.

"Yes, ma'am," both Jason and Thomas spoke simultaneously.

Donna looked at Thomas. "Proverbs 13:24: 'Spare the rod, spoil the child.' Remember that. Now, I will see you all for dinner. Unless you have an objection."

"No, ma'am," Thomas whispered through his clenched teeth.

"I have such good boys. What shall we have for dinner?"

They all walked out of her office, with Thomas walking slowly behind them, sulking as if he were 10 and had gotten scolded for skipping school. He rubbed his back where Evelyn had zapped him.

"Ass-kisser," he groaned as he watched Jason link arms with Donna.

Chapter 19

Back in Texas

Kendra sat in her office, looking over a few new potential clients' profiles. She had been back for a week and, along with planning the trail ride party, had been bombarded with inquiries for service.

Troy was heavy on her, though, and it was hard for her to concentrate on any of her work. After she killed Lisa, she started having regrets, heavily. She had vowed to her mother that she'd do everything she could to ensure that Troy wouldn't have to grow up in the same environment that they had. She should've just minded her business and let Brent deal with his own mess. How could she help Troy when she was no better than his father, Sean?

She sighed and went through a few of her potential client lists. Suddenly a thought hit her. She smiled because, for the first time, the thought of Tyrone didn't hurt. She remembered how enthused he was about learning the business. He wanted to join forces with her and build a dynasty. Troy loved music, and he could be the new face of her music department. Kendra stood up and walked out of her office in search of Taye. She was going to have Taye train him and show him the ropes.

As soon as she walked out, she saw Taye and Bridget huddled up in her office talking. When she tapped on the door, they looked over and waved her in.

"What's up, boss lady?" Taye asked.

"Listen, wait a minute, what y'all two got going on in here?" Kendra asked.

Bridget smiled. "I am going on a date."

"For real? With who?" Kendra asked, sitting down across from her.

Bridget began blushing. "With this guy I met at the seminar that you had me attend. He was very nice, and we started out talking on the phone. Then we met for coffee before work just now. We are going out Saturday night."

"I'm so happy for you," Kendra remarked, smiling hard. "I hope that he is the one for you. You deserve to be happy."

"Thank you," Bridget replied, looking at Tyrone's picture that she had up.

Kendra followed her glance and shook her head. "Nope, baby girl. He wouldn't want you living your life like a nun. Go be happy. So listen, Taye, can you show Troy around starting tomorrow afternoon when he gets out of school?" Kendra asked. "I need him to learn the ropes concerning the management of music."

"You know I can. I got you."

"Thanks. Have you seen Christine by any chance?" Kendra asked.

"I haven't seen her since this morning. She seemed like she was having a serious conversation with someone and rushed out with her phone to her ear," Taye replied.

"I'll try to catch up with her later. Okay, so I'ma talk with Troy when I get home, and just for the record, I'm glad you're here," she told Taye.

"Same here."

Kendra walked out and stopped in to speak to a few of her other employees, and then she went back inside her office. She set a few appointments up with some new clients and worked on some marketing strategies for her current clients. After she finished up there, she decided to go home early, giving everyone the rest of the day off. She knew that they had been working extremely hard, and she wanted them to get some rest before they stepped it up to the next level and branched off into a global economy and clientele.

As she walked out, she saw Christine still sitting at her desk. She walked over and tapped on the open door. "Hey, what's up?"

"Just got a lot on my mind, sis." She sighed.

"Anything I can help with?" Kendra asked.

"Naw, this is something I got to decide for myself, but thanks, babes."

"You know I'm here if you need anything," Kendra told her.

"I love you, sis," Christine whispered, smiling.

"Yeah, yeah, I love you too." Kendra walked away, feeling concerned. She hadn't seen Christine look like that in a long time.

She waved at the security guard as she exited her office building. When she got into her car, she reached into her purse and pulled out her cell phone. She called Troy to make sure that he would be home when she got there. She hoped that he would jump at the idea of learning the ropes at her firm. She felt that it could be something that he could take over when she decided to retire. On her way home, she stopped at the AT&T store to pay her cell phone bill and pick up a new adapter for her charger, and then drove home.

As Kendra pulled into her driveway and drove down to her nice-sized ranch-style home, she frowned, noticing that Troy was in the company of some rough-looking guys. Troy knew that neither she nor John allowed anyone to visit without permission.

When she finally parked and got out, she nodded at Troy and walked into the house. As she entered through the side door of the kitchen, she saw John peering out the window.

"Did he ask if he could have company?" she asked.

"Yeah, he did, but I didn't know he was bringing such a rowdy-looking bunch," John replied, sipping his coffee.

Kendra walked toward the door in a huff.

"Kendra, don't embarrass the boy. Let him have his company. If they start acting up, I'll deal with it myself. Go take a bath and relax. Oh, I closed on my mother's house finally. It's been just sitting there all these years rotting."

"Oh, really? How much you sell it for?" she asked as she tasted the hamburger steak with gravy that he had made. "That's delicious, babe."

"Thank you. Well, I accepted three hundred thousand for it," he replied, pulling the paperwork out of the drawer near the microwave stand.

"Good numbers. What you gon' do with it?"

"Whateva you wanna do. It's our money."

"Why don't you invest in some kinda business venture?" she questioned, leaning her back against the counter.

"Maybe. We can decide once everything clears."

"Yes." She walked to him and kissed him. "I'm going to shower so I can dig into that food. That squash and onions smell divine!"

"Anything to please you, madam," he cooed as he wrapped his arms around her for one more kiss.

Kendra pulled away. "I'll be back in a few minutes."

"Okay. I'll have the table set and ready by the time you get out, unless you want me to wash your back."

Kendra smiled at his attempt to join her as she walked back into her room and undressed. She hopped in the shower, and when the warm water kissed her skin, she closed her eyes and sighed. She had so many thoughts that plagued her mind that she couldn't share with John. She had to figure shit out. She had left Brent in a very bad situation, and she needed to find out exactly who Lisa's family were.

Once she finished her shower, she emerged from the bathroom and walked over to the bed with her full-length towel wrapped around her body. She flopped back on it and closed her eyes. She was physically tired and mentally drained. All she wanted to do was relax. She sighed as she heard her cell phone beep. She sat up and rolled her neck, trying to relieve the tension in it. She got up and grabbed her phone and read the text from Brent.

Brent: I hope everything is good with you. No need to worry. I have my team here, as you know, and we have a plan in motion. I'll let you know if I need you.

Kendra nodded her head as if he could see her and texted back: Okay, I love you.

Kendra got dressed, then walked out of the bedroom and headed down the hall to the kitchen. She could hear John and Troy talking, and John seemed concerned.

She walked in and sat down at the table and glanced at both John and Troy, wondering if they were going to fill her in on what they were talking about. After a brief, awkward silence, she grabbed a forkful of her food that was steaming hot. She blew in and out quickly and grabbed at her water and took a big gulp.

"Fuck, that was hot!" she cried.

Troy smiled and bowed his head to hide his face.

"Goddamn, babe, you hungry for real, huh?" John questioned.

"Shut up!" Kendra groaned.

"Don't get mad at me. You saw the steam." He laughed.

Kendra laughed and watched Troy, who was also laughing.

"You know, you have the perfect smile when you flash it. Makes you look even more handsome."

Troy shrugged. "Yeah."

Kendra dropped her head, and when she looked back up, she sighed. "These past two years have been hard on all of us, but I know it was harder for you. I know that you understand what happened, and in my opinion, you shouldn't. You should be confused as hell, but you're not because you were placed in a position where you had to do things and see things that no one should have to. You lost your family, and I know I can't replace them, but I love you, Troy, and I only want for you what you want for you, but please, please don't continue the trend that our family had. Let it die."

Troy looked at Kendra and nodded his head. "When Pops did what he did to my mom, I wanted to kill him. My brother died because he was disloyal. I didn't feel bad about that. You know he told me that I shouldn't have been born. He hated me, Aunt Kendra." Troy sighed. "The feeling was very much mutual. He deserved what he got. And Pops, well, when Grandma sent me away that day, I knew she was going to kill him, and before I walked out, I looked at him, and all I could think was, 'Good riddance.' I'm not so sad, Auntie, and I'm glad I'm here with you and John. I love you."

Kendra wiped at her eyes and smiled.

"Yeah, yeah, yeah, let's g'on and eat with y'all oversensitive asses," John said after clearing his throat.

Kendra rolled her eyes. "Anyway, what you think about coming to join me at Unique Management? I can place you over the music section, and Taye has agreed to show you the ropes."

Troy took a bit of his food and nodded his head. "Uncle John, you put yo' whole dang foot in this!"

John laughed, "Skills, nephew. Get yours up!"

Troy nodded. "Word. And, Auntie, I'd like that, but I'm planning on going to college."

"Well, until you go, you can come and learn something. After school for an hour a day," she pressed on.

"All right, if that's what you want." Troy shrugged as he ate another bite of his food.

"Thank you," Kendra replied.

They finished their dinner and retired for the night.

Chapter 20

Friday morning, Kendra got up and got dressed, fixed herself a pot of coffee, and prepared breakfast for herself and Troy. John had gotten up earlier, around four, so he could tend to the farm and package the last box of fresh sausage that he had to deliver to Jakes Food Market.

"Hey, Troy. What do you think we should have for dessert tomorrow?" she asked as he walked in and poured a glass of juice.

"Pound cake."

"No, that wouldn't go good with the type of dinner it is."

"Why ask me then?" He shrugged.

She shrugged. "I'on know. What you got planned this afternoon after school?"

"I'on know."

"Well, if you don't know, who does?" she mocked him.

Troy stared at her with his head tilted, his eyes saying, "Really?"

Kendra laughed, "I'm gone. Love you."

"Love you too," he replied.

Kendra got into her car and started it. She sent a message to Christine to see if she had made it safely and waited a few moments for her reply. As soon as she got the thumbs-up and a kissy face, she backed up and pulled out of her driveway and headed for work.

Kendra was two blocks away from her office when a black Acura sped by her, almost hitting her car. She swerved and ran off the road. Her heart began pounding erratically, and her head was spinning.

"What the fuck!" she yelled out. "You stupid bastard!"

It took her a few minutes to get herself together before she could proceed. When she pulled up to her office, Taye was just getting out of her car. Taye waited for Kendra to park so they could walk in together. She frowned when she saw the panic on Kendra's face.

"You okay?" Taye asked.

"Man, some fool just damn near crashed into me. I had to pull off to the side, girl," Kendra replied.

Taye put her arm around Kendra's shoulder. "Well, I'm glad you made it here, boo. Come on, let's get a good old cup of coffee on me."

"The coffee is free, Taye." Kendra smiled.

"Even better," Taye sang.

Kendra laughed lightly.

By the end of her workday, Kendra had pushed the incident out of her head.

Kendra drove home and picked John up. They were going to buy the food for the dinner that Kendra was having for her staff. They first went to Food Crave. They usually stayed stocked with everything, so Kendra was certain she'd be able to get the majority of the things she needed there. They got out and walked arm in arm into the store.

Kendra and John walked through the grocery store, picking up items for their dinner with the staff at Unique Management. Kendra wanted to show her appreciation for all the hard work and long hours that they had been putting in.

"I'ma go to the seafood department, and you can go grab some spices for the lobster tails and meet me up at the register."

"Gotcha, babe," John replied. He leaned in and kissed her on the lips before walking off.

She bit her bottom lip as she watched him. "That man!" She turned her head and walked over to the counter.

"May I help you, ma'am?" a short white man asked as he walked to greet her.

"Yes, how many lobster tails do you have back there?"

"How many do you need? I'm sure I can handle your order."

"Can you handle fifty?"

"I sure can, but they are $15.99 per tail."

Kendra gave him a look that turned his face red before she spoke a single word. "I don't think I asked you how much. I asked whether you could handle an order of fifty tails. It's a simple yes or no answer, sir. If you don't have fifty, give me what you have, and I'll go elsewhere for the rest."

"Yes, ma'am, I'll go see how many I have."

"That's all I need you to do, and thank you."

John approached Kendra as she stood waiting for her tails. He placed the spices in the cart and laughed, "I'm glad I doubled back. I would've been standing at the register looking stupid, li'l lady."

Kendra pointed her finger at the double doors of the seafood department. "Dude takin' his own good time getting the tails. Trying to tell me how much they cost and shit!"

"Is his ego still intact, or did you snatch it?" John laughed.

"When I suck yo' dick, do yo' soul still be intact, or do I snatch it? You look hella good walking away from me," she whispered, but not low enough.

"Damn!" a woman laughed, standing behind them.

Kendra turned and laughed, "Girl, I'm not even embarrassed you heard me."

She looked at John, who had his head down, laughing. "You just not gon' act right, li'l lady."

"Make me act right."

The man returned with Kendra's lobster tails, and Kendra turned her attention to them. "How many are there?" she asked as she inspected them.

"We only had twenty-three tails. I do apologize for that," he responded nervously, looking at John.

John knew at that moment that Kendra had probably said something to him. "I'ma go get a few cases of water and sodas. You need me to get anything else?" John asked.

"No, I'll meet you up front," she replied.

After the man wrapped the tails and handed them off to Kendra, she walked hurriedly to the register. John hadn't made it to the front, so she started putting her items on the counter.

"Taxpayers paying for them to eat like kings," she heard a male voice say.

Kendra turned and saw a tall white man standing behind her. She glanced around to see if there was possibly someone else he could've been speaking of. After confirming that he was speaking to her, she turned fully around to face him. "Excuse me?"

The man looked down at her and smiled, showing his rotten teeth. "You heard me. Y'all use y'all food stamps to eat rich while the working folks like me gotta eat how we can."

"First of all, you raggedy-mouth bum, if you spent more time worrying about what you eat and less time about what's in other people's carts, your teeth wouldn't look so worn out. Bob!"

"My name ain't Bob," he interjected.

"Second of all," Kendra continued, ignoring his statement, "you racist piece of shit, it doesn't matter how I'm paying for my food, but for the record, I'm using cash. I don't need the taxpayers to pay for shit that I buy. If I want it, my pocketbook is deep enough to get it."

By that time, John had walked over and put the stuff he had in his cart on the counter with what Kendra had. He pulled his wallet out and handed her seven $100 bills. "That should be enough," he told her.

The woman behind the counter was standing with a shocked look on her face at what Kendra had just said to the older white man standing behind her.

She rang her items up. "$695.76."

Kendra handed her the money, and when the lady gave her the change, she looked at the rude white man and smiled. "I don't like charity, so allow me to give you back the two cents that you just tried to give me, Bob!" She tossed two pennies in his cart.

John stood there, glaring at Kendra. "Aye, woman, what just happened?"

"Nothing. I took care of it, babe. He just felt the need to speak on something that he shouldn't have."

The white man was staring at John with fear as John refused to move from the checkout line. The man swallowed hard and refused to move forward until John began to slowly walk away.

"Be careful who you fuck with, 'cause er'ybody ain't wit' dat dumb shit."

"Babe, leave Bob alone and let's go."

The young woman who was behind the counter began to snicker, causing the older white man's face to turn even redder than it was.

Kendra and John walked out, and as they did, John walked up behind Kendra and placed his hands on top of hers as she pushed the cart, and they walked to the car. After they placed the groceries in the back, he laughed, "Do you gotta show out everywhere we go?"

"No, babe. Only when somebody shows out on me. We gotta stop at the seafood market to get a few more tails before we pick Troy up from school."

"Shit, whateva you say. I ain't trying to make you mad."
Kendra laughed and hit his arm. "You love me?"

"You know it. You love me?"

"Forever!"

They got in the car and drove off.

Later that afternoon, Kendra was in her kitchen prepping the food that she was cooking the following day. She loved the layout of her kitchen. It was roomie and different. Unlike most modern kitchens, hers had a black cast-iron wood stove as well as a modern stove available. The iron stove was used for cooking a lot of her meats. It gave her food an old country-style flavor. John had installed it himself and taught her how to cook on it. As she was peeling her shrimp, there was a knock on the door.

She wiped her hands on her apron and walked to the sink. "Just a minute," she called out as another round of knocks sounded. After she quickly washed her hands, she grabbed a paper towel to dry her hands off and headed to the door. She pulled back the curtain and smiled as she opened the door. "Hey, boo."

"Hey, sis," Christine replied as she walked into the kitchen. "Damn, it stank in here," she said, complimenting the smell of the food that Kendra was cooking. She had some lobster-filled mac and cheese baking in the oven and some sauces thickening on the stovetop.

"What's up, babes?" Kendra asked.

"Hey, Kendra, listen, I know the trail ride event is coming up, but I need to go handle some personal stuff," Christine informed her.

"Sis, you know you don't have to explain anything to me. You'll be there tomorrow, though, right? You and Taye done put in so much work with my team, and I'd hate for you to miss it."

"Kendra, I'm so proud of you and what you have accomplished here. I'll definitely be at the dinner tomorrow. I don't want to miss those lobster bites."

Kendra hugged her. "I love you, sis. When you leaving?"

"Tomorrow, after dinner," Christine replied.

Kendra nodded, "Okay, boo. Well, that means you gon' have to help me cook."

"Yes, Mom," Christine joked.

Kendra hit at Christine playfully, and they embraced and finished filling and chopping up the lobster.

After the food was prepped and Christine was gone, Kendra took a quick shower. She curled up next to John. While he was reading *The Wall Street Journal,* she was reading *Sin City Dreams* by Trinity DeKane. Reading was her escape from her busy life.

Troy was seated at the table doing his homework with his headphones bumping. Kendra was amazed at how he could listen to his music and still focus on his work. She smiled as things felt normal for once. She knew that she was going to have to come clean with John soon about who really killed Lisa. She just wasn't ready to face that demon inside her or him.

The following day, Kendra showered her team with gifts and food to thank them for all the hard work that they had been putting in. It was the least she could do to put so much work on them. Christine headed out as soon as she ate. She promised Kendra that she would call her once she got settled.

Chapter 21

Tuesday Afternoon

Scottie walked into his mother's house and called out for her. She didn't respond, but the door to her prayer room opened up. He swallowed hard as he walked forward. He hated her dramatics, but he knew that she was angry, and when she was, it was difficult to guess what she was going to do. He shook his head because he had planned for this day. He wasn't going to let her continue to treat him like the black sheep of the family.

"Hello, Mother," he said as he walked in.

She was kneeling on her knees in front of her prayer board. "Amen." She stood and stared at him. "You been out since Sunday night, and you're just coming to see me? Why is that?"

"Because I knew you were going to be acting all you."

She laughed, "You sound just like Thomas, and just like with Thomas, I can help you learn a little respect."

"Okay, Momma." He muttered, "Look, I think that one of the guns they pulled was the one that I used on Li'l Mike."

"Dammit, Scottie! You know, your father died for his family, and may God rest his soul, this is how you reward him? What have I always told y'all from the doe? You never hold on to a gun with a body attached to it. You ain't no amateur. This ain't yo' first or last rodeo with pushing these guns, so why the fuck are you moving like that? Careless! Now not only did I have to bail you out of jail after yo' dumb ass sold guns to an undercover cop, but now I'ma have to get you somewhere just in case they find out that yo' gun was involved in a murder. Just stupid as shit, Scottie! Lucky for you, Thomas needs you out here. Otherwise, I'd have left yo' ass in jail."

Scottie stood. "It's always about Thomas. And for the record, you killed my daddy because you wanted to marry Thomas's daddy. You always treated me like I wasn't a part of your family. You hate me cause I'm so much like you and remind you of him. My dad loved you more than anything in this world. You killed him for a man who left you to be with his own kind! Thomas and them walking around here looking all Caucasian and shit. That white man didn't want you or them, Mother." Scottie glanced at her, and the anger growing in her face let him know that he had hit a nerve.

Donna slammed her fist down on her desk and stood as well. "How dare you speak to me like that! I love you and always treated you just like the rest of 'em."

Donna's eyes bulged, and a huge vein stretched across her forehead. Scottie didn't blink or react to her response, which further angered her.

"You treated me like I was your servant, Mother! Neva yo' son, and it's all good. I'ma make this shit right on my own, and when I'm done, I want out of this family. As a matter of fact, you can best believe that if I do go to prison, you coming with me."

"Is that a threat, son?"

"Naw, Reverend Harris," he sneered, "just trying to keep the family together. Oh, and I sent some information to a friend, so if anything happens to me while I'm out, they will send the information to the police and all y'all going down."

Scottie walked out of his mother's house and got into his 2021 Dodge Charger and started it up. He glanced at the house and rolled his eyes as he saw Donna staring out her office window. He pulled off, blowing his horn as he did.

Thomas

"Ma, what's up? I'm kinda in the middle of something," Thomas asked as he answered the phone.

"In the middle of something? Boy, I don't give a fuck if the archangel Gabriel was sitting on yo' left shoulder and Raphael on the right, with the pope sitting in front of yo' face speaking in tongues. When I call, you answer with respect, li'l boy. See y'all children done got beside yo'selves."

Thomas looked over at his brother Jason and rolled his eyes upward. "Yes, ma'am," Thomas replied.

"I need y'all to go to the club when you finish up there and go talk to Scottie. We got to see where his head is at."

"Yes, ma'am," Thomas replied.

"God loves you, amen. See you at church in the morning," she said before hanging up.

Thomas turned and shook his head. "Yo' momma a trip, man!"

Jason nodded. "I know it."

The middle-aged man who was tied up was shaking his head, mumbling incoherently behind the gag that was in his mouth. Thomas shook his head. "We ain't got time to talk, old boy."

Pow!

Thomas shot him in between the eyes and looked at Jason. "Let's clean this shit up so we can head on to the club. She wants us to talk to Scottie."

Jason nodded. "I really wanna blast on, bruh. How he gon' threaten to take us all under 'cause he got caught slippin'?"

Thomas sighed, "Same here, but Momma wants us to do things her way."

Thomas shrugged as he pulled the gloves that he had on off and grabbed another pair. "You get the legs, and I'll get his arms. We can bury him out in plot one hundred twelve."

"A'ight, bruh."

The two men proceeded to clean up the small storage building located a few yards from the graveyard behind the church. After they were finished, they drove to their home and showered before heading to the club.

Scottie sat at the bar and downed his first shot of Patrón. He quickly ordered another. He kept checking the entrance, knowing that his brothers would be there soon. He was ready for any issues they brought to him. He knew he had taken it a bit too far with his threats toward his mother and them, but he was just furious with how she always seemed to belittle him and his existence. He sighed as he downed yet another drink.

He turned and scanned the club, and his eyes clashed with Thomas's. He was sitting in the VIP area with a woman he had never seen before. Thomas nodded at him and stood. Scottie laughed and met Thomas halfway.

"We need to talk, big bro," Thomas whispered.

"When I'm ready to talk, I'll let you know. What you doing, bro, running errands for Momma?" Scottie sneered.

"Listen, we both know I'd fuck you ova if Momma weren't in the picture, so chill with that tone," Thomas warned.

Scottie laughed, "Yeah, if Momma weren't in the picture, you'd be dead. Play with it."

Thomas smiled and looked Scottie in the eyes. "You gon' learn."

Scottie walked around Thomas and headed to the bar.

Christine

Christine sat in the corner, watching the two men bicker. She had been watching Thomas for a week and a half and had tried to get his attention but failed every time. She smiled. If she couldn't get next to one, she'd get next to the other. She downed her drink and headed to the bar.

"Oops, excuse me," she cooed as she bumped into Scottie.

Scottie looked down at her and smiled. "You're definitely excused, beautiful. What you drinking? I got it."

And I got you! she thought. "A sex on the beach sounds good," she answered sweetly.

"My name is Scottie, and you are?"

"I'm Christine Michaels," she replied, giving him a false last name.

"Nice to meet you. So, where yo' man at, sweetie?"

She held up her hand. "Single."

"Just 'cause there ain't no ring don't mean ain't no man in the picture."

Thomas watched the interaction between Scottie and the unknown woman. Was she the one to whom Scottie was entrusting vital information? He stood and walked over to where Scottie was.

"Um, excuse me, but who is your friend?" Thomas asked once he was standing next to them.

Scottie looked at Thomas and laughed, "If she wants you to know her name, she'll tell you."

Christine laughed and turned to face Thomas.

Thomas's eyes grew wide as he took in her beauty. Her skin was dark brown, and it looked like silk. Her hair was up in a curly bun, and the silky brown dress hung close to her body, showing every thick curve she owned. Her lips were thick and perfectly shaped.

Christine cleared her throat as she looked at Scottie, then at Thomas. "How about this—you keep the drink," she replied, looking at Scottie, and then to Thomas she finished, "and you keep your questions."

She then walked away, putting a little extra oomph in her twist. She prayed that Thomas followed her, as he was the one she initially needed to connect with. She turned and smiled. He was on her ass just like she needed.

"Aye, man, I know you see me," he called out.

She hurried into the women's room and walked into the stall. She needed to figure out her next approach before she stood face-to-face with Thomas. She had a plan, but after being face-to-face with him, she had to admit that he was fine!

She pulled her pants down and sat down on the toilet after placing two toilet protectors down. A few seconds later, she heard the door open and heard stall doors being pushed open. She glanced up, noticing that she didn't lock the stall door behind her, and as she reached out, the door was pushed open.

"There you are. I asked you a question. What is your name?"

She had to think quickly. "Damn, this is the ladies' room. A little privacy?"

The bathroom door opened again, and a woman walked in and squealed.

Thomas shook his head and held up his hand. "This bathroom is temporarily out of order, ma'am."

She quickly apologized and briskly exited the bathroom.

Christine's heart began to race, and she glanced back up. "It's Christine. You got two options at this point. Since you feel so obligated to stand there watching me pee, you can wipe my cooch for me, or you can leave me to do my business."

Thomas laughed, "Since I'm a gentleman, I'll wait for you outside. But another invitation like that won't go ignored."

Christine laughed as he shut the door to the stall.

"And next time, lock the stall door," he called out.

Christine wiped and pulled up her clothes. As she stepped forward, the toilet flushed. She walked out and washed her hands. She checked her reflection and rearranged her short spaghetti-strap dress and tossed the paper towel she used to dry her hands in the trash. As she exited, she saw Thomas standing against the wall.

"So, what brings you to my establishment?" he asked.

Christine laughed, "If you think that you telling me that this is your place will have me falling over you, please attempt that on someone else."

She walked away only to have him grab her by her forearm and pull her back against the wall. "It's rude to just ignore someone. I'm intrigued by you a little bit. And I mean, I don't think you wanna just brush me off like that."

"Is that right?" Christine asked.

"That's a fact. Listen, I'm not gon' let you leave without getting to know you, gorgeous. Just talk to me. I promise if by the end of the night, you don't be trying to take me home, I'll leave you alone for good," he replied, flashing his white teeth at her as he smiled.

She sighed, smiled, then lied, "Fine. I'm from Texas."

"Miss Texas, follow me to my table."

He escorted her to his table and saw the female who was sitting under him earlier sitting there. She turned to him. "Looks like your table is full already."

He looked at his young companion. "You can go."

She glared at Christine, then back at Thomas. "I know you can't be serious right now, Thomas."

"Do you think I'm playing?" He frowned.

The girl stood, and the look on her face told Christine that she knew he was serious.

"How am I going to get home? I came with you, baby," she whined.

Thomas looked at the girl and shrugged. "Pattie and Duke can take you."

"I don't know them."

"You standing on 'em," he said, glancing down at her feet.

"Fuck you! Don't ever call me again." The girl raced off.

Christine sat down and looked at Thomas. "That's why I could never fuck with a man like you. That shit wasn't cute."

"It wasn't meant to be cute," he replied.

Christine shook her head as she sat down at the table. "It's dark out, and the women are coming up missing. The right thing would be to call her an Uber or a taxi."

Thomas stared at Christine. "Right." He picked up his phone and requested an Uber to arrive at his establishment. He then motioned for one of his waitresses to come over. "Make sure that Yolanda gets in the Uber when it arrives. Let her know that it's on its way, and if she doesn't get in it, then my hands are clean if she doesn't make it home safe."

The waitress nodded, and Christine laughed.

"What?" he asked.

"That was so generous of you."

"Damn right. I'on normally do that, but I'm trying to show you I'm an okay guy."

"Why does it matter how I view you? You just met me."

"Let's just say I'm invested in you right now."

"Mm-hmm. I hear you."

"So why are you here in Charlotte?" he asked.

"Talent scouting. I work for a management firm, and we are looking to recruit a few new clients," she explained, half lying and partly telling the truth.

"Oh, okay. Damn, a businesswoman. I like that. So how do you know my brother?"

"Who's your brother? Who are you, for that matter?" she asked, trying to look confused.

"The guy at the bar. And I am Thomas Harris," he replied.

"Nice to meet you, first of all, and secondly, I just met him tonight. I simply bumped into him." She laughed.

"So, you're not here with him?"

"No."

"Wanna dance?"

"I'd like that."

He stood and grasped her hand and pulled her up. As she stood, he looked down at her, and when she smiled, the deep dimple in her left cheek appeared, and for some reason, his dick jumped. *Damn, this muthafucka fine as hell!*

Christine was fighting with the devil at that moment because it was if she belonged to Thomas, but she was there for only one purpose: to kill him and his family.

Scottie watched Thomas and the lady he had been talking to earlier on the dance floor dancing away to Lakeside's "Real Love."

"So how about I show a gentler side? Come to church with me tomorrow. Or you can meet me there. Whichever makes you comfortable."

Christine nodded. "I could use a little church. Give me the address, and I'll meet you there."

"Let me see your phone." He extended his hand.

She laughed, "I'on know you like that. Write it down, and I'll put it in my notes myself."

"Must be scared I'ma find yo' baby daddy numba in there. I promise I won't look at it," he joked.

"No baby daddy. Again, write it and I'll type it," she corrected him.

"Okay, I get it." He laughed.

After he wrote down the address to the church and his number, Christine looked at them and smiled. "Got it. Well, I'ma call it a night. I will see you tomorrow."

"So can I have yo' numba?"

"I'll give it to you after church," she replied defiantly.

He laughed, "You somethin' else, Texas."

"You just don't know, sir." She laughed.

He stood and escorted her to her car. "Damn, you ridin' nasty, baby girl," he said, complimenting her Charger that she had souped up. The twenty-twos were custom made with diamond-style studs, and the paint job was burgundy, but in certain shades of the sun, it looked pink and platinum. She had BAD BITCH on the front plate with an urban Winnie-the-Pooh design as her interior.

"Gotta love Pooh, daddy." She laughed as she opened her door.

"I'm kinda jealous. Pooh getting all yo' love." He laughed.

She laughed as she got in with him, closing the door behind her. She put her keys in and turned the ignition just once and rolled her windows down. He leaned down and smiled. "Geez, you really not gon' give me yo' numba, Miss Texas?"

She shook her head. "I got you after church."

"You gon' show up?"

"I don't lie on God."

"My momma would love you," he whispered.

"Good night." She started her car, and the motor rumbled.

"Damn, she sounds good, girl."

"Thanks," she replied as she pulled off.

Thomas watched her as she pulled off, and so did Scottie, who was sitting in his car watching both of them. Scottie waited for Thomas to walk back into the club, and then he started his car and drove in the direction that Christine had headed. He finally was able to spot her car, and keeping a safe distance, he followed her to the Marriott. When she pulled into the parking lot, he parked on the side of the road where she couldn't see him and watched her walk inside. While he sat watching her, he pulled his cell phone out of his pocket and called Thomas.

"What you want, bruh?" Thomas asked after picking up on the first ring.

"Hell, you said you wanted to talk to me, so talk shit," Scottie replied.

"Naw, not over the phone. I'll talk to you after service tomorrow," Thomas replied, refusing to discuss anything over the phone.

"Who said I'll be in church tomorrow?" Scottie asked.

"You'll be there," Thomas said before hanging up without saying goodbye.

"The fuck you will," Scottie said to himself.

He tossed his phone onto the driver's seat and pulled off. He knew if he didn't show up at church, they'd come to his home, and he wasn't ready to see his mother so soon after their disagreement.

He suddenly busted a U-turn in the middle of the street, and a few moments later, he was pulling into the Marriott parking lot. He figured he could stay there for a few days and get to know the pretty-ass chocolate drop he had met at the club. Thomas couldn't cockblock every second, being that he was a momma's boy, at least in his opinion.

Kendra

It had been a little over a week since Kendra had really been able to talk to Christine. She had texted her here and there, but there wasn't any real communication. She knew that Christine had lied to her and was more than likely to be somewhere doing something for Brent, and although she didn't like the fact that they felt inclined to keep her out of the loop, she was happy someone was there to help him.

She sent Christine a text and waited for her to respond. She just needed to know that she was good.

Christine

Christine was up early Sunday morning. She had spoken with Brent and informed him that she had contacted Thomas and his brother.

"Just see what you can learn about them and let me know if they say anything about coming here. Christine, I appreciate this."

"I'm doing this to keep both you and my sister safe. So no need to apologize."

Truth be told, Christine loved the hustle of the lifestyle. She loved the killing and the adrenaline of not knowing what could happen next.

After she drank her coffee and ate her breakfast down in the dining area of the hotel, she stood to leave and saw Kendra calling.

"Hey, babes. How's it going?" Christine asked.

"It's going okay. I can't wait for you to bring yo' ass back, though," Kendra admitted to her.

"It won't be much longer, sis. I promise," Christine assured her.

"Everything working out for you?" Kendra asked.

"Everything is wonderful, sis." She thought of Thomas and how he held her while they danced. She couldn't get Scottie's sexy ass off her mind as well. "Best of both worlds."

"What that mean?" Kendra asked.

"Oh, shit! I didn't mean to say that shit out loud." Christine laughed. "I got to go, Kendra. I'm on my way to church."

"You what?" Kendra squealed.

Christine laughed, "Don't even do that, girl."

"I'm saying," Kendra laughed.

"You ain't saying shit, girl! Bye, sis," Christine said.

"Love ya!" Kendra said.

"Love you more."

The sisters hung up, and Christine walked out of the hotel and got in her car. As she caught her reflection, she started having second thoughts about the dress she had chosen to wear. It was a royal blue dress that showed off her curves. The dark gray heels that she wore accented her calves greatly. Her hair was in a schoolgirl ponytail, and her Michael Kors pocketbook completed her ensemble. She just didn't like the way her butt poked out from the dress. She shrugged it off and got in her car and drove to the church.

Once she arrived at the church, she double-checked the address. "This can't be it." The church was small and looked like it couldn't hold any more than a hundred attendees. After confirming that she was at the right place, she pulled into the driveway and parked.

When she got out of the car, she grabbed the Bible that she had borrowed from the hotel room she was in and walked into the church with her head high.

As she entered, Thomas, who had been checking the door off and on, smiled and stood as she made her way to where he and his brother were seated.

"Thank you for coming, gorgeous," Thomas said once Christine was standing next to him.

"Thank you for inviting me," she replied.

"Indeed, ma'am. This is my brother Jason."

Christine turned her attention to the young man sitting down. He looked like Thomas, but his hair was shaved close to the sides in a short box fade, whereas Thomas's hair hung downward, with the sides shaved down. "Nice to meet you, Jason."

"Yeah, whatever," he replied nastily.

Thomas gave him a damning look, and Jason challenged his look with one of his own.

"Have a seat, please," Thomas finally whispered, turning his attention from his brother. "I'm sorry for his attitude."

"You don't need to apologize for me!" Jason whispered angrily.

Christine smiled. "Listen, it's okay. He don't know any better. I get it." But in the back of her mind, she was already plotting how she could make him curb his tongue.

Donna stood at the pulpit and continued with her morning sermon, but the interaction going on in the front row of the church didn't go unnoticed. Donna preached her sermon, directing a portion of it on the topic of fornication over at Thomas and Christine here and there.

Christine found it more humorous than degrading since Brent had already told her a bit of information about Donna and her many lovers, not to mention what she had learned on her own. Donna was far from innocent, as she had included adultery on her list of sins. After the service was over, Thomas walked over with a gleam of satisfaction in his eyes. He knew he had touched a nerve by inviting Christine to church. His mother hated competition for their affection and viewed any other woman as a threat to her control over them. He was ready to escape her grasp, and Christine could be the key.

Christine smiled and offered her hand as Thomas introduced her. "Hello. I really enjoyed your sermon today."

Donna eyed her for a moment, then offered her a half smile and nodded and looked at Thomas. "You are coming to dinner, right?"

Thomas could tell it was more of a demand than a question. He smiled. "Yes, but we gon' need an extra plate for my date." He put his arm around Christine's shoulder as he stared at his mother.

"I'm sorry, but today wouldn't be ideal. I have a few matters, personal matters," she added as she gave Christine a quick glance, "so maybe another time."

Thomas frowned. "I won't be rude, Mother!" he fussed.

"Oh, it's okay. I need to handle some things at the hotel anyway. I just really appreciate you inviting me. Will you walk me out?" she asked as she smiled sweetly at Donna.

Thomas sighed as he rolled his eyes. "Sure, come on. I am really sorry that we have to end things so early."

"Mother comes first," she replied.

"I guess. Listen, can I contact you later this week for a redo?" he asked.

"Most definitely. But do you think mommy dearest will mind?" She smirked.

"Jokes, huh? I gotcha, lady." He kissed her on her cheek once they reached her car. "Don't think I forgot. Give me those digits."

She laughed and gave him her number as promised.

Before she got in her car, Thomas hugged her tightly, and as she glanced at the church door, she saw Jason and Donna staring at them. She pulled away and nodded her head in their direction. "I think they are waiting for you."

He turned, and when he noticed that they were watching, he turned back around. "One more hug for the road."

They hugged once more, but it lasted longer than the first. When they separated, she got into her car and headed back to the hotel.

Scottie
Sunday Morning

Scottie woke up the following morning and decided to relax for the day. He had turned his phone off, and the quietness of the atmosphere was more peaceful than he could have imagined. He closed his eyes and mentally made his plans to go to his home and pack a few things and return to the hotel to relax further. He prayed that he would run into his mystery lady en route. Thomas wouldn't get her without a fight.

It wasn't that he found her so appealing that he had to have her. He just couldn't let Thomas have her so easily.

He knew Thomas and the rest of the family were attending church service, but he decided to send a message to his mother by not going. She couldn't manipulate him into doing her bidding. He never understood how so many people could believe in her word when she was nothing more than a hypocrite, in his opinion. It was like the dirtier shit she got involved in, the more blessings she received.

Donna joined the ministry at the age of 23. She hosted several events where she met influential members of the State. The first man was his father, General Noel Colby, who was a general in the Marines first but soon moved to the special ops forces. He traveled a lot and wanted him and his mother to travel with him, but she didn't want to leave her ministry. His father provided for them and was home when allowed, which wasn't often. When Noel was sent to live in Japan, Donna met another man and fell head over heels in love with him. The man was a well-respected white married man who soon impregnated her with Thomas.

The judge promised Donna the world, and he gave it to her. He spent several days a week with her and him. Scottie didn't like him at all, as he often referred to him as "boy" whenever his mother was gone. He prayed that she'd see him as the racist he was, but he didn't have to wait for that day as George proved it the day that she divulged to him that she was three months pregnant.

"Donna, you're going to have to take care of that. Do you know what my wife would do if she were to find out?" he asked her.

"You promised that you were going to leave her anyway. This"—she pointed to her protruding belly—"is your way out."

George looked at her and shook his head. "I could never. You're married, Donna. I'm not going to jeopardize what I have for a married black woman."

"Black woman? You weren't worried about my color before when you were fucking me!" she fussed with her eyes glowering daggers at him.

"No, I didn't mean it like that," he started.

"Well, you need to explain to me just how the fuck you meant it 'cause I'm starting to feel really offended," she replied with her arms crossed.

"Baby, listen, work on getting out of your marriage, and I'll work on getting out of mine," George promised her.

A few weeks later, Scottie's father arrived home to find his wife pregnant. He was furious, and from what Donna told the police after they found her standing over his body with a bloody knife in her hands, he tried to kill her in a jealous rage after learning that she had been unfaithful. But Scottie didn't believe that story and hated his mother for what she did. He knew she had killed him in order to be with George. Being that Donna had formed a relationship with a lot of prominent members of the police department, they took her word as if it were golden, condemning his father's good name and character.

Once Donna buried his father, she reached out to George, who still refused to leave his wife and two kids for her and her baby. Donna's heart began to turn dark after that. She started using her body to trick the wealthiest men into bending to her will. She soon started several outreach programs, two that were centered around prisons. After Thomas was born, Donna volunteered to counsel female inmates, and she held the title of chaplain at Caledonia Central Prison. Everyone loved her, and because they trusted and valued her so much, she was able to bring in food to give to the less fortunate inmates and instruments for the prison choir that she had started. It didn't take long before she befriended two older female inmates, and they hatched a plan to run the yard. They snuck in cigarettes, marijuana, and cocaine. She put them in a power position, and they capitalized on it until the day they were released and became her stewardesses.

In between her charities and job, Donna had met another government official and began seeing him: North Carolina Senator Andrew Dempsey. Unlike George, Andrew was upfront about what he wanted from her. He wanted nothing but a sexual relationship, to which she agreed. But again, she got pregnant, and Andrew's reaction to her pregnancy sent her completely to the dark side.

The day she told him, Thomas and Scottie were sitting in the front room, and their mother and Andrew were in the bedroom.

They could hear Andrew yelling, "That little yellow-ass bastard out there ain't no better than the dark one, and you want me to claim a mixed child you are carrying? I can't have people knowing that I slept with a nigger!"

Donna's face became hot, and her heart rate had increased tremendously. Her hands began to sweat, and every impulse she had told her to kill him right where he stood, but she couldn't. She couldn't kill him and leave her boys behind because she knew they wouldn't let her off with yet another self-defense excuse.

So instead, she blackmailed him along with Judge Potts. They paid her a monthly stipend while also turning a blind eye to what she was doing. She started running guns and drugs for a while, but as the drug game grew, she decided it was time to step back and just focus on what brought in the most loot. And the underground gun business took form and flight. She had her hand in a few murders, but as Scottie, Thomas, and Jason grew older, they became the hitters while their mother and her ladies maintained the business. Donna's congregation began to grow, and during one of her sessions within the prison, Donna was introduced to a woman who was pregnant but was going to death row for murder, and she became a sponsor for her. The woman accepted the counsel and soon agreed to let Donna adopt her daughters, Lisa and Ariana.

Donna treated them like diamonds and the boys as well. As the years flew by, they all had fallen into a routine of hustling and lying in the name of the most high, their mother.

Scottie sat up and swung his feet over the side of the bed. He sat there and rubbed his coarse hair. He had to get something to eat. It was well after one, and he hadn't eaten a thing all day. He had gotten so caught up in his thoughts that he had forgotten about eating.

He got up and put on a pair of jogging shorts and a gray tank top. He grabbed his keycard and walked out.

Chapter 22

Thursday, One Week Later

Scottie walked into Mecklenburg County Courthouse in a black and blue pinstriped Italian suit. The legs of the suit were creased in the front, and the suit fit perfectly around his small yet muscular frame. His Afro was picked out neatly, glistening from the hairspray he had used. The graying of his hair and beard gave him a very distinctive look.

As he walked down the aisle, he noticed that his mother and her two favorite stewardesses were seated in the third row back from the DA's table. His mother was dressed in a red and white skirt set with her ministry shawl around her neck. Her stewardesses were seated to the left and right of her, wearing their Sunday whites. Scottie tried to hide the laughter from his face. They took shit to the extreme. His mother acknowledged him with a reassuring nod.

His attorney finally walked in, and Scottie fumed as he greeted his mother first. The two spoke briefly, and when they briefly hugged, Scottie rolled his eyes upward and whispered, "The damn audacity!" As his lawyer turned toward him and made his way to talk to him, Scottie glanced at his mother, who was looking at the judge. Scottie shook his head.

"What's going on? Why are you talking to her?" Scottie asked his lawyer once he was in earshot.

"It's going to be okay. Listen, I'll explain everything in a few, but you gotta trust me," his attorney told him.

Scottie could hear his mother laughing, and he shrugged his shoulders. "Whateva, man."

He took his seat, and as they began calling the court docket and cases, Scottie watched as his mother walked in and out of the courtroom. Each time she left, her companions followed behind. He respected their relationship. They had been friends and business associates for over thirty years, and they didn't allow anything to get in the way of it.

Finally, his name was called. "Scottie Harris?"

"Not guilty, Your Honor, and may I address the court, sir?" his attorney asked.

Scottie frowned and glanced at his attorney as he dug into his briefcase and pulled out a manila folder. He then turned and glanced at Donna and back at Scottie.

"Your Honor, I am asking for a dismissal of all charges against my client."

"On what grounds?" the judge asked.

"On the grounds that they didn't have a legal right to search my client's home," the attorney replied, passing up a copy of Scottie's lease.

Scottie frowned, wondering how the hell he got a copy of his lease. He didn't wonder long. He knew it was his mother.

"How didn't we?" Detective Gage asked from the DA's table.

"Your Honor, if you take a close look at the address on the warrant and the address on my client's lease, the two don't match. Even the description of the property is vague, to say the least, sir," his attorney continued.

The judge looked over the lease and the pictures that were attached to it, which showed several homes in the neighborhood with similar features.

"Lastly, Your Honor, my client has never been to jail nor been in trouble with the law. All the guns that were pulled from my client's home are registered. Here is the paperwork."

What the hell? Scottie thought.

The judge shared the pictures with the DA, who handed them to Detective Gage. "Why wasn't this warrant processed correctly?" the judge asked.

"Your Honor, I can assure you, this is not correct. Someone has tampered with the paperwork," Detective Gage declared.

The judge sat in his chair, shaking his head as he looked over all the paperwork that was presented before him. "Regretfully, all the charges against Scottie Harris are dismissed. You got lucky today, Mr. Harris."

Scottie stood stone-faced as the judge talked to the DA. He had long since tuned the judge out. After the case was dismissed, Scottie thanked his attorney as his mother and her stewardesses left the courtroom.

Detective Gage was furious. He stared at Scottie with pure hatred.

Scottie smiled and walked out of the courtroom. He pushed through the double doors, and when he exited, he almost bumped into his mother.

"I know that you had something to do with all that. Thanks," he murmured.

"See you in church Sunday." She walked away. "I'm hungry. What y'all got a taste for?" she asked her companions.

Scottie rolled his eyes upward and groaned inwardly. "I told her I could handle this on my own. Goddammit! She couldn't believe in me enough to let me do that!"

At that moment, the courtroom doors opened, and Detective Gage walked out. He looked at Scottie and sneered, "I don't know how you did it, but I'ma keep my eyes on you and your family."

"Sounds kinda like stalking to me, and we both know that's against the law. Fuck off!" Scottie walked off, and once he was halfway down the walkway, he turned back around and smiled.

Detective Gage walked into the station in a huff. A few of his comrades stared at him, realizing that he was in a mood, while others stared at him in disbelief that he had dropped the ball on a case that he'd been working on for over a year. He was always thorough in his job.

As he entered his office, the chief of police, Robert Stakes, walked in behind him and closed the door. He stood with his hands in his coat pockets. "What happened, Gage? Huh? I trusted you with this case, and you dropped the ball. A rookie I can sorta understand, but you aren't an amateur. You've been doing this for years, which is why I handed this case to you. The wrong address? Come on, Gage, tell me why I shouldn't fire you right now."

Gage shook his head, then dropped it. "Sir, I don't know what happened. I had everything together. I don't know how shit . . ." He paused and looked at Robert and grimaced. "I apologize, sir, for the bad choice of words, but I honestly don't have a clue as to what happened. I gave the paperwork to Jackie for processing. I . . . I don't know, sir."

Robert sighed, "Well, I hate to do this, but I think you need to take a few days off. You know that the FBI has been watching us after two of our finest were found guilty of racketeering, and now I have to explain how one of my top detectives managed to put the wrong address on his warrant. Do you know if they find out that you are in cahoots with the Harris family, you could be seeing some serious time in prison?"

"But, sir, I swear I don't know what happened. I can fix this. Just give me a chance. Don't take this case away from me," Gage cried.

"Case? This case is closed. Now that the Harris family knows that we are aware of their illegal dealings, do you think they gon' trust anyone outside of their immediate circle? You are foolish if you think that. If they do fuck up again, I'ma make sure I put someone on it who will catch them and seal a case on them. I'm sorry, Gage, I'm gonna need your gun and shield," Robert Stakes replied.

"But, sir—" Gage started.

"Now!" Robert boomed.

"Yes, sir," Gage mumbled. As he handed his shield over, he felt ashamed and furious at the same time. He felt the hotness of his tear burn a track down his face. Here he was, a grown man crying in front of his superior. A man who he looked at as a father. He looked up and glared Robert in his eyes as he placed his property in his hands.

Robert turned to walk away but paused, and without turning around, he whispered, "As your superior, I have to tell you to stay away from the Harris family, but if you aren't in cahoots with them, then, as your friend, I'm telling you to prove you're not by any means necessary. I'll deny it if you tell anyone I said that."

After Robert walked out, Gage sat down behind his desk and closed his eyes. He had to find a way to fix things. He packed his box, making sure that he printed off everything that he could find from the Harris files. Gage walked out of the precinct with his personal items from his desk.

Detective Gage pulled out of the parking deck of the police station in his 2010 Acura and decided to check up on the man who had cost him his shield. He wasn't going to just sit back and wait for his superiors to make their decision on whether he had a job. He was going to bring the Harris family down if it was the last thing he did. It had gotten very personal for him.

He turned down Kimber Road, and twenty minutes later, he was pulling onto the street where Scottie resided. He drove past slowly and decided to pull up to the salt building across the street and park. There were several cars in the parking lot, and he knew he'd go unnoticed sitting there. He pulled out his notepad and a few files to look over while he waited for Scottie to surface. He pulled his ball cap down on his head and opened up the file that he had taken from his office.

"Where was the fuckup?" he questioned aloud to himself.

As he scanned the documents, highlighting anything unusual, he heard a squealing noise. As he looked up, he saw Scottie pulling in. He grabbed his camera out of his box, and after realizing that his assumptions were right, that he'd go unseen, he started snapping pictures.

Once Scottie was inside, Detective Gage put the folder back in his box and watched the house. When Scottie walked back out, he had two huge duffle bags in his hands. He got in his car and pulled off.

"Where are you going?" Gage whispered as he turned his car on and backed out. He was going to tail him everywhere he went.

After fifteen minutes of following Scottie, Gage turned into the Comfort Inn and Suites and parked a few rows away from Scottie. He watched as he walked in with his bags.

"What are you up to, my guy?" he asked. Again, he pulled out his camera and snapped more pictures.

Detective Gage waited a few hours, and when Scottie didn't walk back out, he decided to get out and do a little investigation of his own. He walked into the hotel and looked around. He spoke with two of the workers there, persuading one of them to call him anytime they saw Scottie leaving.

He walked out feeling somewhat optimistic that he'd once again be back on the force.

Chapter 23

Friday

Christine decided to go out Friday night. She had been out with Thomas and Scottie and figured she'd throw a little wrench in their plans to kill Brent. She saw how competitive they were, especially where a woman was concerned, so she wanted to see if she could cause a bigger divide between the two.

She walked in wearing a cute, short black spaghetti-strap dress with a split on the right side. The back was out, and her red bottom black heels complemented her calves immensely. When she walked in, she sat at the bar. Several men walked over, asking if they could buy her a drink, and each time she declined. After an hour of sitting there, she was beginning to feel like her plan was out the window until she heard a familiar voice behind her.

"Now I know you just not gon' sit here all night. Come on, let's dance."

She smiled as she accepted Thomas's hand and walked to the dance floor. As "It Feels So Good to Be Loved So Bad" by the Manhattans blared from the speakers in Trinity's Lounge, Thomas and Christine swayed to the music and talked. Every so often, she'd dip her head, laughing at something he had said. He pulled her even closer, and their bodies swayed to the melodies as the talking ceased. They both relaxed to the feel of one another's body. Christine could feel Thomas's manhood throbbing.

She looked up at him, and he stared into her eyes. He wanted to kiss her, but before he could, Scottie walked over.

He had stood in the shadows long enough. Watching the two of them dance made him feel something that he had never felt before: jealousy over a woman. He hated the way Thomas gripped her waist. He hated seeing her laugh at his jokes. He hated seeing her with him, period.

"May I cut in?" he asked.

Christine stepped back and cleared her throat. She looked at Scottie, and although she wanted to tell him no, she couldn't, but she wasn't ready to leave Thomas's arms.

"Man, what the fuck is wrong with you? You see me dancing with her. You just can't stand to see two people enjoying themselves." Thomas pushed Scottie, and Scottie advanced upon him, fist balled, ready to strike.

Christine jumped in the middle. "Don't do this. Listen, you are both nice guys, but I am single and can dance with whoeva I want. If you want, we can finish our dance, and then I'll dance with you next."

"Yeah, well, I'm good on the dance," Scottie said and walked away.

Christine watched Scottie walk away in a huff, and she looked up at Thomas. "You wanna end the dance?"

"Naw, I'm straight right where I am. If he don't want the dance, I'll gladly take it," he replied, feeling a great victory over his brother.

Jason, who had been watching the two brothers bickering, called his mother and shared every detail of what had occurred and how Christine was able to defuse the situation.

"Take her the phone," Donna ordered.

"But Thomas is still with her," Jason whispered.

"I don't give a shit! Take her the phone like I freaking said."

"Geez, okay!" Jason groaned as he slowly walked over to where Thomas and Christine were dancing. Jason tapped Christine on the shoulder and handed her the phone.

Thomas shook his head, knowing who was on the other end.

"Hello?" Christine said.

"This is Mrs. Harris. I'd like to invite you to lunch tomorrow."

"Perhaps, what time?" she asked, looking at Thomas smiling.

"About twelve, my house," Donna replied.

"Twelve is fine, but how about we meet at Starbucks on Hoover Road instead?" Christine told her. She wasn't foolish enough to meet the lady in her home. She could cut her head off and no one would know to look there.

"That's fine. We'll see you then," Donna said.

"Definitely. Now I don't want to be rude, but I have a dance to finish. Are you ready, Thomas?" she asked sweetly, taunting Donna purposely. Christine handed Jason the phone and finished her dance with Thomas.

She didn't see much of Scottie after the small incident between him and Thomas. She wished he hadn't shown up. Before she left that night, she and Thomas made plans to meet up the following Tuesday.

The following day, Christine got up and dressed for her meeting with Donna. She had her .22 on her hip. She made sure she had her concealed carry permit in her purse. She wasn't going to go meet Satan without some form of protection. She had learned enough about Donna to know that she didn't want to meet her for the hell of it.

Christine arrived about fifteen minutes earlier than she was supposed to be there. When she walked in, there were about seven people present. A lady to the right of her looked up and smiled.

"Hello," Christine whispered as she walked by.

She found a table near the rear and sat in the chair with the back against the wall. She didn't need any unexpected visitors to pull up on her. She walked up to the counter after placing her shades on the table and ordered herself a muffin and a vanilla swirl chocolate latte.

She sipped her latte and nibbled on her muffin while scrolling through TikTok.

"Hello, Christine."

She looked up, and smiling at her was Donna. "Hello. Would you like a coffee? It's on me," Christine said.

Donna sat down and shook her head. "No, thank you."

"Ohhh, you don't know what you're missing," Christine chided.

Donna's smile faded. "You're a little bigger than I imagined. I wonder what my sons see in you to bicker with each other."

Christine laughed as she bit down on her muffin. "Now, not to be disrespectful, but it appears that your mothering skills are a bit flawed if you just noticed that those two are bickering. Shit, that fight between them has been in them for a long time. I'm just meeting them, and I can see the animosity in both of them."

"I don't want you to see them again. You're a problem, and I can tell you got a dark spirit in your soul."

"Mrs. Harris, I doubt God gave you that kind of power. To read into my soul sounds kind of evil. Are you serving the right one?" Christine fired back.

"Now you listen here, you fat-ass troll, stay the hell away from my boys! You've been warned once. There won't be a second one," Donna hissed.

Christine was wired up with her mouth set on go and her hand itching to shoot Donna in her mouth. "If calling me fat makes you sleep better, then snore on, you shark-mouth heathen! I'll leave them alone when I'm good and ready. Go play in traffic, blindfolded, and pray that you don't get hit, bitch. You got me fucked up if you think I'ma do anything you ask me to do. You wanna know why? 'Cause you didn't ask politely. Pray on it. Good day, ma'am."

Christine stood and downed the rest of her coffee and walked out. She walked briskly to her car and got in. She waited for Donna to leave and watched her walk to her car with the lady who had greeted her when she first walked into Starbucks. It seemed that Donna was one step ahead of her, but she wouldn't get a second chance. Christine shook her head. If she had to take the Harris family out, she'd go straight for their jugular, and Donna would be the first to be picked off.

She waited a few minutes before pulling out of the parking lot and headed in a different direction than they had taken.

When she walked back into her hotel, she bumped into Scottie. "Hey."

"How are you?" Scottie asked.

"Very well, considering I just left from coffee with yo' mom. Why is she so evil? No disrespect." She laughed. "Hey, listen, I didn't mean to make you feel any kinda way last night. It's just that I don't like being put in the middle of y'all sibling rivalry."

"I get it, and I'm sorry that I did that. I should've waited, but hey, fuck him and last night. What you about to get into?" he asked.

She laughed. "I'm thinking a swim would be great," she admitted.

"Can I join you? I'd like to spend some one-on-one time with you."

"I'm cool with that. Give me thirty minutes."

He nodded his head. "See you in a few, pretty lady."

She smiled and walked to the elevator. When she got on the elevator and turned, he was still watching her. She dropped her head, trying to hide the smile that he had caused.

Upon entering her room, she quickly showered and changed into her swimsuit. She grabbed her towel and keycard. She walked down to the swimming pool in a cream-colored one-piece with a see-through wrap around her waist. Her boobs sat up in it nice and perky, leaving her cleavage exposed. Her white and tan flip-flops accented her swimwear. Her hair was pinned in an updo, leaving a few curls dangling down the nape of her neck.

Being a full-figured woman, a few people stared at her approvingly as well as disapprovingly. The ones she caught sneering she smiled at, as they only boosted her confidence. She loved the skin she was in.

As she walked into the area where the indoor swimming pool was located, she searched for Scottie. It didn't take long for her to spot him, as he was already en route to her. She swallowed hard as he got closer. His slim yet muscular physique was dripping wet, and the way his abs contracted as he walked was sexy.

Get yo' head in the game, girl. Don't get caught slipping.

"Don't you look . . . fuck! I'on know what to say. That bathing suit is looking all good wrapped around you," he told her.

She could see his approval in the way he was staring at her. She could feel his eyes trying to penetrate her soul, and she didn't know how she felt about it. Part of her loved it, and the other part hated it because she knew nothing could happen between them. She turned her head quickly and walked to the edge of the pool.

He watched as her hips swayed and her booty cheeks jiggled. He walked over and stood beside her. "Come on now, I know you ain't come down here to just stand by the pool."

She laughed, "Sure didn't." She took her wrap off and slid her flip-flops off and placed them on an empty pool chair. She took her hair down, ran to the pool, and jumped in. When she came up, she swiped her hair from her face and searched for Scottie.

He was still standing by the edge of the pool, nodding. "Let me show you how a pro do this."

She moved to the edge and perched up on the steps near the shallow end of the pool.

As he took off and jumped, he grabbed his knees up toward his chest and hit the water. The water made a loud thud sound, and the water splashed up higher than what she had created.

She turned her nose up playfully once Scottie emerged from the water. He walked over and stood in front of her. She glanced up at him and blushed at how he was staring at her. He didn't say a word, but his body and eyes told it all. She bit her lip and dropped her eyes.

"Don't look away now. You shy?"

She laughed, "Maybe a little bit."

"Baby girl, all I wanna do is ruin you for any other man. I might be the one to tame you."

"Tame me?" she asked.

"Yeah, I know you got some shit with you, missy. For real. It's the way you carry yourself. You got a feminine side, but you kinda rough around the edges. I can tell just by the way you speak at times that you got a li'l ghetto in you. Your eyes tell a story that your mouth don't, which makes you dangerous. You got that stranger danger vibe." He leaned in until his mouth was next to her ear. "But see,

I ain't scared. I'ma figure you out, and then I'ma take you away from the world."

She looked at him defiantly. "That sounds like a threat to my life. I'on know if I want to be taken from the world."

She stood and headed back into the water. As she swam, Scottie watched. He was going to make her his one way or the other. He refused to let Thomas have her.

He stood and joined her in the pool. They swam and played around in the pool for over an hour. Afterward, they went to their separate rooms but not before agreeing to have dinner later that evening.

Scottie

Scottie left the pool anxious about his dinner with Christine. He needed to know more about her. She was mysterious, and it piqued his interest. He had the desire to fuck her, but there was more to her being there, and he was going to find out just exactly what it was.

Before he could get in the shower, he heard his phone chirp. He knew without looking who it was. He could've ignored it, but he decided that it was time to speak to her once again. "Yes, Mother?"

"Hello, son. We missed you at church last Sunday. I would like to see you in church for Bible study tomorrow night. Do you think we can do that?"

Scottie was quiet for a moment but finally conceded to her request. "Yes, Mother, I will come."

"Good. I love you, son," she said before hanging up.

Scottie hung up and glanced at his phone long and hard. His mother could throw one hell of a temper tantrum that sometimes ended in her inflicting pain depending on the state of mind she was in. He knew that the lack of attention, not to mention the disrespect, that he had shown her more than likely had her in her feelings. Therefore, he was gonna feel it too. He just had to brace himself for whatever trauma she was about to inflict on him.

He lay back on the bed and closed his eyes. His mind was filled with so many thoughts, ending with the mysterious lady who had his attention. He smiled as he sat up and grabbed his phone once again. He was going to make this a special night for him and Christine.

Chapter 24

Scottie

Sunday morning, Scottie walked into the church and sat next to Thomas and Jason on the bench in the front row. Donna smiled approvingly as he did so. She started her sermon by thanking God that all of her boys were present. Thomas side-eyed Scottie and let out a low huff. Scottie smiled because he knew that it struck a nerve for him to hear her acknowledge all of them.

After the sermon, Thomas walked over and hugged her and stood back as Scottie followed suit.

"I need to talk to Scottie. You two can go on and enjoy your day."

Scottie and Donna sat down in the front row of the church, and after everyone was gone, she started talking.

"I know I've been hard on you more so than the others, and for that, I'm sorry. You know, you think I went against your father, but you do know that I didn't set out to hurt him. He was trying to kill me," she whispered.

Scottie couldn't believe that his mother was lying in the face of God. "Mother, I know you love me, but I also know you love them more. I'm good knowing that, but you can't keep trying to manipulate situations so that we feel obligated to continue doing your bidding. I'm a grown man, and I can't leave town unless I ask my mommy. No! That's not how it's going to be with me."

Donna sighed, "I understand, and I can respect that. I just need y'all to find your sister and bring her home. Please."

Scottie dropped his head and nodded. "I can do that."

"Thank you. Now will you come have dinner with your mother? We can go wherever you want," she asked with pleading eyes.

Scottie laughed, "Hamlets Bar and Grill."

"Let's go then." She sighed as she stood. He offered her his arm. "You are such a good son," she cooed.

"Aren't I?" He laughed.

They walked out, both feeling victorious in achieving their demands.

Tuesday morning, Christine drove and parked downtown at Bakers Circle, a small parking deck located across from Trinity's Unlimited, a management company with which she had told Thomas that her firm was attempting to partner. It was far from the truth, but she already had her hands full with one Harris brother at the hotel. She didn't need two. At least that's what she told herself. Truth be told, she didn't want any interference with her and Scottie. He had shown her a side of himself that she admired. She knew nothing could grow from their connection, but she needed to have a little fun before she killed him.

When he pulled up, he parked behind her car and got out his pine green souped-up antique 1952 Chevy truck. The motor purred, and the whitewall tires glistened against the sun that was piercing through the gaps of the wall surrounding the parking deck.

"Okay, I see you, Thomas. I love this truck," Christine said, complimenting his stylish ride.

"Thank you. I have a few of these in my yard. So are you following me or riding with me?"

"I'ma ride with you. I'm not gon' pass up the chance to ride in a sexy classic with a fine brother!"

"Shit, say no more and get in." He smiled as he opened the passenger door, but she stalled.

He looked at her questioningly, and she responded by laughing, "I'm trying to drive this classic!"

He shook his head. "You might as well drive yo'self if you think that's gon' happen, shawty."

She laughed, "Well, dayum, a sista can't get behind that wheel?"

"Baby girl, I like you but not that much." He laughed.

"Shit, tell me how you really feel then," she replied, pouting.

"Get in," he whispered as he stared down at her.

She bit her bottom lip, and his eyes focused on them. She moved seductively against him as she slid past him to get in the truck. He grabbed her by her waist and held her steady as she climbed in.

"You know, I could've gotten in on my own."

"I know," he replied. He shut the door and walked over to the driver's side and got in. Before they pulled off, she hit the button on her keychain, setting the alarm on it.

They traveled down the highway listening to King George. "What you know about King G?" Thomas asked as he eyed her, snapping her fingers and mouthing the words to the song.

She glanced at him with a smirk on her face. "I'm familiar with his music. I'm versatile in my music selection. Jazz, old school, R&B, rap, country music, and a little rock and roll."

"Okay, give me a title of a country song you like."

"'Somewhere on a Beach' by Dierks Bentley, 'Tennessee Whiskey' by Chris Stapleton, and 'Firecracker' by Josh Turner," she replied quickly.

"I see you know a li'l something about country music. You grew up in the country?" he asked as he turned off on Old Country House Road and shifted gears. Christine watched him intently. The way his arms looked in his gray T-shirt made her mouth water. He was thicker than Scottie, but they were both sexy. Thomas's curly black hair was thick in the middle with the sides shaved down. His lips looked inviting, and the way his dimple peeked out every time he smiled made her stomach flip. He was fine. His deep voice and personality made it hard for Christine to keep things in a non-sexual realm. Truth be told, she wanted to fuck both of them, but she wasn't there for all that. She was there for one purpose, to find out what they knew about Lisa and Brent and then kill them.

But could she?

"No, I didn't. I'm from Texas, remember? And my family had a farm. You'd be surprised about the things I've learned and done on a farm."

"Oh, really? Maybe you can show me a few things."

"No doubt. Trust me, I plan on showing you so much." She smiled innocently.

"Lady, don't play with me," he mumbled.

"Trust me. I don't play period, handsome," she cooed.

Thomas turned his attention back to the road, feening for the woman next to him in the worst way.

They turned down a short, newly paved road leading to a huge cottage-style home. The landscape was neatly and beautifully decorated with small ceramic fixtures with flowers adorning a few of them. He had a dark blue F-250 that was chromed out throughout, and the tag read DIRTTRAP.

She glanced around and took in the layout: the homes next to his and across, the trees and the way they opened up into the neighbor's yard. She knew that there had to be a fence blocking the two yards, and if she had to jump it, she was sure she could in record time.

When they parked, Thomas got out and walked around to open Christine's door. Christine jumped out of the truck and smiled as Thomas grasped her waist to steady her. She turned and found herself engulfed in his chest. *Damn, he smells good as fuck!* She groaned inwardly.

"Welcome to my home. I figured since we didn't get to have dinner the other day, I'd make it up by cooking for you." He let his arms slide around her hips.

"So what are you making?" she asked as she grasped his upper arms seductively.

He pulled away and led her toward his backyard. "Let me give you a tour. Just know that whateva I fix gon' be fire!" He laughed.

"Fire, huh? We gon' see," she replied jokingly as she clasped her arm within his.

He showed her his chicken coop and let her feed them. He then walked her over to where his goat Hilda was. She supplied him with fresh goat milk every morning. Christine was impressed with his small farm. He had a few hogs, and when he showed her his stables, she couldn't help but ask if they could take a ride one day.

Thomas stood back and shook his head in amazement. "Oh, you ride, too?"

"I do," she started, then paused. "Very well, I might add." She walked away, leaving Thomas watching her ass.

He shook his head, groaned, and thought, *she is a ten in every way!*

He followed her in a quick, short jog. "You wanna go now?"

She turned and looked at him as he approached her. "Hell yeah!"

He laughed, "I'll help you saddle one up."

She gave him a whimsical glance. "I can do it myself. Are you trying to play me, dude? I'ma need you to respect my country swag, patna!"

He threw up his hands. "A'ight, gangsta! Calm down, shawty."

They laughed and walked into the stall. Thomas pointed to the horse that she was going to ride and showed her where the saddle was located as well as the reins. She surprised him with everything that she knew about horses. She saddled that horse quicker than any average ranger. Once she climbed on top of the horse, she looked around to see what was keeping Thomas and laughed as she caught him staring at her ass.

"No disrespect, but goddamn I'm jealous! That goddamn horse's back is strong, shit! Man, you are one gorgeous woman, that's for damn sure."

Her smile faded, and she looked at him sternly. "You can finesse me later, but right now I'm ready to ride."

"That's what I'm trying to tell you!" He laughed as he got up on his horse.

They rode for twenty minutes before Thomas suggested they head back to the house. He had enjoyed seeing her body bounce to the rhythm of the horse's trot, but he was ready to chill with her in a more sensual setting.

After they put the horses back in the stables, Thomas locked the stables up, and he and Christine headed to his home. As he unlocked the door, he stood to the side, allowing her to enter first. As she entered the kitchen area, she was shocked at how homey it was. Although it was a large home, it wasn't as lavish as she imagined it would be. The decor was just as country as Thomas carried himself. It was clean yet cluttered here and there.

"It lacks a feminine touch," she informed him.

"It's the right touch of my masculinity. Until I find the right missus, that feminine touch isn't necessary."

"Touché," she laughed.

"Come on, let me show you the rest of the house, and then you can wash up and wait for dinner."

He showed her around, and she took in all the hunting medallions and awards on the wall in his sitting room. He had a trophy for the best groomed horse in the county. She could tell that he was a simple man with too much time on his hands. How could he or Scottie cause Brent to fear them? She didn't get it.

After showing her his home, he took her to one of the bathrooms so she could freshen up before dinner. Fifteen minutes later, they were both in the kitchen talking about dinner. Christine was posted up on a stool behind the counter while he stood by the stove, putting his cabbage on.

As he began to pour the water into it to let it boil, Christine interjected, "You know, if you have some chicken broth, it will make the cabbage taste better."

He stooped and looked at her. "I think I know what I'm doing, ma'am." He turned his head but reached up in the cabinet and searched for his chicken broth. He didn't say a word as he opened it up and poured it into the cabbage.

"Come on," he said after he had the cabbage cooking. He grabbed her by the hand and took her to the front room. "I got over five hundred channels. Find something to watch 'cause I'on need you taking credit for my meal."

After she was seated with the remote in her hand, he left her alone. She laughed as he danced away. As she searched through the channels, she spotted a picture of Ariana over the fireplace. She stood up and glanced toward the doorway, then quickly walked over to the fireplace. She took out her phone and snapped pictures. There was a picture of Brent and another girl who wasn't Lisa. She was going to ask Brent about her later.

"You want something to drink?" Thomas asked as he walked back into the sitting room, startling Christine.

"Um, no. I got to go," she stuttered.

"Why? What's wrong?" he asked.

"Is that your wife?" she asked, acting angry in an attempt to get him to talk about the mysterious woman with Brent.

Thomas walked over. "The women in those pictures are my sisters. I'm not married. I'm not the type of man who would entertain another woman if I had one. I'm not gon' make her share me 'cause I damn sure ain't gon' share her. You hear me?"

She nodded. "Indeed."

He stepped closer and bent down and kissed her. He pulled her into him, and she allowed him to. She wrapped her arms around his neck, running her fingers through his curls, gripping them each time he gripped her ass.

She finally pulled away and stepped away from him. "You should go check yo' food."

He frowned but nodded his head, turned, and walked away.

"Damn!" she groaned as she bent down and started waving her private area as if she were putting out an invisible flame.

"You didn't say if you wanted a drink," Thomas said as he walked in, catching her in the act. She stood up quickly, face flushed and her bun sideways. He cleared his throat, trying to stifle his laughter.

"Whatever!" she said. She tossed her head and snatched the remote up and sat back down.

He walked up behind her, bent down, and whispered close to her ear, "I feel the same way."

She shivered as his breath caressed her neck as if he had really kissed her. He smiled as he watched her body shiver.

"You want a drink?" he repeated.

"Yes, yes, a . . . umm, a glass of ice water," she stammered.

"Gotcha! Be right back."

She watched him as he walked away. She felt a weird attraction to him that she hadn't felt for Scottie either time she had been with him.

Thomas walked out again, and she looked around more. Minutes passed before Thomas walked back in. "I'm so sorry, Christine, but we gon' have to do this another day. We have an emergency at the church. I am so sorry, love."

She waved it off disappointedly. "It's okay. I understand, but," she said as she walked over to where he stood, "we definitely gotta finish this date."

"Fuck," he whispered as he stared at her. "You making it real hard for me to go."

She smiled. "We got time, trust me."

He nodded. "Well, at least I got to enjoy a little bit of your time today."

"I say the same."

"Come on and let's get you back to your car." He waited for her to collect her things.

Thomas reluctantly dropped Christine back off at her car. He was going to give his mother a piece of his mind when he saw her. He didn't care who she thought she was, but she wasn't going to keep making demands of him, especially when he was trying to get his mack on.

When he pulled up to the church, he noticed that no one else was there. *What the fuck does she have going on?* He got out and headed into the church. He saw his mother placing the Bibles into the wood sleeves of the pews. She looked so angelic at times, but she was pure evil.

"What's this about, Mom? I thought you said it was an emergency."

"Whatever it takes to get you here. Come to my office."

"I mean, dang, I was on a date, and I cut it short because you made it sound like there was something going on. You gotta stop this," Thomas complained.

"Thomas, just come on," she instructed as she walked toward the back.

Thomas looked around and shook his head as he followed her. Once inside, he sat up on the table beside her desk. He looked so comfortable to Donna.

She sat down and eyed him. "Well, tell me about this little tramp you've been seeing."

He shook his head. "Why you always gotta be like this?"

"My job is to protect y'all at all costs, and that's what I'm gon' do. You don't know shit about this girl, yet you brought her to church. Thomas, let me ask you this—have you even talked to Brent Love?"

Thomas turned his head and then stared at her. "I called a few times, but he hasn't returned my call. His boys ain't been seen in weeks."

She sighed, "You know what the deal is if it's discovered that he has hurt Lisa. We already know that Ariana is dead, and he gon' have to pay for that, but if he has hurt Lisa too, I'ma torture his ass. I just need y'all to get on y'all shit and find him."

"Ma, the police are already heavy on our ass. You gotta chill."

"Do you think I care about the police? Have they ever stopped us or taken one of y'all down? No, 'cause I kept them at bay. Now I want my child or revenge against the man who hurt them."

"Revenge isn't always the answer, though. Look how close Scottie came to going to jail."

"'Vengeance is mine . . . saith the Lord.'"

"Yeah, but you aren't God, Momma," Thomas retorted.

"Boy, I work for Him, which is the same thing as being Him."

"No, it's not," Thomas argued.

Donna walked over to him, and once she was standing just a few inches away from him, she asked, "Why do you always have to challenge everything I say and do, Thomas?"

Thomas swallowed hard as he looked at his mother. "It's all too much. I'm tired of living like this," Thomas whispered.

"Living how? Boy, you got everything you could ever want. You grew up in a world where you didn't have to want for anything. I made sure of that."

"Yeah, but it's time to try something else. I'm ready to live life without the guns, killings, and cops," he cried.

She reached up, causing Thomas to flinch. "I'm not gon' hit you, boy. If this is about that foul-mouthed tramp you brought for church Sunday, she isn't the one for you, son. I'll make a deal with you. If you help me find Lisa, like I've been asking, I'll let you go off and be with anybody else, just not her."

"Why not her? What the heck is so wrong with Christine?"

Donna rubbed Thomas's face and walked away without answering. "Do we have a deal, son?"

Thomas dropped his head and sat down in the chair next to the door. "Yes."

"Good," she said. "In the morning, I need you, Scottie, and Jason here. I did a little research, and I found out that Brent's family owned a farm a few hours from here. If he hasn't contacted you back within a few days, you will go down there to see if he is there."

"Scottie gon' be hard to convince to show up," Thomas groaned.

"If you want out, you'll make sure he's here."

"Where is Jason anyway? I haven't talked to him in two days."

"You know how he is. He pulls a disappearing act every other day," she replied, looking over the church's financing.

"Why is it that he can dip out whenever he wants? That's not fair."

"Because he never questions nothing that I request of him, Thomas."

Thomas stood up. "Love you. I'll see you tomorrow. "

After Thomas left, Donna sat back in her chair and took her glasses off. She loved her boys and fought so hard to ensure that they could live life comfortably. She couldn't believe that Thomas was talking about leaving the family. She knew it was because of the newcomer, and she was going to have to take care of her as well. No one was going to come between her and her boys.

Right then, Evelyn walked in with a weird look on her face. "Read this. You won't believe who this girl really is."

Donna looked over the information and clicked her teeth. "We got some plans to make."

Evelyn nodded. "Tell me what to do."

Donna and Evelyn began to talk about various ways to handle Christine, but she had to be more subtle about it. If she moved the wrong way, her boys would never forgive her. She didn't know what kind of hold Christine had on her boys, but she didn't like it.

Chapter 25

Texas

Tuesday

Kendra walked out of her office, and as she headed to her car, she heard a very annoying familiar voice.

"What's good, momma? You miss me?" Devon called out.

His voice reminded her of how egotistical he was, thinking that she'd fall for him and then trying to attack her when she didn't. She had warned him to stay away from her, and here he was lurking around. She wished she had her gun because she'd shoot him dead where he stood.

"Boy, if you don't get the hell away from me, I'ma leave a hole right in the middle of your underdeveloped forehead!" She started reaching in her purse, pretending to be grabbing a gun.

He pulled off and yelled, "I'll be back, beautiful."

Kendra shook her head and walked to her car. When she got in, she sighed and prayed that he wouldn't make her kill him. She started her car and pulled off. She checked her mirror to ensure that he wasn't following her.

When she finally arrived home, John was out in the backyard, fixing the doors to their horse stall. He had his shirt off, and every muscle in his body was flexing. His thigh muscles blessed her sights as he bent down to grab his hammer. She turned her car off and unbuckled her seat belt. She watched as John worked and moved. Her heart nearly jumped out of her chest as he turned and caught her staring. He gave her a smile that made her feel amazing.

She laughed, "The nerve of that young nigga thinking I'd give up the opportunity to be with this man." She looked at the diamond wedding band on her hand and laughed, "The fucking nerve!"

She got out and walked over to him and gave him a kiss.

"How was your day, babe?"

She hugged him, but then pulled back quickly. "You need to bathe."

"Yeah, love my funk too." He grabbed her up. She screamed and playfully fought to escape his sweaty embrace. He laughed and let her go. "So?"

She crouched as she attempted to catch her breath. "It was okay." She knew that telling John about Devon would only cause him to act out, and she didn't need the trouble. "I'm going in to take a shower. You wanna come?" she asked seductively.

"Wish I could. Gotta finish this up. Next time." He patted her on her butt.

She pouted. "So why tease me like that?"

He laughed, "See you up at the house, li'l lady."

She shrugged. "Okay then." She walked to the house. All thoughts of Devon were erased from her mind.

For three days, Devon called, sent flowers, and rode by the office a few times. Bridget and Taye tried to convince Kendra to call the police, but she refused.

"I ain't studded that li'l bitch-ass boy," she told them. Taye and Bridget shared their concern repeatedly, but it seemed to fall on deaf ears. It was tense at work and at home. It was hard trying to keep Troy from knowing as well as John finding out. She knew that she was going to have to deal with Devon, but it couldn't be until after the trail ride event. Nothing was going to ruin her weekend.

Friday morning, Kendra and John were both dressed in a pair of jeans and long-sleeved flannel shirts. Kendra's black knee-high boots fit snugly around her legs. She wore a black hat to complete her ensemble. John looked handsome in his orange and black flannel shirt, his brown boots, and a matching Stetson brimmed hat.

Kendra was excited about getting her weekend started. She just wished that Christine could be in attendance. But she understood that she needed to handle whatever business that she had to deal with.

Taye and Troy

"We gotta stop by the office and print a few contracts off so we can have a few available at the trail ride. You should expect this from time to time. Everyone else is there for the party. We are there for work," Taye told Troy once she picked him up. Kendra and John had left earlier that morning with Bridget in tow so they could finish helping their team set up, while Taye and Troy were to arrive later in the evening after handling some things in the office.

As they pulled up to the office, Taye hopped out and grabbed her keys. "Listen, I'ma go in and clear the alarm while you go into my office, look in my desk drawer, and pull out all the pages of the contracts that we will need. We should be in and out within an hour or so," Taye said.

They walked into the office, heading in different directions to get their work done so that they could go join the festivities. In doing so, Taye forgot to set the alarm again after she disarmed it.

The Trail Ride Event

The huge field that Kendra and John purchased a year earlier had two entrances: one on the north side and one on the south. The north entrance was for the drivers who weren't interested in the trail ride but still wanted to participate in the camp-out party, as well as for the staff there to oversee parking, security guards, cooks, and the performers. The south was for the trail riders. They had one of the most reputable horse breeders allowing them to use some of his horses. Kendra made him an offer and paid him well, not to mention the exposure it gave his company and farm. They had close to a thousand overnight campers already confirmed, and they expected to have more by the end of the day. They had a few people already at the site cooking dinner: deep-fried fish, homemade coleslaw, hamburgers, hotdogs, barbecue ribs, mac and cheese—with lobster chunks in one pan and a second pan without—cowboy baked beans, and corn on the cob on the grill.

Soon the crew arrived to set the stage, and she watched and asked questions about the setup and asked them to make sure that it was safe for the artists scheduled to perform.

"Hey, you ready to check out the trail?" John asked, looking just as excited as she felt about the events that were about to take place for the weekend.

"Sure am," she replied.

They walked over to where the horses were in the trailer. After guiding them safely down the trailer ramp, they tied them up at the hitching post and proceeded to grab their saddles and harnesses. After getting the horses ready to ride, they made one last round around the site, hopped on their horses, and headed down the trail with one guy leading them in a horse-pulled wagon. They had bottles of water along with music playing from a battery-operated boom box.

Once they arrived at the meeting spot, the man who was loaning them the horses was already in place and had several horses already saddled and prepped for riders. They had a total of fifty people who wanted the whole trail ride experience. They all got acquainted with their horses by feeding them lumps of sugar and patting them down. As they began mounting their horses, the man who rented the horses led them down the trail. They lined up and started trotting down the trail. Kendra smiled and beamed as everyone spoke highly of how she had everything organized. It confirmed that she would definitely make it a yearly event.

Back at the Office

While Troy went to Taye's office to get the items she requested, Taye went to Kendra's office and typed up the meeting minutes that she had forgotten to do. She figured that since they were already running late, an hour more wouldn't hurt.

A little over an hour later, she had completed all the tasks. She grabbed Kendra's note tablet that she had left, and as she turned to close the blinds, she saw a shadow in the doorway.

"I'm finishing up now," she started.

"Well, lookie here. I was looking for Kendra, but dayum, you fine." Devon admired her from the doorway.

Taye frowned. "Why are you here? Kendra doesn't want to be bothered with you."

Devon smiled as he sauntered in. "Mouthy as hell, I see. Let's see if we can fix that." Devon approached Taye, and she screamed.

Troy was walking out of the restroom when he heard the rustling coming from Kendra's office. He took off running, and as he approached, he saw a man strangling Taye. He rushed forward, grabbed the letter opener on Kendra's desk, dived on Devon, and started stabbing him repeatedly in the back of his neck. The amount of force behind each jab sent the sharp letter opener deep into his flesh. With one final blow, blood spurted out, and when Troy moved away, Devon's body slumped over.

"Nooooo! Noooo!" Taye screamed. She was covered in blood, and Devon's body lay on top of hers. Troy pulled and yanked until Taye was free from beneath him.

"Oh, my God!" Taye screamed as she hugged Troy. "Thank you! Thank you!"

Troy didn't move. He couldn't speak. Taye realized that he was in shock. After she collected herself, she called Kendra, but she didn't answer. She then called John and then Bridget. After the seventh call, she was able to get through to Bridget.

The trail ride event was going off without a hitch, and Kendra had met over ten new potential clients. They took to the stage in what Kendra called the South Side Gong Show. Several people took to the stage platform and sang, rapped, and acted, and the crowd either cheered them to the next round or rang their cowbell, which was distributed earlier in the day to move them off the stage. The ones who were sent off were escorted off by a few models Kendra had recently signed. Kendra had someone live streaming the event off and on via Facebook, Instagram, and X. She wanted to spotlight the event in hopes of bringing in new clients as well as potential contracts from companies abroad for her clients and upcoming clients.

She hugged John as she took to the stage to thank everyone who performed and congratulated the winners. As she spoke, she saw Bridget rushing forward with her phone glued to her ear and panic on her face. Her heart began to thud as she assumed it was something amiss with Christine, but when Bridget finally approached her, out of breath, she sputtered, "It . . . it's Troy."

"What about Troy?" Kendra asked.

"Taye says he had a run-in with Devon, and—" Bridget stuttered.

"Give me the phone!" Kendra ordered. She snatched the phone, hands trembling as she braced herself for whatever she was about to hear. "Taye, what's going on?"

Taye explained what was going on, and Kendra froze in her spot. Her brain started clicking, and pain seared through her temple. Kendra walked down from the platform with the phone glued to her ear, looking dazed, and her head was spinning. Her chest began to hurt as her breaths became shallow. John was already en route to the platform when he saw her facial expression change when Bridget initially approached her.

"We got to go to the office. Bridget, you need to stay here and keep things going. We will be back as soon as we can," said Kendra.

"What's going on?" asked John.

Bridget shook her head at Kendra. "I can't do that."

"Do what? What the fuck is going on?" he asked again.

"I can't stay here and do this alone!" Bridget cried.

"I ain't got time to even discuss this. Either you do it, or you're fired! We have to get to the office!" Kendra pushed frantically through the crowd with John on her ass.

"What's going on?" he asked again more aggressively.

"I'll explain when we get to the car," she hollered over the music and noise of the crowd.

Once they were both in the car, she turned to John as she started the car. "Troy just killed Devon, the man who was trying to get with me a few years back when we first met."

John's brow furrowed as he thought back. "The young boy?"

"Yes. He started threatening me, sending me flowers recently, and I ignored him. I didn't want to tell you 'cause I thought that he'd get the picture and leave me alone, but . . ." She sighed, shaking her head, trying her best not to cry. "I should've gone to the police, but I didn't think he'd actually try anything." She drove down the highway doing seventy-five all the way.

"And why didn't you tell me, Kendra?" John asked.

Kendra trembled, as she had never heard his voice so steady and controlled when he was angry. She could deal with his fussing and rants, but the way he was at that moment, she was afraid. "I didn't want anything to interfere with our event. I worked too hard to let that get in the way."

John laughed, "You know, you think you know everything and that your way is the only way. Look at what you not telling me has led to! A man is dead, and Troy is now a murderer, Kendra. You don't know every damn thang."

"That's not—"

"Shut the fuck up, Kendra!" he growled.

Kendra opened her mouth to check him but snapped it closed quickly. She didn't want to poke the bear, especially when he was that angry.

She didn't say another word as they drove to her office. She was glad that no one was at the office other than Taye and Troy. At least they'd have time to clean and get rid of the body. As they pulled in and got out of the car, John walked around and opened Kendra's door. He wanted to slap the back of her head, but he vowed never to put his hands on a female. But the desire to do so burned through his veins. Kendra walked a few steps ahead of him as if she felt his desire to touch her. After they walked in, she quickly locked the door and set the alarm. Kendra walked quickly to her office and stopped at the door. Troy was sitting back on the chair in her office, and Taye had already gone to the supply room and was rolling Devon up in a huge piece of plastic and was about to wrap duct tape around it. John rushed forward to help. She also had a huge brown roll of paper. Once they finished, Devon looked as if he had been prepped in a meat market, packaged for delivery.

While John and Taye wrapped Devon's body, Kendra removed Troy from the room. "It's okay, Troy. I know how you feel. I won't let you go down for this. Do you hear me?" Kendra could feel his heart beating so hard, and his hands were sweaty and trembling. "I love you, Troy. I'm so sorry," she cried.

Troy lifted his head and looked Kendra in her eyes. "The worst part is I enjoyed it. Each time I hit him in his neck with the letter opener, the better I felt. It was like therapy. But now I feel like the worst damn person."

"But if you hadn't done what you did, Taye wouldn't be here," Kendra replied.

"I don't feel bad about what I did, just how good I felt doing it. What's wrong with me?" he asked, finally letting out all his emotion. "Uggggghhh!" He began hitting himself in the head. Thankfully John rushed in and grabbed him.

Kendra walked out slowly, feeling like she had let Troy down in the worst way. Taye walked up to her. "What do you want me to do now?"

Kendra didn't stop her stride as she replied, "Get my nephew away from here. Take him to the farm. Tonight!"

Taye stood watching Kendra as she walked back into her office. Kendra stood in the doorway, staring at Devon's body. "I should've killed you a long time ago!" she cried out. Taye rushed by her side and sat with her while John consoled Troy.

Twenty minutes later, Taye and Troy were heading to North Carolina, and John and Kendra stayed behind and cleaned. The ceramic floors were scrubbed and disinfected and scrubbed again. Taye had grabbed Devon's keys from his pocket before wrapping his body up, and John used them to drive his car into the office's private garage and popped the trunk. He and Kendra used one of the large mail baskets on wheels to take Devon's body down. Once they put him in the trunk and closed it, John looked at Kendra. "Follow me back to the farm. My hogs about to have a feast."

"Okay."

"Stay close behind me, Kendra, 'cause if we fuck this up and I get pulled over, I'm going out like a G, guns blazing." He raised his shirt to show his Glock.

Kendra's heart began to pound. The look in his eyes told her that he was speaking nothing but the truth. She tried to kiss him, but he pushed her away.

"You better pray that this works 'cause you won't be able to live with yourself if I die. Kendra, I am disappointed that you didn't trust me enough to know that I would have never done anything to mess up this weekend, but I could've made sure that something like this would have never happened. I am your husband, and this ain't gon' work." He got in the car and told her to go lock up and meet him at the side entrance.

Kendra watched him with tears in her eyes, feeling like he was probably done with her and her bullshit. She had one more secret to tell since he was probably gon' leave her once the weekend was over. The drama-free weekend that she was trying to avoid had just taken a turn that had probably destroyed her marriage and her nephew's life forever.

She walked back into the building, grabbed the tapes that they had taken out of the security cameras, and walked out to follow John back to their home.

Kendra followed close behind John and made sure she damn near rode his ass. She wasn't sure how the night would end, but she could pray about how she desired it to.

They reached the house, and John drove around to the far right toward the barn. He jumped out and opened the trunk, exposing Devon's wrapped body. John grabbed his corpse up and slung it to the ground with a force that Kendra was sure was meant for her.

John didn't say a word as she rushed forward. He grabbed two pairs of John Deere gloves and grabbed an ax. "Go start a fire over in the pit while I chop him up."

Kendra nodded and ran to the shed and grabbed the gas and matches. There was a stack of wood already in place, so all she had to do was douse it with the gas and light the match. Once the flames began to dance, she walked back to where John was chopping the last few pieces. "Here, grab the bottom of the torso, and I'll get the top."

She and John fed the hogs while feeding the fire a few pieces. By midnight, they had almost gotten rid of Devon. John poured acid over a few pieces and then tossed them in the fire. John removed the tires from the car along with the plates and inspection sticker from the windshield. He tossed all the objects as well as his wallet in the fire. He replaced the tires with some he had on his old truck and used tags from his car and spray painted the hood of the car, then the back. He wanted to alter the look of the car and would ditch it on the side of the road.

Kendra again tailed John to a secluded area deep in the country. John wiped down the interior, the handles, and the lugs. He then grabbed a gasoline container from the back and doused the car all over. He lit a match and threw it, then made a dash for Kendra. As soon as he jumped in, she pulled off before he could get his foot in good.

"Goddamn, you trying to kill me?" he growled.

"Sorry. Dang! I was just trying to get away before the car blew up."

"Whateva!"

They drove back to their home, showered, and decided that they needed to head back to the trail ride event. The more they were seen, the better off they'd be if anyone came looking for Devon.

Saturday went by with more coverage, more dancing, and more performances. Kendra's heart was hurting, and pretending to enjoy herself was hard. She and John had already gotten tickets to Greensboro, North Carolina, scheduled to leave Sunday afternoon, arriving in Charlotte at 2:30 p.m. with an hour layover before heading to Greensboro. John had a car waiting for them at the airport that he rented online.

Chapter 26

Charlotte

Christine and Scottie

Saturday

Scottie met Christine in the lobby, and when he greeted her, her heart began to thud. There was something about the way he made her feel when he smiled. His deep dimples made her tingle every time she saw him.

"Hey, you ready?" he asked as he placed his arm around her waist.

"Indeed."

"Come on. I want to take you somewhere." They walked out of the hotel hand in hand.

They made small talk as they walked to his car. As they approached, Scottie slowed his advance as he noticed that there was a slip of paper under his driver-side windshield wiper. He hurriedly unlocked the passenger door, and once Christine was inside, he briskly walked to the driver's side, snatching the note and putting it in his pants pocket.

Christine couldn't help but wonder what was on the paper. She had to get her hands on it.

Scottie got in and looked over at her. "You're so beautiful."

She smiled. "Thank you."

"No thanks needed."

They drove down the interstate with Charlotte's city lights flashing by. Soon the city was behind them, and twenty minutes later, they were entering the small town of Shelby, North Carolina, close to the South Carolina border.

Christine turned the music down. "What's out here?"

"You'll see." He turned the music back up.

Christine clutched her purse tightly against her body with her fingers gripping the latch just in case she had to get in it in a rush and pull out her .22.

Five more minutes passed before they finally turned down a wooded, rocky road. As he drove down, he glanced over at her and laughed. He turned down a small opening and parked in front of one of the most beautiful ponds she had ever seen. It kind of reminded her of Kendra's family pond.

"Soooo, what are we doing here?" she asked, ready for any bullshit he had with him.

He smiled. "Don't worry, shawty, I'd never hurt you. I just wanted to bring you to one of my getaway spots. When I wanna escape life's distractions, my mother and brothers, I come here. My dad used to bring me here when I was small. Before he died."

"What happened to your father?" She had already heard rumors after digging around a bit before she actually met him, but she wanted to see if he would tell her his truth.

"Let's just say betrayal can be a monsta," he answered. "It's beautiful here, ain't it? Come on."

Christine stared him in his eyes, and for some reason, she felt safe with him.

They got out and leaned against the front of his '79 Oldsmobile. Christine noticed that he and Thomas both liked the classic cars. She stood next to him, and he pulled her back against her. He wrapped his arms around her waist, and her hands instantly clasped his, and she leaned her head back against his chest.

"You know my family drives me crazy, but Thomas . . . I think we are so similar that we feel the need to compete with one another. I love him, but I don't respect him. He will do anything our mother tells him and then whine about it. He should learn to say no! Like now, my two sisters are missing, and she, rightfully so, is demanding that we try to find them and bring them home. I honestly don't think my sister Ariana is still alive. She was dealing with a scum who was in debt and was using our family to get out. Man, shawty, I shouldn't even be telling you all this, but I feel like I can tell you anything, and you gon' keep it to yo'self. My life has been so fucked up being around my family, but I'm stuck with 'em, and I got to do my part."

Christine listened, taking in how controlled Scottie was speaking about his family, fears, and dreams. She also paid attention as he listened to her speak about her father and brother's bond and how she felt like an outcast. She shared parts of her real life, and as she did, she realized that they had more in common than she thought.

After talking for almost an hour, Christine laughed, "I see why you like coming here. It's so calming and peaceful. Got us out here sharing our life stories."

"Ain't nothing wrong with that. Out here, nature makes it calming. Listen," he said as he placed his finger to his mouth. "You can hear the crickets, frogs, the fireflies creating a natural light show, and the way the moon casts its reflection over the pond. Nothing like it."

Christine nodded. "I agree. So what else do all these natural surroundings do for you?"

He caught her meaning and shook his head and stared down at her with a fire in his eyes that would've set the trees ablaze. "See, don't play with me like I'm a city boy. Suppose we go there. You mine. Ain't no leaving."

She kissed him on the lips and suckled the bottom lip seductively.

"Man, Christine, don't play with me. Are you good on leaving Thomas alone? 'Cause I'on got time for this back-and-forth shit."

Christine didn't answer, but instead stood in front of him and kissed him once again, only this time she pressed her body into his and wrapped her arms around his neck.

Once they separated, Scottie looked at her. "Say no mo'." He grabbed her by her hair and pulled her head back. "Can I have you?"

"Yes."

Wait, what? she screamed in her head.

It was the eyes. The way he snatched my head back. What have I done?

Scottie buried his head in her neck, and she slowly wrapped her arm around his neck. All the breathing and kissing he was doing to it had her coochie talking in Spanish. "*Fóllame, papi.*"

They stayed at the pond an hour more. Scottie had shared more of his family life with her and even unknowingly shared some very disturbing things about hers. Brent wasn't the man she thought he was. He was a bitch, and never would she have thought that her loyalty to him was misplaced. She had to talk to him ASAP. She knew it was all true because Scottie had no reason to lie to her about a man she wasn't supposed to know. She had been fighting with herself about going through with Brent's plan, but Scottie's affirmation of Brent's bullshit-ass character decided her. She was ready to go back to Texas. She decided that she'd leave within the next two days.

"You ready to go?" she asked him.

"Oh, yeah, I'm ready."

She smiled. "I'm definitely not ready for this night to end. Just ready to get comfortable."

"You aren't hungry?"

"We can order in."

As she walked and got in the car, Scottie smiled. He was glad that he was prepared.

Brent

Brent was getting overwrought with anticipation waiting for Christine to contact him. She had been in Charlotte for close to a month and still hadn't killed Thomas or any member of his family. He had chosen Christine because of her background in the game. She had shared stories of the numerous things that she had done for their father, Clinton, and he thought she would be the perfect person to take the Harris family out. Plus, she was expendable to him. He initially was going to send Kendra out on that mission since she was the one who had killed Lisa, but she was married to big John, not to mention the fact that Kendra wasn't a thinker. She was moved by her emotions and would've been killed before having the opportunity to kill them. She was no match for Donna.

Aaron called him every day for three weeks, leaving voicemails and text messages instructing him to contact him. The first few times that Brent had reached out, Christina assured him that she was on it. But for the last few days, she hadn't answered his calls or texts. Had they discovered her treachery? If so, he could easily assume that Christine was dead. Donna wasn't one to prolong anything, especially taking out those who betrayed her.

"Fuck it. I'ma have to call Christine tomorrow," he told Aaron.

"Listen, we ten toes down with you, bruh. I think we can take them. I'm ready for war," Aaron told him.

Brent laughed, then snarled, "Nigga, if you were frightened of Kendra, how the hell you ready for war with the Harris family?"

"Bro, I know if I had been aggressive with her, especially here, I could have very well ended up in the same field that we buried Lisa in. That big-ass husband of hers didn't seem friendly either! I ain't crazy. This y'all land. I just didn't want to end up being another example. My soul wouldn't rest. I'd be walking on y'all grounds haunting the shit out of y'all," he replied jokingly.

Brent laughed, "You sound like her. She has always said that this land was tainted with lost souls."

"Listen to bruh. We can plot our next move if yo sista don't come through. I'm just tired of hiding out like cowards," Savage suggested.

"I'm with you on that," Aaron agreed.

"Well, let's get something to eat. We can stress tomorrow," Brent said.

They all sat down and ate the food that they had fixed, and they did not mention the Harris brothers for the remainder of the night.

Scottie and Christine

Christine and Scottie arrived back at the hotel and headed for her suite. Once inside, Christine turned to Scottie. "You know where everything is. Pour me a drink also, please, sir."

"You got it. What would you like, pretty lady?"

"Gin and cran-peach juice with lots of ice."

He nodded his head in approval as he watched her walk away. After he fixed their drinks, he carried them to and placed them on the small table in front of the small two-seater couch, then sat down on the couch, waiting for her to come back out of the bathroom. Her one-bedroom suite was clean, and it smelled of her scent, exotic and sweet.

When she finally returned, she was wearing a white T-shirt, and the ends of her hair were wet, visible signs that she had taken a quick shower. He knew that he was about to get some, and he had come prepared. She sat down next to him, and he closed his eyes as her perfume blessed his nose. He stared hungrily at her lips and then in her eyes. "So this is really what you want?"

She sipped her drink and smiled. "You're here, aren't you?"

"Yes, indeed I am. You smell so damn good."

"Thank you. Just a li'l cherry blossom lotion."

He sipped his drink and smiled. She asked, "Can I taste your drink?"

He frowned nervously. "Huh?"

She leaned in and kissed his lips, suckling the bottom lip seductively. When she sat back, she licked her lips. "A Henny man, I see."

"Girl, if you knew what was going on in my head right now, you'd ask me to leave." He laughed.

"Well, if I didn't already know what was on yo' mind, I doubt we'd be here together. I want all the smoke tonight," she whispered. Since she was going back to Texas by the end of the week, she decided she'd take full advantage of Scottie's body.

"Shidd, you ain't got to say no mo' for real," he admitted.

He stood up, looming over her as she remained seated on the couch. He began to undress and grinned as Christine kept her eyes glued to his torso. He knew he wasn't the biggest, but the thickness of his eight-inch dick had caused many pussies to tremble earthquake-style. He felt his stroke game was one to be proud of. Before he pulled his pants down, he pulled a Magnum out of his pocket.

"Came prepared, huh?" she asked.

"Ma, I'm always strapped."

Christine cringed inside. His sensual side had just crept over to the lame side, causing her to feel a twinge of regret for what she was about to do.

She lay back and opened her legs, exposing her trimmed pink moist fun tunnel. She moved her fingers down until they were inside her wetness. As she moved her fingers inside and out slowly, she never removed her eyes from his.

"Damn!" he exclaimed.

She slid her hips down until her ass rested on the edge of the couch. He kneeled and rubbed the head of his dick across her clitoris, the edge of her pussy opening. After he put the condom on, he slid his dick inside her, and he cried out.

Her eyes flew open, and she was further irritated as he began making noises like a female. She closed her eyes and concentrated on getting her nut. His dick felt so good as he slow stroked her. It didn't take long for her to cum, but as she tried to speed his stroke up, he refrained.

His body lay on top of her, making it hard for her to breathe.

Damn, this nigga ain't trying to switch it up. Does he think this shit is sexy? she wondered as he continued to slowly grind on her. "Come on now, let's switch it up. You trying to make love. I'm trying to fuck," she finally blurted out, shocking herself more than him.

He pulled out, and she had a very brief moment of guilt, hoping that his dick hadn't gone soft. She wasn't trying to hurt his feelings, but as quickly as the thought entered her mind, it flew out even quicker as he ordered her on the floor, on all fours. She smiled wickedly and moaned, "Yes, sir." She got up and positioned herself in a doggie-style position. He posted up behind her and slapped her on the ass.

She smiled and bent her head downward, bracing herself for his entrance. He reached down and grabbed her hair and yanked her head up as he entered her. He slipped in and out feverishly, and he was hitting every nook and cranny of her pussy, talking to her as he did.

She was about to cum again until he jumped on her ass and switched from doggie-style to what she called froggy-style. *What the fuck!* she thought. *Damn!* Pain shot up her spine, causing her to cry out.

Her knees buckled, and she fell down on her stomach only to hear him say, "Uh-uh, don't run. Take this dick."

What the fuck? He was killing her back and telling her not to run. Shit, she no longer cared about getting a second nut at that point. "Move! Get off me!" she cried.

"Take this dick. It's yours. It's all yours, baby."

"I'on want it!"

She moaned inwardly. For some reason, her discomfort seemed to turn him on more, and within minutes, he was cumming. He moved as he gripped the condom as he pulled out.

They lay on the floor in silence for a while until he sat up. "I'm sorry I was so rough. I don't know what came over me."

"Me either," she commented, wanting to tell him that he had fucked her back up with that lame-ass froggy-style position.

"Can I take a quick shower?" he asked.

"Yes," she answered, lifting her head up.

As he walked away, she waited for the door to close and then reached over by his shoes and grabbed the piece of paper that was previously on Scottie's windshield. It had fallen from his pocket when he pulled the condom out. She saw it and prayed that he hadn't seen it.

She glanced at it.

You should give me a call.
Detective Gage: 704-940-7722.

She stood up slowly, and after stretching and popping her back, she grabbed a pen and wrote the number down on a hotel pad on the desk.

Detective Gage? Christine was dumbfounded. Why would a detective be leaving notes on a car? If he needed to talk to Scottie, he could easily take him down to the police station. Something just didn't seem right about it. She placed the note back next to his shoes and lay back on the floor like she hadn't moved.

When Scottie finally walked out of the shower with just a towel wrapped around his waist, Christine sighed as she thought, *such a waste.*

He walked over to her seductively, grabbed her hand, and attempted to pull her up off the floor and to the bedroom.

"Once is enough, Mr. Harris. Besides, it's my turn to bathe," she said with a smile.

"You can bathe after round two," he replied.

He pulled her up, and her lower back began to ache slightly, reminding her of how he had hopped up on her ass like a toad.

Again, she refused. "Naw, dude, I need to bathe first."

She walked into the bathroom and closed the door. She turned the water on, all hot, and filled the tub midway.

She then took off her T-shirt and climbed in. The water felt so good to her and relaxed her muscles completely. The pain began to disappear, but she began wondering if she would ever sleep with Scottie again.

Fifteen minutes later, she got out of the tub and put on her cotton nightgown. She normally wouldn't wear such a garment around a man, but she wasn't trying to turn him on.

To her joy, when she emerged, Scottie was fully dressed. "What's going on?" she asked.

"Gotta make a quick run. I can come back later if you want," he told her. "I mean, I'd love to wake up to you."

She smiled. How could a man be so sexy, so sweet, a male version of herself, and be such a downer in the bedroom?

"Sure, just call me. If I'm still up, we can definitely wake up together," she lied.

He walked over and kissed her deeply. She wrapped her arms around his neck and moaned.

She could lie to herself all night, but she knew that if he did call, she was going to let him come up. She really liked him outside of the sex, but even that could be worked on.

Scottie left, leaving Christine to clean up their mess and ponder what had him leaving so soon after they'd fucked.

After she lay down, she turned her phone up and started watching television.

Chapter 27

Scottie, Thomas, Jason, and Donna

Scottie arrived at the church, frustrated and angered that his mother had messed up his night with Christine. When he arrived, he noticed that Thomas and Jason had parked around the back of the church, which led him to believe that they were going to have to clean up a mess that his mother was about to create.

He wanted to tell Thomas so bad what he and Christine had done, but he was going to let her tell him.

Thomas, Jason, and Scottie walked into the basement of the church and walked into the hidden room where they transformed themselves. No one knew about it but them, Donna's sidekicks, and their mother. If anyone else was unfortunate enough to walk in the room, they weren't walking back out.

Once they entered the room, they found a tall white man tied to a chair, swollen and bruised. His left eye was closed and purple, while the left was bleeding and bloodshot. Thomas could only imagine what they had done to him. Donna was standing, leaning back against a table with her feet crossed, smiling when they walked in.

"Glad y'all decided to join us. Tommy, does he look familiar? Huh?" she asked as she stood straight up and walked toward her sons. As she approached Thomas, he flinched automatically because she seemed to always have a reason to hurt him.

Donna frowned. "Don't flinch. It makes you look like a bitch. I ain't raised no bitch."

Thomas shook his head. She hugged him, then Jason, and finally Scottie.

"This the muthafucka who snitched on you. He set you up, and his name is the only one on this indictment." She showed them a copy of the original warrant.

The man's head drooped, and she rushed over and grabbed him by his hair and yanked his head back. "You look at my sons, boy, so they can see what a rat looks like. You tried to have my child taken away from me!" She grabbed him by his face and forced his head up. "I'ma make sure you regret the day you decided to betray my son. You a rat, and I think you should eat like one."

Evelyn walked over and handed her a piece of aluminum foil, and as she opened it, a piece of cheese was revealed.

"Eat!" Donna growled as she shoved the thick piece of cheese in his mouth.

The man's eyes bulged as tears wet his swollen eyes and face. He tried to clamp his mouth shut, but Evelyn Tased him, causing him to cry out. Donna forced the cheese in his mouth. "Scottie, this is your mess, and you need to make your pet eat!"

"Yes, ma'am," Scottie replied. He was shocked at how hard his mother was going to prove her love for him. Had he been wrong about her?

As he approached the man, he whispered, "You can die the easy way or the hard. I suggest the easy way because the hard way could last for days. She won't be gentle with you at all."

The man began to eat the cheese slowly.

"Eat that shit up!" Donna sneered.

As Thomas, Jason, Donna, and Evelyn talked among themselves, Scottie couldn't help but watch the man. He knew it was poisoned, and he was curious to see how it affected him. They had shot, cut, beaten, burned, and drowned niggas, but this tactic was new. After about five minutes, the man's head snapped back, and an agonizing moan escaped his mouth. His body began jerking, and saliva slid from his busted lips. The saliva began to thicken into a foam that had a hint of bright red blood in it. He began to gasp for air using quick breaths. He began to shake, causing the chair to topple over.

"Interesting, huh?" Donna asked as she bent down to look into the man's face. "Rat poison and antifreeze. Does it hurt?"

As the man's body convulsed as he took his final few breaths, Thomas stared at his mother and cringed as she took pleasure in watching the man die. It was becoming a bit much for him.

Christine
Sunday

The following morning, she was startled awake by continuous banging. She glanced at her phone and saw that it was 5:46 in the morning. Scottie hadn't called, so it couldn't be him. She grabbed her pants and put them on under her nightgown along with her .22 by her side. She tiptoed to the door, and when she looked through the peephole, she frowned as she hurriedly unlocked the door.

"What are y'all doing here?" she asked, staring at Taye and Troy.

Taye's face was red, and her eyes were swollen. Troy looked scared and bewildered.

"Is Kendra okay? What's wrong?" she asked.

"Christine. Oh, my God, Christine, it's so messed up. We are on our way to see Brent, but this drive got me tired. Can we stay here for the night? We'll leave tomorrow," Taye whispered in a shaky voice.

Christine nodded her head, but the look on her face told them that someone needed to explain what was going on.

Troy walked over and plopped down on the couch in the room and dropped his head in his hands.

"What the fuck is going on?" Christine asked once more.

"He killed . . . he killed someone," Taye whispered with her eyes glued to Troy. "Kendra told me to take him to Brent while they deal with everything."

"Who?" Christine whispered.

"This young dude named Devon. He was a client of hers a few years back and fell in lust with Kendra. She eventually let him go but recently, he has been calling and asking to speak to her. We did our best to intercept his calls as much as possible, but he came in yesterday demanding to see her. Christine, he was going to kill me. He was literally choking me, and that's when Troy came in and stabbed him."

Christine's face scrunched into a scowl then, and she looked concerned as she walked over and put her arm around Troy. "Don't feel bad or beat yo'self up about this. You did what you had to do to protect Taye." She looked over at Taye and smiled.

Troy looked up and sighed, "I'm not mad at myself for what I did. I'm upset because I enjoyed it, Aunt Christine. I don't want to grow up living like y'all. No disrespect at all, but I want to go to college and make a difference in this world. But how can I when this mess will always be hanging over my head?"

"Kendra will fix it, Troy. You can believe that," Taye told him.

"But she shouldn't have to. It was self-defense. I didn't do it because I wanted to harm him. I did it because he was harming Taye. I don't want to run from this, but they are forcing me to. It's not right, Auntie."

Christine nodded. "It's a li'l too late now, Troy. If you tell the cops now, everyone will probably go to jail, and it's gonna be harder now to prove self-defense. You gon' have to make peace with this, Troy. Some kinda way."

"I know. Dammit! I don't want this lifestyle! Always running. Always wondering if I'ma end up like my daddy. Please help me figure this out because I'm confused." Troy sobbed and crumbled in Christine's lap. Christine rubbed his hair and comforted him until he fell asleep.

Taye sat across from them and watched as Troy fell apart. She didn't know what to say and was glad that Christine was available to calm him.

Once Troy was asleep, Christine walked into her bedroom with Taye close behind. "What are you gon' do?" Taye asked as she sat down on the bed.

"I'ma call Kendra. She shouldn't make him run away from this if he wants to man up and take responsibility for what happened."

"Yeah, but what if they don't see it as self-defense? He was trying to protect me," Taye cried.

"Oh, geez, I'm sorry, boo. I have been so busy worrying about everything else. How are you doing?" Christine asked.

"I was so scared, Chrissy," she replied.

"I can imagine. I am so sorry that happened to you."

"Yeah, and Troy doesn't deserve to go down for something he was forced to do. He saved my life, Chrissy."

Christine hugged Taye as she broke down. After consoling Taye and leaving her in the room to sleep, she decided to take a quick shower.

Thomas and Christine

Thomas called Christine to ask her if he could take her to dinner. When she answered, she was seemingly out of breath, and it took him calling her twice before she answered. He wasn't used to a female being so elusive. Most women enjoyed his company and attention, but Christine was different, which made her interesting. Not to mention, Scottie was awed by her, and he'd do anything to show him that he wasn't the man for her.

"What's good, juicy?" he asked.

"Juicy? Where'd that nickname come from?" she asked, laughing.

Because you are. All that thickness. I need to taste some of it, he thought but didn't dare speak aloud. Instead, he laughed, "It's a compliment, love."

"I know," she assured him. "So what's up?" she asked as she checked her reflection in the mirror.

"Shit, just trying to see if I can come and pick you up tomorrow for lunch."

"Well, I got a meeting over by where we met the other day. We can meet there if you like."

"You got a husband lurking where you're staying? Got a nigga curious."

She laughed, "Again, sir, ain't no man lurking anywhere. I can meet you there if you like. No biggie. It was just more convenient for me since I was going to be out most of the day." She remembered the first night that they met and how he had made a similar statement about a husband.

"I got you. We can meet there if you like. What time?"

"Nope, you wanted to pick me up at my hotel, and that's what we're going to do. I don't want you to think all that extra shit you just mentioned." Suddenly there was a knock on the door. "Listen, pick me up at the Hilton over on Melrose Street. I'll meet you in the lobby. I gotta go because my food just got here," she lied.

She didn't know who was at her door, but she didn't need him hearing Scottie's voice at all. Although they knew about one another trying to woo her, Scottie didn't want anyone to know that he was staying there, and she was going to honor his wishes. Plus, she didn't need both of them on her because she was there to pull a job.

"Okay, juicy, text me when you're ready," he told her before hanging up.

After Christine got off the phone with Thomas, she ran to the door, and when she opened it, the maid was standing before her, asking if she needed her room cleaned.

"Oh, no, thank you. I've done most of the cleaning myself, but thanks."

The lady smiled and walked away. Christine took a quick shower and got dressed. She walked into the bedroom and saw Taye fast asleep, and Troy had filled the front room up with his loud snoring. She could tell that the two of them were tired, so she decided to just leave them a note and one of her keycards on the desk just in case they decided to go get a bite to eat once they awoke.

Christine walked out of her room, hoping that she wouldn't run into Scottie. He had called and texted her numerous times, but she didn't answer due to everything that was going on. She had forgotten to call him back.

As she exited the hotel, she bumped into a handsome man who looked Italian to her.

"Whoa, you okay?" he asked her.

"Yes, oh, gosh, I apologize for not paying better attention."

"What's your name, if you don't mind me asking?"

She looked him up and down, and for some reason, he favored Thomas and Jason to her. She squinted her eyes and stepped back a bit more. "After you tell me yours."

He smiled. "Of course, I'm Thomas Gage."

He eyed her hard, trying to see if she recognized his name, and by the reaction in her eyes, he knew that she had.

"Well, nice to meet you," she mumbled as she walked by.

"Hey, wait a minute, that was a rude way to introduce yourself," Gage said in an attempt to carry on his conversation.

"Wasn't trying to be rude, just got somewhere I need to be."

"Well, maybe we will talk another time," he said as he eyed her.

"I doubt it, but have a great day." She walked off.

Detective Gage watched her walk off and smiled. He enjoyed making her nervous. As he turned, he saw Scottie walking to the bar. He took his lead and followed him in there. It was time that he riled Scottie up a bit. He was going to get his job back and would stalk all the members of the Harris family if he had to.

Chapter 28

Charlotte

John and Kendra

Sunday, Last Day of the Trail Ride

Kendra called Taye and checked on them repeatedly. Taye assured her that they were safe and would be heading to Greensboro soon. She hated that she didn't get to talk to Troy more about the situation, but she had to get him to a safe location. He looked as if he was about to freak out, and she understood why. He wasn't like her or the rest of the family. He was more like Tyrone than anyone else, and she wanted to give him the lifestyle that Tyrone wanted but didn't get—a life away from drugs, killing, and running.

When Sunday finally arrived, Kendra made a quick speech thanking everyone for coming and making a promise to see them the following year. She had made a few connections that she never imagined she'd make. She and John asked Bridget and the team to oversee the cleaning, and they'd make sure they were paid extra for all the work that they had put in. Kendra was proud of Bridget and how she worked under pressure.

She walked over to her before they left and pulled her to the side. "I know I've been hard on you. You've been working extremely too much, and when I get back, you will be getting a long-overdue paid vacation, and when you return, I wanna offer you a deal: you be my partner, and we run a check-up. What you think?"

"I think that sounds like a deal. I love you, Kendra." Bridget smiled as she hugged her.

"I have to go, but we will talk when I get back." Kendra winked at her and smiled as she walked off. Kendra rushed to John's side. "You ready?"

He nodded, and they left the event. They drove to their home so that they could pack, and they were going to call an Uber to the airport. John hadn't spoken to Kendra much since finding out that she had been keeping secret the fact that Devon had been stalking her, so she decided to just blurt out her secret. "I killed Lisa, and Brent covered it up for me."

John swerved as he stared missiles at Kendra. If she could shrink ten sizes down, she would have. He made her feel like a child the way he was staring at her. She suddenly began to get angry. She loved him, but she was growing tired of his judgmental attitude.

"Look, I did everything that I did to keep my family safe. Be mad all you want. I really don't care. If you want out, just tell me now so I can remember to deal with that emotion after I deal with the shit I gotta deal with behind Troy!"

John stared at her as if she had lost her mind. "Just shut the hell up!" he retorted.

She threw up two fingers aggressively. "That's two, you asshole. Don't tell me to shut up again."

"Or what? Huh? What the fuck are you gon' do?"

She watched his eyes and could see he was at his end. She bit her lip, looked back at him, and replied, "Two, nigga!"

They rode the rest of the way in silence. After they parked and John applied a bit of lye around the area where he had chopped Devon up, they headed in to pack. Although she was mad at John, she packed his bag. They sat at the table, waiting for the Uber to arrive.

Christine and Thomas

Christine and Thomas arrived at Jennifer's, a five-star restaurant that Thomas had always enjoyed. He wanted to show Christine what it would be like to be with him—a lot of wining and dining, romance, and some sexual stimulation.

As he parked and exited the car, Christine smiled as she noticed how both Thomas and Scottie were true gentlemen. They knew how to treat a lady. She smiled at Thomas as he grasped her elbow gently and pulled her up against him.

He kissed her, and although there was indeed a spark, it wasn't like when Scottie kissed her. She pulled away. "I'm starving. What type of restaurant is this?"

He smiled, and they walked hand in hand to the door. "Soul food," he replied as they reached the door.

She nodded. "It sure smells delicious."

After they walked in, she excused herself and headed to the restroom. She stood in the mirror as she washed her hands and shook her head as she whispered, "You got to tell him he's not the one."

She cracked her neck and walked out. Thomas was on the phone when she walked out and quickly got off before she reached the table. He cleared his throat. "I took the liberty of ordering us drinks."

"Okay. Thanks. This is a lovely place."

He sat back, looking at her with confusion on his face, but he quickly smiled. "Yes, it is. So, where did you say you from again?"

She glanced around and then back to him. "Texas."

She clasped her hands in front of her on the table, and Thomas looked at her fingers. They were beautifully shaped and manicured, and he needed to feel them on his body.

"Your accent isn't Texan. That's why I ask," he continued but changed the subject once the waitress arrived with their drinks.

"Thank you," Christine said as the waitress handed her the drink.

Once the waitress walked away with their food order, Thomas grabbed Christine's hand. "I have been enjoying your company lately, and I want to apologize for all the interruptions, but today is your day. What you wanna do when we leave from here?" Thomas's fingers lightly traced a path from finger to finger.

Christine knew she had to tell him, but she decided that it could wait. She was going to enjoy his company at least for a day.

They talked and talked as they ate their lunch. An hour and a half later, they were back in the car, heading to their next location. As they eased onto Route 49 South, Thomas's phone rang, and Christine signaled in on the voice. She knew it was his mother, and she sounded furious.

"I'm busy right now, Mother," he yelled.

"I don't give a damn what you're doing. Get over here at the church now!" she heard Donna scream before hanging up in Thomas's face.

Thomas sat stone-faced, and just like a kid, pouting, he turned the car in the direction of the church without saying another word until they reached the church.

"I'll be right back. I'm sorry about this, but I won't be long."

She nodded. "I truly understand. Handle your business."

He smiled. "Be right back."

Once he walked away, she picked up her phone and called Taye. After the third try, she gave up. She looked up toward the church after catching movement in her peripheral vision and saw Thomas, Scottie, and Jason walking out the back of the church and down a path. She slowly grabbed her purse and took out her ID and any other items that could identify her and placed them in her back pocket, then took her gun out. She eased out the door, ducked down, and raced toward the direction that she saw Thomas and his brothers going in. Once she hit the path, she began dipping and dodging behind trees until she got to the back side of an old wooden shed-like structure. She crept up to the rear window and almost vomited at what she saw.

Inside, Donna had Taye and Troy tied up and was moving them to another area of the shed.

She quickly ducked back down, trying hard not to panic. She knew that if she ran in alone, all of them would surely die, and she wasn't ready to check out. She had to think. She eased away from the shed and quickly but as quietly as possible through the woods until she came to a small opening leading to a major highway. She scanned the area and saw a fire station across the street. She jolted out through the clearing and raced across the highway once the light changed in her favor.

She had to think quickly as she ran into the station. "Please help me!" she cried out as she pretended to collapse on the floor.

As one of the men inside lifted her up, her eyes fluttered open.

"Someone just tried to kidnap me. I need you to call my uncle, please," she lied.

"I think we need to call the cops," he told her.

"He is a cop," she replied as she slowly sat up.

"What's his number?" the man asked as she closed her eyes pretending to be a bit incoherent. "Ma'am? Do you need an ambulance?"

"No, no, his name is Gage, Detective Gage, and his number . . ." She gave him the number, and the man waited with her until Gage arrived.

While they waited, Christine asked if she could use the restroom to wash her face and cool down. The man escorted her back and showed her where to go. As soon as she walked in, she began to run the water, and as it ran, she called Kendra.

Chapter 29

Scottie stared at his mother and then at Thomas. "Did you know about this?"

"No, I didn't. Mom, what are you doing?" Thomas asked.

"Your little bitch ain't who she said she is. She is actually the sister of Brent Love, the man who is responsible for both y'all sisters' disappearances. I told y'all to find Lisa, but you been so bewitched by Christine that you dropped the ball. But thanks to Evelyn, we found out exactly who she is. I sent Evelyn and Jason to bring her to me, but they found these two there instead. "

"Yeah, well, how did you get them here without any fuss?" Thomas asked, keeping his eyes averted from theirs.

"I told them that we had Christine and if they wanted her to live, they'd come with us willingly. Love is a deadly thing, I guess." Donna smirked darkly.

Thomas frowned and rushed out the door as he remembered that Christine was in the car. He stomped the ground hard as he saw that his car was empty and she was nowhere in sight.

Scottie walked out behind him. "What's with yo' momma?"

"I don't know, but I wonder what Christine's whole ulterior motive was for being here. I'm also wondering where the fuck she at being that I left her here in the car."

Scottie frowned. "Left her where?"

"We went to lunch, and I was about to take her out for a relaxing drive until Momma called me to come here," Thomas explained.

Scottie shook his head. He was more concerned with why Christine was with Thomas after their night together, more so than he was about why she was there. In his opinion, if it was to kill him or Thomas, she had had several opportunities to do so. Then he remembered everything that he had shared with her about Brent and smiled. "If she's anything like Brent, it wouldn't be hard to get the truth from her. Brent was a weasel, and if she was acting on his behalf, she had to be one too. Let's go find her."

"I'd rather do that than sit here. What do you think she gon' do to them two?" Thomas asked.

"Hell, I don't know, but I'm not gon' have any part in her killing two innocent people," Scottie said.

Thomas huffed, "I don't give a shit about them, bruh, and you shouldn't either."

"Yeah, well, we aren't the same, bruh."

"Call me if you find her." Thomas walked and got into his car.

Scottie couldn't believe the mess that they'd made for themselves over the years living the way their mother raised them. He had to get away from under her thumb, but first, he had to find Christine so that they could talk with Donna and deal with Brent once and for all.

Charlotte
Kendra and John

Kendra and John touched down in Charlotte at 4:13 p.m., a few minutes ahead of schedule. They walked through barely talking to one another. John was livid that Kendra had kept so many secrets from him, and Kendra was disappointed that he didn't understand why. "I'ma go check on our flight to Greensboro," she told him.

"Cool." He went and found a spot close to the window but far away from anyone else. The airport was packed but not to the point where they would be sitting on top of anyone else.

Kendra stared at her husband as she watched him turn and walk away from her. She knew that she may have pushed him too far. She walked toward the check-in counter and was third in line when her cell phone rang. "Hey, boo. You okay? I have been so worried about you."

"Listen, I can't talk long, but long story short, Taye and Troy stopped by and stayed the night with me, and now they have been kidnapped," Christine hurriedly whispered.

Kendra stood unmoving and speechless.

"Hello? Did you hear me? Kendra!" Christine whispered sharply.

"What?" Kendra replied, emotionless.

"Kendra, you need to come now! Like right now!"

"I'm already here," Kendra said quietly before hanging up.

She stood in the same spot for a few seconds before a woman walked over. "Honey, are you okay?"

Christine

When Christine exited the restroom, Detective Gage was waiting for her. When he saw her, he held a look of satisfaction as well as a look of curiosity as to why Scottie's companion had sought him out. How had she gotten his number? He had questions and hoped he'd get his answer.

Christine decided that she'd tell Detective Gage enough to get his assistance to get her safely to her hotel, in her car, and back on the road. She had to pick Kendra up at the airport and get Troy and Taye back home in one piece. "Hello, do you remember me?" she asked.

"Sure, you're my long-lost niece. What can I help you with?" he asked as they walked out.

"So you know that I've been seeing Scottie Harris, and I think I can help you out with finding out a few things that you should know. Like, who Thomas's father is," Christine said.

He eyed her. "I'm listening."

"I'll tell you everything while you drive me to my car. I need you to make sure no one tries to kill me as I get in my car."

"Let's go. Do you mind if I ask your name?" he continued as they drove away.

"I'm sure you already know it, and if you don't, well, you don't need to know it." She began to talk, and Detective Gage was flabbergasted at what she shared with him.

Detective Gage

As soon as she got in her car and was on her way, he contacted the FBI, but before he could make the call, his phone rang. "Yeah, this is Gage."

"Meet me at the library."

"Who is this?"

"Just meet me there. Memorial Drive in ten minutes."

Gage's day was about to get even more interesting.

John and Kendra

John was on his feet in a flash. "Move! Move out the way!" he growled as he fought his way through the concerned crowd that was forming around her. "Get the fuck out da way, dammit!" Once he was beside her, he shook her calmly. "Kendra. Kendra!"

He turned and, with her nestled against his broad chest, walked to the closest empty chair. "Baby, what's wrong? Talk to me," he said as her eyes fluttered open and closed as he gently rubbed her hair.

As she focused on his face, she shook her head, and tears began to drop from her eyes. "I gotta get outta here!" she cried as she pushed through a few people who were still lurking and being nosy.

"Kendra?" John called out.

Kendra turned. "Let's go outside."

Kendra told John everything that Christine had said to her. John stood and began pacing back and forth, clenching his fists. Kendra knew she had to pull herself together, and after vomiting in an outside trash can and gargling a bottle of water she had, she and John called Christine back and formulated a plan that meant that John would go ahead to meet up with Brent and Kendra would stay in Charlotte. John didn't like leaving Kendra behind, but he had no other choice if their plan was going to work.

Before parting ways, he tried to kiss Kendra, but she shook her head, not wanting him to kiss her after she had recently vomited, but he pushed her hand away and kissed her anyway.

"I love you," he whispered.

"I love you too."

She watched as he walked to the gate to board the flight to Greensboro. She sighed, and with each step she took away from him, the angrier she grew, and the colder her heart became. She wasn't going to let the people who held her family hostage get away with what they had done.

Before John boarded the plane, he moved to a secluded area and called Brent to let him know about what was going on. "Aye, bruh, I ain't got long, so listen, there has been a mishap regarding Troy."

"A mishap? What kinda mishap?" Brent asked.

"Man, whoever those Harris folks are you're after kidnapped him and Taye," John started.

"Wait a fucking minute. How the fuck . . ." he boomed.

"They were visiting Christine when it happened. But that's neither here nor there right now. We need you to get the basement ready for guests," John told him.

"All right, man, where is Kendra now?"

"She is meeting up with Christine. They got something planned, and you know how Kendra can get. I'm on my way to you guys now. I'll be there in about two hours," John advised him.

"All right, man. Damn, I can't believe this shit," Brent said.

"Me either," John replied, then hung up.

When he finally boarded the plane, he realized that no matter how angry he was with Kendra, he knew he couldn't live without her.

Brent

After Brent got off the phone with John, he shook his head. Things had gotten out of control. If Christine had done what she was supposed to have done, none of this would be happening. He never wanted Troy to get involved, but somehow, he had. He was furious, but he couldn't switch up his plan to survive the wrath of Donna Harris.

"Aye, bruh, help me get the den set up for Kendra."

"Your sister?" Aaron asked.

"Yes, my sister. Is that an issue for you?"

"Uh naw, man. I'm good. She just still scares me for some reason," he admitted.

Brent laughed, "Rightfully so."

Big T walked over and grabbed an apple off the table and washed it off, drying it with his shirt. "Man, these apples are so good. Never tasted one so delicious."

"It's all in the soil." Brent laughed as he led them down to the basement. "Let's just clear some room right here, and I'ma need you," he said, pointing to Aaron, "to go get some firewood so we can get this woodstove heated."

"Man, it's hot enough, though!" Aaron replied.

Brent looked at him long and hard. "You worried about the wrong shit. Just go do it."

Aaron walked out, and once he did, Brent and Big T continued to get the basement ready.

"Aye, bruh, what yo' sista got going on?"

"Listen, she just told me to get the basement straight. That's what I'm doing," he lied.

Truth be told, Brent was having a hard time trusting either man currently in his company. He knew that once they saw who Kendra had with her, the snitch who told Donna Harris about Ariana's death would be exposed, and he'd deal with them accordingly.

Chapter 30

John

Once John got off the plane and was securely in his rental, he began traveling to Guilford County. He was furious because Kendra was placing him in the same predicament that he had sworn he'd never return to once he relocated to Texas with Kendra. Since the age of 16, he lived with revenge in his heart. He was raised by a single mother who did her best to provide him with all the things he desired. He didn't want for anything while his mother went without the majority of the time. He never much cared about the needs of anyone else until the day that his mother didn't come back home. She had left for work on a Tuesday morning and was killed by a serial rapist. The man left his mother's body bludgeoned and naked, but due to technicalities, the white man walked. Having no other real family willing to take him in, John was placed in the custody of the State until he turned 18. Although the living arrangements and the situations were indeed different, he felt that he and Kendra shared a common past. They were both shut away from family in their teen years.

The first year after John was released from being a ward of the State, he got a job and used the money from his mother's insurance to pay off the taxes on the home that his mother had purchased right before her death.

One day, after leaving CVS, he spotted the white man who was accused of killing his mother. He was with a tall, slim white woman and two kids. They all looked so happy. He was stunned for a moment, standing gawking at the white man who walked right by him and smiled.

"Good afternoon," he had said.

John frowned. His nose crinkled, and his lips curled. He clenched his fist, gripping the bag tightly. From the moment John was released from foster care, he began conducting his own research on his mother's case. He Googled and found pictures that had recently surfaced on Facebook of Benjamin standing with the sheriff of Alamance County at an event held each year by the city. He also discovered that Benjamin Teil had two previous rape cases against him, and each time, the police dropped the ball. As he read over the news articles, it was always "Due to a technicality," and each victim was a young black woman. But unlike his mother, they lived to talk. Although it did no good, from the cozy picture of Benjamin and the local sheriff, he finally knew why he hadn't spent a day in prison.

Darkness set in John's heart, and he knew that the only justice that Benjamin was going to get was the one he was going to deliver. How dare he look so fucking happy when he had destroyed so many lives? He could only imagine what kind of fear they lived in daily.

Finally, he started walking back to his car. When he got in, he hit the steering wheel and yelled loudly. John sat in his car and watched the door of the pharmacy. When Benjamin Teil and his family exited the building, he waited for them to pull out, and he followed them to their home in Guilford County. They had a beautiful home, and the children seemed to enjoy playing in the yard. Something that was stripped from John's life by their father.

For the next week, John drove past their home and, at times, sat across the street in a huge field. He took note of when they left and when they returned. He watched his mother's murderer each day love on his wife and kids, and they let him! They knew what kind of man he was. They had to know. On a Thursday afternoon, John sat across the street and watched as the family drove away from home. His car was hidden behind a huge apple tree, and as they drove by, he gritted his teeth. He waited until they were out of sight, and he put on a hoodie, gloves, and a pair of goggles. He walked across the two-lane country road and raced behind the small bush located by the stairs. He walked around and pried the side of the wooden back door open with a crowbar. Once he was inside, he pulled out his gun and sat down in their living room and waited.

John began to get nervous as he waited for the family to return. He didn't have a particular plan of what he was going to do, but he knew he couldn't walk out with Benjamin still breathing. That, he was sure about.

He waited about two hours, and around nine, he heard their car pull up, but they weren't alone. They had company. John hurriedly snuck out the back door unseen. As they entered the front of the house, he ran around to the side and waited for everyone to go in. He crept around to the side where the driveway was. He moved cautiously toward the cars. He crouched down and used his pocketknife to poke several holes in the front and rear sides of the tires. He glanced quickly back at the house before he raced across the street to the field where he had left his car.

John leaned back against his car and sighed. Maybe revenge isn't the answer. God has to be trying to tell me something, he surmised.

He closed his eyes, and for a split second, he heard the sound of leaves crunching. He glanced up and searched the area. After a few seconds, he saw three dark figures approaching him. He noticed that the man to the left had a shotgun at his side. He moved his hand to the gun at his hip.

"I wouldn't do that if I were you," the man with the shotgun warned him as he pointed the gun.

John threw his hands up in the air as the men moved closer.

"No need to raise your hands. Just don't reach for that gun. I have been seeing you posted up on my property. Why?" the man asked him.

John blurted out the first thing that came to mind. He looked at the street and saw a HELP WANTED *sign and looked at the man. "I was thinking about applying for the job. It's very peaceful, and I could really see myself living out here."*

"Yeah, I could go for that, but it's nighttime, my guy. So how about we go down here at the pond and talk? I'm Sean, by the way, and you are?"

John looked at the man and dropped his head.

"Come on now. I gotta know who I'm hiring," Sean said with a smirk on his face.

"But you don't know anything about me," John replied.

Sean took a step back and looked him up and down, then rubbed his chin. "I know that I need an extra hand around here. I know that if you fuck over me, you know you will die, and I also know that you aren't here looking for a job, but you got one if you need one."

John nodded and laughed. "I do need a job," he lied. "I do know that if I fuck over you, you will possibly kill me, but I also know that you know it won't be easy."

Sean laughed, "Goddamn, I like you! This is my li'l brother, Tyrone, and that over there is Derek. Come on, let's talk. We were over at the pond drinking a few beers."

"I could take a drink," John said as they walked down to the pond.

They sat down by the pond until the wee hours of the morning. Sean showed John where he'd be staying, and John immediately agreed. He figured that he could use the time working for Sean to plot how he was going to kill Benjamin.

A few months after being employed by Sean, he had learned exactly what kind of farm they ran. He had helped bury more bodies in the cornfield than he had planted corn. He had boxed up more cocaine than he could count, but the money was his motive for him. They had a really nice setup, and all the drug money they made, blood money, and company money all contributed to the sweet lifestyle they lived. He had seen Kendra's pictures daily as he moved in and out of the house over the years, but he never would've imagined that he'd be married to her.

Seven months into his employment, Sean approached him one evening while he was sitting at the pond.

"I'm glad I met you, John. You've proven to be a great asset to the farm," Sean said as he pulled out two beers from the bag he was carrying.

He sat down on the log bench next to Sean and watched as two of his workers drove down the small dirt road leading to the area where John first met Sean. He didn't pay much attention to their movement.

Sean handed John a beer, staring straight ahead as he started talking. "So, when are you gon' do what you really came here to do?"

"What you mean?" John asked as he sipped his beer.

"I watched you daily as you watched that house across from my land. Why do you think I hired you? I could see

in your eyes what you were planning to do. Do you still plan on doing it?" Sean asked as he dipped his head and looked back up.

John knew he could tell Sean the truth. *"He raped and killed my mother. He didn't spend one day in prison, and I was without my mother and placed in foster care. Home after home! Yes, I'm still doing it."*

Sean nodded his head and took out his phone. He pushed a few buttons and looked at John. "Keep staring straight ahead."

After about ten minutes, brightness filled the background.

John's eyes grew wide. "What did you do? There were kids in there!"

"You wouldn't want them to be left as orphans like you were, would you?" Sean said after a few moments.

John figured that what he was currently going through with Kendra was his karma for agreeing that those kids were better off dead than living without their parents.

Christine

Christine called Scottie, and after the fourth ring, he picked up. "You need to come to talk to Mom now," he said quickly.

"Not before I see you. Is my sister okay?" Christine asked.

"For now."

"If you don't want the police involved, I suggest you bring her to me," Christine warned him.

"I'm sure you don't want them involved either. We know exactly who you are. So when we get our sister, you can get yours," he stated flatly.

"Tell that bitch she got one hour to get here, or I'ma start practicing my swordsmanship on her sister here!" she could hear Donna yelling.

"If she touches her, I'll kill all y'all dead!"

Kendra shook her head. "Hang up and call the other brother. I got a plan," she mouthed.

"What?" Christine mouthed.

"Just hang up!" Kendra mouthed.

Christine hung up without saying another word.

"Call the other one," Kendra said as she sat on her phone, texting.

"Why? What's going on?"

"I'll tell you once you call the brother and ask him to meet you at the hotel."

Chapter 31

Christine and Kendra

Christine nervously waited for Thomas to pull up at the hotel. She had been in some murderous situations but not to where someone she loved was being held up. She just prayed that Taye was okay. At first, she thought that Kendra would've been livid and acting her craziness out more than she was, but she was actually calmer than she could've imagined.

Christine was parked by the front of the hotel to ensure that Thomas didn't come with anyone and that he wouldn't shoot her in plain view before Kendra had a chance to join them. Christine saw a pair of headlights turn in behind her and park. She sighed as a big white man exited the vehicle and entered the hotel. She began shaking her legs as nervousness took over. She peeped through the doors of the hotel and saw Kendra talking to a man in the lobby.

Tap, tap, tap.

She jumped as Thomas knocked on the window. *Where the hell did he come from?* She motioned for him to get in on the passenger's side. As he walked around, she looked into the hotel, and Kendra was already en route.

Thomas got in the front seat and looked over at her. "You gotta straighten your face with my mother. Who the fuck are you?"

Christine looked at Thomas and smiled. "My brother is Brent Love. But you already knew that."

Before he could respond, there was a commotion starting up between the white man who had walked in earlier and the security guard outside the hotel. While Thomas was distracted, Kendra hopped in.

"Do me a favor, put yo' hands on the dashboard now!" she ordered once securely in the back seat.

"What the fuck is this?" Thomas growled.

"Pull the fuck off, Christine," Kendra ordered with her eyes glued to Thomas, who slowly complied with her demands.

As Christine headed out of the parking lot, Kendra moved behind Thomas. "Taye, is she alive?"

Thomas didn't say a word at first until Christine looked over at him. "You should answer her. Her fuse is shorter than yo' momma's."

Thomas sneered, "She's fine."

"Good!" Kendra responded before hitting him across the back of his head twice, knocking him unconscious.

Thomas's body slumped forward, Christine pushed him back, and Kendra grabbed him and worked at tying his hands behind the seat and taped his head to the head-rest as Christine drove down the dark roadway. Before they jumped on the interstate, Kendra placed a hat and shades on Thomas. They didn't want any unnecessary attention drawn to them.

"I hope you got a plan because we can't leave Taye with them folks, Kendra."

Kendra gave her a 'did you really just say that?' look and nodded. "I got this, Christine. Just drive to the farm." An hour later, Thomas began to stir and groan. Kendra sat up in the back seat and pulled her gun back out of her pocket. She lay back against the seat and pulled Thomas's cell phone from her pocket. She watched and waited for Thomas to become fully awake and smiled as he struggled against her ropes that held him firmly against the seat.

"Aye, you can relax, or I'll smack yo' ass across the head again. You might as well relax and chill the fuck out."

"Fuck you, bitch!" he growled, still trying to snatch out of the ropes.

Kendra shrugged. "Okay."

"Wait," Thomas shouted, but it was too late. Kendra clocked him harder across the head, knocking him out cold.

Another hour and a half passed by before they were turning down the long, rocky back road leading to their family farm. When they pulled up, John and Brent were waiting outside for them. Kendra got out, and John quickly pulled Kendra to the side.

"I have a bad feeling about this. Promise me that you won't do anything outside of what we're here to do."

Kendra didn't answer him as she turned her head.

"Kendra!" he growled.

"I got this, John." She walked into the house.

John watched her as she walked calmly into the house. He knew at that moment that she was definitely on some bullshit.

Once they had transferred Thomas to the basement, she walked over to where he was tied up. She had tried swiping his cell phone, but she couldn't open it without a passcode.

"Untie him," she told Aaron.

"Do what?" Aaron squeaked, looking at Brent, questioning this.

"You heard what I said! Why the fuck you look at Brent? He didn't tell you to do it. I did."

John huffed, annoyed, and walked over and untied Thomas. Kendra rolled her eyes at him and stared at Aaron until he eased next to Brent.

"You know, I'm starting to think you kinda sweet on my brother. I hope it's one-sided," Kendra said icily.

"You sound about stupid as shit!" Brent growled.

"Yeah, okay. Type in your passcode and call yo' momma," Kendra said as she stood next to Thomas with his phone.

"I ain't doing shit. Fuck you, bitch," Thomas retorted.

"Fuck me? Nigga, I'll kill you right where you stand!" Kendra threatened.

"Bitch, like I said, fuck you. I ain't giving you shit. Kill me, and you can believe my ma gon' make sure yo' people die an awful death and then kill you! Fuck all y'all, especially you, Brent. I bet they don't know what—"

Bam! Big T punched him in the face.

"Kendra, I got Lisa's phone. We can call Donna using her phone," Brent said as he pulled Lisa's phone out.

"Fuck that shit! I want his phone!" Kendra growled as she kneed Thomas in his nuts.

Thomas dropped to his knees, moaning in pain. Thomas groaned as he stood back up.

Brent was already dialing Donna's number using Duo video. He wanted to show her just what was going on and who was doing it. He knew that if Kendra killed Thomas, Donna was gonna want to know who did it, and on the flip side, if for some reason Kendra won against Donna, it would look as if he had her back. Either way, he was covered.

As Thomas faced Kendra, Brent called out to her, "Kendra, Donna is on the phone."

Kendra turned and glared daggers at Brent. He had the phone facing him. "Listen, Donna, there's someone—"

Kendra walked over and snatched the phone from Brent, frowning at the woman on the other end of the phone. "So you're the wench who took my nephew? Bitch, do you know who the fuck you dealing with? Where are my nephew and friend?" Kendra asked.

"Where is my daughter? You got her phone. Where is she?" Donna questioned.

"Where is my nephew at?" Kendra repeated, ignoring Donna's question.

"They are safe for now. Where is my daughter?" Donna repeated.

"Show me and I'll show you," Kendra replied as she turned to face Brent.

Donna walked a few steps and opened a door. Sitting in straight-back chairs was a battered Troy and a swollen Taye.

Kendra's eyes watered, and the darkness that shadowed her eyes was frightening. She smiled at Donna, who at that moment hadn't realized that Thomas was with them.

Kendra turned, keeping the phone averted from Thomas as she walked to where he was being held by Big T and Aaron. "Come hold this," she demanded, looking at Brent.

Brent walked over and grabbed the phone, turning it so that Donna caught a full view of Thomas.

"An eye for an eye, right? Reverend?" Kendra asked.

Donna's eyes grew larger than silver dollars. "What? Noooo! You let him go, or I swear to God . . ." she fumed.

"You swear to God what? Huh?" Kendra growled as she clawed viciously at Thomas's face, leaving deep lacerations across his cheeks.

"Uuugggg!" he cried out as he fought to be freed to charge Kendra.

As Big T and Aaron wrestled to control Thomas, John rushed forward and scooped Kendra kicking and swinging her off her feet and removed her from the room.

Christine stood back, watching Brent during the altercation. His demeanor was snakish, and she couldn't wait until his secrets emerged from the shadows.

Donna could be heard screaming, and Christine rushed forward and grabbed the phone from Brent's hands. "If you don't want yo' son hurt, I suggest you listen and do as you're told."

"I knew your hoeish ass would be bad for my son, and I can't wait to kill you," Donna replied coldly. Big T and Aaron had Thomas secured and tied back up and sitting in a chair.

John and Kendra returned, with him looking just as furious as Kendra was, but Kendra didn't seem too concerned. Kendra grabbed the phone. "I swear on yo' kids' lives that if something happens to my nephew and friend, if you or any of your fuck niggas touch them again, I'll kill them slowly. They'll meet Satan before you will, Reverend. I've lost family members, and I refuse to lose any more, especially for some shit that doesn't concern them. Tomorrow afternoon, I'ma text you this address, and y'all better come alone. You and yo' sons. If anyone else is with you, you won't make it in to see yo' kids," Kendra warned her.

Donna agreed, and once they hung up, Kendra grabbed her cell phone and began to type. She looked over at Christine, who nodded to the door. "I need to tell you something. Can we go outside?"

"I'm behind you, sis," Kendra whispered. Kendra walked past John without looking at him.

"I been watching Brent, and he ain't on board like we think he is," she remarked.

Kendra looked at her and smiled. "I got something special planned for him. Don't worry about him."

They walked back in, and Kendra and John slept in her old bedroom while Christine slept in LeTera's old bedroom. They had twenty-four hours to get prepared for the Harris family's arrival.

The following day, they put together a plan that Kendra and Christine both weren't going to stick with. As the hour neared when they were to meet Donna Harris, Kendra told everyone that Christine would be sitting with Thomas while they rode off to collect their guest.

"I know the hell you ain't gon' trust her with him! It's her fault we are in this shit as it is. Had she gone down there and killed them like she was supposed to instead of trying to get laid, Troy would be safe!" Brent growled.

"You always trying to blame somebody else for your fuckups, Brent! Fuck you!" Christine shouted as she lunged at him.

Before she could grab him, Kendra grabbed her up. "Not tonight you won't. We ain't here for this."

Before Christine could get offended, she caught the gleam in Kendra's eyes and calmed down. "Fine, but you better get that bastard outta here, before I really forget that I'm his sister."

"Let's go on down here. We got about twenty minutes before they pull up, and we need to stop them at the gate," Kendra said. "Agreed?"

Everyone agreed, and they grabbed keys to the four-wheelers and ATVs that they had gassed up and prepared to retrieve their guest. Kendra also grabbed a can of gasoline to set the car on fire. The trailer that they had on the back of two of them had three sets of hand-cuffs, and anyone outside of Taye and Troy left standing without a pair of handcuffs, Brent had decided, would be killed. At the end of the night, he planned on more than one person dying.

Kendra put on her gloves and ski mask, bulletproof vests, and her black leather Timbs. She then grabbed her Draco and loaded it. She was going to post up in an area in the woods where she could see everything from a few feet from their driveway. She could easily kill them once Taye and Troy were freed, but she knew John was at his wits' end with her thoughtless decisions. If they died, it would be in somebody else's hands.

She had one of the walkie-talkies that Sean used to use when he was working out on the field with the farmhands, and John had the other. Once they arrived at the gate, John pulled the four-wheeler sideways, blocking the entrance to the farm. He turned it off and leaned forward on the steering wheel on his elbows as he waited for everyone else to get in position. He sat up once Brent rode up and pulled his Glock out and made sure the safety was on. He and Aaron hopped off their rides and walked over to Big T, who was on an ATV. They pulled the shotguns off the trailer and walked to the bushes at the corner of the road.

As they waited, Brent began to get antsy. He didn't know why Kendra just didn't want to kill them, but whatever she had planned for them, he hoped she was prepared for the backlash if they lived beyond that night.

After ten minutes of waiting, they heard a car slowing down and saw lights turning down the road. As the car hit the small curve in the dirt road, Brent moved quickly to open the gate with Aaron and Big T standing by his side with their guns drawn.

As the car slowed to a stop, Kendra used the scope on her gun to search the area for any other vehicle, and once she was sure no one else was following them, she started her four-wheeler and joined the others by the gate.

"Turn that shit off!" Brent ordered.

Scottie had driven, and he did as he was told. He looked at Brent and frowned. "What the fuck now, nigga?"

Brent laughed, "Toss the keys out, nigga! Then get your bitch ass out."

Donna opened her door, and Aaron pointed his gun at her. "I'on think you wanna get out right now. Close the door and put yo' hands up, Reverend."

Donna stared at Aaron and smirked as she did what he said. Aaron turned his head and caught Kendra looking at him. He pointed the gun back at her and sneered, "You can smirk all you want, but the wrong move gon' send you right to the man you been praising, and I ain't talking about the Lord. Your evil ass won't make it to heaven."

She huffed, and Kendra couldn't help but think of her mother. Everything that Donna had done was for her kids the same as her mother, but just like her mother, she had to answer for leading her boys astray. If it hadn't been for her taking Taye and Troy, Kendra wouldn't have an issue with her.

After Scottie got out and was seated and handcuffed to the trailer, they applied the same tactic with each individual. Taye and Troy were the last two to get out of the car. Kendra rushed over and hugged Troy and looked him over. "Did they hurt you much? Are you okay? My God, I have been so worried!" She grabbed Taye and hugged her as well. "I'm so sorry you and Troy had to go through this. I'ma have Aaron take y'all somewhere safe 'til this is over with, okay?" She looked at Aaron, who also drove an ATV. "Take them to the trailer on the other side of the house and don't leave them alone."

"Let me see those keys," John told Big T after he pulled the four-wheeler that he had ridden back into the woods.

Big T walked over and handed him the keys, and he proceeded to walk over to the trunk, motioning for Big T and Brent to stand by with their guns as he checked the trunk. After making sure no one else was in the vehicle, he drove it to the house, following Big T, Brent, Kendra, and Aaron, who veered off the trail.

Back at the house, Christine was doing her best to avoid Thomas's eyes. She had the chairs set up for the rest of his family. She busied herself for a good while, yet he hadn't taken his eyes off her since Kendra and everyone else had left. She sat down and finally looked at him.

"Don't look at me like that. I had every intention of leaving Charlotte and leaving y'all be until yo' momma took it upon herself to kidnap my nephew and best friend. Y'all started this war."

Thomas was staring at her as if he could tear her apart with his own hands.

"I tell you what," she continued, "you and Scottie are more alike than either of you want to admit. Y'all both felt trapped under your mother's thumb and wanted out. You should've done that. Now look at you." Christine had grown to respect the Harris brothers just a bit and regretted their current situation.

It wasn't long before Christine heard a car pulling up. She walked to the window and peeped out. "Looks like we got company." She walked to the door and opened it up. She could hear the roaring of the ATV with the two four-wheelers trailing behind.

She walked out and helped Kendra with Donna. She smiled at Donna as she approached. "Hey, momma. I told you that you were going to reap what you sow, didn't I?"

"Girl, you just don't know the can of worms you've opened," Donna replied before Kendra jerked her forward. As they ushered her into the house, John and Brent grabbed Scottie, while Big T dragged Jason. As they tied each one up, Kendra gazed at Brent. John noticed that Christine was standing close to Brent. He didn't know what was about to happen, but he knew something was about to erupt.

"I used to think that me and you were more alike than anything. We both wanted out of the 'family,' and we did what we had to do to get that," Kendra started.

"Kendra, what the fuck are you talking about?" Brent asked as he took a step forward.

"Sit the fuck down," Christine growled as she placed the barrel of her gun to the back of his head.

John rolled his eyes upward and gritted his teeth. He knew something felt off earlier. Kendra just wasn't going to ever do what she was told.

"Bitch, I know you done lost yo' goddamn mind!" Brent growled as he attempted to turn around.

Bam! Christine hit him across the back of his head, and he fell to the ground.

"Get his feet, niggas!" Kendra ordered Aaron and Big T.

They stood still for a minute, and Kendra pulled the handle of her gun and shot it in the air. They hurriedly did as they were told as Christine kept her gun on Brent's face.

John walked over angrily with his pistol raised and pointed in the direction of Aaron and Big T. He was pissed but not so pissed that he wouldn't put a slug in either of them if they tried Kendra.

As soon as Brent was seated and tied to the chair, Kendra sat down in front of him. Tears filled her eyes as she spoke. "You wanted Clint's love and money so bad that you set our brother up to be killed. You were the one who called him and told him to make a stop for you. You owed Mrs. Harris some money, and you were afraid they were going to kill you, so you set Tyrone up. You're the biggest rat in this room. You walked around here crying and acting like the victim when Clint denied you yet again after you did that fuck shit!" Kendra punched him in the face. She looked at Brent and stood up. The lie she was about to tell would be worth the trip to hell that she'd surely face.

She turned and looked at Donna. "Your daughter is buried out in the sunflower field. He killed her after she told him that she knew he had killed Ariana. There's your truth. My problem is that you had the audacity to put my nephew in a situation he had no business being in. Taye either! Untie her."

Aaron untied her with no questions asked. Brent laughed and shook his head. "So I'm guessing you're the one who told them about Ariana."

Aaron didn't say a word as he finished untying Donna. She handed her a gun after John placed his against Donna's temple.

"You wanna kill him? There he go! Shoot his ass right between the eyes." The look in Kendra's eyes was indescribable. Hate, love, and pain were all wrapped up in one look.

John's heart ached for his wife.

"Go on. Shoot him!" she cried as she forced Donna to raise her arm. Donna looked at Kendra as if she had lost her mind.

Brent closed his eyes for what he knew was about to happen.

Bam! Bam!

Suddenly, there was a loud bang, and the door flew open. But before the police could get to the basement, Donna shot Brent three times in the chest and dropped the gun. She couldn't let him live after killing her girls. She just didn't like the fact that someone was forcing her to do so.

"Everybody get on the floor! Now! We need the crime scene here ASAP!" the first officer yelled as he walked in. After the third officer walked in, Detective Gage walked down and smiled at Scottie.

"I told you I'd see you again."

Scottie shook his head and then dropped it.

"I got the whole clan in one swoop." He laughed. "With the exception of one."

Donna frowned as she was being handcuffed.

Christine acknowledged Detective Gage, and it was at that point that John realized that most of what she and Kendra had done was planned. Yet another lie she had told him.

Detective Gage laughed, "When I learned that you all were going to rendezvous here, I had to go through a lot of shit to get sworn in as an Alamance County Detective. I mean, it wasn't that hard to do, being that I know a few people in high places. Kinda like what you had, Mrs. Harris. A judge, a senator? I'm sure they are regretting their decision to bend the rules for you and your boys right now. You couldn't have chosen better fathers for your boys."

"I don't know what you're talking about."

"I'm sure you don't, but a DNA test will tell it all. We are halfway there. We just need the DNA from your other son," Detective Gage mused.

Donna glanced at each one of her sons. Which one was the snitch? It couldn't have been Scottie because neither of the men mentioned was his daddy.

"I'm sorry, Momma," Jason replied. "I couldn't pass up on the deal he offered. I contacted him after I saw Scottie meeting with him."

Detective Gage cleared his throat and laughed, "Young man, you think I'm giving you a deal after you told me everything I already knew? Scottie beat you to it. I just needed your DNA."

The officers uncuffed Scottie, who walked out of the house. Christine watched him as he left. She wanted to go after him, but she couldn't. She felt that too much had happened.

Everyone had to give a statement, and once they did, they walked outside so that the crime scene investigators could access the murder scene.

Kendra sat in a daze watching the paramedics load Brent's lifeless body into the ambulance. She turned and looked around to see where Aaron and Big T were and noticed that they were leaving. She prayed a thousand times over for forgiveness for the lie she had told. Before the police pulled off with Donna, Jason, and Thomas, the police were bringing in an excavator tractor and were mapping out the site Aaron had shown them where Lisa was buried.

Donna dropped her head as they drove past. She closed her eyes and said a prayer that her daughter had made it to heaven.

Christine walked outside and saw Scottie getting in the back seat of Detective Gage's car. If he looked at her just once, she felt that would be a sign. *Look at me,* she silently prayed.

She opened her eyes as the car pulled away. Scottie never looked her way.

She slowly walked over to Kendra, and they embraced one another tightly.

The police stayed there for about three hours, collecting evidence and removing Lisa's corpse from the field. The guns that were found in their house were registered to her mother and stepfather. They never kept an illegal firearm in the house. Before her mother turned the main house into a slaughterhouse, that was the only sanctuary from criminal activity.

Two days later, Kendra, John, and Troy were on the plane back to Texas. Christine and Taye decided to hang back. Taye went back to her mother's and decided that she'd be better off staying in North Carolina.

Chapter 32

Texas

Kendra, John, and Troy arrived back in Texas, and Kendra asked John to sit in on a discussion she decided to have with Troy. She knew he had been through a lot, and she had decided that the best way to help him was to ask him how he wanted to proceed in the future. If he wanted to leave and never return, she wouldn't stop him or blame him for that matter. Their family seemed to be cursed, and she didn't want it to become Troy's life. She had been so busy trying to protect him from the past that she hadn't noticed the severity of the mental issues that Troy had suffered due to the past. He said he was okay, though he clearly wasn't.

"Troy, I think you need to talk to a therapist. You got so much built up inside that you need to learn how to deal with it. I don't want you to explode."

"It's too late for that, don't you think?" He sulked.

"Listen to what you did to Devon. You had to. He was trying to kill Taye."

"I'm talking about the way it made me feel. I wanted to keep jabbing at him until his head fell off. What kinda person visualizes taking somebody's head off?"

"A lot of people, actually," Kendra mumbled.

"Not while they stabbing a man to death," he countered. Kendra leaned forward. "Okay, okay, listen, we kinda losing focus. You see how you just shared that with me? I'm here for you, baby boy. You gon' be okay, I promise, and I'ma always be here for you."

Troy hugged her. "I'm about to head out. I'ma go chill at Laura's house. And I will talk to you more. I promise."

"Okay. That's fine, but call me when you get there," Kendra said.

John really hadn't said much since they left North Carolina. He was still pissed at Kendra for all the lies and secrets she had been keeping.

"I wish you would talk to me. I have apologized several times."

John kept walking as if she hadn't said a word.

"See, now you pissing me off!" she yelled.

"You know what, Kendra? You can be mad all the fuck you want, but it wasn't me who jeopardized our marriage!" John growled.

"After everything you just learned, you still feel like I did the wrong thing?" Kendra asked confusedly.

"Goddammit, Kendra, you know that's the part I hate the most. That I fucking understand why. But it still hurts to know that, at the end of the day, you lied to me and felt you couldn't tell me anything! That's some real fuck shit."

"John—" Kendra started.

"If you can't put us first, then what do we have?"

Kendra closed her eyes, allowing her frustration and pain to show. Her face went from sad to angry, from angry to pained. She clenched her fist, and when she opened her eyes back up, John was closing the door to the bathroom. She shook her head as she tried to process everything. Was John thinking about leaving her?

She stood up and walked into the bedroom and grabbed a towel and rag and walked to the second bathroom. She ran a hot bubble bath, and when the tub filled up, she sank down into the calming waters.

She lay back with her eyes closed for a few moments before washing herself off. As relaxing as it was, she was ready to talk to John. Kendra got out of the tub and dried off. She tossed her dirty clothes in the hamper and walked out with just a towel wrapped around her. When she got to the bedroom, John wasn't there. She peeped around the corner and saw the light shining under the door.

She walked quickly into the bedroom, dimmed the lights, and lit two of her jasmine-scented candles. She turned on her stereo, and as the sounds of Lakeside's "Real Love" blared from the speakers, John walked in butt naked.

He ignored Kendra as he walked over to the dresser to get his deodorant and hairbrush. As he stood in the mirror grooming himself, Kendra whispered, "Can I give you a massage?"

As he shook his head and continued brushing his hair, Kendra walked up behind him and placed her hand gently on his back and stepped so that her breasts rested on his naked back. She wrapped her arms around his waist and laid her head on his back.

She kissed his shoulder blade. He turned and stared down into her eyes, which seemed to hold just as much pain in them as his heart was feeling.

"Please?" she whispered.

John suddenly felt selfish. Kendra had lost almost everyone who had ever meant anything to her. Her brothers, her mother, and her nephew. He knew when he married her that she was a part of that lifestyle. It was just terrifying thinking that he could lose her.

He stared at her, and as "Real Love" faded out and "Honestly" by Boney James began, he walked to the bed and lay face down.

Kendra turned and grabbed her lavender-scented oil and a wet wipe. She climbed on the bed and got in between John's bowlegs and opened the top to her oil. As she squirted a bit on John's back, she admired the way his muscles curved around his arm and the small love handles on his sides.

She slowly began to massage his lower back and upper buttocks. She dipped deep and rolled her fingers, getting lost in her task. She massaged his back and arms, paying extra attention to the spots where she got the deepest moan. She bent over and kissed the back of his neck.

"You are my priority. I'll never go against you again. I love you."

John began to turn, causing Kendra to readjust herself.

Once he was on his back, she grabbed her oil and squirted some on her hands, and as she began to work her way up from his thighs, she couldn't ignore the growth of his third leg.

She bit her lip and moved her hands to his dick and began to slowly massage it. Up and down. Finally, she moved up and straddled him, sliding down on his dick slowly, never removing her eyes from his. As she steadied herself with a rhythm that was new to John, he closed his eyes, enjoying his wife's apology.

He grabbed her hips as she began to speed up. "I love the way your pussy feels when it grips my dick. Damn, this shit was made just for me."

John flipped Kendra over on her back, and her legs went instantly on his shoulders. He slid in her, inch by inch. Kendra moaned as he fucked her, slowly, bending his head to kiss her here and there.

"You like the way I make you feel, baby?"

"Yes, daddy." She gasped as he plunged deep inside her.

"I can get used to you calling me daddy," he moaned.

She stopped moving, and feeling her body's response, he stopped.

"You are a daddy, you know. Well, will be in about six months," she told him.

"What?" he exclaimed.

John started pulling out, but Kendra wrapped her thick thighs tightly around his waist and used them to hold him in place.

"Na uh, big country, we gon' finish this." Kendra began to grind her hips, causing John to react by moving his. And just for a little while, they allowed their bodies to mend every heartache they were feeling.

Afterward, Kendra lay curled up in John's arms. "A daddy, huh?" John beamed.

Kendra turned to face him. "Yes, I found out a few weeks ago."

John didn't respond.

Kendra looked up at him. "I know you're angry, and sex can't fix everything, but I do love you so very much. I appreciate everything you've ever done for my family and me. I'm fucked up, John. I am hurting so damn bad. My sister and Taye are back in North Carolina. I got no one

left except you, Troy, and, well, my upcoming arrival. I'm
so very blessed that I have you all, and I don't want to
lose you."

"We got some things to work out, but I ain't going
nowhere. I'm here for the long haul, but dammit, when
you said, 'to obey,' that's a lie you told."

Kendra laughed, "I don't remember that part being in
our vows, sir."

"Little lady, don't play now." He laughed.

They sat up until the wee hours of the morning, falling
asleep after they made their first decision as soon-to-be
parents. If they had a girl, she would be named Christina
Lynn, and if it was a boy, Shawn Alexander. As a couple,
they made the decision that they'd never go to bed angry
and that any issues they had would be worked out before
sleeping.

Christine

Christine hung around for a few weeks. She spent time
with Taye and found that she was more devastated by
the recent events than she had said. She spent countless
hours with her as she couldn't sleep due to nightmares
and her concern for Troy was overwhelming. Christine
kept Kendra updated about Taye, and the three of them
FaceTimed one another more than once a day.

Several weeks later, Christine decided to take a ride to
the south. She didn't have a destination in sight, but soon
she was hitting the Charlotte city limits. She hadn't heard
from Scottie since that night, but she had thought of him
often. His mother and brothers were in jail awaiting trial
on numerous charges, one being murder as they dug

up the body of Kent—the man who Donna called a rat and fed rat poison to. The DNA test that was taken from Jason and Thomas both confirmed that Judge Potts and Senator Dempsey were, in fact, Thomas's and Jason's fathers. After the FBI obtained enough evidence, both men were arrested for conspiracy and collusion with the Harris family. Scottie hadn't gotten off totally free. He was going down for five years in prison and five years' probation for the gun charges. It was a deal he made in order to avoid murder charges and facing over thirty years to life in prison like his family was facing. They gave him twenty days to get his affairs in order before he had to turn himself in to begin his time.

Christine drove past the road where Scottie had taken her on their very first date. She pulled over to the side as she contemplated whether to back up and drive down to the pond. Giving in, she backed up slowly after ensuring that traffic was light, and as soon as she had enough room to maneuver onto the road without causing a wreck, she headed to the pond. She slowed as she recognized the area where he had turned. As she turned down the driveway leading to the pond, she saw that the tobacco around the property was being pulled, and the emptiness showed an opening to the pond that wasn't visible before. The weird thing was that she could see and feel the energy from being on the land. It was serene, and the air seemed to smell different, raunchy yet fresh. When she parked, she got out of the car and walked around to the hood. She jumped up on it and closed her eyes. She couldn't help but smile. She looked around, and the beauty of the land didn't seem as beautiful as the night that she spent with Scottie. He was rough around the edges in the bedroom, but she could work with him on that. He had the potential to be everything she desired in a man. They were similar in a way, she surmised.

She sat by the pond for over an hour, and by the time she had decided to leave, she had also decided that she was going to reach out to Scottie. He'd either forgive her or not, but she had to see if there was something that they could build together. They were both tainted by the savage life. She figured they could ride the rest of their lives being savage together. She got in her car, and as she started to back up, a pair of headlights blinded her.

She stopped and frowned. She thought Thomas was locked up. His green truck was posted up behind her, blocking her exit. She turned and frantically searched for her gun, but before she could get it, her door was snatched open.

"Why are you here?" Scottie fumed as he bent down, glaring at her.

She leaned back a bit and peeped out at him. "I remembered you said this was where you came to get away. I figured I'd use it for a li'l while."

"Christine, you were supposed to kill me?" he thundered as he walked backward, watching her. He seemed a bit off-balance, and she jumped out just as he stumbled backward to the ground.

"Oh, fuuuuckk!" he groaned.

"Oh, shit!" she exclaimed simultaneously with Scottie. She raced forward and stopped to hold her nose. "You're drunk!"

"I ain't either. What you want, Christine?" he asked as he started to sit up.

She helped him sit up and wondered just how in the hell he had made it to the pond without killing someone or himself.

"I saw you when you pulled up, and it took everything in me not to come over here and drag you by yo' hair and sling yo' fucking ass in the pond. I swear to God! You just don't know," he sneered.

"Saw me how?" she asked, ignoring his rant.

Finally on his feet, he pointed to a small cabin area that would be missed if you weren't looking for it.

"So you just been sitting there watching me?" she asked, kind of terrified but flattered at the same time.

"Every time I thought about drowning yo' ass, I took a drink. I should still do it." He walked up to her.

She placed her hand up and pushed at his chest, but although he was staggering, he managed to grab her wrist with a grip that caused her to wince.

He released her. "I'm sorry, man. I don't want to hurt you, Christine. Please leave," he whispered.

She could feel the tears stinging because she felt the hurt in his voice when he said, "Leave."

She turned and then turned back around to face him. "I would never have hurt you. I knew the first time we talked I was meant for you."

He snorted as if her words disgusted him.

She turned and walked to her car, but as she opened the door, he slammed his body into hers, knocking the breath out of her. "Hurts, don't it?" he sneered in her ear as her body slumped a bit.

He lifted her body up and turned her to face him. He grabbed her by her chin and snatched her head up. "If you ever try me like that again or lie to me again, I'll kill you!"

She blinked and frowned. She snatched her head backward from his grip and pushed him. He stumbled and fell once again. She bent down to help him up, and as he placed his hands in hers, she dug her nails into his flesh. "Ditto, nigga!"

She helped him up and helped him into Thomas's truck. She had to leave her car where it was, as she had to drive the truck back over to the cabin because he wasn't in any shape to do so. When she got in the driver's side, she thought back to the day she asked Thomas if she could drive and he told her no. She laughed at the situation.

When they walked into the cabin, Scottie pulled her into the bedroom and got undressed. His dick was hard as shit, and her eyes locked in on it. She took her clothes off, ready to pounce, but Scottie was halfway to sleep. She gazed down at his dick, which was still erect. She smiled, climbed on top of him, and asked, "You asleep?"

"Huh?" he whispered with his eyes half closed.

"Can I have you?"

"Damn right!" He sighed.

She shrugged. "Say no mo'."

She climbed up on him and slowly slid down. She began to ride him, slowly rocking her hips. Somewhere in between the sixth and the seventh rock, Scottie's eyes were open, and his hands were on her ass.

"Do what you want to me, baby," he moaned.

"Yes, sir." She moaned as she began to speed up the pace, just a bit, lifting her ass up enough so he could slap her ass. She leaned forward and placed her hand on the headboard as he began to thrust upward. He lifted his head and took her right nipple in his mouth and began sucking. She cried out as he began to take control. He was different this time. More controlled, more intense, but in the most sensual way. He pleased her over and over again

"Baby, wait!" she cried as he was preparing for round three.

"Naw, you wanted to take some dick, now take the dick!" He slid inside of her from the back and laid a pounding on her that had her pussy farting and her legs quivering.

Once they were drenched in the funk of sex, Scottie looked over at her. "You know I got to do five years in prison, right?"

She nodded. "I had heard something about it."

"What you gon' do while I'm gone? And don't say you gon' hold me down and keep that pussy free from other niggas. Don't promise me that shit 'cause I couldn't promise that to you if the shoe were on the other foot. All I ask is that you write and don't fall in love."

She looked at him and said, "I promise that even if I do fall in love, I'ma still fuck with you. We locked in, babe."

He nodded. "I respect that."

They fell asleep.

The remaining time Scottie had free he spent with Christine. The day he walked in the gate, she made him a promise that she never imagined she'd make: "I promise I won't fall in love."

He laughed, "Better not. And I don't expect a visit every weekend, but maybe every now and then."

She laughed and waved as he walked through the gates of the jail.

She drove off in Thomas's truck and kept her word. She was there at the prison three times a month. She stayed true to her feelings for Scottie. And on the day he got out, they decided that they couldn't live together without being married, so three days later, they were married. They got matching wrist tattoos. His read, "Her Savage," and hers, "His Savage."

Thomas Harris received thirty years in prison for gun racketeering and money laundering. Jason received ten years for the same charges after taking a plea deal. After learning of the many ill transactions, Judge Potts was stripped of his honor and received twenty years for his cover-up in the many crimes that the Harris family was involved in. Senator Dempsey received fifteen years in prison for money laundering and aiding funds to the Harris family.

The day Donna Harris walked into Women's Correctional Center in Greensboro, North Carolina, she felt weird being on the other side of the realm. She had received a life sentence for murder, gun racketeering, coercion, money laundering, and attempted murder of a government official.

When they escorted her to her cell, the guard turned. "Anything you need, I got you."

Donna smiled. "Thank you."

The guard walked away. "Okay, ladies, y'all make Miss Donna feel right at home."

Two ladies walked to her cell door and smiled. "Miss Donna, Evelyn sends her love. We have been asked to take care of you here. So we got your back."

Donna smiled. "Well, thank you, but y'all think you can protect me from the masses if they wanted to get at me?"

The girls laughed. "Not us," the taller female said, pointing at her and the other girl. "*Us.*" She pointed to the entire dorm. "That's why you were put here."

Donna smiled. She knew Evelyn wouldn't forget about her. She hadn't ratted her out and took her lick along with her boys. She left her home and money to Evelyn, and it seemed that Evelyn had utilized the money that she had left her. Donna always thought about the what-ifs, and the "if I get caught" played a part in why she kept her money in the very place no one would ever think to look: Evelyn's bank account. She had helped Evelyn form a fictitious business and began sending money to it as if she were purchasing online products.

She knew in her heart that Evelyn would do right by her, and she was right. She wondered about her sons and tried to keep in touch with them through Evelyn, but they never responded to her. She prayed that they'd find it in their hearts to one day forgive her, but until the day she took her final breath, they had stayed firm on casting her out of their lives.

Thomas and Jason lived out years of their lives in prison. They never spoke to one another again, but for Jason, the prison was a blessing. He became a pastor while in prison, and once he was released, he took over the church that his mother once handled. He helped the youth in the community become more than street kids. He and Scottie linked up once, and he thanked Scottie for doing what he did. He knew that if it weren't for Scottie, he'd be dead.

Thomas continued to live the lifestyle that he lived on the streets behind bars. He ran a few blocks and was the leader of a mob. One late Thursday evening, a fight broke out, and Thomas was killed.

Troy took Kendra's advice and started seeing a therapist. He talked about the death of his father and mother. He talked about his father killing his brother and mother. He shocked the therapist a few times, but even with all the truths he told, he knew he couldn't be totally honest about his family. He went to college and found that he had a desire to help others who felt trapped in life, as he had felt. He opened a center for mentally ill children who had suffered from abuse, abandonment, and those dealing with self-esteem afflictions that affected their existence in society. He felt that by helping them, he could redeem himself in the eyes of God for killing Devon.

His center grew, which allowed him to branch off to five other states, creating group homes and support-ive programs for youth in the 911 crisis, among other programs focused on the youth. He never got married because the one trait that he seemed cursed with was womanizing.

Kendra and John had two more kids, two girls and a boy, and they kept a real tight grip on them. John loved having someone to teach the farm to. He would've loved for John Jr. to be the one, but his oldest, Nadia, was the only one interested in knowing things like why slop was better for the pigs than the store-bought feed. She took to the horses and had perfected riding by the age of 8. She loved the farm life, but their other children seemed to gravitate to Kendra's company. Siena wanted to be a model, and as beautiful as she was, they knew she would be a success. They allowed her to pose in a few clothing magazines, but she was taught that beauty and brains made you unstoppable. John Jr. learned the business aspect of what Kendra did. She started her children off young in learning what it meant to work and be respon-sible individuals. They had created their own brand and family legacy. She knew that she'd never look back.

The End